P9-DCM-348

#1 *NEW YORK TIMES*
BESTSELLING AUTHOR

LISA JACKSON

NEW YORK TIMES BESTSELLING AUTHOR

ELLE JAMES

DANGEROUS
TEMPTATION

Previously published as *A Twist of Fate* and
Deadly Fall

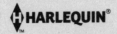

ISBN-13: 978-1-335-00887-9

Dangerous Temptation

Copyright © 2019 by Harlequin Books S.A.

First published as A Twist of Fate
by Harlequin Books in 1983
and Deadly Fall by Harlequin Books in 2017.

The publisher acknowledges the copyright holders of the individual works as follows:

A Twist of Fate
Copyright © 1983 by Lisa Jackson

Deadly Fall
Copyright © 2017 by Mary Jernigan

Recycling programs
for this product may
not exist in your area.

Printed in U.S.A.

www.Harlequin.com

CONTENTS

Lisa Jackson is a #1 *New York Times* bestselling author of more than eighty-five books, including romantic suspense, thrillers and contemporary and historical romances. She is a recipient of the *RT Book Reviews* Reviewers' Choice Award and has also been honored with their Career Achievement Award for Romantic Suspense. Born in Oregon, she continues to make her home among family, friends and dogs in the Pacific Northwest. Visit her at lisajackson.com.

Books by Lisa Jackson

Illicit
Proof of Innocence
Memories
Suspicions
Disclosure: The McCaffertys
Confessions
Rumors: The McCaffertys
Secrets and Lies
Abandoned
Strangers
Sweet Revenge
Stormy Nights
Montana Fire
Risky Business
Missing
High Stakes

Visit the Author Profile page
at Harlequin.com for more titles.

A TWIST OF FATE

Lisa Jackson

Chapter 1

The telephone receiver was slammed back into its cradle with such force that the paperweight sitting next to the phone slipped off the desk. Two framed pictures of a round-eyed, blond-haired girl rattled and then dropped onto the corner of the desk. The tall man who had slammed the telephone so violently righted the portraits with care, clasped his hands behind his back and resumed his pacing. *Would it ever be possible to communicate with Krista again,* he wondered. His shoulders were slightly slumped, and there was a pained darkness just beneath the anger in his eyes. He swore an oath, aimed for the most part at himself, and continued pacing in front of the wide plate-glass window.

For a moment he paused to look out the window and try and control his rage. A fading California sun was dispersing the final rays of daylight inland as it settled peacefully into the tranquil Pacific Ocean. Long lavender shadows had begun to deepen against the white sand of the beach, and the first cool hint of autumn hung crisply on the air. Kane closed his eyes tightly, as if to shut out the serene view. Turbulent emotions stormed through his body. He kept telling himself that he couldn't change the past, that he couldn't blame a dead woman for his daughter's condition, and yet he did.

A solid rap on the door interrupted his black thoughts, and automatically Kane called out a terse acknowledgment. A moment later Jim Haney marched through the door carrying an ungainly sheaf of papers and a long manila envelope. Jim's tired face held a genuine smile, although he also noted the severe lines of stress that contorted Kane's body. Kane's normally impeccable wool suit was wrinkled and his expensive silk tie askew. Harsh creases webbed from the corners of Kane's deep-set gray eyes and there was a cold, hard determination in the set of his jaw. It wasn't hard for Jim to surmise the reason for Kane's obvious annoyance. Jim knew Kane well enough to recognize that Kane was angry and concerned over his eleven-year-old daughter. The guilt that Kane bore silently was beginning to show. Kane needed to think about something else—anything else—and Jim hoped that he had found the solution to Kane's studious disinterest in anything other than the near-fatal accident that had left his daughter disabled.

Jim's smile remained intact as he met Kane's annoyed gaze. "I guess this about wraps it up," Jim announced, fanning the air with a smooth sheaf of computer printouts. Kane's cool eyes followed the green and white pages with only feeble interest while Jim continued. "The Seattle sale—it's final—and all of the loose ends are tied up...except for one."

"So quickly?" Kane asked skeptically as he settled

into the worn leather chair behind his desk and began scanning the printout.

"For once it looks like we may have gotten lucky."

"Good!" There was a note of finality to Kane's words. He looked up at Jim with a grim smile. "Then there's really no reason for me to wait, is there?"

Jim coughed nervously before meeting Kane's unwavering gray stare. "Are you sure that you're making the right decision?"

Involuntarily a muscle in Kane's jaw tightened. "Let's just say that I'm making the only decision possible."

"But to just pack up and leave all of this…" Jim's voice trailed off as he waved expansively. The gesture encompassed the entire gray concrete office building of Consolidated Finances, the understated but costly furnishings and the calm ocean view.

Kane's eyes swept the office, noting the leather furniture, the thick plush carpet, the book-lined cherry-wood walls, and then fell back on his friend. "Think of it as a prolonged leave of absence, if you like."

"Then you will be back?" Jim asked guardedly.

"When I have to be," Kane agreed, with an expression of distaste. "No doubt the board of directors will insist that I come back and oversee the operation from time to time." Kane returned his attention to the computer sheets before him. Quickly shuffling through the smooth, flat pages, he located the report that he sought. A dark furrow etched its way across his forehead as he reread the printout. "Still losing money in the legal department?" he asked, almost to himself. "I thought that we had cleared up that embezzling scam last week and had gotten rid of Cameron—or whatever his name was. Didn't we?" He turned his sharp eyes on Jim.

"That's the one loose end that's still dangling. It looks as if Cameron has an accomplice."

"What?"

"I had a hunch from the beginning that someone was working with him, but I couldn't prove it until I made sure that Cameron was out of commission. I'm not sure who the culprit is—haven't been able to dig up any tangible proof—but I've narrowed it down to a few possibilities." Jim handed Kane the manila envelope. "Here's some personnel information on some of the suspects."

Kane reached for the envelope. "Well, whoever he is, he must be a damned fool! You would think that with all of the hubbub about Cameron, anyone else involved would be busy covering his tracks rather than taking any further risks. This guy must get his kicks by flirting with danger."

"It may not be a man," Jim suggested.

Kane cocked an interested dark eyebrow. "A woman?" A satisfied, almost wicked smile crept over his lips.

"Like I said before, I'm not sure, but it looks as if Cameron has always been…fond of the ladies. He's had a reputation for promoting women."

"Whether they're qualified or not?"

Jim shrugged. He didn't like the glint of inquisitive interest that had stolen over Kane's features. "I haven't had Cameron arrested as yet, but he's being watched. Hopefully his colleague will surface soon."

"So you're telling me that Cameron is still on the payroll and that although you're sure he hasn't taken any more funds, someone near to him has." Kane Webster was beginning to show his anger.

Jim squirmed only slightly as he went on to explain. "That's about the size of it. We're watching Cameron round the clock, night and day. We know that he hasn't pocketed the funds himself, because we've kept him tied up with auditors and the like ever since it became apparent that he was embezzling trust funds. So far he hasn't become suspicious."

Kane wasn't convinced. "And his *friend*?"

"Somehow she's still manipulating the accounts and taking money." Jim shook his head and grimaced. "I haven't been able to trace it to her as yet. She's very clever."

Kane sat thoughtfully in his chair and pulled out the personnel files that Jim had handed him. He didn't doubt Jim's assumption that Cameron had a woman accomplice. He'd worked with Jim too many years not to respect the younger man's opinion. Jim's suspicions had always paid off in the end for Consolidated Finances.

The names on the personnel reports meant nothing to Kane, and at first glance, all of the files seemed to hold nothing out of the ordinary. "You're sure that the thief is one of these people?"

Jim nodded his head in affirmation. "No one else has the authority to move bank funds so freely."

"But couldn't someone else forge a superior's order?"

"I thought about that, too. I had it checked out, but the auditing system of the bank is too complete. No, our misguided embezzler is sitting right there in that envelope. All we have to do is figure out who she is."

Kane puzzled over Jim's recent discoveries in what had appeared to be a sleepy little Seattle bank. His eyes narrowed as he thought about the trap that he would set for Cameron and his accomplice. The fact that it was a woman interested Kane. He had learned several years ago that women could be a devious lot, and it only reinforced his bitter opinion of the opposite sex to learn of the female embezzler.

Jim Haney watched the play of emotions that traversed

Kane's dark features. He had worked with Kane for over ten years and had come to know his boss as well as anyone. Kane was a fair employer, but Jim knew from past experience that Kane could be ruthless if crossed. Right now, as Kane's lips thinned, Jim was thankful that his name wasn't Mitchell Cameron. And he couldn't help but feel pity for the unfortunate woman who had gotten tangled up with Cameron. Jim had his own opinion about the accomplice's identity, and he had met the woman. It was damned hard to believe that such an intelligent, sophisticated woman would be involved with the likes of Cameron. Oh, well—that was Kane's problem. "Did you want me to have the police go to work on Cameron?" he asked.

"No." Kane shook his head, still immersed in his thoughts. "I'll see to it personally. I'm leaving for Seattle tonight." A satisfied grin moved over Kane's features.

"You're really going to enjoy throwing the book at Cameron, aren't you?"

"And the woman! I don't like any thief—especially when she's got her hands in my pockets!" Kane retorted. "This just gives me one more reason to head north as soon as possible."

"That's something I don't understand at all," Jim admitted. "Why you bought that miserable excuse of a bank—it's been losing money for years—just so you can freeze your tail off in Seattle."

"California lost its sparkle for me quite a while ago," Kane muttered tersely, then softened his tone as he caught the wounded look in Jim's eyes. "You know of course about Krista. The doctor thinks a change of climate would be good for her. As soon as I have a permanent residence, I'll send for her."

A personal question died on Jim's lips as he noticed the sober tone of Kane's final words. He hadn't gotten to be vice-president of Consolidated Finances by asking questions that were none of his business. He'd heard the rumors associated with Kane: a glamorous ex-wife, a sticky divorce and an unfortunate accident. But Jim had never pried. He was too interested in self-preservation to open doors that Kane preferred locked.

Kane pushed the manila envelope into his briefcase along with a small portrait of his daughter. He paused for a minute and looked at the eager young face before tucking the picture into a side pocket in the leather case. That accomplished, he snapped the briefcase closed.

"The moving company will take care of the rest of this litter," Kane observed, looking around his office for one last time. "If you need to get in touch with me, Carla has the number of my hotel in Seattle."

"Good luck," Jim said, clasping Kane's hand warmly.

"Let's hope I don't have to rely on luck!" With a smile that didn't reach his eyes, Kane walked out of his office for the last time.

The early-model Volkswagen Rabbit skidded to an abrupt halt, splashing dirty rainwater from the street up onto the sidewalk. The driver of the little yellow car was a slim, striking woman who pulled the emergency brake, slung her purse over her shoulder and slammed the car door shut without taking the time to lock it. She hastened through the damp September evening toward the cozy Irish bar.

There was a determined and slightly mysterious gleam in her large eyes as she hiked her raincoat up and clutched the collar tightly to her throat. Sidestepping a puddle of water as if it were second nature, she pushed her way through the stained-glass door of the restaurant.

The familiar interior was dark, but Erin's eyes became

quickly accustomed to the dim lighting and the air thick with cigarette smoke. Loud, tinny music was coming from a rather bedraggled-looking band reminiscent of the late fifties.

Unconsciously Erin wiped away a few drops of rain that still lingered on her cheeks, while she moved her gaze over the Friday night throng of customers that was heralding the beginning of what promised to be another rainy Seattle weekend.

Appreciative glances and admiring smiles followed her movements, but she ignored everyone other than the distinguished man of about fifty sitting before the polished bottles and the mirrored backdrop of the bar. Erin's eyes met his in the reflection, and for a moment a dark, guarded look crossed over his distracted blue eyes. Finally he smiled tightly and motioned for her to take the vacant stool at his side.

"Mitch," Erin sighed almost gratefully. "What on earth are you doing here?"

He hesitated, and in that instant, any warmth in his eyes faded. "How did you know where to find me?"

"Olivia Parsons thought you might be here," Erin replied. Her smile disappeared at the thought of the leggy brunette.

"Oh, I see. Dear old Livvie," Mitch mumbled sarcastically. "Your friend and mine! Here's to friendship." He waved his glass theatrically in the air and signaled to the bartender for another drink. "What can I get you, Erin?"

"Nothing," Erin whispered, trying to keep the conversation as quiet as possible and yet be heard over the din of the band.

"Nothing?" he echoed, mimicking her. "Not going to join me for old times' sake?"

"What are you talking about and why are you here?" she asked, confused by his cynical attitude. Where was the kind man with the soft voice and the dry sense of humor whom she had known for over eight years? Mitch didn't bother to answer her questions. He seemed intent on evading the issue, but she persisted. "Mitch, what are you doing here?"

"What does it look like?"

"It looks suspiciously like you're getting smashed," she replied honestly.

"Very astute, young lady. I always did say that you were a smart girl, Erin." Mitch drained his old drink and reached for the new one. "Are you sure you won't join me? The Scotch is excellent!" Erin shook her head, but Mitch accosted the bartender. "Bring the lady a glass of Chablis," he commanded over Erin's protests.

Erin was having trouble hiding her annoyance with her boss and his unpredictable mood swings, but she kept her temper in check and tried a more subtle approach with him. "Why did you leave the bank early today?" A glass of chilled white wine appeared on the bar before her.

"You haven't heard?"

"Heard what?" Erin asked uneasily. There was a menacing quality about Mitch that she wasn't accustomed to and didn't like.

Mitch shrugged and Erin noticed that his shoulders drooped. "Why don't you ask Kane Webster, if you're so interested."

"Webster? The new president of the bank? What does he have to do with the fact that you left the office and your clients in order to promote a hangover?" she inquired. Mitch had changed dramatically in the last several months. His behavior had become erratic, almost secretive, and his work had suffered. However, until today Erin had never had to cover for him with a client or track him down in some bar. Erin counted Mitch as one of the few close friends she had in the world, and it pained her to witness his deterioration.

She couldn't forget that Mitch had helped her through an agonizing period in her life by offering her a challenging job and a chance to bury herself in her work. He had encouraged her to do postgraduate work in law and keep busy in order to forget about Lee and the embarrassment and heartache she had suffered while she was married to him. Mitch had helped Erin realize that when Lee had left her eight years before, it hadn't been the end of the world. When she had needed a friend, Mitchell Cameron had been there. And now, if Mitch had a problem, Erin vowed to return the favor.

"Mrs. Anderson was in today," Erin stated, and took the glass of wine from the bar. "She was very disappointed that you weren't able to meet with her yourself. Somehow she didn't really think that I was a suitable replacement for the head of the legal department, and I can't say that I blame her. I certainly wasn't very knowledgeable about her grandfather's will or the estate…"

"That's her problem," Mitch stated blandly and again focused his attention on the bottom of his glass.

"It's not Mrs. Anderson's problem," Erin corrected.

"Well, it certainly isn't mine!"

"But the bank…"

"To hell with the bank," Mitch spat out and slammed his glass on the polished counter. Several of the patrons close by turned interested eyes on Erin and Mitch. Erin felt herself shrink. The last thing she wanted to do was cause a scene.

"I don't understand what's gotten into you lately," Erin began in a low whisper. "And I don't know what Kane Webster has to do with you coming down here to drown your sorrows, but if there's anything I can do—or if there's something you want to talk about…"

"I don't want to talk about anything! You're the one who came looking for me," he reminded her crossly. "I didn't invite you!"

"I was worried about you."

"Well, don't worry over me. I can take care of myself!" Mitch's voice was bitter.

"Mitch, what in the world is going on?" she asked. Erin was stung by his acrid words, but compassion held back the sharp retort that had entered her mind as she watched Mitch order another drink. It was apparent that something was eating him, and because of the kindness he had shown her in the past, she held her tongue. She reached for his sleeve and in a quieter voice asked, "Won't you please tell me what's wrong?"

"Wrong?" The word ricocheted back at her followed by Mitch's mirthless laugh. "What could possibly be wrong?" His blue eyes glittered like ice. "Unless, of course, you think that being fired from a bank that you've given twenty years of your life to is a problem."

The meaning of his words struck her like an arctic blast. "Fired? Webster fired you? But why?"

"Like I said, ask him—if you've still got a job. Who knows, you could be next!"

"But he hasn't even come up from California yet."

"Oh, he's here all right, and mark my words, all of the employees at First Puget—oh, excuse me—Consolidated First Bank better be ready!" he pointed out sarcastically.

Erin sat for a moment in numbed silence. The thought of Mitch being fired was absurd, ludicrous. Mitch had been prominent in building the legal department of First Puget to one of the most prestigious in the city. It was true that for the first time in over a decade the legal department had lost money, but certainly the new president wouldn't hold Mitch solely responsible, would he?

Nothing made any sense to her anymore. Mitch caught the look of confusion and pity in her eyes. His attitude softened momentarily.

"Look, Erin. Don't waste your sympathy on me. And it's really not a good idea for you to be seen with me. Believe me, it would be in your best interests to just leave me alone."

"You look like you could use a friend," Erin suggested.

"What I need now is a good attorney, not a friend."

"But you are an attorney," Erin replied, still completely perplexed.

Mitch looked her squarely in the eyes. "I'm a lawyer, yes, but I specialize in civil law. What I need now is a criminal lawyer."

"I don't understand…."

"You don't have to," Mitch answered abruptly and stood up. "I told you before, I don't need your sympathy or any of your self-righteous friendship!" He turned his back on Erin, fumbled in his pocket for a moment and threw a wad of crumpled bills onto the bar. "See ya around," he called over his shoulder, but Erin didn't think he directed his words at her.

"Mitch…wait," she began, but his long uneven strides carried him out of the door and into the night. As she watched him leave she was still recovering from the shock of his dismissal. Why would he have been fired? It was hard to believe that she wouldn't see him on Monday morning, sitting behind his large oak desk, puffing on a slim cigar and perusing *The Wall Street Journal*.

"Looks like you've been stranded," a smooth male voice suggested intimately. "How about a drink with me?"

Erin turned in the direction of the voice and murmured a firm "No, thanks" to the young man with the clipped mustache. He shrugged his shoulders at her denial, as if it was her loss, and manipulated his attention to a lanky blonde sitting near the dance floor.

Erin made her way back to the car. The drizzle had turned into a downpour and the late-afternoon sky had blackened. The drive home was automatic, and as the windshield wipers slapped the rain off the glass, Erin thought about Mitch and what it would be like without his presence in the bank.

She had suspected for several months that Mitch was in the throes of some personal problem. At least it had appeared that way. He had seemed tired and worried— no, more than that—tense, tightly coiled. The closer the final date for the imminent bank sale had drawn, the more tightly wound Mitch had become. Erin had told herself at the time that it was only her imagination, that all of the employees of First Puget were bound to be a little anxious about the new management. But now, as she drove through the dark, slick side streets, she chided herself for not seeing and acknowledging what had been so transparent: Mitchell Cameron was in deep trouble. Its exact nature she couldn't guess, but it was serious enough to have cost him his job.

Without thinking, she killed the motor of the car as she pulled up in front of the Victorian apartment house. Closing her eyes and rotating her head, Erin tried to relieve the tension in her neck and shoulders. She wondered about Kane Webster. What kind of a man was he? What did she really know about the man, other than the few neatly typed memos with the bold signature that had crossed her desk?

She hadn't heard much about his personal life. Apparently he preferred his privacy. Occasionally Erin had seen his name in print—in the financial pages. If she had read anything about him in the social pages, it usually had to do with his ex-wife, a gorgeous model who had made an unsuccessful attempt at becoming an actress. But that was several years ago, before an accident that had killed Jana and left the daughter disabled, or so it was rumored.

Erin frowned to herself as she thought about her new employer. One thing was certain: Kane Webster had made his fortune on his own, spending the last decade purchasing failing financial institutions and transforming them from operating in the red to operating in the black. He had gained a reputation in financial circles for being something of a rogue because of his unorthodox methods of operation. But if results were the measure of success, Kane Webster was prosperous. It was as if King Midas had reached out and touched the ailing banks himself.

Wearily Erin got out of the car and locked the door. She started up the short shrub-lined walk to her home and smiled at the elegant old house. It was a lovely Victorian manor, perched on a hill overlooking the city. The front porch was comfortable and trimmed in ornate ginger-bread. The turn-of-the-century home had been fashioned into apartments twenty years before, and the contractor had taken care to accentuate the nineteenth-century charm of the house. Erin had fallen in love with it the first time she had laid eyes on it. Ignoring opposing arguments from just about everyone she knew, she had used her small inheritance as a down payment and purchased the building two years ago. Or to be more precise, she and First Puget Bank had purchased it; there was still a sizeable mortgage against it.

Even in the drizzle of early twilight the old manor looked warm and inviting. The white three-story build-ing with its gently sloping roof and deep gables had a picturesque aura that was distinctly "Old Seattle." Upon close inspection it was obvious that the house was in sad need of many repairs, but tonight Erin overlooked the chipped paint and the rusty drainpipes. She had applied for an employee loan with the bank to make the needed improvements, but she knew as well as anyone that her loan would be a very low priority to Kane Webster. With a bank that was already losing money, how could he possibly make any low-interest employee loans?

Erin's own apartment, located on the uppermost floor of the stately house, was an attic converted into a cozy loft with a bird's-eye view of the city. She climbed the stairs slowly, sifting through the various pieces of junk mail and complaints from her tenants. Her mind was only half on the stack of mail in her hands, when she heard the telephone ringing. Racing up the final steps, she hurriedly unlocked the door, threw the mail on the table and grabbed the phone.

"Hello?" she inquired, breathless from her dash up the stairs.

"Erin, honey, it's good to hear your voice. Where have you been? I've been calling for hours," a friendly male voice said.

"Lee?" Erin asked hesitantly.

A good-natured laugh bellowed from the other end. "Hi! How've you been?"

"Fine, Lee," she managed, wondering why he persisted in calling her. After the last call two weeks ago, she thought he understood that she didn't want to see him again.

"What do you say we get together? You know, have a couple of drinks and a few laughs. I'll come by and pick you up in a half-hour," he suggested.

Erin was tempted. There had always been something seductive about Lee, not in the sexual sense, but in the fact that he was such an outgoing, likable kind of guy.

The same qualities that made him great fun at a party made him an immature husband. Erin could almost picture Lee's college-boy good looks—thick blond hair with just the right amount of wave and laughing blue eyes.

"I don't think so," she replied, trying to take a firm stand with him and failing.

"Why not? Don't tell me you've got other plans?"

"No…" Erin responded, and wondered why she hadn't lied and just gotten rid of him. After all these years and all of the heartache, why couldn't she just slam the receiver down and end the conversation?

"Then, let's have a night on the town…"

"I can't, Lee. I'm sorry. I've got a pile of work to catch up on before Monday."

"But it's the weekend," he coaxed in a honeyed voice. "You know what they say, 'All work and no play makes Erin a dull girl.'"

Lee chuckled, but something in his words brought Erin crashing back to reality. Suddenly she remembered just how little she had in common with a boy who refused to grow up. She recalled the shame and humiliation she had suffered while playing the role of dutiful wife.

"No, Lee. That's not what *they* say at all. That's what you said eight years ago."

"Hey, baby, that's all water under the bridge. Come on, what would a drink hurt?"

Erin sighed audibly. "Look, Lee, I'm not in the mood. Not tonight—not ever. I thought I made that clear to you a couple of weeks ago."

There was a pause in the conversation and Erin could almost hear the wheels turning in Lee's mind.

"Just what is it that you want from me?" she asked.

"I told you—we could have a few laughs."

"Why not just turn on the television and catch reruns

of *Gilligan's Island*," she suggested and immediately regretted the sarcasm in her words. Nervously she began tapping her fingernails on the tabletop.

"I have to see you," he pleaded.

"Why? It didn't matter eight years ago. Why the sudden interest?" Erin's voice had begun to shake. Memories began to wash over her.

"You really want to do this the hard way, don't you?" Lee accused.

"I don't even know what you're talking about," Erin sputtered, but an uneasy feeling was growing in the pit of her stomach. This wasn't just a friendly call. He wanted money from her—again. Suddenly Erin felt a deep pang of pity for the man who was once her husband.

"Look, honey," Lee cajoled with only a trace of uncertainty in his voice. "You know I lost the job in Spokane, and well, since I've been back here, my luck hasn't been all that great. I thought that…you could loan me a few bucks, just until I get back on my feet."

Erin swallowed hard before answering. "You haven't paid me back from the last time that I helped you 'get back on your feet.'" Erin's voice was flat. She hoped she sounded unshakable.

"Things just didn't turn out in Spokane. You know how it is, what with the lousy economy and all. It's just hard to get started."

"Oh, Lee," Erin sighed, and felt herself wavering.

He sensed the change in her voice. "I just need a few hundred to get started…"

"Spare me the sad story, Lee," Erin interrupted. "I can't loan you any money right now. I just don't have it."

"Don't have it—or won't lend it?" Lee asked desperately.

"I'm sorry, Lee."

"I doubt it!"

"I don't think that you and I have anything more to discuss. You were the one who made that decision several years ago. Good night."

Erin hung up and noticed that her hands were trembling. Why did he always affect her this way? It was as if she was reliving those last few months before the divorce had become final all over again. Why didn't Lee just disappear from her life completely? Was it her fault? Did he notice her hesitation and somehow construe it as an invitation? While they were married, he had wanted his freedom so desperately. And yet, since the divorce had become final, he kept showing up, trying to rekindle the dead flames. When he finally moved to Spokane, Erin had breathed a sigh of relief. She thought that finally he would make a life away from her.

That was why she had made the mistake of loaning him fifteen hundred dollars, hoping that he would establish himself in Spokane. But his plans had backfired, and he was back in Seattle. It hadn't lasted six months.

Erin shook off her raincoat and started taking the pins from her hair. She couldn't worry about Lee right now. She had too many other pressing problems, the first of which was to get up early in the morning and straighten out the mess that Mitch had made of the Anderson will. That meant that she would have to go back to the bank on a Saturday, but she saw no other solution. With the new boss in town, it wouldn't do to have him walk in on Monday morning and face an angry beneficiary.

Erin shook her hair down to her shoulders and made her way to the bathroom for a long hot bath. It had been a tiring and disturbing day.

Chapter 2

In the silent city, the stark marble building knifed upward through the early-morning fog. Workmen were already removing the old lettering to announce formally that First Puget Bank had become one more cog in the banking machine known as Consolidated Finances. Erin felt a surge of sadness as the final gold letter was lifted off its marble support. It was disheartening to realize that an institution with eighty-year-old roots on the banks of Puget Sound could be so easily transformed into a new, slick piece of financial machinery. Erin couldn't help but feel that some of the personality of the bank would be lost in the transition. Quietly she let herself into the building with her own key and waved to the security guard near the door.

The large foyer of the bank was conspicuously quiet without the usual din of customers, tellers and ringing telephones. It was an eerie, tomblike feeling, and usually gave Erin a feeling of peaceful tranquillity, but today she felt somber.

The elevator was waiting for her, and with a vibrating groan, it whirred into motion and lifted her to the twenty-third floor and the maze of offices that comprised the legal department. She walked in the glow of the security lights, not bothering to turn on the bright iridescence of the outer office fixtures. As she passed Mitch's office she lingered for a moment, experiencing a stab of regret and bitterness. Why couldn't things have worked out better for him? Why did Webster let him go? She wondered about the circumstances surrounding his departure. Was Kane Webster really on a witch hunt of sorts, or was there more to the story? She touched the brass doorknob but released it quickly. What good would it do to go snooping in Mitch's office—it would only stir up unwelcome feelings. The best idea would be to do her work and leave the building before depression really did settle on her shoulders.

Erin's office was dark, but she clicked on the brass desk lamp rather than the overhead fluorescent fixture. The lamp bathed the desk area in a gentle warm glow and gave the room a more intimate and less businesslike atmosphere. She adjusted her reading glasses and pulled out Mitch's dog-eared copy of the Anderson will. As she began to read the verbose and tangled document, Erin became totally consumed by her work. She pulled out several large volumes and unconsciously began humming to the airy notes of the piped-in music. Within minutes she settled herself comfortably on the carpeted floor of her office and became oblivious to anything other than the interesting terms of the document.

Kane stepped out of the cab and handed the driver a healthy tip. He stood for a moment on the curb and squinted up at the tall building he had purchased. With stern satisfaction he watched while the new sign for Consolidated Finances was put into place. He couldn't help but wonder if, as Jim had suggested, he had made a mistake in purchasing this particular bank. It had lost money for nearly two years through terrible mismanagement and was teetering on the brink of bankruptcy. It would take a great deal of finesse on his part to avoid the collapse of the entire organization. Perhaps he had been rash in his decision to acquire the bank. In his eagerness to get away from a glittery lifestyle in California, and in hopes of favorably relocating his daughter, it was possible that he had been too hasty in his decision.

It was too late to start second-guessing himself at this point. With a determined grimace he let himself into the newest in a series of West Coast branches of Consolidated Finances.

As the elevator took him upward he reflected on the position of the bank. Certainly it was salvageable. The first order of business was to plug the embezzling leak. Kane smiled to himself. Nothing would give him greater satisfaction than to deal with the woman who was attempting to steal money from the account holders of the bank. He'd already dealt with Cameron, just yesterday, and fired the bastard. Unfortunately Cameron hadn't given Kane any clues as to the identity of his accomplice. Kane had underestimated the man. He had expected Cameron to crumble into a thousand pieces and give him any information he required in return for immunity from prosecution. But Cameron was made of sturdier stuff, it seemed.

Cameron's attitude had reinforced Jim's opinion—the accomplice had to be a woman, someone Cameron cared enough about to try and protect. Kane hoped that there might be a clue in Mitch's office, just one tiny shred of evidence as to the identity of the woman.

The steel doors opened and Kane stepped into the

dimly lit reception area of the legal department. As he
was about to snap on the lights, he paused. Was it his
imagination or was someone actually humming? His
eyes swept the reception area and the adjoining offices
until he saw the golden glow of a desk lamp illuminating a partially opened door. The humming continued, a
soft womanly quality in its melodic tones. Kane's mind
speculated about the woman. Who would be here alone
on a Saturday, early in the morning, when the bank was
closed? Security personnel? A custodian? Unlikely.

Kane smiled almost evilly to himself and left the hallway in darkness. Maybe for once he had gotten lucky.
It was about time for his luck to change. Perhaps the job
of finding Cameron's accomplice was going to be much
easier than he had first supposed. Stealthily he strode on-
ward toward the beckoning doorway. His jaw tightened
and he cautioned himself to be wary. It would be easy
for a thief to cover her tracks if she was smart enough to
realize that he could be suspicious of her. He would have
to tread lightly. Silently he made his way to the door, un-
prepared for the scene that met his eyes.

A small woman with thick black hair brushed loosely
over her shoulders was sitting on the floor of the office.
She sat cross-legged with her back to the door, and she
was poring over an enormous pile of open-faced legal
documents and books. The office itself was an incredible
tangle of notes, books and loose papers. The object of his
inspection wasn't what he had imagined. Wearing tight-
fitting jeans and a bulky violet sweater that hid none of
her soft curves, she was so absorbed in her work that she
didn't hear his entrance. A pair of reading glasses perched
tentatively on the end of an upturned nose and a pencil
caught behind one ear kept her hair from falling in her
face. Absently, to herself, she continued humming. To

Kane she appeared more like a college student preparing for final exams than a businesswoman, and she hardly looked the type who stole. There was a tranquil but nevertheless faintly disturbing beauty about the young woman.

Kane's reflexes hardened. No matter who this woman was, he had to force himself to keep his objectivity about her. Right now she had unwittingly assumed position number one on the list of embezzling suspects, and Kane couldn't forget that fact. No matter how innocent or vulnerable she seemed, she was most likely to be the snag in the legal department. It didn't matter that the elegant curve of her jaw conformed to her regal bearing, or that her obsidian hair shimmered with streaks of indigo.... Before he let his thoughts wander any further, he caught himself. The last thing he could afford at this point was to feel any interest in her whatsoever.

He coughed to get her attention, and immediately she swung her startled head in his direction. Her eyes met his, and just for a moment he felt as if he was slipping into their lilac depths. Even over the top of her reading glasses, he could see that there was a tremor of fear in those luminous eyes, and involuntarily he wanted to reach out and comfort her. But he forced himself to remain standing, unwavering.

Erin had been completely oblivious to anything other than her work, but a soft cough interrupted her thoughts. She whirled to face the intruding noise, half expecting to see a familiar face.

"Mitch?" she called from habit.

The man standing in the doorway was a stranger and a ripple of alarm broke over her. Her surprise was revealed by the barely concealed gasp. Whoever the tall man was, he had evidently been standing in the doorway for several minutes. He had been right over her, silently appraising her. The thought of his eyes traveling unrestricted over her made her uneasy, tense.

"Were you expecting someone?" he asked.

"Yes...no...you surprised me."

He cocked an eyebrow and leaned against the doorjamb, still watching her intently. He was a tall man, and even in his casual clothes Erin could tell that he was well-proportioned and lean. Strong, broad shoulders supported the expensive weave of his open sport coat. As he stood somewhat insolently, his supple legs strained against the light weight of his tan corduroy slacks. His hair was thick, burnished auburn, laced with traces of gold that gleamed in the warm light of the room. His face was tanned and angular to the point of being harsh, and his gray eyes held hers in a severe gaze that spoke of power and hinted at arrogance. For a moment neither spoke, and Erin felt the spark of electricity in the air.

"May I help you?" Erin inquired in her most coolly professional voice. She guessed at the identity of the intruder and tried to present a calm and efficient demeanor to her new superior. It wasn't an easy task, considering the fact that she was sitting cross-legged in a semicircle of legal documents. She rose as gracefully as possible, without letting her eyes waver from the calculating face of the man who just last night had fired Mitch.

"You're Miss O'Toole?" he continued his inquiry, not answering her question, and only breaking the power of his gaze by a glance at the carved nameplate on her desk.

"That's correct," she agreed, for some reason unable to smile. "I assume you're...Mr. Webster?"

"Kane," he suggested. His silvery eyes drove more deeply into hers and she could feel that he was watching her response, almost anticipating her reaction. "You were expecting me?"

"No, of course not."

"Then...you were waiting for Mitchell Cameron?"

"I told you before, no."

"Then what exactly are you doing here?"

She paused for a moment. It had to be evident that she was busy with legal work, didn't it? Perhaps it was the way that he asked the question that made her feel a need for caution. "I was working."

"I can see that," he scoffed, and for a minute a smile threatened to creep over his face. "But I guess my question should be more specific. Why are you working—" his eyes scanned the office "—seemingly alone, on a Saturday?"

"I am alone!" Was he relieved? "And the reason that I'm here is that there has been a tremendous increase in my workload with the conversion to Consolidated," she replied, but he didn't seem to be listening. To her consternation he came into the room and casually hooked one leg over the desk corner, as if to remind her that he owned the place—literally.

She felt a need to back away from him—to put a little space between his body and hers, but she ignored the temptation. Intuitively she knew that she couldn't show him the least sign of vulnerability or weakness. The harshness in his attitude and his tight-lipped questions made her stiffen and become increasingly wary.

"I see," he mused as if he really didn't. He tented his hands under his chin in a thoughtful and, in Erin's opinion, overly dramatic pose. "Then you're saying that you're overworked?"

"No..."

"No?" He smiled broadly, but the grin didn't light the cold depths of his eyes. "Then you must be inefficient," he suggested.

"I beg your pardon!" Erin blurted, the color draining

from her face. What was he doing to her with all of these insane questions and inaccurate accusations?

"Well, it has to be one or the other, doesn't it?"

"Of course not!" she rifled back at him, and suddenly felt as if she had just swallowed a well-placed morsel of bait. He was toying with her for some reason, and it frightened her. To hide her nervousness she began stacking the legal volumes back on the shelf and tidying the scattered papers. She started to arrange her desk in brisk, sure movements, all the while aware that his eyes touched her face, her hands, her neck, her breasts....

She pulled her attention back to him. "I explained that I had a little extra work to finish up. For some reason, that apparently irritates you. I had no intention of offending you so...."

"You haven't offended me." His voice was softer.

"Then what is it with you? I'm just trying to do a decent job, for your bank, I might add, and you march in here unannounced and start an interrogation!"

"Have I been interrogating you?" he asked gently, and reached for her wrist.

"You still are!" she retorted as his hand captured hers. His fingers were a warm, soothing manacle and her pulse began to heat with his touch. Her eyes flew to her wrist, to his eyes, to his fingers and back to his eyes. Then, as abruptly as he had reached for her, he let the hand drop. The intimate gesture had startled Erin, but the release was a disappointment. Unconsciously she drew away from him. He was too commanding, too powerful, and her response to him was too violent.

"I'm sorry," he apologized, and his dark brows drew together. "I didn't mean to make our first meeting an inquisition. I didn't expect to find anyone here today."

"Neither did I," she breathed. "And that's precisely

why I came in—to work without interruption—from the telephone or…anything else." Her breathing was still uneven; the man made her nervous. She tried to control herself and avoid overreacting.

"Do you come in after hours often, Miss O'Toole?" Another question!

"Only when I feel it's necessary!" she responded cuttingly, and then feeling immediately contrite, added, "Please call me Erin. Everyone else does."

"Fair enough. I like to keep things on a personal level."

Erin's black eyebrows shot skyward with his last remark, but she decided it would be wiser not to comment. She had only to remember his grip on her wrist and the storm of emotions that had seized her with his touch. She didn't understand why she was overreacting to him, but she knew that it would be best to put distance between them.

He rose to leave, and Erin felt the air slowly escape from her lungs. She needed time to collect herself, to be alone. However, before reaching the door he paused.

"What was your relationship with Mitchell Cameron?" he asked.

Erin swallowed hard and met the chill in Kane's eyes. "He was my boss," she replied curtly.

"That's all?" Kane's angular face was tense, his jawline firm.

Erin narrowed her eyes. "No…that isn't all!" she said defiantly, watching his gray eyes grow a shade more calculating.

"Somehow I didn't think so."

"Mitchell Cameron is my friend. That fact won't change, even if you did fire him!"

"So you know about that," he thought aloud. "Did Cameron tell you?"

"That's right."

"Did he explain why?"

"I thought maybe you could answer that one." Now she goaded him.

Kane slammed the door closed, reversed his stride and came back to Erin's desk. He planted his hands firmly on the polished surface and pushed his face to within inches of hers.

"What exactly did he tell you, and when?"

"I don't really know if it's any of your business," she shot back at him. Why was he so angry with her? She didn't understand it, but she felt her temper rise with his.

As quickly as a cat springing, he reached out for her and pulled her face nearer to his. "Anything about this bank is my business!"

"But Mitch doesn't have anything to do with the bank anymore, does he?" she asked rhetorically. "You took care of that!"

She felt his closeness, the warmth of his hand against her chin, the light pulse in the tip of his fingers, the heat and magnetism that seemed to radiate from him.

"Why don't you tell me about 'your friend,' Mitch," he coaxed, and suddenly the fingers that had been rough became gentle. His thumb persuaded her to relax as it moved sensually along the line of her chin and jaw, stopping just short of her throat.

"There's nothing to tell," she whispered, trying to think coherently and disregard the intimate persuasion of his hand.

His eyes, flooded with passion, cooled. "Just how good friends are you?"

"Good friends—just that," she managed, and seeing the clinical hardness on his face, pushed his hand away, adding, "Nothing more. And I resent the implication."

"Implication?" he mocked.

"That I sleep with him. That is what you were getting at, isn't it?" she asked with a bitterness she couldn't conceal. "Not all successful women sleep their way to the top!"

"I didn't mean to imply…"

"You certainly did! I really don't understand what all of these suggestive questions are about. I came in here to get some work done!" Erin began gathering the loose papers on her desk as she attempted to stem her anger. She knew it wouldn't do anyone any good to let her temper surface, but she couldn't help but feel a deep-seated resentment toward the man who had fired Mitch. She wondered fleetingly about her conflicting reactions to the man—his touch, his words—but she pushed those provocative thoughts aside as she snapped the desk drawer shut, locked it and retrieved her car keys from her purse.

"I'm only trying to find out firsthand how the staff of this bank works," he explained.

"So that you can fire us all?" she rifled back at him.

A twinkle lighted his steel-colored eyes. "Is that what you're so upset over? You're angry because I let Cameron go?"

How could she explain that everything about him upset her, threw her off balance. "It's really none of my business," she admitted, her poise and professionalism back in place.

"If it makes any difference to you, I have no immediate plans for—how shall I phrase it—restructuring the personnel of the bank. At least not until I see firsthand exactly how efficiently each department runs."

"Except in Mitch's case," Erin prodded, still confused.

"Cameron was different, and as you so aptly stated, 'it's none of your business.'"

Kane pressed his hands together and his lips thinned. "Do you make a practice of working here alone?"

He prepared to analyze her response, but it seemed innocent. "Not usually. But as you must realize, Mitch had been wrapped up with your auditors and computer people."

"And you had to assume his duties alone?" Kane guessed.

"Not entirely," Erin conceded. "Olivia took over a few of Mitch's clients…"

"Olivia? Parsons? The executive secretary?"

"She's more than that. Actually an assistant officer," Erin explained, thinking about the sultry woman who had once so openly flaunted her affair with Lee before the divorce was final.

Kane's eyes never left Erin's face. He noticed the embarrassed burn on her cheeks, the furrowed brows and the slight droop of her shoulders. Something was definitely bothering Miss O'Toole, and he meant to find out exactly what it was. He noticed that she picked up her purse, a gesture that indicated she intended to leave. She couldn't, not yet.

"If you'll excuse me, Mr.…Kane," she requested. She started to walk past him, but his hand reached for her arm.

"You're leaving?"

"That's right," she agreed but remained standing still, conscious only of the warm touch of his hand on her arm.

He grimaced. "I was looking forward to having someone here while I set up my desk."

"But you didn't expect anyone, did you?" she reminded him.

"No, I didn't. But since you're here, you might as well give me a rundown on exactly how this department functions—or at least the way it did in the past."

"Sorry—I've got plans this afternoon," she lied. He was still touching her and the feeling was delicious, warm, inviting. The dimly lit room was beginning to close in on her, and she knew that she had to get away from him and clear her head.

"What about tonight?" he persisted.

"Still busy." She smiled up at him but felt her lips begin to tremble. He eyed her curiously and she wanted to shrink away from him and melt into him all in the same motion. As if he understood her feelings, he pulled her a little more closely and asked his final invitation in a whisper, his breath fanning lightly across her face. "What about tomorrow?"

Her eyes reached for his and she found it impossible to lie. "I...I don't know."

"Come on," he persuaded. "I'm new in town. You can show me the sights."

"I thought you wanted to discuss business...."

"We will."

"I don't date anyone I work with." His eyes touched her forehead, her cheeks, her chin, her throat.

"Don't think of it as a date," he murmured enigmatically. "Consider it...an orientation meeting."

"But..."

"I won't take no for an answer. I'll pick you up at ten."

"No!"

Kane released her. "I'll see you in the morning," he stated as if it were already a fact.

She didn't answer. Couldn't. But she found the strength to tear herself away from the imprisonment of his stare and walk out of the office with as much pride as she could muster. She wasn't thinking clearly; her thoughts were tangled in a web of emotions. Her mind was as ragged as her breathing, and there was an impulse and yearning that she had never experienced in her lifetime.

Once outside the building she hurried to her car and only paused to take in full, mind-clearing breaths of fresh air. Her fingers trembled as she fumbled with her keys. She kept telling herself that her reactions were bordering on insanity. She had met a man, a very attractive and charismatic man, under tense circumstances. The feelings that had flooded through her were merely a release of that tension—that was all.

But the more she tried to convince herself that she was once again in command of her feelings, the more helpless and vulnerable she felt. Not since her marriage to Lee had she let any man come so close to her, and the powerful magnetism and raw energy that she felt when she met Kane frightened her. She couldn't, wouldn't, let her emotions get so out of hand. She had to avoid being alone with him, for she couldn't trust herself around him. In the past she had always scoffed at the kind of chemical attraction that had received so much public acceptance. Now she wasn't so sure.

She started the engine and roared out of the parking lot, all the while mumbling to herself that she was acting irrationally.

Kane sat at his desk long after Erin had made her hasty departure. He had waited by the window until he had seen her actually leave the building and drive away. Now that she was safely gone, he lifted the long manila envelope from his briefcase.

The ordinary printouts that had seemed so dull yesterday had taken on a new luster and significance today. The desk chair groaned as he settled into it and pulled out the neatly typed report marked O'TOOLE, ERIN. He reread the information on its pages, slowly turning the facts over in his mind.

One piece of information leaped out at him. It seemed that Miss O'Toole had for a while been Mrs. Lee Sinclair before reassuming her maiden name after her divorce. Kane frowned deeply and inexplicably to himself. Erin had been employed by the bank for over ten years. In the past eight, with the aid of Mitchell Cameron, she had been rapidly promoted until she had reached her present position as second in command of the legal department. Quite an accomplishment for a thirty-two-year-old woman.

Kane rubbed his chin thoughtfully as he continued to study the file on Erin. It seemed that she had purchased a building a couple of years ago—with the help of an employee loan granted, of course, by Cameron. And just recently she had again applied for more funds, to renovate the building.

Several items didn't add up in Kane's mind. Erin seemed forever in need of money, but she had loaned her ex-husband a tidy sum about a year ago. A copy of the canceled check made payable to Lee Sinclair had been included in her file; Jim Haney had done his research well. The fact that she seemed always in debt was a bad sign. Also, for such a young woman, she had been promoted rapidly—too rapidly. Bad sign number two. And, from Cameron's comments on her personnel evaluation reports, Mitchell Cameron had trusted her completely. Bad sign number three.

And what about today? She had called out Mitch's name when Kane had entered her office. Was she expecting him, or had she merely been sent by Cameron to continue his dirty work? She had obviously spoken to Cameron last night; she admitted it herself. Just how deep was she in with Cameron and how much did she know? The suspicious questions rattled around in Kane's head until he scowled to himself and threw the report on the desk.

It was difficult to imagine Erin O'Toole Sinclair as an embezzler. Although the evidence was stacking up against her, he couldn't forget her delicate features and surprisingly innocent eyes.

Thoughtfully he rubbed the weariness from the back of his neck. Somehow the satisfaction that he had expected to feel while tracking Cameron's accomplice was missing. He chided himself and accused himself of being a fool. He was beginning to soften where Erin was concerned, and he couldn't let that happen, especially since she was probably robbing him blind at this very moment.

He slanted another severe glance at the file. The name that seemed to leap from the page at him was Sinclair. His lips drew into a thin, hard line. It was ludicrous, but the piece of information that bothered him the most wasn't the incriminating evidence against Erin, but rather the fact that she had been married at one time. It was infuriating for him to imagine another man making love to the dark-haired woman with the wide eyes and provocatively defiant tilt to her chin, even if it had been years ago. He chuckled to himself humorlessly. What did he expect, anyway? That any woman that attracted him be a virgin?

It was the word that his own mind had used that jarred him back to reality. He was *attracted* to Erin, and he couldn't allow himself that luxury. He couldn't let her get under his skin, especially if she was indeed what he suspected her to be.

With a disgruntled shove Kane pushed the file back into the drawer and slammed it shut. Then, after shaking himself mentally, he locked his desk, somehow wishing he could throw away the key.

Chapter 3

It was late afternoon by the time Erin arrived home. She had spent the day window-shopping and walking through the heart of the city, mindlessly watching the crowds of shoppers and breathing the salty air from the Sound. She had avoided going home, content to wander among the tourists as she attempted to sort out her confused feelings. She didn't want to deal with anything or anyone until she had set her uneven emotions back in balance. But try as she would, she was unable to push Kane Webster out of her thoughts.

Erin was angry and resentful of the way Kane had so high-handedly dismissed Mitch. She was offended by his insinuations that she had compromised her morals for career advancement by sleeping with Mitch. And, perhaps more than anything else, she was afraid of and uncertain about the feelings that he could stir in her with only a look or a touch of his fingertips. It was as if he were

attracting her and repelling her at the same time. What
was it about him that caused such warring emotions to
battle in her weary mind? Something about him excited
her, fascinated her, and she felt helpless as a moth compelled to an irresistible flame. It was a flame that would
surely burn her with a molten passion until she was consumed by heat and fire.

Even the old Victorian apartment house didn't seem
as comforting as usual. As Erin was about to mount the
stairs to the loft, Mrs. Cavenaugh, oldest of the tenants,
opened the door of her apartment and called to Erin before she could escape.

"Erin, honey," Mrs. Cavenaugh cajoled sweetly while
leaning heavily on her cane. "It's already getting dread-
fully cold in here. I thought you were going to do something about that insulation. The floor is just like ice, and
it's starting to bother my arthritis again." The kindly, be-
spectacled old woman smiled at Erin.

"Yes, Mrs. Cavenaugh, I know," Erin sighed as she
paused on the lowest step. "And I promise that I'll get
some bids on the insulation this week. There…uh, have
been a few changes at the office. I've been pretty busy
and I guess I've been neglecting my duties around here.
But that's no excuse. I'll take care of it."

Wise, faded blue eyes scanned Erin's face, and Mrs.
Cavenaugh shook a slightly crooked finger at the younger
woman. "I could tell that something was bothering you
from the moment you dragged yourself through the door.
It's not that ex-husband of yours again, is it?"

"Oh, no! This has nothing to do with Lee…"

"Humph! Always said that boy would come to no
good."

Erin began to protest again, but Mrs. Cavenaugh would
have none of it. "You know what you need, don't you? A

cup of my chamomile tea. A good strong one." She gave Erin a knowing wink. "You're in luck—I have a pot brewing this very minute." A crafty look came over the wrinkled face, and she turned to lead Erin into her apartment.

"Oh, no, Mrs. Cavenaugh, I couldn't…"

"Nonsense!" Mrs. Cavenaugh sputtered. "Now, you come in here and tell me what's really bothering you!"

Erin stopped protesting to smile and follow the bent figure into her apartment. The poor dear woman wasn't really looking for Erin to complain about the cold floors at all, Erin realized. Mrs. Cavenaugh just wanted some company to brighten the long afternoon and evening. Erin decided the least she could do was enjoy a cup of tea with her elderly tenant, even if it was the foulest concoction ever to be poured from a silver teapot.

As Erin expected, the long, lace-covered coffee table was already set for two. A service of shining silver teapot and fragile porcelain cups adorned the table, and the air was scented with the strong aroma of chamomile.

Erin sat graciously in the floral side chair while, with slightly shaking hands, Mrs. Cavenaugh poured the pale ochre liquid into one of the cups. "Sugar?" she suggested, and without waiting for an answer, dropped two lumps into the light-colored brew.

Erin took the cup and sipped at the tea while Mrs. Cavenaugh settled herself into her favorite worn rocker. "So now, Erin, tell me about your problems at work." Light blue eyes sparkled with interest as Erin briefly sketched out her morning at the bank. Erin glossed over a few of the details, carefully omitting any references to the bevy of emotions that her new boss had aroused in her. But Mrs. Cavenaugh's knowing eyes saw more than Erin had hoped to divulge.

"So this new boss of yours…what's-his-name…" Mrs. Cavenaugh began.

"Mr. Webster." Erin supplied the missing words.

"Yes…what's he like?" Eyes, crinkled at the corners, stared earnestly at Erin over the rim of the tiny cup.

"Oh, I don't know," Erin said with a shrug, hoping that she appeared aloof. "He's…all business, I suppose. You know, the typical banker type."

"I wonder…" The old woman paused dramatically, but Erin refused to rise to the bait and defend her position. "You say that he let Mitchell Cameron go? Why?"

Erin frowned into her teacup. "I don't know," she replied earnestly. "But I intend to find out!"

Mrs. Cavenaugh's laughter crackled through the apartment. "And I don't doubt that you will." Why did Mrs. Cavenaugh seem so pleased? "Do you expect to corner Mr. Webster at work on Monday and get to the bottom of this?"

"I hadn't really thought about it. He wants me to meet him tomorrow—show him the city, let him know firsthand about the bank. But I don't think it would be a good idea. You know how I feel about my free time…"

"Oh, nonsense!" The sweet, wrinkled woman smiled and waved her hand, dismissing Erin's argument as if it were a bothersome insect. "Yes, I know all about your need for privacy, and I know why. But, Erin, it's been eight long years since that louse of a husband walked out on you, and you can't hide away forever. Why not have some fun with this Mr. Webster? How could it hurt?"

"I have no intention of 'having fun' with Kane!" Erin exclaimed, bristling. Mrs. Cavenaugh's eyes seemed to dance at Erin's familiar use of her employer's first name. "*If* I were to go, it would be strictly as a business meeting!"

"Call it whatever you will, it doesn't matter. But for goodness' sake, honey, *go!*" Mrs. Cavenaugh seemed to sense that Erin was wavering, and she added one final incentive. "How else do you plan to find out about Mitchell Cameron, unless you confront this Webster? I would think that you would prefer to do it while you were alone with the man." She seemed thoughtful for a minute, letting her teacup rest in her hand. "This isn't the kind of thing that you would want to start a scene over—now, is it? It just wouldn't do to let on to all of the employees. It's too scandalous, don't you think? What would it do to employee morale?"

Erin laughed at the thinly veiled attempts of the kind but conniving old woman to persuade her. "Why is it that I feel manipulated?"

Mrs. Cavenaugh spread her palms upward in a helpless motion, suggesting that she didn't have the faintest idea what Erin was implying, but a devilish twinkle remained in her eyes.

"Look, Mrs. Cavenaugh, I just may go with Kane tomorrow. But don't make anything more of it than what it is—a business meeting. I've seen that look in your eyes before, so don't go playing matchmaker for me," Erin warned with a pleasant smile as she set her empty cup on the table.

Mrs. Cavenaugh chose to ignore Erin's bit of advice. "More?" she asked, holding the teapot in midair over Erin's cup.

"No, thank you. I'm sorry, but I really do have to get upstairs. But you're right," she added, placing her palm on the hard wood planks of the floor, shiny with patina. "I think there's a draft coming from the bay window." She walked over to the window in question and ran her fingers around the sill. The cold air made her frown. "I'll see to it that somehow we warm this place up before winter really sets in." Erin rose and dusted her hands off against her jeans. "Thanks for the tea."

"Don't mention it," the elderly woman responded with a wave of her hand. "You know you're welcome here any time." She was smiling smugly to herself, seeming quite pleased.

Erin let herself out of the quaint little apartment and headed up the stairs. She glanced at her watch and realized that it was too late in the day to get anyone out to weatherize Mrs. Cavenaugh's apartment this weekend. She jingled the keys in the lock and gave a hefty shove to her own sticky front door. There were so many things that needed to be done to the apartment house and so little time and money to do them with.

With a sigh she took off her jacket and headed for the kitchen. As she made herself a quick sandwich she thought about Mrs. Cavenaugh. She was right, of course. The only logical way that she would find out the circumstances surrounding Mitch's dismissal would be to confront Kane directly, especially since Mitch was so mysterious and cynical about the situation. However misguided Mrs. Cavenaugh's motives were, Erin had to admit that the little old woman made sense. And, no matter what, she couldn't run away from private discussions with her boss forever, could she? Any emotions that had started to entangle her would just have to be straightened out and dealt with in a professional manner.

The pastrami sandwich that she created tasted like mustard-covered cardboard, and after a few nibbles she put it back into the refrigerator. Mrs. Cavenaugh's biting words came into her mind. "It's been eight long years since that louse of a husband walked out on you. You can't go on hiding forever!"

Is that what I'm doing, Erin wondered as she flopped down on the soft cushions on the couch. *Am I hiding? From what—or whom?* Ever since her personal life had been thrown open to the public, and she had become the object of speculative gossip, Erin had vowed to keep her privacy securely guarded. Lee's open affair with Olivia had scarred Erin so badly that even today, eight years afterward, she refused dates with co-workers in an almost paranoid way. With the exception of a few close friends no one at the office had any ideas about her love life.

Some love life! She had to laugh at herself at the thought. Except for a couple of men who had interested her only slightly, she had hardly dated since the divorce. It was easier, and she preferred to keep her feelings under tight rein, thus avoiding any further conjecture about her personal life.

Eight years ago Lee had seen to it that Erin was the topic of conversation in the bank cafeteria. Whether he had intended that she discover his affair with Olivia, Erin couldn't guess. But it hadn't taken long to find out about his clandestine meetings with one of the most seductively beautiful women in the bank. When she had discovered the affair, Erin had crumbled. But Lee had seemed to blossom and feed upon her humiliation. Even during the first confrontation he hadn't been upset or contrite but rather smugly proud. Erin and Lee had separated, and Lee's fascination with Olivia continued to thrive. He was forever throwing the affair in Erin's face as if, somehow, she was to blame for the failure of their marriage. For a while she had tortured herself with the same thoughts.

But as Lee's attraction for uncomfortable confrontations with Erin increased, Erin realized that he drew a malicious satisfaction from taunting her. He saw to it that he and Olivia were everywhere that Erin went. During working hours he would come into the bank and meet Olivia for coffee. At office parties he would escort the sultry Olivia, never missing a chance to display his affection for her with a gentle kiss or a whispered endearment—always within eye and earshot of his former wife. At the time Erin told herself that it shouldn't bother her, and during the day she kept up a seemingly unconcerned and professional appearance. But at night, after long lonely hours working toward a law degree, she would find herself alone in the bed that she had once shared with Lee and she would cry bitter tears of frustration.

That was years ago, and somehow the pain had lessened. Now, looking back on the past, Erin wondered if she had ever really loved Lee. She had cared about him, yes, and her pride had been severely bruised by his betrayal. But she doubted that she had ever loved him, and certainly not with the passion that she knew he had found with Olivia.

After the liaison with Olivia had cooled, Lee had come back, hoping to rekindle the ashes of their broken marriage. Erin had waited for that day, falsely thinking that she would feel a vengeful satisfaction from slamming the door in his face. But when he had actually arrived on the doorstep, he looked tired and ragged. He was unshaven and had large purple circles under his eyes. His clothes were disheveled, and even his perfect blond hair had seemed to lack its usual luster. It had taken all of her strength to close the door on him in his embarrassed and confused state. She had turned him away, and instead of feeling the grim satisfaction of sweet revenge, she could only feel empty, dry and sad for her ex-husband. After locking the door, she had run into the bathroom and been sick for the rest of the afternoon, retching until her stomach had emptied and her body shook from the ordeal.

Erin stretched out on the couch and shook her head, trying to dislodge those vivid and melancholy memories of the past. She ran her fingers through the thick tangle of her black hair. The long evening stretched ahead of her as she clicked on the television to clear her head. The selection of sitcoms and variety shows was dismal, so she picked up a mystery novel that was guaranteed to interest her and curled up again on the antique sofa. But the spy thriller that should have held her attention, didn't. She found her thoughts traveling backward in time to her marriage only to jump forward again to this afternoon and to Kane Webster. With a disgusted sigh she tossed the book onto the coffee table and stared into the dusk. She let her mind wander at will until late in the night.

The doorbell chimed precisely at ten o'clock the next morning. Erin paused for a moment as her defenses wavered at the thought of facing Kane alone. Impatiently the doorbell sounded again, and she forcibly steeled herself before opening it.

"I thought that just maybe you had run out on me," Kane joked. He seemed affable, yet there was still that underlying hardness about him, a doubt that she had felt yesterday.

"I wouldn't think of it," she quipped back lightly, but felt her stomach tighten as she realized just how many times last night she had thought of avoiding meeting him.

"Good. Now, how about a cup of coffee?" he asked as he walked into the apartment and rubbed the chill out of his hands.

"Are you offering me one, or asking for one?"

Hearing the sarcastic tone of her voice, he cocked his head in her direction. "Are you angry with me already?"

Erin hadn't realized until then that she *was* angry with him for setting her life off balance. "No...of course not. I didn't mean to snap at you," she apologized.

"Then you won't mind if I use your phone?" he inquired. "I promised to call my daughter this morning, but I didn't want to disturb her earlier."

"The phone is in the bedroom," she replied, and smiled at him for the first time that morning.

He excused himself and threw his jacket over the hall tree before he set off in the direction that she had indicated. Not wanting to intrude, she went into the kitchen and began brewing the coffee. The apartment was small, and it was impossible for her not to overhear part of his conversation, although she purposefully turned up the volume of the radio. The last thing she wanted to know about was Kane's personal life. She had to try to keep things on a business level with him. Unfortunately even the classical music couldn't drown out Kane's voice as it rose in volume and unsuppressed anger.

"Krista! Don't even suggest such a thing! I'll be back in two weeks, and then we'll move you up here..." There was a long pause, and then Kane's voice softened. "I know how you feel, honey, honestly I do. But Dr. Richards thinks..." Another long pause. The conversation was extremely one-sided. "Look, Krista, I know that Aunt Sharon would like to have you stay until Christmas.... But the doctor and I think it would be best to get you into school here as soon as possible." Silence. "We'll talk about it later. Goodbye, honey."

It was several minutes before Kane came out of the bedroom, and in that time the lines around his eyes had seemed to deepen. Although he managed a smile, Erin could see that it was forced. He was preoccupied and tense. Through the soft folds of the fabric of his light-weight sport shirt, Erin could see the contours of his muscles, and they were tight. He walked into the living room and stared out of the window without seeing.

There was something in the droop of his shoulders that made her want to reach out and place a comforting hand against his cheek. He was having problems with his adolescent daughter—that much was evident—and Erin wanted to soothe away some of the mental pain he was experiencing. But she hesitated and remained in the kitchen, dawdling over coffee that was already brewed. It was safer somehow, watching him from a distance, wishing that any pain that he might be feeling would disappear.

When at last he turned back to face her, some of the strain had left his face. He ran his gaze over the apartment, appearing to study its contents. At that moment Erin sensed that her life was laid bare to him. The dusty rose couch, her weathered volumes of Shakespeare, an array of slightly disheveled plants, the antique rocker—everything was explored by Kane's cold gray eyes. It was as if, from the objects in the room, he could understand her and penetrate her soul. A part of her wanted to be examined by his eyes and touched by his mind, but another, more suspicious side of her objected to his appraisal.

Thoughtfully he picked up the discarded paperback mystery novel from the coffee table along with a worn volume of poetry by Keats. He opened the poetry book slowly and settled himself uncomfortably on the couch, with his long legs cramped under the coffee table. "You read this?" he asked, half to himself.

Erin poured the coffee but remained in the kitchen, still unsure of how to handle the conflicting emotions that surfaced each time she was alone with him. To answer his question she explained, "I read a variety of things, depending upon my mood."

"So I see," he agreed, eyeing the paperback spy thriller.

Suddenly she knew that she had made a mistake by seeing him in the intimacy of her own home. She felt too vulnerable, too transparent, too visible. Kane was alone with her, looking into the secret corners of her life, and unexpectedly she felt threatened. She had overheard part of his disagreement with his daughter, and she felt a desire to comfort him, and yet a need to turn her back on him and his problems. She couldn't let his life get tangled with her own; hers was too complicated and too precarious. She had to work with him as an employee; she couldn't let her emotions carry her away. She braced herself as she carried the two steaming mugs of coffee into the living room. "Kane," she began, placing a cup near him, "I don't think that it would be a good idea to go out today"

"You want to stay in?" he asked, deliberately misinterpreting her. "That would be fine with me.... Thanks." He reached for the cup and took an experimental sip while still watching her.

"No... I don't want to stay here. What I mean is I don't think that you and I should see each other..."

"Why not?"

"Because, for one thing, I make it a practice not to date anyone I work with."

He smiled to himself. "Then obviously, you're not as insecure about your job as you pretended to be yesterday. Wasn't it just yesterday morning that you accused me of plotting to fire you, along with all the other employees of the bank?"

"You're avoiding the issue," she challenged, a feeling of exasperation beginning to wash over her. "I'm not up to playing word games this morning!"

"Then let's be honest with each other, shall we? Why is it that you won't go out with me?" he asked, his silvery eyes capturing hers.

How could she tell him what she herself really didn't understand? Was it possible to explain that she felt a desire to be with him and an urge to run from him?

"Are you afraid of me?" His voice broke into her thoughts.

"No!"

"Well?"

"I just don't think it's a good idea to mix business with pleasure."

"Then," he seemed to agree, "let me assure you that you'll have a very unpleasant afternoon!" He placed his cup down and smiled at her in a perfectly sickening and victorious manner.

"Be serious...."

"I am! So far, you haven't given me any viable excuse for not spending a quiet afternoon together."

"But I thought..."

"It doesn't matter what you thought." Kane reached for her hand across the table, stifling her protests. "I just want a chance to get to know you better. Is that such a crime?" His angled face was earnest and open. Any doubts she had conceived earlier were quickly cast aside with the touch of his hand on her palm and the peaceful serenity of his gaze.

"No..."

"Good! Then let's go, shall we?"

She pulled her hand away from his and reached for her jacket. He pulled his legs from their bent position under the table, stood up and let his eyes roam over the apartment. His perusal was slow, steady and deliberate. Erin felt herself once again becoming more uncomfortable as the silent minutes passed.

"Do you like living here?" Kane finally asked, all of his attention drawn to the features of her face.

"Why do you ask?"

"I guess because this apartment house isn't exactly

what I expected." He lifted his shoulders and shrugged into his jacket.

"Just what did you expect?" Erin was intrigued by the conversation. Perhaps if she could draw him out, he would explain his feelings about her and wash away those last traces of doubt that nagged at Erin's mind. She could sense that there was something he wasn't telling her. It was as if he was purposely being wary with her.

"Oh, I don't know," he began in answer to her question. "But this place—it seems a little out of character," he remarked, looking at the faded Persian rug and running his fingers over the antique craftsmanship of the lead-glass windows.

"Out of character?"

"You're a career woman, right?" he asked, and Erin nodded her head in agreement, all the while wondering what he was leading up to and somehow not wanting to know. "This apartment—for that matter, the entire building—just doesn't fit with my interpretation of today's liberated woman..."

"Why not?"

"Truthfully," he chuckled, "because it looks like the set for one of those black-and-white slice-of-life movies of the forties."

Erin arched an inquisitive black eyebrow. "And you expected smoked glass, chrome fixtures and black vinyl upholstery?"

"Something like that."

"Sorry to disappoint you," she quipped, leaning against the door.

"You haven't disappointed me—not at all." His eyes found hers for an instant, and then his gaze swept the loft. "I knew when I met you that there was a darker, more private side of you. A side that you prefer to keep hidden away. Am I right?" His hands came up to the door, pressing on the wood and creating an imprisoning barrier near her head.

Erin met his questioning gaze with defiance. He was too close to the truth, too close to her. She drew in a deep, trembling breath. "You're right. I am a very private person, and I like it that way. What I don't like is anyone coming into my home and attempting to psychoanalyze me!"

A smile tugged at the corners of his mouth, but his eyes revealed only arctic cold. His breath whispered across her face. "Is that what I'm doing?"

"I hope not," she breathed, trying to still her racing heartbeat. Surely he could hear it—he was so near.

His finger reached out and stroked her cheek and his eyes covered her face and throat. "Maybe it would be a better idea to stay here today," he suggested silkily, but abruptly changed his mind. "On second thought it might be too dangerous to stay here…come on. I don't like being late."

"Late? For what?"

"You'll see…" There was just a hint of intimacy in his tone.

Erin pulled her jacket tightly around her shoulders, as if she were experiencing a sudden chill. "What have you got planned for today? Where are we going?" she demanded.

"You really don't want to know!" He moved one of his hands and helped her with the light calfskin jacket. His fingers brushed against her arm and lingered. Or did they? She pulled abruptly away from him and cinched the belt securely over her waist.

"Of course I want to know! Where are you taking me?"

"Just come along. And don't try to kid me. I haven't

known you very long, but believe me, I know you well
enough to realize that you like surprises and mystery in
your life."

"I'd just like to know what makes you such an expert
on me," she muttered and reached for the door angrily.
She was angry because he was correct in his assumption about her, but she hated to admit it. Before she could
open the door, he grabbed her forearm and whirled her
around to face him.

His eyes reached into the depths of hers. "You can't
hide from me, Erin," he whispered. "I won't let you." She
could feel herself trembling at his touch. Her lips parted,
but the denial that was forming in her mind died.

He lowered his head slowly, and his lips melted into
hers in a kiss that was soft, beckoning and full of promise. She found herself yearning to respond to the warmth
and tenderness of the embrace, but she forced herself to
pull away. If he had any questions about her reaction to
him, he didn't ask them. Instead he pulled her tightly
against him and led her down the steep steps of the apartment building.

There were many thoughts that crossed her mind, and
just as many questions that didn't have answers. She ignored the flood of emotions that carried her out of the
house and into the sleek black sports car. Kane helped her
into the car and then slid into the driver's seat. He started
the engine and the sporty machine roared to life. Neither
Erin nor Kane spoke, and the silence was as heavy as the
gray Seattle fog, but Erin discovered an inner warmth
that she didn't know existed.

Chapter 4

Kane drove steadily toward the heart of the city, carefully maneuvering the sporty little car down the steep inclines of the hills in order to save the muffler on the roller-coasterlike grade. Through the fog the gray waters of Elliott Bay lapped lazily against the waterfront. As they crested a final hill Erin was able to see the wharf and the bustle of activity along the crowded and colorful piers.

After parking the car, Erin and Kane strolled on the boardwalk that flanked the water's edge. Kane's hands were pushed deep into his pockets and his gaze slid over the water. Salt spray brushed against Erin's cheeks in a chilling embrace. Seagulls marauded the shore, calling out their lonesome cries. White, gleaming ferryboats plowed their way through the water, leaving only a frothy wake on the gray-blue waters as they disappeared into the fog.

Kane led Erin into a tiny bistro on the wharf. The warmth of the cozy restaurant was a welcome relief from the chill of the seawater and fog. They were seated at an intimate table near the window where they could watch the activities along the piers from the shelter of the bistro.

As the waiter brought the fresh seafood omelettes, Kane studied his empty coffee cup before looking into Erin's eyes.

"I suppose that you overheard my conversation with Krista." It was more of a statement than a question.

"Part of it."

"Why didn't you ask me about her?"

Erin met his gaze unwaveringly and noticed the rigid line of his jaw. Was he always so tense when he thought about his child, she wondered to herself. Aloud she responded, "I didn't want to pry."

Kane took a deep breath and looked out over the waters. He seemed to be wrestling with a weighty decision. Finally he turned his head back toward Erin. "Krista's disabled."

A startled look threatened to possess Erin's features, but she managed to make her voice steady. "I'm sorry," she whispered.

"So am I," he groaned and threw his napkin on his empty plate.

"Do you want to talk about it?"

"Do you want to listen?" His face was a mask of indifference, as if he suddenly regretted his outward display of emotion. *No,* she wanted to scream. *I don't want to know anything more about you. I'm attracted to you and I'm afraid of the attraction. I can't learn anything more about you that might bind me more tightly to you. I have to push away from you... I have to.*

"Of course I'll listen," she murmured, quieting the voice of suspicion that nagged at her.

"Krista is eleven. She was ten when the accident occurred." A dark, faraway look crossed his features. As he continued, his voice was flat, betraying no emotion. It was almost as if the words were part of a well-rehearsed speech, devoid of feeling or life. "She was riding in the car with her mother, my ex-wife. They were going to some 'retreat' or 'support group' meeting for the weekend. I really don't know much about it except it was the latest self-improvement seminar to be offered. Jana, my ex-wife, was forever following the latest self-improvement craze. It was one encounter group after another. Maybe I'm in part to blame for that, too."

Kane shook his head, as if clearing out unpleasant memories. Erin waited in silence as he continued.

"Anyway, it doesn't matter what new kick she was on. It just so happened that she had called and told me where she was going. I was angry. I didn't think that Krista needed to be exposed to all of that pseudopsychiatric garbage, and I told her so. We got into a helluva fight and she hung up on me. Two hours later I got a phone call from the police telling me that Jana was dead and Krista was in the hospital. To make a long story short, Krista's been in and out of the hospital ever since. She's still unable to walk unassisted."

"She's paralyzed?" Erin asked cautiously.

"Not exactly." Kane's eyes clouded for a minute. "It seems that she was lucky—nothing was actually broken in the accident. Jana was thrown out of the car and killed instantly, but Krista remained in the car, and other than a few cuts and bruises and a sprained left wrist, the doctors can find nothing physically wrong with her."

"But…"

"I know." Kane nodded his head. "It seems as if the cause of her paralysis is mental."

"I don't understand." Erin's brows knit in concern. What was Kane actually saying?

"I don't either. But what I can gather from the doctors is that she blames herself, or perhaps me, for the accident."

"No! That's not fair!"

Kane shrugged his shoulders. "Why not? Maybe if Jana and I hadn't fought, she would be alive today. Maybe the argument was the catalyst for her reckless driving."

"You can't blame yourself," Erin argued.

"Then who can I blame?"

"No one. It was just an unfortunate accident…"

"Try explaining that to a ten-year-old girl who has just lost her mother."

"Oh, Kane," Erin sighed, and reached for his hand.

Her hand was warm and comforting, and for a moment Kane forgot that he suspected Erin O'Toole of thievery. What was it about her that had made him open up to her and tell her the story of Krista's paralysis? Why was it so necessary that she know about him, that she care?

The waiter came to remove the dishes and bring the check. Kane helped Erin out of her chair and smiled disarmingly down on her. "I'm sorry," he apologized. "I didn't meant to bore you with my problems."

"You didn't bore me," Erin admitted.

"Well, let's push all those black thoughts aside for the day, shall we?" he asked, and took her hand powerfully in his. "I'm sure that when Krista gets up here and settles in, she'll be fine." Convincing as his words were, he didn't seem to believe them himself.

It was nearly afternoon, and they hurried down the boardwalk to catch the Blake Island ferry to visit Tillicum Village. Once on the island, they were entertained by the folklore and art objects of the native inhabitants.

Erin was fascinated by the blending of the modern and ancient cultures. The fog had lifted and the day was cool, but pleasant.

They spent the day hiking over the island and watching the everyday rituals of life in a tribal village. Late in the evening Erin and Kane, along with the other tourists, were guests of the tribe and feasted on baked salmon cooked in hot coals, as they had been for centuries. As twilight descended, the torches were lit, and Kane wrapped his arms possessively around Erin's waist. They sat on the hand-carved stone steps of the amphitheater and watched the colorful display of folk culture as enacted by the inhabitants of the island. In the flickering light of the stars and the torches, Kane's features looked stronger, more masculine. The scent of his cologne wafted over Erin, and involuntarily she pressed closer to him.

Darkness covered the island as the entertainment faded. Erin and Kane made their way back to the waiting ferry. The warm lights inside the vessel winked at them, but Kane led Erin onto the deck. The wind had become stronger, sending a salty spray into their faces as they stood on the deck of the boat and watched the sparkling lights of Seattle call to them across the narrow stretch of water.

Kane held Erin tightly, the power and warmth of his body molding to hers. During the day all of her defenses had melted. Ever since he had opened up to her and explained about his daughter, she had felt a kinship and warmth toward him. And the doubts that she had experienced were withering.

He stood behind her with the strength of his arms wrapped securely over her waist. They were silent as they watched the distance and felt the giant boat move through the black water. The engine of the large vessel whirred noisily and rhythmically and the darkened waters churned white as the ferry headed inland.

A light drizzle had begun, but Erin didn't move, afraid to break the spell of the evening. Although the September nip in the air was cool, Erin was warm, pressed firmly against the heat of Kane's body. It was as if they had made an unspoken pact that neither wanted to violate by speaking.

The drizzle increased into raindrops, and even the hardiest of the tourists shuffled into the interior of the ferry. Erin and Kane remained outside alone, content to feel the salty breeze against their faces and the heated promise of each other's body. Kane nuzzled the back of her neck, letting the wind whip her hair over his face. She could feel her skin become alive with his touch, her blood begin to warm with his caress. Unconsciously she leaned closer to him.

He murmured her name, seeming to give it a special and intimate quality as it caught on the wind. She pivoted to face him and he cupped her chin in his hand before pressing the moist tenderness of his lips firmly over hers. She parted her lips involuntarily, letting his tongue trace a silken path over her mouth tentatively before slowly and sensuously exploring the moist recess and enticing her to do the same. He wrapped himself more closely around her as his tongue stroked and danced with hers.

The rain came down in silvery droplets, sliding over Kane's face and past Erin's cheek to her throat and finally to hide below the collar of her blouse. Kane's kiss deepened and his hand moved gently but persistently against her back. His lips roved over her face and neck, kissing and licking the drops of rain from her eyes, cheeks and throat. An urgent moan escaped from his lips, and he finally pulled his face away from hers. His eyes slid over her body, seeming to probe every inch of her being. They had darkened to misty gray, and a pulsating passion was blazing in their dark depths.

A raindrop passed over Erin's neck, and Kane stooped to kiss it away, his lips brushing over the hollow of her throat. She shuddered, more from his delicate kiss than from the cool night air. Her knees buckled and he pulled her to him, but a blast from the ferry's horn announced that they were docking. All too soon the jewellike lights of the city had blossomed into streetlamps, and the intimate water journey was over.

They walked back to the car in silence, each absorbed in private thoughts. Erin wondered how she could possibly work for a man she needed so passionately as a woman. And what about his daughter, who blamed him for his wife's death? And Mitch—could she bring up the subject of Mitch's dismissal with Kane, or would it be the wedge that would come between them? For, as unlikely as it seemed, Erin was unwittingly beginning to look upon herself and Kane as a man and woman with a deep understanding of each other. *But that's crazy,* the realistic side of her mind argued. *You don't even know the man.*

And Kane wondered about Erin. Could this enigmatic and beautiful woman really be a viable suspect in the embezzling scheme? She seemed so…innocent, if that was the right word. It was so easy to talk with her; he had already confided in her concerning Krista. That was probably a mistake, he thought now. But for the moment he didn't want to believe anything about Erin other than what he felt. She was bewitching and he meant to find out all he could about her—tomorrow. Tonight he just didn't give a damn whether she was embezzling or not.

The black sports car whipped through the quiet streets,

sending sprays of water as its tires slashed pools of standing water. The windshield wipers moved in tempo, pushing the raindrops off the glass. Night closed in on Erin
as the black interior of the car seemed to melt into the
darkness of the evening.

Erin's senses were heightened. In the warmth of the
enclosed sports car, she could smell the tangy scent of
Kane's cologne and the masculine essence of his rain-
drenched body. For the entire short ride Erin was aware
of the man next to her. As he shifted gears, she could see
the long hard lines of his fingers and the athletic slant
of his legs straining against the fabric of his pants. She
had trouble concentrating on anything other than his potent masculinity.

As they approached the apartment house, he killed
the engine and sat motionless, his hands still gripping
the steering wheel. He glanced toward the windows of
Erin's third-floor apartment.

Erin cleared her throat. "Would you like to come in?
For a drink—or a cup of coffee?"

He rotated to face her, and even in the darkness she
imagined flames of smoldering passion burning in his
eyes. "I'd like it very much."

He opened the door for her and they walked up the
long staircase noiselessly. Although they didn't touch,
Erin felt a bond between them bridging the inches of open
air that separated their bodies. She licked her arid lips as
she reached into her purse for her keys. Many emotions
had come and gone since he had hurried her out of the
apartment this morning. God, was it only twelve hours
ago? Erin had hesitated only slightly when she thought
about asking him up to her apartment. She knew how
precarious it was for her to be alone with him, but she
couldn't resist extending the invitation and the evening.

Mrs. Cavenaugh had been right; she had hidden herself away from the world of men for much too long.

Her fingers shook as she tried to unlock the door, and Kane took the keys from her hand. He escorted her through the doorway and into the small apartment. Erin went through the motions of taking off her jacket, but her mind was on Kane and the intimacy of the apartment. There was no place to hide. "Could—I offer you a drink?"

He took off his jacket and let it fall casually across the arm of the couch. "Sure."

Erin moved into the kitchen and opened the liquor cabinet, but her thoughts didn't leave Kane. Although he was in the living room, the air was charged with electricity and anticipation. It was difficult to think, to move. Why had she asked him up to her loft, and why had he accepted?

She managed to put together some Irish coffee, and the cups were steaming as she carried them into the living room. Kane was standing at the window, looking into the night as if he could penetrate the darkness. His shirt was moist and clung to his body, and the ripple of his muscles was evident through the fabric.

When she entered the room, he turned to face her. His face was ragged, torn with emotion, and she knew that he was as tense as she. "Anything wrong?" she asked.

"Nothing," he whispered, but the besieged look on his face didn't disappear. "Thanks," he said with a tight-lipped smile and sampled the hot drink.

"There is something wrong," she challenged. "I can feel it. It's something about me, isn't it?"

"You're imagining things," he retorted, and took a long swallow of his drink.

"No... I'm not. It all started yesterday, at the office."

His gray eyes bored into her, daring her to continue. "I don't know what you mean."

"I think that you do. You were angry that I was at the office—don't deny it. And all of those ridiculous questions about Mitch. It has something to do with him, doesn't it?"

"Why don't you tell me," he suggested huskily. "What do you know about Mitchell Cameron?"

"Nothing—except that you fired him, and I don't know why!"

He set his cup down on the table and strode quietly over to where she was standing. His voice was barely audible, but he pinned her with his gaze. "You can't even hazard a guess?" he coaxed.

"No!"

"Why don't you try?" His fingers reached upward and found the nape of her neck. He lifted her hair from her shoulders and clasped both of his hands gently around her neck, massaging her shoulders through the light rain-washed fabric of her blouse.

"I have no idea. I only know that the legal department wasn't profitable..." His gray eyes snapped.

"Is that it? Would you let him go because of one bad year?"

"What do you think?"

"I don't know. I don't know how you work..."

"Sure you do," he suggested smoothly, and Erin felt that she had known him all of her life.

"Aren't you going to finish your drink?" she asked, not able to concentrate on anything other than the warm enticement of his hands. His thumbs traced lazy patterns of seduction along her throat, gently persuading her mind to think of nothing other than his overpowering maleness.

His eyes looked over at the half-full cup of Irish coffee. "Is that my cue to leave?"

Erin braced herself, trying to ignore the dizzying sensations that seemed to build up from within her and explode at his touch. "It's…it's getting late."

"And you'd like to go to bed?" he cajoled, his dark eyes alive.

"I…you…we have to work in the morning," she stammered, her senses reeling from his closeness.

"That we do," he agreed.

Erin's pulse was beginning to dance wildly as Kane's hands coaxed her to newer heights of sensuality. She could feel his breath, smell his clean masculine scent, and she knew that he was going to kiss her.

His arms moved to her waist and coiled possessively around her as his mouth brushed velvet-soft kisses down her cheek and throat. Her head fell backward, and he rained kisses up and down the length of her exposed neck. Erin's chest grew tight, and her breath began to whisper in short, shaky breaths.

His hands toyed at the hem of her blouse, at first tentatively, and finally with determination as he tugged the blouse out of the waistband of her slacks. His fingers explored the soft, supple muscles of her back, warming her skin to a rosy glow. Her knees began to give way, and he caught her, pushing his lips over hers in silent union. She moaned, and at the invitation of her parted lips, his tongue found hers, flicking and dancing with moist sparks of unfettered passion.

Moving steadily upward, his hands inched up her spine in a delicious spiraling motion. Her skin heated and caught fire. All her nerve endings ignited in hot boiling passion. His fingertips slowly and sensuously moved forward until he was kneading the tight muscles of her abdomen.

Her breasts ached against the confinement of her bra, and when at last his fingertips played with the lacy garment, she sighed. He pushed her gently and persuasively to the floor, and she felt the cool floorboards press against her fevered flesh. Slowly he let his hands slide to the buttons of her blouse, slipping each button easily through the buttonholes. As the blouse parted he unleashed her breasts from the lacy bra. "God, but you're beautiful," he moaned, looking directly at the full white curves of her soft breasts.

She felt her fingers working at the buttons of his shirt. When at last it was opened, and the expanse of golden bronze skin was visible, she moaned with pure animal pleasure. "So are you," she said huskily, watching his firm muscles flex under her admiring gaze.

His thumbs idled over her nipples as he fondled her breasts. Masterfully, he enticed her nipples to erection, and a smile of triumph lighted his eyes as he noticed them harden. He looked once into her eyes, the smoky gray of his gaze blending into the lilac-blue passion of hers.

It was as if she were drugged; all she could concentrate on was taking and giving pleasure. Her female body was overshadowing her mind. As Kane loved her, explored her, exulted in her, she, too, took satisfaction from touching and enticing him. Body was controlling mind in the sweet dreamlike mist of lovemaking.

They rolled together on the floor, and he rained kisses upon her face, her neck, her breasts. His tongue licked paths of fire over her body and kindled an aching need in her innermost core.

Endearingly his mouth descended on her breasts, and he suckled as if a babe, kneading the sensitive tissue with his hands as his lips lured love from her nipples. His body was upon hers and she felt the bittersweet pain of his weight over her. The cold floorboards touched her back, and his warm, naked torso inflamed her soul, causing boiling currents of lava to course through her veins.

"Oh, Erin," he called against her, and her pounding heart was triggered to a more passionate rhythm. He tore himself away from her and saw the disappointment in her eyes.

"I want to go to bed with you," he breathed, "and I want to make love to you."

"Are…are you asking me?" she gasped, drawing much needed air into her lungs.

"I've been asking you all night." He levered himself over her and leaned on one elbow while one hand still massaged her breasts.

"I want to…" she murmured, closing her eyes and trying to think rationally. Would the ache subside? Would she really be able to make love to him? Would she be able to stop?

"But…" he prodded, his breath ghosting over her hair.

"But…" She breathed heavily. "But…I'm afraid."

"Of what? Me?"

"No…"

"Then it must be that you're afraid of your husband," he guessed.

"Lee? How did you know about him?"

"A small surname discrepancy in your personnel file."

"Oh," she murmured, pulling her blouse over her breasts. Suddenly she felt conspicuously naked.

"He is the problem, isn't he," Kane asked gently, but there was a cold and calculating edge to his voice.

"No… Lee has nothing to do with us," she managed, but her mercurial temperature had cooled.

"You're still in love with him, aren't you?" His eyes regarded her gently, and he pulled her closer to his body and rocked her.

"No...you're wrong. You've got it all wrong. I'm not in love with Lee. Sometimes I wonder if I ever really was." His eyes followed hers to look out the window. "Oh, I thought I loved him, once, but some of the things that he did...that he said..." She still couldn't talk about it without getting a catch in her throat.

"Erin, honey. It's been a long time, and still he affects you. Are you sure that you're not still emotionally involved with him?"

Tears began to flow from her eyes, and he brushed them away. She tried to look away from him, but he forced her head in his direction, softly cupping her chin in his fingers. His movements were gentle, but his thoughts were grim. Lee Sinclair, whoever the hell he was, had scarred Erin, and Kane meant to know all about him.

"Have you seen him recently?"

"No...he moved to Spokane about a year ago." For some reason Erin couldn't tell Kane about the phone calls and the fact that Lee was back in Seattle.

Kane continued to rock her in silence, only the thin line of his lips belying his calm and comforting actions. Slowly Erin composed herself. She wondered how she had ever let things get so out of hand. She felt an embarrassed burn on her cheeks as she realized that she was sitting half-naked on the floor of her apartment with her new boss, weeping like a teenager, nearly jumping into bed with him. It was frightening and confusing, completely out of character.

"I'm sorry," she sniffed, managing a feeble smile. "I really don't know why I fell apart."

"It's all right. Here." He pulled the afghan from the

couch and wrapped her in its rainbow-colored tiered folds. "Are you sure that you're okay?" She nodded, and he rose from the floor, pulling her with him. "Why don't you go in and get in bed? I'll bring you some tea."

"No! Oh, no... I'm fine, honestly." She was embarrassed by her emotional outburst, and the last thing she wanted was that her boss should wait on her. She hiked the awkward blanket over her shoulders, but it seemed determined to slide to the floor.

"You're sure?" he asked, cocking a suspicious eyebrow in her direction and buttoning his shirt.

"I'm sure." Her voice was still husky, but the firm quality and tone that he recognized as control were back in her words.

She could tell that he was reluctant to leave, but after a final kiss to her forehead, and his hastily scribbled hotel phone number, he left her alone.

After he closed the door, she listened to the sound of his shoes clicking down the steps. Silently she counted them. Finally she heard the front door open and close with a thud. A sporty engine roared to life and faded into the night. Erin felt more alone than she had in years.

Chapter 5

The morning newspaper was spread before her as Erin sat down to a light breakfast of toast and jam. Her eyes wandered aimlessly over the headlines on the front page, but her mind refused to budge from the intimate moments she had shared with Kane. What had seemed a natural and beautiful lovemaking experience in the darkness had somehow lost its enchantment in the morning light. It wasn't that she regretted getting to know Kane, not at all. But he was her boss, and she couldn't let her body control her mind where he was concerned. Professionally it just wasn't sound judgment to get emotionally involved with an employer. And, although she could still conjure up the enigmatic image of his tanned masculine body and mirthless gray eyes, she wouldn't let it control her.

She applied a healthy spoonful of raspberry jam to her toast as she turned to the financial section. As her eyes met the black-and-white photograph of Mitchell Cameron, she let the knife fall to the table. The picture was several years old, and Mitch was smiling with his pleasant self-assured grin, but the caption in black boldface print captured her attention. FINANCIAL LAWYER ALLEGED THIEF—and in smaller print—Mitchell Cameron Accused of Embezzling Bank Funds.

"Oh, no!" Erin gasped, and her eyes read and reread the newspaper article several times. "There must be some mistake," she murmured to herself. "There has to be!" According to the article Mitch had been manipulating bank funds for the better part of two years. When the bank was sold, an audit found him out, and the new president, Kane Webster, had fired Mitch. The police were summoned and Mitch would be arraigned for indictment within the week.

Erin raced to the telephone and dialed Mitch's number. A busy signal beeped flatly in her ear. Either Mitch had taken the receiver off the hook, or he was already being plied by inquisitive friends and reporters.

As quickly as possible she scooped up the paper, grabbed her purse and slipped on her coat. She took the steps two at a time and nearly ran over Mrs. Cavenaugh on her way out the door. On the run, she apologized to the startled old woman and hurried out to the car. She turned on the ignition, the little car sparked to life and Erin proceeded on a mad dash to the bank, hampered only by the early-morning rush-hour traffic.

When she got to the bank, it was already crawling with employees. Although it was still early, it seemed that everyone had arrived with time to spare on this first day of new bank ownership. Erin pushed herself into the crowded elevator and wedged herself between two women.

"Have you seen the paper today?" a middle-aged woman with a faddish, curly hairstyle asked her friend.

"Not yet—I usually wait until coffee break. There's just not enough time in the morning, what with getting the kids off to school, you know," the shorter woman in a pink raincoat replied.

The elevator started its upward motion. "Then you haven't heard about Mitchell Cameron?" the curly-haired woman asked.

"Cameron? The head of the legal department?"

"That's right. Seems that the new president—that Mr. Webster—had him fired."

"No!"

"That's right," the taller woman said with a firm shake of her head. Her voice lowered, and she looked over her shoulder as she continued. "They suspect that Mr. Cameron was involved in some embezzling scheme…"

"The head of the legal department? Are you sure?"

Erin pretended not to hear the conversation. The elevator stopped on the seventeenth floor and the two women continued their conversation as they disembarked. Erin closed her eyes for a minute. By this time the entire bank staff had heard about Mitch. Could it possibly be true? She fervently hoped that Kane was wrong about Mitch.

The elevator stopped with a jolt, and Erin walked into the legal department. She was early, and only a few of the more aggressive young employees had made it to their desks. There were a few new faces in the crowd, probably some of Kane's imported troubleshooters from California, Erin guessed as she passed by the reception area and picked up her telephone messages. The most compelling of the notes was a handwritten memo from Kane indicating that he wanted to see her in his office immediately.

After taking off her coat, she armed herself with the

newspaper and marched into his office. An eerie, nostalgic feeling gripped her when she discovered that the familiar brass nameplate of Mitchell Cameron had been torn from the door. Only two fine drill holes remained in the wood panels to remind Erin that just last week Mitch had occupied this office.

Kane was sitting behind the desk when she entered. He motioned her to be seated in one of the side chairs as he finished scribbling some notes on a legal pad. But instead, she remained standing with her arms folded against her chest. The rolled newspaper was clamped firmly under her left arm.

"Have you seen the paper?" she asked him, echoing the conversation she had overhead in the elevator.

"Yes," he replied, looking up from his work.

"And you read the article on Mitch?" she accused.

"I've read several, starting last evening," he replied evenly. His eyes searched her face and he studied her intensely.

"Is it true?" she asked, her incredulity registering on her face. "Did Mitch really embezzle? How do you know—and why did you let the press find out about it? Do you know what you've done? You've ruined his career. He worked for this bank for over twenty years, and in one clean sweep you destroyed him!"

Her voice had risen with her emotion. She flung the paper onto his desk and turned her head away, biting on her fingernail and trying to piece together her shattered poise. Kane rose from the desk and crossed the room to close the door. He came back beside her and placed his hands on her shoulders. Gently he rubbed the tension out of her neck and shoulders.

"Don't," she implored. "Don't touch me—just give me answers, preferably straight ones!"

His fingers stopped their comforting motion but remained against the back of her neck. Her hair was pinned into a businesslike knot, twisted behind one ear, and Kane rested his hands on her exposed neck. Her head was bent, and she pressed a hand to her forehead as she waited for his explanation.

His voice was low and soft as he began to speak. "You've met my associate, Jim Haney?" His fingers felt the barest of movements as she nodded. "During the conversion, while Jim was still working here in Seattle, he... discovered that funds were being funneled out of some of the larger trust accounts. It took Jim quite a while, but finally he tracked down the culprit."

"Mitch?" she asked in a voice that was barely audible.

"Yes."

"But...how can you be sure?" She pivoted her head upward to find his face, and there was an unhidden pain in the depths of her eyes.

"Erin. We caught him red-handed. There's no doubt." The words were spoken softly, but there was an almost cruel hardness in his features.

Tears threatened to spill from her eyes, but she forced them backward and vainly attempted to keep her voice from shaking. "I...I just can't believe it." She averted her face from his intent study.

Kane propped her chin between his fingers and let his thumb rub it caressingly while tracing the line of her jaw. "You were very close to him?" he asked gently.

Erin shook her head faintly and bit her lip. "He's been a good friend to me." Her eyes were shining with unshed tears when she looked up at Kane's face once more. "He...he helped me through a very difficult time in my life..." she explained, and gave in to the urge to lean against him. His arm wrapped securely around her, and for a moment Erin forgot everything other than Kane's comforting presence. This couldn't be the same cold-hearted man who had fired Mitch, could it? Had Mitch really stooped to thievery?

"The difficult time," he whispered. "The divorce?"

She nodded mutely against the smooth fabric of his jacket.

A knock resounded on the thick mahogany door, and before Kane could respond, the door swung open. Olivia Parsons, with all of her self-assurance and poise in place, breezed into the room with only a brief apology.

"Excuse me, Mr. Webster... Erin." She included Erin out of courtesy. Her cool green eyes swept over the intimate scene before her, and although they reflected a glimmer of interest, her professional aplomb never wavered. Erin moved away from Kane with as much grace as was possible, but she was sure that Olivia hadn't missed the tender embrace between employer and employee. "I didn't mean to disturb you, but your secretary indicated that you needed these financial statements before the board meeting this afternoon." The tall brunette with the svelte figure and sleek Halston original dress handed Kane the stack of papers that she was carrying. The confident smile that she was wearing never left her face.

"You must be Miss Parsons," Kane surmised, his eyes traveling appreciatively over the neatly typed pages.

"Please call me Olivia," she responded. She gave Erin a fleeting head-to-toe appraisal, as if seeing her for the first time. Turning back to Kane, she continued. "I really didn't know that you were busy," she apologized again, and Erin felt a tide of crimson creep steadily up her neck.

"No problem," Kane assured Olivia, and escorted her out of the room. "Thank you for taking the time to bring the reports by."

"Anytime," Olivia suggested in a voice so throaty that Erin barely heard it.

Once Olivia had made her exit, Kane closed the door and deliberately turned to face Erin. His back was pressed firmly against the polished wood grain of the door, as if he were using his own body as a barricade against another intrusion. His body had stiffened, and all of the familiar fondness had escaped from his features. His face had become a mask devoid of emotion, and his words were no longer tender or caring. They were brittle in the air.

"I don't think that my office is the place to continue this discussion," he said tersely.

"I think it's a perfect place to discuss Mitch—right in the middle of his office!"

"Is that how you still think of it, as Mitch's office? If so, you had better change your mind. Mitchell Cameron is gone. He was an embezzler—a thief—and he's no longer with Consolidated Finances. I hope that fact doesn't hamper your work." He strode across the room to the desk. "We can discuss this later…tonight if you like. But right now I'm very busy." He sat at the desk and started reading the reports that he had received from Olivia.

Erin watched him with disbelieving eyes. How could he change so rapidly? It was as if he were a kind, considerate gentleman one moment and a heartless bastard the next. He looked up at her and flashed a perfectly condescending smile at her, but she knew it was an act. She had been with him enough to recognize the cool distance in his gray eyes.

"You're the one who called me in here," she reminded him, and waved the green personal memo in the air. "Just what was it that you wanted to discuss?"

The petrified smile fell from his face and a darker,

more volatile expression took over. "I wanted to ask you to dinner tonight."

"You've got to be kidding! First you call me in here. Then you nearly throw me out. And now you expect me to go out with you?" Sarcasm dripped from her words. "Not a chance!"

"Why not?"

Erin sighed wearily, tired of the argument. "For the same reasons that I spelled out to you yesterday."

There was a pool of darkness in his eyes. "You're afraid of me, aren't you?" he suggested, and then continued. "Or is it yourself who scares you?"

"It has nothing to do with fear, and you should know it! It's just that I don't think it would be good for either of us, professionally that is, to be the subject of office gossip or speculation."

"Don't you think that you're putting the cart before the horse?"

"I don't know what you mean," she sighed.

"In order for there to be any gossip, there's got to be a glimmer of truth. Someone has to start the rumors, and since I'm not one to 'kiss and tell,' I've got to assume that you are. Otherwise, there would be no cause for concern, would there?"

"You don't understand," she accused with a vehemence that interested Kane. "Gossip...it can be vicious— ugly! It can ruin your life!"

"Only if you let it—the same as anything else. Now, why don't you be honest with me—no, make that honest with yourself—and tell me what's really bothering you. I can't believe that a little innocent speculation about what you do after-hours is all that traumatic. For God's sake, Erin, you're a thirty-two-year-old divorcée, not a whimpering virgin! What kind of lily-white reputation are you trying to create?"

Her eyes narrowed and she planted her hands firmly against her hips. "The point is that I like to keep my personal life just that—private! And even though you and I won't go around telling anyone that we're seeing each other, believe me, the word will get out."

"And everyone will just naturally assume that because we're dating we're sleeping together, right?" he surmised, elaborating on her logic. He threw the neatly stacked reports down into an unruly pile on his desk and covered the floor space that separated them in long, swift strides. He didn't touch her, but he was close enough that she could feel the delicious warmth of his breath as it fanned against her hair. She stood her ground, not moving an inch, but every nerve ending in her body was rigidly aware of him and his nearness. "And even if some of the people around here think that we sleep together—" his fingers touched the silken skin of her cheek softly "—what's so bad about that? What do you care what other people think?"

Erin's lips thinned into a white line. She tried to control her temper and ignore the warm feelings that Kane was commanding from her. She pushed herself away from him in order to think clearly and avoid the compelling magnetism that seemed to surround him. "I've worked very hard to get where I am with this bank, and I don't need the frustration of knowing that co-workers think that I sleep with the boss to promote my career."

"Would you mind it if they thought you slept with the boss because you wanted to and not for career reasons?"

"You can't possibly understand!" she whispered, and turned on her heel to leave.

As she pushed open the door to make her exit, she

heard Kane's parting words. "You, Miss O'Toole, are paranoid! And I'll pick you up at seven-thirty!"

Kane's voice boomed through the open door. Several of the secretaries looked up from their typewriters to stare openly at Erin. She tried to ignore their curiosity and continued toward her office. She could feel their speculative glances boring holes into her back, but she managed to return to the security of her office with a modicum of poise.

Outwardly she controlled her ragged Irish temper, but once in the sanctity of her own office, she could feel the fumes of anger rising steadily within her. No doubt half of the legal department had already sized up her situation with the new boss, and it wasn't even ten o'clock yet! She tried to concentrate on her work, and she told herself not to be childish, but she couldn't help but feel that Kane had betrayed her trust by announcing that he planned to see her after work. To make matters worse, he had brushed off the subject of Mitch's dismissal with an arrogant wave of his hand and very little explanation.

During the remainder of the day Erin saw little of Kane. All of his contact with her came via his secretary in the form of interdepartmental memorandums. They had no personal contact. She had seen him only in passing, and he had smiled at her with the same polite but less than enthusiastic smile that he rained upon all of his employees. He showed her no special attention, which was exactly what she had wanted. And yet, a small and very feminine part of her yearned for the vaguest sign of emotion from him. Affection, endearment, friendship—anything that demonstrated that he cared for her in a more intimate way.

For most of the afternoon she attempted to bury herself in her work to avoid any further confrontations with

Kane. It also helped her ignore the whispers about Mitch and the speculations about the embezzlement.

It was long after five o'clock when she rose and tucked away the paperwork that was still spread unfinished on her desk. Although she had worked diligently, she had accomplished very little because of her preoccupation with Kane. He had asked her out early that morning, and she had refused, but her mind had wandered relentlessly back to the invitation. *What would it hurt?* her persuasive mind taunted.

But what good would it do, her more rational nature inquired. Yes, Kane was an interesting man, and yes, she would like to spend some time alone with him, and perhaps she would, if circumstances were different. But as things stood, she couldn't reconcile herself to live a double life of daytime employee and nighttime lover. No matter how she would try to convince herself otherwise, she was attracted to Kane as she never had been to any other man. Given an alternative set of circumstances, she knew that she could fall deeply in love with him. But, as fate would have it, she couldn't allow herself the pleasure of falling in love with a man for whom she worked.

It had taken her all day to come to the decision that she would have to explain her position to Kane once and for all. She threw her coat over her arm and clicked off the lights to her office. Most of the staff had left the building, but she knew that Kane was still working. She could hear his voice through the door. Rather than disturb him, she continued past his office toward the elevator.

Before the elevator doors parted, the door to Kane's office opened. Erin quickly resolved to herself that this would be as good a time as any to have it out with him. She turned to face him and discovered that he wasn't alone. Olivia Parsons was with him, looking as if she was hanging on his every word. Rather than intrude, Erin whirled and faced the elevator. Just as the doors were opening, Erin heard Kane call out to her.

"Erin, wait!" Kane hurried to Erin's side. "I'm glad I caught up with you. Do you need a ride home?"

"I've got my car," Erin replied, a little tartly. Why did Olivia always seem to be a part of the conversation? She looked cautiously at Olivia, but the calm expression on the brunette's face didn't appear to hold the slightest hint of interest.

"Then I'll see you at seven-thirty," Kane rejoined.

Erin looked from Kane to Olivia and back to Kane. "I...don't think so...not tonight." Olivia's eyebrows raised just a fraction of an inch. The gesture was almost unnoticeable, but Erin caught the movement and the silent gleam of fascination in Olivia's perfect green eyes.

"Going out?" Olivia asked casually. "I don't blame you. Who wants to cook after a full day at the office?"

Erin couldn't resist the temptation of disagreeing with Olivia. "Oh, I don't know. I've always enjoyed cooking."

Olivia's face registered disbelief, but it was Kane who answered. "Good!" he interjected. "I haven't had a home-cooked meal in ages. We'll eat at your place."

Erin was about to reject Kane's suggestion, but Olivia stilled Erin's tongue. "That's terrible!" she sang out sweetly to Kane. "I tell you what. Why don't you come over to my house for a special dinner? We'll have fresh seafood from Puget Sound..."

"Thanks, Olivia. I appreciate the hospitality." Kane seemed to agree, and Erin could feel her heart beginning to shred. Kane shot Erin a questioning look and continued, "But I've got other plans." His response was gentle but firm.

"Some other time..." Olivia persisted, only slightly dejected.

"Some other time," Kane agreed evasively.

There was a slight pause in the conversation, and finally Olivia broke the silence. "I guess I'd better be running along. I'll see you in the morning." Although the farewell was meant for both Erin and Kane, Olivia's warm green eyes looked directly into the cool gray depths of Kane's gaze. Erin could almost see the invitation in those emerald pools.

Olivia slipped into the elevator, and it started its descent before Erin began. "Look, Kane. I've made a decision. You can't come over tonight...and I can't go out with you. It's as simple as that!"

She pressed the elevator call button and waited for Kane's reaction. She expected that he would be violent, but when he spoke it was with quiet deliberation.

"You...would deny me a home-cooked meal?" he asked, and there was a mischievous smile in his eyes.

"Of course not, but you've got to understand..."

"It's settled then. I'll bring the wine." He slipped his hand beneath her elbow and guided her into the elevator. As the doors shut he wrapped his arms tightly around her and kissed her feverishly on the lips. All of the warmth and intimacy that had been denied during the day was surfacing again in his passionate embrace.

Before Erin could respond, the elevator stopped on the fifth floor, and Kane released her to smile at two of his new employees. Erin was sure that even in the slightly dimmed elevator light, the two young women could see her swollen lips and the trace of passion still lingering in Kane's eyes. When she stepped out of the building she hurried to her car, and Kane didn't follow. How was she going to deal with him and the web of emotions that was entangling her more tightly each day?

It was crazy and she knew it, but she felt that she was beginning to fall in love with Kane Webster. The thought made her shudder as she reached for the headlights and the windshield wipers. *You're a damn fool, Erin O'Toole,* she chided herself. She couldn't be, wouldn't be, in love with her boss. It was an impossible and ridiculous situation, but nonetheless, it existed.

She was still arguing with herself as she stopped the car in her familiar spot in front of the apartment house. She bent her head against the wind and slight drizzle of the evening. A welcome light came from Mrs. Cavenaugh's window and Erin stopped at the doorway to the little old lady's apartment. She waited several minutes before Mrs. Cavenaugh's voice called through the door.

"Who's there?"

"It's me, Mrs. Cavenaugh… Erin," she responded, and immediately heard the click of locks as Mrs. Cavenaugh opened the door. The old woman peeked timidly through the crack in the door before removing the final chain and opening the door widely.

"Come in…come in," Mrs. Cavenaugh welcomed her.

"I can't… I'm having company tonight."

"Oh?" Mrs. Cavenaugh didn't even have the decency to hide her interest. "Mr. Webster?"

Erin eyed the half-bent old woman with loving suspicion. "How did you know?" she asked.

"Lucky guess," the old woman murmured, her blue eyes dancing with pleasure. "Don't you have just a minute to tell me all about it?"

"No, I'm sorry, truly I am." Erin's face was earnest, and Mrs. Cavenaugh didn't doubt her sincerity. "I just dropped by to tell you that I got hold of someone to install the insulation. They'll be here by the end of the week."

"Good!"

"Look, I've really got to run."

"I understand," was the kindly reply. "Oh, by the way, Erin, did you know that Mr. Jefferies is planning to move out by the end of the month?"

"Oh, no," Erin sighed, and then quickly hid her disappointment. "I knew that he had been thinking of moving in with his daughter and her husband, but I didn't think that he had made up his mind."

"Seems they made it up for him," Mrs. Cavenaugh asserted. "I'm sure he left his notice in your mailbox."

"Oh, thanks for reminding me." Erin crossed the hallway and opened her mailbox. Among the various bills was Mr. Jefferies's notice of vacancy. The last thing she needed right now was one more empty apartment. She needed the rental income just to keep up the mortgage, let alone the repairs and upkeep. But she couldn't show her worries to Mrs. Cavenaugh. She called out to the friendly elderly woman as she mounted the stairs, "I'll let you know exactly when the repairmen will be here."

"Thanks, honey," Mrs. Cavenaugh responded before closing the door to her apartment. Erin raced up the remaining stairs, anxious to get into the familiar and secure surroundings of her own apartment.

Kane pulled the small black sports car to the curb and snapped off the motor. He sat in the darkness for a minute, staring at the apartment house that Erin called home. He was angry and he was tense, but he tried to control his emotions so that Erin wouldn't become suspicious.

Erin was already home. The lights in her apartment glowed in the night, and the Volkswagen Rabbit was sit-

ting where she had parked it in front of the house. Kane's
eyes moved from the car back to the building. Even in the
unearthly glow of the streetlamp he could see the signs of
age and disrepair in the large old home. Was this apartment house the cause of Erin's financial woes? Could she
possibly be moving funds out of the bank for the upkeep
on the costly old house?

He had thought he would feel a deep satisfaction in
catching Cameron's accomplice in crime, but as he came
closer to the truth, the satisfaction had soured in his stomach to a feeling of sickening disgust. He knew now that
Erin was lying to him, and somehow he had to find a
way to prove his theories about her, as much as he de-
spised the idea.

He took in a long breath as he thought about Lee Sinclair. Erin's ex-husband was supposedly in Spokane, but
with a little checking, Kane had discovered that Lee had
moved back to Seattle over six weeks ago—about the
same time that Erin had applied for her employee loan.
Could she still be involved with him, and was he the
drain on her money? Perhaps he was the catalyst in the
partnership with Cameron.

Kane's hands tightened on the steering wheel until
his knuckles whitened. He could only hope that he was
wrong and that someone else was the embezzler. God,
how he hoped so. There were still a few more possibilities, but unfortunately, right now the evidence was stacking up very heavily against Erin O'Toole.

Angrily Kane pushed his disturbing thoughts aside
and got out of the car. He was furious at himself, at Erin
and particularly at Lee Sinclair, whoever the hell he was.

Erin had just placed the pan of lasagna in the oven
when the doorbell rang. Before she could cross the room,

the door swung open and thudded against the wall. Kane strode into the room and closed the door just as angrily as he had opened it. Erin had begun to smile, but when her eyes met his, her face froze. His gray eyes were guarded, a stormy fog clouding their depths. His casual clothes, the same ones he had been wearing earlier, were disheveled and his tie was loosened rather haphazardly. "Don't you ever lock your door?" he muttered.

"Of course I do…but I was in a hurry…"

"That's no excuse!" he rifled back at her.

Erin was confused by his only slightly suppressed anger, and she felt her temper rise to meet his. "Look, Kane, thanks for your concern, but it's really not your problem."

"It is my problem, when it concerns your safety."

"I'm all right. I just forgot to latch the door. That's not such a crime."

A more contrite look softened his features. "I suppose you're right," he sighed, raking strong fingers through his coarse brown hair. "I didn't mean to jump down your throat." He walked over to her and brushed a light kiss across her forehead. "But I do wish that you would be more careful."

"I'll try," she agreed in order to ease the tension that was building between them. She could see that he was beginning to relax, but the lines near the edge of his eyes looked deeper than they had this morning. She tried to tell herself that it was probably just the first day at the bank that had taken its toll on him, or possibly that he was concerned about Krista. But she couldn't help feeling that there was a larger problem storming through his mind—a problem that concerned her.

"Would you like a drink?" Erin suggested.

"Oh." He slapped a palm against his forehead. "I forgot the wine—something came up at the bank. Forgive me?"

He was teasing, Erin knew, but she could sense an inner turbulence below his light attempt at humor. "Consider yourself forgiven," she agreed, "but my liquor cabinet isn't all that great."

Kane walked over to the cupboard that she indicated and searched through the bottles. "Saying that is being kind. It's downright pathetic."

"I don't see that you have much room to complain, since you were the one who forgot the wine in the first place," she reminded him, trying to suppress a smile.

"Touché, Miss O'Toole. Now let's see what we have in here." His voice was muffled as he pushed aside partially filled bottles of liquor and finally pulled out an unopened bottle of brandy. With a triumphant flourish, he held out the bottle for Erin's inspection. "Look at this. Maybe the evening won't be a total loss after all!"

"A loss? You practically insisted on inviting yourself over to a home-cooked dinner, and already you're insinuating that the evening will be wasted?" She could feel him looking at her, but she didn't turn around and started slicing the greens for a salad. She was only kidding, of course, but he deserved a shot after barging in that way.

In a moment his arms were encircling her waist and his breath moved her hair as he whispered in her ear. His voice was low and full of promise as he spoke. "I don't think that any time would ever be wasted if I could share it with you."

She let the knife slip to the counter. His touch was warming her abdomen, and the feel of his hot breath against her neck made her heart race. She tried to keep her head and recapture the light mood of the minute before. "That sounds like a line if I ever heard one."

"A line? Oh, Erin, don't you think I'm a little too old for lines? Don't you know what you mean to me?" There

was a torture in his words as if he was admitting something that he himself didn't want to hear.

His hands persuaded her body to rotate and face him,
and when her eyes found his, she saw that his gaze had
darkened with a smoky passion. Smoldering embers lit
his eyes as he bent his head slowly downward to capture
her trembling lips with his. The warm, seductive pressure of his mouth roving passionately over hers made her
dizzy. She tried to blink and restore some sanity to her
emotions, but she couldn't. It was as if her entire body
began and ended where her lips met his. Her knees began
to give way and melt beneath her. And as he tasted her,
an aching need began to consume her.

Her response was complete. Her blood warmed in a
swirling moist heat. She began to return his kiss, hesitantly at first. But as he kindled the fires of desire within
her body, she responded in kind. Her kisses became anxious pleas for a more intense lovemaking. Boldly her
fingers crept up his chest until her arms encircled his
neck. She felt the thick muscular cords near his spine
and unconsciously began to massage away the tension
that seemed to devour him tonight.

Kane groaned with pleasure, his voice an echo of hers
as she gasped for air. His tongue met hers and danced
hungrily in a torrid fever, first flicking light touches to
hers and finally molding it with a moist and fevered need.
"Erin," he breathed, letting her name whisper against her.
"I need you…tonight."

Erin's mind continued to remind her that she should
stop him now, while she still had the chance, but she found
herself resisting common sense and embracing temptation. Never had she felt so ignited, so completely female.

His lips scorched a trail of featherlight kisses from
her eyes to her throat and on to her tender ear. His deli-

cious breath tingled her inner ear, sending shock waves of passion resounding through her mind. She let her head fall away from him, hoping to somehow make her neck and earlobe more available to him. His thumb traced the hollow of her throat, gently at first, but with increased pressure in tight little circles…around and around, until she thought that she wouldn't be able to breathe.

Erin sighed briefly and resigned herself to the fact that her mind wanted him as much as her body did. "Oh, Kane," she murmured, "I need you, too." She succumbed body and soul to her desires and arched her hips against his. His breath ruffled her hair and he smiled down at her before lifting her off her feet and carrying her into the bedroom.

"I know that you need me, Erin. I thought that you would never realize that we were meant to be together."

"Together?" she breathed.

"As man and woman. I knew it from the first time I saw you, sitting amid that ridiculous pile of books in your office."

Together as man and woman, she thought, *but for how long? For an hour, a day, a week?* Her mind raced forward, but her body wouldn't let go, not tonight. She felt him pressed hotly against her, smelled his warm clean scent and saw a stormy passion in his face that she had to capture. She needed him every bit as much as he needed her, and perhaps much, much more.

Erin let herself follow the path of her emotions. The magic of his kiss had aroused her to the point of no return, and she was heedless of anything save his sensitive touch. She couldn't deny herself any of the pleasures that he could spark in her. Since that first moment in her dimly lit office, she, too, had been aware of him first and foremost as a man. His sensuality couldn't be ignored, not for a second. His dark eyes, well-muscled body and virile self-assurance had enticed and beckoned to the center of her femininity, and she was tempted beyond reason to respond.

Erin's body seemed to warm from the inside out, melting in fevered washes of heat and desire. Any reservations that might still have lingered in her mind were slowly and unconsciously stripped away from her as he rained liquid kisses over her skin.

The bedroom was bathed in moonlight. Kane laid Erin on the bed, and she felt the cool satin of the comforter through the sheer silk of her blouse. She was still dressed, although as he stood over her, she felt naked. Naked to the pain of needing him. Naked in the knowledge that she loved him. And naked in the recognition that her love was unreturned. His heavy-lidded eyes were unreadable, but Erin was very certain that although there was a smoke of passion in his gaze there was no flame of love.

Regardless of that fact, she couldn't and wouldn't deny the urges of her body. She loved him, despite his lack of love for her. The bed sagged beneath Kane's weight, and Erin felt herself tremble. His finger traced the length of her arm, but his eyes never left hers. He was watching her, almost studying her, seeming content to let his gaze caress her.

"Tell me no if you want me to stop," he commanded in a hoarse voice. His lips brushed tentatively over hers.

Her response was a grateful moan. Their lips met in a hot embrace, and she let her arms wind around his neck in a display of total abandon. She wanted all of him with a burning need that she had never before felt.

He let his hands stroke her face and throat in moth-soft caresses, until at last they reached her collar and finally the buttons of her blouse. He opened the blouse slowly, letting the fine silky fabric part of its own accord. And then gently he raised her shoulders to let the blouse slip to the floor. His eyes watched her torso as her breasts rose and fell with each of her gasping breaths.

"Erin... God, but you're beautiful," he sighed, fingering the lacy bra that was still a seductive barrier between his flesh and hers. His fingers teased and finally unclasped the skimpy piece of lingerie, until at last her aching breasts were unrestrained.

A groan escaped from his lips as he slowly massaged each dark-nippled breast to arousal. When he could feel the hardness of her breasts, he cuddled them softly and buried his head between the two feminine peaks. Erin arched against him, unable to control the hot urges that were firing her. She reached for his shirt, and as quickly as possible, removed it from his body, until her anxious fingers found the thick soft mat of fur that covered his chest and the male nipples beneath it.

As he enticed her, so did she him. She let her fingers touch and caress the firm muscles that flared rigidly over his body. Her hands traveled up his spine, vertebra by vertebra, feeling the hardness of his back through the moisture of his sweat.

The room was dark; only the soft glow from the partially opened door mingled with the moon glow to add a shimmering pallor to the night. But Erin could see Kane as clearly as if it were a bright summer day. All of her senses were alive to him. His touch fired her, his scent encouraged her and his salt-sweet taste lingered on her lips and tongue.

His hands traveled to her skirt and pantyhose, quickly discarding a portion of the clothing that separated them. He cast off his pants as rapidly, never for a moment leaving Erin alone. Always one part of him was pressed warmly and possessively over her.

Her blood was boiling through her veins, spiraling

upward from the deep mercurial well that was vibrating from the essence of her femininity. His lips traveled over her breasts, teasing and tasting each one while his hands slowly and rhythmically rubbed soft patterns against her abdomen, dipping deliciously below the elastic of her panties, and then letting the fabric snap tantalizingly against her skin.

Kane toyed with her last article of clothing until she thought she would go mad with the urgency of her need for him. When the agonizing last flimsy barrier was finally freed from her body, she groaned in pure animal pleasure and desire. He let his lips graze the muscles of her abdomen to circle her navel. His tongue warmed her flesh and she pulled him more closely to her.

All thoughts of anything but the mastery of his lovemaking were torn from her mind, pushed aside as quickly as her clothing. She was conscious of only one thing: the bruising, pulsating desire that dominated her mind and body. Time had ceased. Doubts had fled. All that she cared about was Kane: the skillful play of his fingers on her thighs and buttocks, the searing brand of his kiss over her breasts and abdomen, the enticing lure of his strong body.

She could feel the granitelike touch of his naked leg against hers, the soft hair tickling her cleanly shaven skin. She could also tell that he was holding back his physical needs to give her the utmost pleasure. In the half light of the moon she could see his arousal and feel the warm length of him brushing against her.

Just as she felt that she would surely melt with need of him, he came to her, fusing the fine muscles of his body with hers in a hot, rhythmic blend of passion. She felt him push her over the delicate edge of desire to fulfillment, and in the warm wash of exploded passion, he came with her in a burning torchlike shudder of surrender.

Erin felt a sigh flow from her lips as she held him tightly and securely, holding on to him as if her life depended on him. It had been many, many years since she had made love to a man, and never had she felt the wonder or the magic that Kane had aroused and satisfied in her tonight. Although she felt an incredible bliss, her torn emotions got the better of her, and she began to feel the hot sear of tears burn at the back of her eyes.

Embarrassed at herself, she tried to move away from Kane and blink back the unwanted tears. But as she slid against the satin comforter, his arms locked over her, imprisoning her.

"Where do you think you're going?" he whispered silkily, his voice still holding the satisfaction of afterglow.

Erin's voice caught in her throat and she couldn't force herself to answer him.

"Erin?" Kane's voice was more aware than it had been. "Is something wrong?"

She shook her head negatively, but when she did, she felt his strong fingers reach up and stroke her face. His hands stopped their movement as his fingertips encountered the first tear that had slid unrequested down her cheek. "Oh, no," he murmured.

"It's not…what you think," she managed to sigh.

"Did I hurt you?" His voice was uneven in the night.

"No…no… Kane…"

"Then why? I don't understand." His words were raw with concern.

"Neither do I," she admitted as the tears began to flow freely past the web of her lashes and down her cheeks. She shook her head in self-deprecation, letting the ebony curtain of her hair fall loosely around her face. How could she do such a thing to him, she asked herself silently. And how, when she was so deliriously happy, could she feel so confused and torn?

"Erin." His voice had lowered an octave, and he brushed her hair away from her face so as to kiss the tears from her cheeks. "Is something wrong?" He held her gently to him, letting her skin press tightly to his, while he covered them both with the comforter. In the quiet room, he rocked her in the cradle of his arms.

"No...nothing...nothing's wrong..." Her voice wavered.

"What is it? You're not ashamed of making love to me, are you?"

"No...no...never." She felt his breath feathering the back of her head as he sighed with relief. "It's nothing I can explain," she continued. "The last few weeks have been hard...." Could she tell him about the badly needed repairs to the building, the confusion she felt about Mitch or the taxing telephone calls from Lee? "...I guess I've been tired." She wanted to explain how she felt, but there were so many conflicting and unsettling emotions warring within her that she didn't want to think about them. Not tonight. She just needed to feel the peaceful security of Kane's arms around her.

Kane clutched her more urgently to him in a protective embrace. He could feel the beating of her heart, a warm pulse fluttering lightly under his fingertips and vibrating against the velvet smoothness of her breasts. He wanted her to speak—to confess. He needed to assure her that he could make everything right. He would find a way to help her out of the mess that Mitchell Cameron had created.

Kane's voice rumbled against his chest, and she could feel the deep manly tones pulsing against her naked back. "I want you to know that if you do have a problem—any problem whatsoever—you can come to me." His last words sounded like a confession. "I'm on your side."

"Oh, Kane," she breathed, wanting to confide her innermost thoughts and share everything with him, yet unable to bare her soul any more than she already had. "There's really nothing to tell. I'm…just a little keyed up. That's all…." She could feel herself smiling at him through her tears.

Outside a cloud crossed the moon, giving a misty aura to the light that passed into the bedroom. She turned to face Kane, and his eyes looked all the more omniscient in the unnatural moon glow.

"I hope you realize that if you ever need a friend, you can count on me," Kane murmured, before lowering his head to hers and kissing away the final tears that stained her cheeks.

As his lips found hers, she tasted the salt of her own tears, mingled seductively with the uniquely male taste of Kane. She parted her lips, and in a moment the kisses deepened to rekindle the fires of passion that possessed them.

With a gentleness that belied the tension that pushed against him, Kane caressed Erin and together they discovered the secrets of inflamed desire and glorious love. Erin fell dreamlessly to sleep in the warm strength of Kane's arms. But Kane didn't sleep. Too many uneasy thoughts about Erin strained against his mind. He looked at her asleep and brushed an unruly wisp of raven hair off the perfect alabaster sheen of her face. Sleeping in the moonlight, she seemed so childlike, innocent and vulnerable.

But his mind continued in its ugly pursuit of the truth. Why had she lied to him? And why did he care so much?

Chapter 6

Erin felt comfortably warm and drowsy as she stretched lengthwise in the bed and tucked the silken comforter more cozily around her neck. She sighed softly to herself in pleasure as she slowly awakened. All the tension that had been gathering in her body over the last six months had somehow ebbed gently away from her. She smiled to herself contentedly before realizing that she felt so dreamily happy because she had made love to Kane Webster—her new boss!

Her dark lashes flew open as the reality of the situation dawned upon her. The bedroom was dark and the bed was empty. Kane must have left her and disappeared into the night as she slept. A feeling akin to desperation cascaded over her, and the bed, once warm and comforting, seemed cruelly cold and empty. She wondered silently to herself how she could have been so foolishly naive to expect him to stay with her. She was achingly aware that she loved him, and although she didn't want to care for him so deeply, she accepted the naked truth of her love. But she wasn't so foolish as to expect that he could possibly reciprocate her feelings of the heart.

Erin mentally chided herself for her thoughts of love. For all she knew, Kane might consider her just another easy conquest. The infuriating phrase "one night stand" crept into her mind. For all her bold talk of not mixing business with pleasure, she had invited Kane all too easily into her heart and into her bed.

You're an idiot, she swore at herself as she decided to get dressed. She reached for her teal blue skirt that was still lying in the discarded heap of wrinkled clothing at the side of the bed. After pulling her pantyhose on furiously, she began to step into the skirt.

"Don't get dressed on my account," Kane's voice whispered across the darkness to her. Her disappointed heart leaped at the sound of his voice, and she whirled toward the doorway to find Kane leaning casually against the doorjamb, his gaze wandering recklessly over her body. Involuntarily she crossed her free arm over her breasts, while with the other she tugged vainly at the skirt.

"I...I thought that you'd gone," Erin murmured, and feeling somewhat embarrassed by her partial nudity, she hastily grabbed the sheet from the bed and pulled it toga-like around her body. Kane watched her swathe herself with the white sheet, and in his mind he likened her to a Greek goddess.

"Now, why would I want to leave?" he drawled huskily as his eyes traveled lazily over her one exposed slim leg and up to her eyes. Her fingers tightened around the sheet and yet she felt naked.

"I don't know," she admitted, "but when I woke up, you were gone and I didn't hear any noise. I thought that you must have..." Her words died as she interpreted the expression in his clear gray eyes.

He stood still in the doorway watching her. One well-muscled shoulder rested against the doorjamb. The light from the living room was behind him, and his silhouette in the darkness seemed to intensify the broad strength of his shoulders and the powerful play of muscles on his chest. His shirt was still unbuttoned as if he were just in the process of getting dressed when he heard her awaken. Erin found it hard to concentrate on anything but his tanned skin and the invitation of his open shirt. Unconsciously she gripped the sheet a little more tightly.

"I'm not going to leave you," he replied seriously, and then wondered at the promise he heard echoing in his words. He could see Erin's face in the cloud-shadowed moon glow—a delicate, regal oval placed in relief by the tangled mass of black hair that cascaded down to rest against the marble texture of her bare shoulder. The hollow of her throat beckoned him, but he resisted reaching for her. She was beautiful, almost an inspiration, and Kane had difficulty reining in his emotions. Her lilac eyes shimmered in the half light, and Kane was sorely tempted to go back to the bed and crush her passionately against him. How could he ache so much for one woman, he asked himself. And how could any woman who appeared so innocent and vulnerable be mixed up with something as gut-wrenchingly dishonest as embezzling? The onerous thoughts that battled in his mind must have been evident on his face because Erin's expression changed from innocence to wariness. God, why did he want her so badly?

Kane cleared his throat, and in an attempt to break the heady silence that was entrapping him, tried to lighten the suddenly tense moment. He cocked one dark eyebrow in mock suspicion and effectively changed the subject.

"So you thought that I had left you, did you? Wishful thinking on your part, wasn't it?"

"Wishful thinking? What do you mean?"

"You've been trying to weasel out of fixing dinner for me all day, but it won't work. I'm here and I'm famished!"

"The lasagna! Oh, no! I forgot all about it!" Erin wailed. She started to hike her skirt upward over her hips, while still grasping the sheet.

Kane stood, unmoving and bemused, in the doorway. His silvery eyes never left her body. Erin sucked in a deep breath. Although she was uncomfortable about dressing in front of him, intuitively she knew it would be useless to try and dissuade him from watching her. She gave him an irritated glare that only seemed to amuse him further as she tried to squirm into the tight blue skirt and attempted to keep the sheet positioned modestly. Her efforts were in vain, and a deep chuckle erupted in his throat as he unabashedly studied her dismal efforts at privacy. Finally, when she slipped the skirt up to her waist and tried to tug at the zipper, it got caught in the sheet and Erin gave up. After the passionate intimacy of only an hour before, Erin realized that her modesty must appear slightly neurotic. With a burning flush of scarlet on her cheeks, she untangled the sheet from the zipper and let the sheet fall to the floor.

"Damn!" she swore under her breath when the skirt was in place at last. She raised her deep round eyes to him and met his gaze unwaveringly. Her breasts, two white soft mounds, were unshielded, and she moved slowly as she finished dressing. "You're not making this easy, you know," she accused, her eyes never leaving his. He met her challenging gaze with an amused twinkle in his eyes. "The least you could do," she continued, "is take the dinner out of the oven so it doesn't burn!"

A condescending smile touched the corners of his lips. "You expect me to help with the cooking?"

"Why not? You obviously intend to help with the eating," she bantered back at him, and attempted to hurry through the doorway. Just as she tried to pass him, he placed a strong arm across her path. The action effectively barred her passage and barricaded her into the bedroom.

"Not so fast," he murmured seductively. Erin felt her throat tighten.

"But the meal—the lasagna. It's probably cremated!"

"It'll keep," he breathed, his eyes holding hers. His head dipped downward, and before she could utter any further protest, he kissed her softly. His lips lingered over hers for only an instant before he dropped the imprisoning arm and pulled his head away from hers. "I just wanted to thank you."

"For what?" she asked breathlessly.

"For just being you." His words warmed her, and she felt more than a little light-headed and dizzy, but the steady pressure of his warm hand against the small of her back forced her into the living area of the apartment. She couldn't help but smile as she noticed that he had set the table for two and pulled the slightly overcooked casserole from the oven. Candles graced the intimate table. The wine was poured. The meal was already served.

"You did this?" she asked, surveying the table that he had set with enviable care. "And I slept through it?" Amazement was evident in her voice.

"Surprising, isn't it?"

"That's putting it mildly." She shook her head in concentrated thought. "I'm normally a light sleeper," she murmured as she walked into the kitchen.

"That's because you haven't been keeping the right company."

"And just what is that supposed to mean?" she inquired cautiously as she put the finishing touches on the meal and placed the salad on the table next to the lasagna and warm bread.

"Just that you'd probably sleep more soundly with me."

Her eyes jumped to his face as she took the chair opposite his at the table. She took a deep breath and decided that it was time to set him straight about her. Perhaps he had gotten the wrong impression and thought that she was somewhat promiscuous.

She began slowly and deliberately. "Kane, I want you to understand something about me," she requested.

"Such as?"

"Contrary to what you might think…" She struggled with her next words as they caught in her throat. "I don't normally… I mean…" She shook her dark curls in frustration. "What I'm trying to say is that I don't make a habit of sleeping with a man whom I barely know." She watched for his reaction.

"Oh?" His voice was interested, and he pushed his plate aside to give her his full attention. She saw no criticism in his misty eyes, only concern.

"I hope that I haven't given you the wrong impression about me…."

"You mean because you slept with me?"

Two dark scarlet points of color brightened her cheeks, but she bravely continued. "That's exactly what I mean." Her words were hushed, and for a moment she was forced to look away from him. When she brought her eyes back to his, she held his gaze steadily and her voice became

coolly even. "I don't really understand why I think that
you have to know this, but for the sake of my own somewhat Victorian morals, I want you to realize that I don't
have casual affairs. In fact, other than my ex-husband,
there has been no one. Until you."

"I know that," he assured her in a voice as grave as
the night.

She fingered her wineglass and took a long swallow
of the rosé. She studied the pale pink liquid and swirled
it in the long-stemmed glass before continuing the conversation. "Then why did you ask me all of those insult-
ing questions about Mitch?"

At the mention of Mitchell Cameron's name, a scowl
darkened Kane's features. Once again his face was
guarded and his eyes became two silver shields. "I didn't
know you then," was the terse reply.

"And in just three days you know me well enough to
evaluate my love life?" she returned, and heard the sarcasm in her voice.

"I probably know a lot more about you than you think."

Her lilac eyes fastened on his, and a rush of indignation that she couldn't conceal colored her words. "You
haven't been checking up on me, have you?"

"No more than I have any other employee of the bank."
It was a lie and he knew it, but he couldn't let her think
any differently at this point. He hated himself for the lie,
but he was trapped by the web of suspicions that plagued
him and by the storm of emotions that captured him every
time he looked into her eyes.

"Then why all the insinuations about Mitch? Can't
you believe that a woman can make it on her own without sleeping with the boss?"

He arched an expressive dark eyebrow, and she felt
immediately contrite. The question that was unspoken

hung between them on a charged electric current. Unashamedly Erin answered it. "You know that I didn't make love to you because of my job."

"Then tell me, why *did* you sleep with me?" he coaxed.

"For the same reason that *you* slept with *me*," she responded, lifting her chin proudly. "Because I wanted to." His tight frown seemed to relax, and he took a sip of his wine as he surveyed her over the rim of the wineglass. His gray eyes concentrated on her. She seemed so honest. It was impossible to think that her beautiful face would lie. Why hadn't she been truthful about her ex-husband? Erin O'Toole was an enigma, a ravishing, seductive enigma.

Erin struggled with her meal. Why did she feel such an uncontrollable urge to explain everything to Kane? And why did she feel the need for caution? As she put aside her fork, she spread her hands outward on the table, her fingers reaching up in a supplicating gesture. "Mitch was my boss, and he was and is a very dear friend. No matter what he's done, nothing will change that. But there was never anything more between us than personal friendship and professional respect for each other. Can't you believe me?"

"Of course I do—now," Kane replied. "But you can't blame me for my suspicions. Until I met you in the bank last Saturday, I didn't know anything about you other than what was in your personnel file. I knew that you had been promoted rapidly—perhaps too quickly—and I wanted to know why. You have to understand that no matter how close you are to Mitch, he is a thief!" Kane's cold gray eyes grew dark. "It's my responsibility to the bank, the stockholders, the savings customers, everyone, to know everything I can about each employee. It would be ridiculous to think that I would rely on Mitchell Cameron's judgment."

Kane's words hit Erin like a splash of cold water. She was stunned, and her voice was brittle as she asked the question that was uppermost in her mind. "Are you trying to tell me that you don't think I'm qualified for my position, that the only reason you could see that I would get the job was because I might have slept with Mitch?" she challenged, stricken at the thought.

His voice was strangely devoid of emotion. "I'm saying that it's difficult for me to believe that a thirty-two-year-old woman is second in command of the legal department of a major Seattle bank...."

"And if I were a man?" she fired back at him, her eyes deepening to the color of a midnight storm.

"Sex has nothing to do with this!"

"Sex has everything to do with this," she argued, slapping her palm against the table and rattling the silverware. "You seem to overlook the fact that I spent the last six years of my life in night school, for the most part doing postgraduate work in corporate law! If it weren't for the fact that you bought First Puget Bank, I would probably be a practicing attorney today!"

It was Kane's turn to be angry and his words sliced through the air. "I don't see how I could have possibly hindered your legal career! What does my ownership of the bank have to do with it?"

Erin swallowed with difficulty and licked her arid lips. She tried to think calmly and took a long swallow of wine to quench her parched throat. Getting angry wouldn't solve anything, she told herself, and giving in to her sometimes volatile temper would only hinder the situation. Carefully she explained her position. "There are several reasons that I haven't been able to take the bar exam."

"And somehow they are all my fault," he surmised.

"I'm not blaming you," she insisted, and began toying with her napkin. "First Puget was paying my way through school. Any class I took that pertained to my job was paid for by the bank. Other classes I paid for myself. That is—until the bank sale."

"You mean, until Consolidated Finances bought out First Puget?"

She nodded.

"Lack of money prevented you from taking the exam?" His jawline hardened and a tiny muscle began to work in his jaw as he clenched his teeth together. One more reason Erin needed money, as he saw it. Just how desperate was she?

"Money isn't the only problem," she sighed, wishing there were some way to avoid this particular discussion. "You see, in the past six months, there have been several departmental changes...and Mitch wasn't around a good deal of the time. I had to spend a lot of my free time at the bank, working."

"And you didn't have time to study for the examination?" Was there a slight undercurrent of sarcasm to his question?

"It's not as simple as going out and getting a driver's license, you know!" she snapped back at him, her strained temper unleashed at last. Viciously she speared a portion of the lasagna and forced the bite into her mouth.

For a few seconds neither she nor Kane spoke, and they finished the remainder of the meal in silent battle. When she hazarded a surreptitious glance in his direction, she felt her anger flow out of her. Perhaps it was the deep concentration of his knit brows, or the play of light on his gold-streaked chestnut hair. Or maybe it was the seductive way his mouth curved, or his bronzed chest as it peeked out from beneath his shirt. Whatever the reason, she felt her temper cool as she watched him. Her heart was torn and she ached to understand the man whom she loved so urgently.

Why, she wondered, did she feel that he was holding something back from her? Why did there always seem to be a dark, unasked question in his eyes? Was he like she was, insecure about a commitment to a fellow employee? Was it possible that he had a girlfriend, or perhaps a fiancée, waiting for him in California? Or was it a brooding concern for his daughter that made him seem so remote at times? How could she love a man so desperately and still feel that he wasn't being completely honest with her?

She finished her meal, excused herself and began brewing some coffee in the kitchen. Despite the uncomfortable conversation, Kane ate hungrily and Erin was pleased. What was it about preparing a meal for the man she loved that made her feel so satisfied? Some age-old maternal instinct, she supposed and smiled to herself. She had experienced the same satisfied sensation with Lee in the first few months of her marriage. It hadn't lasted long, she reminded herself!

At a time like this why would she remember her ex-husband and the few good times that they had shared? She tried to dispel her mood of melancholy remembrance by pouring the coffee and carrying it into the living room.

Kane had risen from the table and was standing at the window, staring out across the darkened Puget Sound. From his position, he could see the jeweled lights of Seattle winking on the quiet black waters. A deep blanket of fog was beginning to roll into the Sound.

"Even at night this is a spectacular view of the city,"

he thought aloud, accepting the coffee that Erin offered. She, too, looked into the misty night.

"That's one of the reasons that I had to have this place," she agreed, and then laughed. "Along with a very long list of other things."

"Such as?"

"The charm of this old house. Everything about it speaks of a different time, a more romantic period in history." She ran a caressing finger across the cool wood of the windowsill. "The craftsmanship is exquisitely ornate, and I doubt that it could be duplicated today. This house was built with love. Look at the woodwork, the carved stairs, the beveled windows, everything! Even the builder who separated it into apartments and added all the modern conveniences took enough care to keep the flavor and the grandeur of the house in mind. I fell in love with it the minute I saw it," she admitted, and was surprised at how easily she had opened up to Kane about her feelings for the old mansion.

"Didn't anyone warn you about the expensive upkeep of such an old building?" he asked cautiously as he sat down on the couch. She took a seat next to him and shook her head thoughtfully.

"Everyone I knew tried to talk me out of it. Even my parents, who live on the East Coast, flew out here to try and dissuade me. They all told me that I was throwing money away. How does the expression go? 'Good money after bad'? They swore that the upkeep of the place would ruin me financially." She shrugged her slim shoulders and looked out the window again. "But the more people tried to talk me out of it, the more I absolutely had to have it!"

"Watch out," he cautioned with a smile. "Your rebellious side is beginning to show."

"Is it?" she asked, turning her attention back to him.

She had considered herself many things, but never rebellious.

"That dark, private side of you that I told you about yesterday. It's surfacing," he suggested.

Once again the conversation was becoming too intimate for Erin. She was beginning to feel claustrophobic, as if he were closing in on her. Something made her draw away; she tried to change the subject. "In any event I bought this place and haven't lived to regret it yet."

"And were all those people who gave you advice correct?"

"What do you mean?"

He took a long, experimental sip of his coffee and studied her intently. "I mean, has this house become a financial burden to you?"

Erin swallowed before answering. Just how much did she want him to know about her, and how much did he already guess? "It hasn't been easy," she admitted reluctantly.

"Tenant problems?"

She shook her head negatively. "Not really. Most of the people who rent here have been with me for years, and they are very nice people who take pride in their homes. Once in a while I have a vacancy problem, but the primary difficulty with this place is the repairs. You see, I'm not exactly handy with a hammer or a saw."

"I wouldn't worry too much about that," he teased and lightly touched her shoulder. "You have talents in other fields." His whispered words were tender and comforting, and she felt that she had known him all her life. His fingers touched her hair. He felt himself drawn to the ebony sheen of her curls. They were as black and inviting as the night itself. He caught himself and struggled to maintain his objectivity where Erin was concerned, but found it difficult to put his feelings for her in their proper perspective. She had lied to him and he knew it. Whether she admitted it or not, Lee Sinclair was back in Seattle. Kane felt that he had to press Erin tonight, before he became all the more entangled in her mysterious womanly charms. He couldn't let himself forget that it was imperative that he understand what devious thoughts were being spun in that regal head of hers.

"What about your ex-husband?" Kane prodded.

"Lee?" she asked, perplexed. "What does Lee have to do with anything?" Nervously she pushed an errant strand of hair back in place. Why did Kane continue to bring up the subject of a man whom Erin would rather forget?

"What did he have to say about this place and your purchasing it?"

"He couldn't say much. We were divorced at the time," she responded with a finality that she hoped would effectively close the subject. But still he persisted.

"Tell me about the divorce," he coaxed.

"Why?"

A smile toyed with the corners of his mouth. "Because I want to know all about you…" he suggested silkily.

"I don't like to talk about Lee."

"Why?"

"Are you interrogating me again?" she asked, promptly regretting the acidity in her words. She got up from the couch and shrugged her shoulders. "It bothers me…to talk about Lee."

"Did he hurt you so badly?" he asked, his voice gentle.

Her eyes glazed over with the shame that she had borne. How could she explain the embarrassment of Lee's affair and the messy divorce? "Yes," she whispered, "I suppose that he did hurt me, but only because I let him."

"By loving him too much?" he asked severely.

"No, by being so young and naive. At the time I thought that all marriages were made in heaven, and I didn't think that I would fail, or that he would *use* me...." She found that she was trembling. The cup of coffee shook in her fingers, and she was forced to set it on the bookcase in order to hide her reaction from Kane.

"There was another woman?" he guessed, and Erin, with her back to him, let her shoulders droop as she nodded.

"My pride was wounded very deeply." She pulled her lips into a thin line of self-deprecation and squared her sagging shoulders. "I just never thought that I would end up as a divorce court statistic!"

"You didn't want the marriage to end?"

She turned and faced him. "You don't understand. I didn't want to fail, but I *had* to get out of the marriage to Lee. I couldn't bear the hypocrisy!"

Quickly Kane moved off the couch and reached for her. He pressed her quietly against the strength of his chest. Although she was still shaking, she could hear the steady beat of his heart, and his silent support helped calm her.

"Erin," Kane breathed, sharing in the agony that had embittered her.

"It's all right," she murmured against him. "I don't know why it still bothers me...at times. The pain has been gone for a long while."

She felt his arm tighten around her, and his voice was barely a whisper when he asked the question. "Do you ever see him?" Kane asked with an urgency she couldn't understand.

"I haven't seen him for over a year, since he moved to Spokane." The pressure of his hands against her back increased and she felt compelled to continue. "But he has moved back to Seattle, and he has called me."

His grip slackened, but the deep lines of concern that etched his forehead remained. "He wants to see you again?" Kane asked, and his eyes narrowed a fraction.

"I don't want to see him," she sighed. "So I haven't."

"Is he being overly persistent?" There was a thread of steel in Kane's voice.

"Yes…no…no, not really…" She rubbed her temple in confusion. "Couldn't we talk about something else? I really don't like to be reminded of that period in my life. What about you?" she asked, her lilac eyes searching his. "What was your marriage like?"

Kane released her and scowled. His lips formed a thin line that was neither a smile or frown. "I suppose that's a fair question, since you bared your soul to me."

He strode purposefully back to the couch and raked his fingers through the thick waves of his hair, before picking up his lukewarm coffee and staring into the black liquid.

"My marriage to Jana was a mistake from the beginning," he admitted with a frown. "I guess I probably knew it at the time, but I was much younger then, and it took me quite a few years to finally admit to myself that we had made an error that was destroying us."

He looked vacantly out the window into the fog before continuing. His dark brows pulled together in concentration and carefully Erin came closer to him and perched on the arm of the sofa as he began to speak.

"In the beginning I was attracted to her because she was an incredibly beautiful and famous woman. You know, the glamorous model. I was just getting started in my business at the time, and I was flattered that she would even give me the time of day. I convinced myself that I loved her, when actually there was never any love between us. I was young enough to think that beneath all the glitter was a beautiful person hidden in that gorgeous body. A typical male mistake. And of course I was wrong.

"We had a whirlwind romance, I guess you might say. Lusty affair would be more exact. In any event just as I was beginning to suspect that we were too different ever to get along, it was too late—she was pregnant. I talked her out of the abortion and into marriage."

His lips thinned and he shook his head derisively. "I guess that I was a damned fool to think that a baby would change things between us, that our differences would work themselves out. And as it turned out, Jana and I had very different impressions about family life. She resented having to give up her figure and her career for the sake of her pregnancy, and she resented being a mother and a housewife. After five years of battling with her I agreed to the divorce that she wanted so desperately. As I said before, the marriage was a mistake from the beginning, and I knew it. But no matter what, it was worth every minute of the arguments—because of Krista."

He cleared his throat as he thought about his daughter and a sadness stole across his features. Erin felt an urge to brush away the signs of strain that seemed to age his face. The line of his jaw tensed as he spoke. "The biggest error in judgment I made was that at the time I didn't fight for custody. I subscribed to the same myth as the rest of the world: a young girl needs to be with her mother, regardless of the weaknesses or the frame of mind of the woman." A tortured look came into his steely eyes. "And then, to compound the mistake, I threw myself into my work, trying to erase the memories that had become painful. My attitude—it wasn't fair to Krista. To put it bluntly, I neglected my child. Not because I wanted to, but because I wanted to hide from the memories." He closed his eyes for a moment and rubbed the back of his neck to ease the tension that had knotted at the base of his head as he thought about the divorce and his child. He seemed tired and weary; Erin felt the burn of tears threatening to spill from her eyes.

His voice was a muted whisper when he continued. "I saw Krista occasionally of course, but not nearly as much as I wanted to or should have...it was just too difficult, too much of a struggle." A dark eyebrow cocked sardonically. "A selfish attitude, wouldn't you say?" he asked her rhetorically. His next sentence was one of self-condemnation. "I was a bastard of a father!"

He hesitated only slightly, and that was to wave his arm emphatically, stilling the protest that was forming in Erin's throat.

"Within a year Jana was trying to rebuild her career. It was difficult for her because she was six years older and slightly out of shape. Modeling, for the most part, is for the very young woman with an almost boyishly slim figure. No one in the New York or Los Angeles agencies was interested in Jana. As far as they were concerned, Jana was yesterday's news.

"Then this Hollywood actress obsession took hold of her, and unfortunately she failed, dismally trying to remember her lines as the cameras rolled." He rubbed his chin thoughtfully. "It was at about that point that she began making the self-help and group therapy rounds. She went through periods of fad diets, deep depression, sensitivity groups—you name it and she was into it. I suggested that she go to a respected local psychiatrist, but she ignored my advice as usual and preferred to stick with the most faddish encounter group of the day.

"That's when I decided to do something about Krista. As poor a father as I had been, even I knew that all Jana's neuroses couldn't be good for an impressionable nine-year-old girl. Damn!" He swore at himself and bit his lower lip in annoyed remembrance. "I should have seen it earlier. Maybe I could have prevented all of Krista's problems. Perhaps if I had been paying a little more attention to my kid rather than my business interests, Jana would be alive today and Krista would be walking like a normal and healthy eleven-year-old!"

"You can't blame yourself," Erin objected. "You tried to help."

Steely gray eyes flashed fire at her. "'Too little, too late,' as the saying goes."

Erin had trouble keeping her silence. She saw the emotions that were ripping him apart as he thought about his past. His fist clenched tightly before he thrust it into the pocket of his pants.

"There's really not all that much more to tell," Kane admitted in a softer, more controlled voice. "I was concerned, and I suggested that Krista come and live with me, at least for a while, until Jana could—how did she phrase it—get her head together. But she wouldn't have anything to do with it. Krista was a burden to her, and both she and I knew it, yet she wouldn't allow my own daughter to come and live with me! Sometimes I felt that Jana was using Krista as a weapon against me." An almost evil look stole over his lips. "And it worked! Not only did it bother me, but Krista became steadily more introverted. She always had been a somewhat shy, quiet child, but it seemed that she was withdrawing too deeply into herself, becoming sullen." There was a long pause while Kane drew in a steadying breath. "And then, of course, there was the accident. Up until that time, at least I could talk to Krista." His eyes darkened with a quiet rage at the circumstances that had led to the isolation from his only child. "But since the accident and her paralysis, I have trouble communicating with her about anything. It's as if she's punishing me for what happened to Jana…." He shifted his weight uncomfortably on the couch before murmuring, in a barely audible voice, his own self-condemnation. "I suppose that I deserve it!"

"No!" Erin challenged.

"For God's sake, Erin. Krista watched her mother die!"

"Oh, Kane, don't go on blaming yourself for something that no one could prevent," she begged.

"Easier said than done," he muttered.

Telling the story had been an ordeal that Kane hadn't prepared himself for. He was nervous and amazed at his own confessions to Erin. It was never his intention to divulge so much of himself to her. He didn't want her to be able to see into his mind, and yet he had just given her the chance.

Kane had told himself that he needed to get to know Erin to find out more about the embezzling scheme at the bank, but the pleading look of innocence in her eyes, the soft, petulant curve of her lips, and her clear-sighted, intelligent mind all trapped him into admitting things that he had hidden from the rest of the world. Why was it so damn easy to talk to her, to confide his most introspective thoughts to her?

Erin was obviously moved by his story; he could see that in the caring look of pain she directed toward him and the unshed tears in her eyes. God, he reminded himself, he had to get away from her while he still could.

He cleared his throat and put his empty coffee cup on the table. Avoiding her eyes, he reached for his jacket and slipped the sport coat over his shoulders. "I guess that we had better call it a night," he declared with a touch of tenderness in his voice. He fought the urge to draw her into his arms and kiss away the tears she was trying courageously to hide.

"You're leaving?" Was it a surprise or disappointment that made her touch her lips provocatively?

"I think it would be best."

"Why?"

"I thought you were the one who wanted to keep our relationship strictly business...."

"It's too late for that now," she whispered, and her wide violet eyes touched his.

"Convince me," he coaxed huskily, and mentally cursed himself for his own weakness.

"What would it take to convince you?" she teased, still blinking back the tears that pooled in her eyes.

"Use your imagination...."

A slow seductive smile lit her eyes. "You're wicked," she accused. "You know that, don't you?" She crossed the living room and let her fingers slide inside his jacket to press warmly against the light cotton fabric of his shirt. Powerful muscles tensed under the sensitive touch of her fingertips.

A slow groan of agonized pleasure escaped from his throat before he lowered his head to hers and captured her lips with his. "Oh, Erin," he whispered as he swept her off her feet and carried her toward the bedroom, "why is it that I can't resist you?"

Chapter 7

The bed creaked and shifted in the darkness.

"What are you doing?" Groggily she asked the question. Erin's eyes fluttered open as she felt Kane stir and move out of bed.

"I have to get up—I have work to do today," Kane replied and rubbed her tousled head fondly. In the inky blackness of the predawn hours, he could see her. Even after a passionate night of lovemaking, she looked serenely enchanting against the stark whiteness of the bedsheets.

She groaned and rolled over. "But, oh, God, it's only—" Erin reached for the alarm clock and pulled the luminescent dial within inches of her face and sleepy eyes "—four-thirty in the morning." There was another agonized groan as she pushed the clock back on the nightstand. "No one in his right mind gets up at this time of day," she moaned, and stuffed her face back into the downy softness of her pillow.

The bed sagged under Kane's weight and he pressed a warm kiss against her forehead. "Do you want me to stay until dawn?" he asked quietly. "What about your tenants, not to mention our fellow bankers? You were the one who didn't want our relationship open for public viewing," he reminded her. "Besides all of that nonsense, I need a shower, shave and a change of clothing."

Even to Erin's cobweb-filled mind, Kane's reasoning seemed logical and clear. She propped up her head with her hand and tugged at the quilt close to the base of her throat. An autumn chill stung the morning air.

It took a little time, but slowly she began to awaken, and with interested eyes, she watched him get dressed. It was strange how comfortable she felt just being with him, how natural and right it all seemed. But he was correct. The fewer people who knew of their relationship, the better.

Kane left just as dawn was stretching its golden rays through her bedroom window. She listened as his car roared off down the hill and faded in the distance. It was a faraway, lonely sound that retreated into the misty morning air.

It was impossible to fall back into the heavy slumber that had come to her in Kane's arms. And so, with one final assessing and dubious glance at the clock, she got up, showered and dressed for the day.

Surprisingly, with only a few hours' sleep, Erin felt wonderfully refreshed after the hot needlelike spray of the shower pulsated against her skin. She toweled herself dry, applied a thin sheen of makeup, twisted the ebony strands of her hair into her businesslike chignon and stepped into her favorite burgundy suedelike suit. As she tied the broad white bow of her silk blouse she glanced in the mirror, and the woman in the reflection smiled back in genuine fondness. Erin felt good about herself this morning.

Fingers of fog still held the city, but the bright morning sun sent prisms of colorful light streaming heavenward in what promised to be a gorgeous fall day.

Unwittingly Erin smiled as she pushed her way through the large plate-glass doors of the bank building. The dismal feeling of trepidation that had been with her during the transition of ownership of the bank seemed to have disappeared. Even as she brushed by Kane's office, she felt only a tinge of regret for Mitch. She still had a fondness in her heart for her ex-employer, but she realized that there was nothing that she or anyone else could do to help him. He had never returned any of her calls, although she had left several messages on the mechanical answering device that Mitch had installed. She had tried her best. Now, surely, if he needed to get in touch with her, he would.

As she passed by the outer reception area, she reached, by habit, for her messages stacked neatly on the main reception desk. She smiled inwardly as she read the bold scrawl that she recognized immediately as Kane's handwriting. It was concise and stated only "Tonight, eight o'clock." Erin couldn't restrain the blush that slowly climbed up her neck nor the look of satisfaction that touched the corners of her eyes. She wondered how transparent she must appear.

The secretary who had compiled the messages for her was a professional woman of about sixty, who neither commented nor indicated in any manner that she had read or interpreted the intimate message in Ms. O'Toole's slot. Relief washed over Erin as she read the look of total disinterest in the gray-haired woman's smile and the professional "Good morning" that was her usual greeting.

Nothing appeared out of the ordinary. Even before Erin began to move toward her office, the secretary resumed the quick staccato rhythm of her lithe fingers on the keyboard of the typewriter.

It was midafternoon before Erin actually saw Kane again. He was conferring in the hallway with a man whom Erin recognized as a vice-president of the loan department. For a quick instant Erin's mind traveled to the employee loan that she had requested and wondered fleetingly if it was the topic of conversation. From Kane's reaction she doubted that he was discussing her need for funds.

As she passed the two bankers Kane gave Erin a perfunctory nod of his head to indicate that he had seen her, but there was nothing the least bit intimate in his gesture. It was an act of courtesy to acknowledge an associate. For a moment Erin's temper began to rise, and she felt angry until she understood the reasons for his discretion and feigned lack of interest in her. It was what she had requested, insisted upon—that their relationship remain secret, clandestine—and he was adhering to her request to the letter.

As she closed the door to her office she found herself still thinking of Kane and the tenuous relationship that existed between them. How could something so wonderful as falling in love with Kane seem so wrong? Why did she feel two conflicting urges warring within her mind? One feminine part of her wanted to share the happiness she had found with him with the world. The other more cautious and rational side of her nature urged her to silence. After all he was still her boss, the man who signed her paychecks, and it would be easy for anyone to misconstrue her feelings and relationship with him. She had been the target of curious and malicious gossip before, and she had vowed never to let herself be put in such an emotional and compromising position again. She knew how devastated she had been eight years ago, and she steeled herself against any intrusions into her private life. She hadn't wanted to fall in love with Kane; it had just happened. Perhaps, together, they could avoid the speculation and gossip. Surely it couldn't be that difficult to keep things on a professional level at the office, could it?

Erin lulled herself into a sense of serenity. It was a brilliant autumn afternoon, and other than the slight snub from Kane, the day had gone well. It wasn't until late afternoon that her tranquil mood was destroyed.

Contrary to what she had expected, Erin had accomplished more work this day than she had in weeks. Kane Webster had seemed to more than amply fill Mitchell Cameron's shoes, and all the disturbing telephone calls and interruptions that Erin had become used to had vanished. For the first time in over six months she could devote all her attention to the piles of probate work that had accumulated in her "Incoming" basket.

Erin was actually giving herself a mental commendation as she surveyed the clean desktop and slipped into the burgundy jacket before leaving the building. Just as she reached into the open desk drawer for her purse, there was a sharp rap on the door, and Olivia Parsons, not waiting for an invitation, glided into the room.

At the sultry brunette's entrance, Erin felt a cold tingle of apprehension at the back of her neck. Olivia was holding a clipboard pressed firmly to her breasts and jangled something metallic in the air.

"New keys!" Olivia announced, and dropped a ring of keys with a jingle onto the desktop. The green shimmer of Olivia's street-length designer dress matched the emerald essence of her eyes. "I'll need all your old keys," she stated flatly, and waited, somewhat impatiently, with her long fingers resting against her hip. The action emphasized the long, seductive curve of her leg.

"My keys? Why?"

"Standard procedure, after something like this embezzling thing with Mitch. Who can guess just how many sets of keys he's had made for any door in this building?"

"Of course," Erin agreed, and found herself relaxing a little as she realized that Olivia was just doing her job. Erin understood the liability of the bank. Even if Mitch had turned in his set of keys, he could have a dozen copies hidden away. The bank couldn't take the chance that he might sneak back into the building or the vaults.

"Here they are," Erin stated, producing the keys from the side pocket of her purse. She handed them to Olivia and the dark-haired girl frowned as she counted them. "Where's the other one?" Olivia asked, a puzzled expression crowding her neatly arched brows.

"I don't have any others. Just the key to the front door, the probate file cabinet, and Mitch's office—unless you want my desk key."

"No," Olivia answered, checking the corresponding numbers on the keys against her chart. "What about the key to the securities cart?" she asked, her green eyes reassessing Erin.

"I haven't had the key to that cart in years," Erin said, thinking aloud. Absently she rubbed her temple. "It had to have been over seven years ago." Again a chilly feeling of apprehension swept over her and her stomach began to knot.

"But the ledger here indicates that you should have a key to that cart," Olivia maintained. Laying the white formal sheet of paper on Erin's desk, she pointed to a line showing that Erin did, in fact, receive the key in question within the last year.

"It's a mistake…" Erin sighed. "I never had that key!"

"But aren't those your initials next to Mitch's signature?" Olivia pressed.

"Yes…it looks like I signed out for the key. But I didn't. There must be some mistake…." Her voice trailed off. She knew that she had never had that key. The whole situation was absurd. And a little frightening. Anyone with that key could withdraw negotiable stocks and bonds from the cart if given the right opportunity. A perfect plan for embezzlement. The thought sickened her.

Olivia studied the report for a few seconds more and then, with an elegant wave of her hand, dismissed the subject. "I guess it really doesn't matter since all of the new locks have already been installed. Just sign here for the new keys and I'll see that this securities key matter is cleared up." Erin scribbled her initials next to Olivia's, relinquished the old set of keys to the leggy brunette and snapped the new ring of keys into her purse.

Just as she was about to leave Olivia paused at the door. She thought for a moment before turning to face Erin once again. Her voice was low as she asked, "What do you think about Mitch?" Her normally lively green eyes had deadened. "Isn't it awful…."

Erin slowly shook her head and rubbed her chin nervously. "I don't like to think about it—or even talk about it. It's something that I don't understand at all," she confessed, and hoped that the conversation with Olivia had ended. Something about the brunette always made Erin uneasy. But Olivia wouldn't let the subject die.

"I know what you mean." Olivia seemed to agree. "I would never have guessed—not in a million years." She paused once again, her gaze flicking up the length of

Erin's figure as if something else were on her mind. A flame of life leaped into her eyes. "It must be especially hard for you," Olivia intimated.

"It's been hard for all of us," Erin agreed cautiously.

"Yes, but with you it's a little different, wouldn't you say?"

"I don't know what you're getting at."

"Oh, sure you do," Olivia replied as she brushed back an errant wave of thick copper hair. "You don't have to play naive with me. I know how close you were to Mitch."

Erin's patience, which had been thinning ever since the lanky girl had entered her office, snapped. She pulled the strap of her purse over her shoulder and said with a coolly professional voice that suggested the subject was closed, "Mitch is a good friend of mine—nothing more!"

"Oh?" The question seemed innocent enough, but the curl of Olivia's petulant lips suggested disbelief. "The same way that Kane Webster is your good friend?" The color drained from Erin's face, confirming Olivia's vicious accusation. "Well, honey," she continued with an exaggerated wink, "no one can accuse you of not knowing which side of the bread the butter's on!" After her final invective, and with a self-satisfied smile, Olivia slipped out of the office.

Erin stood in stunned silence in the aftermath of Olivia's remarks. Although she was alone, she felt a storm of scarlet embarrassment climb up her neck. It was happening again! Already! The gossip had started, and who better to start it than Olivia. Erin swallowed hard, and sagged against the desk. Why had she been so foolish—she should have seen it coming. All the gossip, the knowing glances, the snickering laughter behind her back, all over again!

She let her forehead rest on the palm of her hand as

she slowly tried to recompose herself. It had been a good day, she reasoned, and she shouldn't let Olivia ruin it. But that was the trouble, Olivia had ruined it. Why, after all the years that had passed since the divorce from Lee, did any little biting comment from Olivia still wound her? Eight years had passed since Olivia's tempestuous affair with Lee. Although at the time, Erin had blamed the slim brunette for the breakup of her marriage with Lee, she knew now that she had been grossly unfair. If Lee hadn't taken up with Olivia, another pretty face would have caught his wandering eye and lured him away from the bounds of the marriage. Lee was only too willing. It was just unfortunate that Lee had been reckless enough to choose to have an affair with someone whom Erin saw on a daily basis. It seemed to compound the pain.

The problem with the marriage had not really been Olivia, but rather the differences between Erin and Lee. Although Erin recognized that now, she still found it hard to accept Olivia for what she seemed to be: a very knowledgeable and efficient assistant officer of the bank. Although the problems of the past were long dead, Olivia's presence at the bank and her vicious tongue continued to plague Erin. She never felt that she could completely trust Olivia.

Was she being unfair? Erin asked herself as she once again gathered her purse over her shoulder, straightened her skirt and headed out the door. Perhaps Olivia's attempt to communicate with Erin about Mitch was only natural. Both Olivia and Erin had cared very much for Mitch, and each had worked for him for nearly a decade. Perhaps Olivia felt the need to lash out because of Erin's cool attitude toward her. It was just possible that Erin was holding too much of a grudge against the sultry woman who wore the designer dresses and tailored suits with such seductive bearing. Erin sighed heavily to herself. Maybe she had never given Olivia a chance.

But the knot in Erin's stomach continued to tighten. She just intuitively didn't trust Olivia. It wasn't so much what Olivia said that managed to get under Erin's sensitive thin skin, but the way the words came out. Double entendres, sly winks, suggestive innuendos—all at Erin's expense.

As Erin found her way downstairs and out to the parking lot, she tried to dismiss the anxious feeling that had seized her with Olivia's interruption. But as she unthinkingly put the key into the ignition switch of the car, she hesitated and watched, nearly hypnotized, as the other keys jangled and swung near the steering column. How had her name gotten on the list of people who had keys to the securities cart? Try as she would to remember otherwise, she knew that she had never, in the last few months, signed out for that key! And yet the presence of her own initials negated her perception. Would someone within the bank use her good name for his own purposes? Could someone have forged her initials? Mitch, perhaps? Would Mitchell Cameron stoop so low? With a disgusted grunt to herself and a firm shake of her head, she started the car and dismissed her traitorous thoughts. Where had her loyalty gone? Mitchell Cameron had been kind to her, a friend when she needed one most. She wouldn't turn her back on him now—nor would she imagine that he would use her name for his own advantage. But then, how could she explain about the key? Could it be, as Olivia said, just a mistake? Probably. And yet...

There were still slight traces of fog along the waterfront and in the downtown area of Seattle, but as Erin's yellow VW climbed the hill that supported the apartment house, the mist thinned and by the time she was home the evening was cool but clear. Only a trace of fog could be seen in the wisps that clung to the dark waters of the distant Sound.

It was nearly seven, and Erin wanted to dash up the stairs to get ready for Kane, but propriety stopped her. She set her purse and briefcase on the lowest step of the staircase and knocked softly on Mrs. Cavenaugh's door.

A curious blue eye peeked at her through the peephole. Then quickly the door opened, and the slightly bent figure of Milly Cavenaugh greeted Erin with a warm smile.

"Good evening, Erin. I didn't expect to see you tonight," Mrs. Cavenaugh said cheerily, and winked broadly at her young landlady.

Erin's face creased with anxiety. "Why not? Didn't the repairmen show up?"

"Did they ever…" Mrs. Cavenaugh replied with a disapproving purse of her lips. Disgust darkened her eyes and she shook her head as she remembered. "They were here…an entire battalion of them…tracking in mud and heaven-knows-what-else into the house!" Erin's eyes followed the sweep of Mrs. Cavenaugh's hand as it included the front porch, entry hall and stairway. The oaken planks of the hallway were, indeed, imprinted with scrambled tracks of mud-laden, booted feet.

"Did they finish the job?" Erin asked, dragging her eyes away from the mess on the floor and back to her elderly tenant.

"Partially, I think. It seems that it's going to take more work than the original estimate showed," Mrs. Cavenaugh announced, thinking carefully.

"More work? Why?" Dollar signs flashed in Erin's mind.

"Something about dry rot in the floorboards, I think," Mrs. Cavenaugh explained with a shrug of her bent shoulders. "I'm sorry, dear, I really didn't pay too much attention—I was too busy trying to get them to wipe the dirt off their boots."

Erin felt her heart sink. Dry rot? What was that exactly? Something to do with the condition of the subfloor and support beams, she thought. It sounded like it would cost money—lots of it.

"Is something wrong, Erin?" Mrs. Cavenaugh asked, assessing the worried look that had appeared on Erin's face. "Would you like to come in and sit for a moment? I could brew a pot of tea...."

Forcing herself to smile, Erin shook her head. "Nothing's wrong, Mrs. Cavenaugh. I was just a little surprised to find out about the dry rot."

"Oh, it's probably nothing to be concerned about anyway," the elderly lady thought aloud, dismissing the subject with an expansive wave of her hand. Her pale blue eyes took in the concerned look on Erin's features before asking the question that had been entering her head ever since she had seen Erin through the peephole.

"How did things go at work today?"

Erin was still concentrating on the bad news of the dry rot, wondering how extensive the damage was and just how many hundreds or thousands of dollars it would take to correct the problem. Mrs. Cavenaugh's question startled her.

"Pardon me?"

"Work. The new boss. How're you two getting along?" Thinly veiled interest sparked in her kindly blue eyes.

Erin pulled out of her reverie at the mention of Kane. "Everything's going just fine, I guess. Mr. Webster seems to be quite capable."

"And Mr. Cameron?" the old lady coaxed inquisitively. Once again concern clouded Erin's violet eyes. "I don't know," she replied honestly. "I haven't been able to reach him."

Mrs. Cavenaugh played with the strand of pearls at her neck and clucked her tongue. She wagged her head in disbelief. "I read about it in the papers. Embezzlement— it's a nasty business."

"I just wish that I could talk to him," Erin sighed, and leaned heavily against the banister of the staircase. "It's all so hard for me to accept."

"But your Mr. Webster..."

"He's *not my* Mr. Webster," Erin interrupted, her cheeks coloring in indignation. Mrs. Cavenaugh's blue eyes sparkled more brightly.

"Whatever," she replied with a dismissive shrug. "What does he think?"

"Oh, he's convinced that Mitch is guilty," Erin murmured, her slim fingers running along the clean cool lines of the wooden railing. Talking about Mitch and the embezzlement drained Erin, and she realized that she shouldn't be discussing bank business with her neighbor. She straightened her shoulders and changed the subject to a less personal issue. "Have you seen Mr. Jefferies?" she asked Mrs. Cavenaugh, and motioned toward the apartment on the other side of the staircase. "He hasn't changed his mind about vacating his apartment, has he?"

"As a matter of fact, I saw him this morning when I was getting my mail," the gray-haired woman replied importantly. "No, his daughter insists that George will be better off closer to his family." With a catty wink the wrinkled woman continued, "He is getting on in years, you know."

Erin suppressed the smile that tugged at the corners of her mouth. She knew for a fact that Mr. Jefferies was a good ten years younger than Mrs. Cavenaugh, although the sprightly little old lady would be loathe to admit it.

Erin lifted her shoulders in a dismissive gesture. "Oh, well, you win some and you lose some. I guess I'd better put an advertisement in the *Times* and put the Vacancy sign back up. It seems that I just took it down!"

"Has anyone ever told you that you worry too much?" Mrs. Cavenaugh asked, shaking a knowing and gnarled finger in Erin's surprised face.

Erin laughed in spite of herself. "Everybody and anybody. Or so it seems."

"Well, they're right! And what does all that worry get you? Nothing but stomach ulcers and trouble! Now, you take my advice, and—what is it they say these days— you loosen up!"

Erin grinned and impulsively gave the little old woman a bear hug. "You're right," she murmured, and patted the elderly woman's frail shoulder.

"Of course I am! You should do yourself a favor and listen to me more often," Mrs. Cavenaugh rejoined with a proud lift of her chin. "And...if you're as smart as I think you are, you'll put your hooks into that Webster fellow in a big hurry!"

"Mrs. Cavenaugh! Have you been spying on me?" Erin inquired with mock dismay.

The older woman shook her gray head savagely. "Just looking out for your best interests, honey. That's all!" Then, with a dismissive shrug of her thin shoulders, she added, "Call it spying, if you will. But somebody's got to take care of you. I saw the way that ex-husband of yours treated you—and I want to make sure that you don't get hurt again..."

Erin tried to protest, but the severity of Mrs. Cavenaugh's wizened blue eyes held her tongue.

"Now...this Webster fellow, I've seen the way he looks at you."

"And?"

"Unless I miss my guess, which isn't very often, I'd say he's fallen head over heels for you!"

"You can't be serious!"

But the knowing and pleased look on Mrs. Cavenaugh's weathered face added silent conviction to the little old lady's words.

"I...I had better be running along," Erin said a little breathlessly as she thought about Mrs. Cavenaugh's words. Could she possibly be right? Erin picked up her purse and her briefcase and called over her shoulder, "Don't worry about the mess in the hallway, Mrs. Cavenaugh. I'll have the janitor clean it in the morning...."

"Oh, Erin," the lady at the bottom of the stairs beckoned.

"Yes." Erin turned to look back down at her, and she could tell that the woman was struggling with some sort of decision.

"I thought that maybe you'd want to know—Lee was here today, asking about you."

"What?"

"He left you a note, I think." Her blue eyes beseeched Erin. "Everything's okay, isn't it?"

Erin hesitated only slightly. "Of course," she managed, but she heard the hollow sound of her own words. As she mounted the final stairs to her apartment, she heard Mrs. Cavenaugh's door close and the sharp sound of a bolt being turned in the lock. All of the airy feeling that had cascaded over her from Mrs. Cavenaugh's suspicions about Kane's feelings for her had vanished at the mention of Lee. As she thought about it Erin wondered how the little old lady had even seen Kane, but there was something in Mrs. Cavenaugh's pale blue eyes that bothered Erin. The dear little woman really believed that Kane was falling in love with her. But how would Mrs. Cavenaugh even suspect?

Erin shook her head and pulled the pins from her hair as she closed the door to her loft. If only she could believe that Kane could love her or at least learn to love her. Erin's vivid imagination began to run wild.

But just as her heart began to race in anticipation of Kane's love, her rational mind cooled her response. What about the wariness she had sensed in the steely depths of Kane's gray eyes? Why did she always feel that he was studying her—trying to read her mind? Why did she feel that he didn't completely trust her? Her blood cooled and a shudder raced up her spine. The situation was impossible.

It was then that she noticed the white envelope that had been shoved under her door. The note from Lee.

Chapter 8

It had been nearly two weeks since Erin had found the note thrust intrusively into her apartment. The message was a simple request, "Please call," and a number that she recognized as a suburban Seattle telephone listing. She had tried to call Lee once, but was relieved when no one answered. Several other times she had been tempted to try and reach him once more, but before she had found the nerve to dial the number, she had changed her mind and left well enough alone. If he really needed her, she reasoned, he would get in touch with her again. A few times she had wadded up the note in an effort to throw it away, but she hadn't. This morning the note was once again before her as she leaned against the kitchen counter, studiously stirring a bit of honey into her tea. It sat menacingly on the counter, inviting her to make a call that she knew would only bring her more heartache. Was she a coward? Why did she let him linger near her to remind her of the past and the pain.

She took an experimental sip of the warm amber liquid. As the hot tea slid down her throat, Erin thought about the past two weeks of her life. The days had gone fairly well. On the surface it seemed as if everything in the office was running efficiently, just as a well-oiled banking machine should. For the first time in months Erin had cleaned out her pending probate file along with a series of other nagging paperwork problems that had been building on the corner of her desk for several weeks. Her fear over gossip or rumors spreading concerning her relationship with Kane had been unfounded, other than the one unfortunate and vicious incident with Olivia. Kane proved himself to be a capable and fair employer, and outwardly Erin appeared to enjoy working for him. It had even been possible for her to work professionally with Kane by forcing her personal feelings for him into the background and never letting her emotions color her objectivity or judgment. It had been excruciatingly difficult at times not to reach out and touch him or smooth the worried look from his brow. But she had managed to look the part of a disinterested employee. At least she hoped so.

It was the nights that disturbed her, she realized now as she moved restlessly from the kitchen, taking the teacup and the crumpled note from Lee with her. Then, after carefully setting the teacup on the coffee table, she spread out the crushed piece of paper and smoothed its creases against the arm of the sofa. The seven digits of Lee's home phone leaped out at her, and in a moment of sudden decisiveness, she shredded the note into tiny pieces and tossed them disgustedly away in the wastebasket, something she should have done two weeks ago!

Erin sunk into the soft rose-colored cushions of the couch and continued to reflect on the changes in her life. When she was alone with Kane, she felt a freedom and a rapture that were hard to describe, an enthusiasm and exhilaration that she thought had been lost with her teens. Just the light touch of his hand on her shoulder or his throaty whispered voice could send her spiraling into an emotional bliss that was both wonderful and frightening. Never had she given her heart so willingly or so easily. She knew that a part of Kane wanted to love her; she could feel it as they made love. But for some unknown reason, he wouldn't let himself enjoy the pleasure of loving her. At first she had thought that the failure of his marriage had hardened him against a commitment to the future, but lately she had sensed that it was a more personal problem that made him withdraw. A problem somehow directly relating to her.

She shook her tangled curls and looked into the teacup as if she might find the answer to her dilemma in its amber-colored depths. Why the restlessness? Why did she feel like an aerialist carefully balancing her life on a flimsy tightrope and knowing that sometime, although she couldn't be quite sure exactly when, the tense, frail wire would snap and send her catapulting downward into an empty black emotional abyss? The conflicting roles of daytime employee and nighttime lover were constantly at war in her mind.

Erin sighed deeply and ran her fingernails in deep grooves along the overstuffed arm of the antique sofa. There were times when she was alone with Kane that the stone wall of wariness in his eyes would weaken, and she would feel an exquisite happiness, the blush of love. But on other occasions, when she lay alone in her bed, listening as he drove off into the night, she discovered a sense of desperation and loneliness that caused feverish nightmares to disturb her sleep.

Why the torment? Where was the relationship leading them? Why couldn't she come to grips with and accept the affair for what it was—a pleasant, sensuous experience? Why did she insist on coloring her feelings with love?

A key turned in the lock. Kane had returned. Erin could feel herself beginning to coil in tension. Nervously she waited for him to enter—just as he had every night for the past two weeks. But tonight would be different, she vowed to herself. Tonight she would insist upon answers. Why was there always a darkness in his eyes?

Kane entered the room and shut the door behind him. The stern look on his face only made Erin's heart hammer more wildly. He was dressed casually in jeans and a tan pullover sweater. His chestnut hair was slightly messy as if he had forgotten about it over the last few hours. It was obvious that he had hurriedly stopped by his hotel before coming to see her. Unusual. The pattern of their life together had been established over the last two weeks, but this Friday night was obviously different to Kane as well as Erin. Even under the intensity of his gaze she reminded herself that she had to know, tonight, what it was that held him away from her.

"Pack your bags," Kane commanded without even a smile as a greeting. She jumped at his abrupt command, and for a moment his arctic gray eyes collided with hers. She felt a chill of dread pass over her body. His mouth was a tight, grim line that was neither a smile nor a frown. The grooves across his forehead seemed deeper tonight, as if he, too, had been wrestling with a troublesome and weighty decision.

"Do what?" she asked incredulously. Surprise and indignation registered in the startled expression that crossed her face. She was still sitting on the couch with her legs curled up and tucked underneath her. She almost dropped her teacup at his abrasive command.

Kane ignored her question. Preoccupied, he paced distractedly in front of the couch, his fists balled deeply in the pockets of his jeans. As he passed in front of her, Erin couldn't help but notice that his jeans, slung low in the waist, strained against his thighs and buttocks with each of his long strides. As he paced she was reminded of a caged animal, and she could almost visualize his tightly controlled muscles rippling beneath the fabric of his clothing. Forcefully she pulled her attention away from his virile male anatomy and tried to read the expression on his face.

"Didn't you hear me?" he growled, and stopped his absent pacing. "I asked you to go and pack."

"No, you didn't," she corrected, her eyes locking with his. "You *ordered* me to pack without so much as a greeting or explanation!"

Anger snapped in his eyes, but his reply was strangely soothing. The rage that was burning quietly within him was controlled. "You're right," he expelled in a long breath, "and I'm sorry. I…I'm a little distracted this evening," he offered as an apology.

"I noticed!" she retorted, and then seeing the worried creases that pulled his thick dark brows together in concern, she amended her hot retort. "I guess it's my turn to apologize," she admitted wearily. "I didn't mean to snap. I've been a little distracted myself."

"Oh?"

"Nothing to be concerned about," she averred with a wan smile, and wondered why she didn't have the strength of character to lay her cards on the table and confront him with her unanswered questions about their relationship and the future. Instead she chose to sidestep the issue. "Now." She smiled feebly, luminous lilac eyes looking pleadingly up at him. "What's been bothering you?"

"Oh, God, Erin," he moaned and let his forehead drop to his hand in a gesture of total defeat. He raked long tense fingers through the wheat-colored highlights of his burnished hair. How could he explain that he was only a hairbreadth away from confirming his suspicions about her? Could she imagine how close he was coming to finding all of the pieces of the puzzle that would tie her into the embezzling scandal? Although everything was still circumstantial, it was stacking together so neatly that it was actually beginning to scare Kane. Although no more money had been taken from the bank, the most damning piece of evidence that he had found so far—a discrepancy in the securities cart key registration—proved as well as anything that Erin had been lying to him. How long did she expect the charade to work? How could he help her and get her out of this mess? What could he do? It would all be so much easier if he just didn't give a damn!

"Kane," Erin said unsteadily, still sitting, looking both childlike and wise at the same moment. Oh, God, he thought, was she going to confess? Could he bear it? His muscles tensed, and he could feel the pressure as his jaws tightened together in a viselike grip. "Is there anything I can do?" she offered in a whisper.

Erin had noticed Kane stiffen at the sound of her voice, and she was aware that the wall between them was rigidly back in place, but she felt a strangling need to climb the invisible barrier and reach out to him. Why was he suffering so?

"There's nothing you can do," he stated flatly. "There's nothing anyone can do."

She twisted her fingers together. "Is it Krista?" she asked with a shaky breath.

His gray eyes smoldered with indecision. "That's part of it," he conceded, and hated himself for his duplicity. Dropping his body down on the couch next to her, he let his head fall backward as if it were too heavy to support. He sat staring ahead, with only inches separating him from her. Her senses were alive to him, her nerve endings stretched taut. Erin could feel the heat of his body, smell the inviting scent of his aftershave, see the darkening shadow of his beard. But he still didn't touch her. His hands rubbed thoughtfully against his knees, and he looked straight ahead through the window into the late-afternoon sky. "I talked with Krista again today," he said in a voice that seemed remote.

"And?" Erin prodded, not knowing why she should be concerned with Kane's reclusive daughter.

"She doesn't want to move to Seattle," he sighed, and drummed his fingers against his thigh. "Absolutely refuses!"

He turned his head to look in her direction and their eyes met in a chilly embrace. "I'm going to California next week to get her and move her up to Seattle with me."

"And you're worried about her and the adjustment," Erin guessed.

"Wouldn't you be?"

"That goes without saying. Is…there anything I can do to make it easier on you?"

"Would you come to California with me?"

"To get Krista?" At Kane's cursory nod, Erin expelled a long breath and shook her head firmly and negatively. "I don't think that would be a very good idea. She's going to have to adjust to a whole new city. I think you should be alone with her. She doesn't need the intrusion of a virtual stranger."

She could see in his eyes that she had convinced him and she continued, "But if there's anything else that I can do...."

"There is something," he suggested, and for a moment the tension seemed to vanish.

"What?"

"Pack your bags for the weekend" was the brief reply, but the passion that had been lurking in his eyes came alive. His silvery eyes embraced hers, and he reached for her hand. His thumb drew slow, lazy circles on the inside of her wrist, and heat began to climb up her body. "Oh, Erin," he breathed, and his lips found hers in a feverish kiss that seemed to pulsate with need and urgency. When he dragged his mouth away from the supple curve of her lips, he looked savagely into her eyes, asking questions that she couldn't understand. Then a softness stole over his features as he took a handful of her hair in his palm and pressed her head against the protection of his chest. In a ragged breath he asked, "Do you know how hard it's been for me, forcing myself to keep my hands off you at the office?" He growled deep in his throat. "There were times when I thought I would actually go insane, having you so close and not being able to touch you...."

Her arms circled his waist, and she kissed the swell of his cheek. "I know..."

"No, I don't think that you can imagine what it's like—seeing you every day and not being able to touch what is mine."

"Yours? Possessive, aren't you?" she quipped sarcastically.

"Absolutely!" His grip on her tightened, and when she tilted her face to meet his, the warmth of his lips captured hers in a passion that spread fire through her veins. With great difficulty she pulled her head away from his.

"What did you say about packing my bags?" she inquired, trying to ignore the warm intimacy of his breath as it tickled her face.

"You and I are getting away for the weekend," he stated, and with apparent effort he released her from his tenacious embrace. "Hurry up," he ordered. "We don't have all day. I want to get moving before we run out of daylight!"

"Kane!" Erin said with mild irritation. "What are you talking about? Where are we going? Why do I need to pack?"

His smile twisted grimly and Erin saw the weariness and cynicism deep in his crystal gray eyes. "You and I are leaving this city, the bank—" his eyes swept the homey apartment "—this house, everything! We're going to get lost in the wild for a couple of days!"

"The wild?"

"That's right!" Half dragging her into the bedroom, he opened the closet, against her protests, and found her suitcase. "I'm tired of sneaking out of your bed in the middle of the night like some...gigolo!" He ignored Erin's gasp of indignation and began opening her bureau drawers. She caught his reflection in the mirror and saw that a hard, tense mask had come over his angular features. He looked up, his gray eyes held hers and he said with disgust, "And I'm tired of not being able to touch you in the light of day!" His hands were pressed firmly on the dresser top, and he pinioned her with his gaze, cold and distant, in the looking glass. Tense fingers slowly rubbed the wooden surface of the dresser. "Damn it, woman!" His fist pounded against the cool wood. "I'm sick of hiding, and I won't do it anymore! So, beginning tonight, we are not going to keep this affair in the dark, as if we're ashamed of it! You and your paranoia over rumors can go to blazes!" He spit the words out as if they were a bad taste in his mouth. His anger was burning in the darkness of his gaze.

"Kane," Erin implored. "Why are you so upset? What…"

"Look, Erin. We've played the game your way for nearly two weeks, and it's tearing me apart!" His entire body tensed for a second before he took in a long steadying breath and controlled the note of rage that had entered his speech. In a softer voice he continued, "Let's have an entire weekend alone together—what do you say?"

"I don't understand…"

"Let's go somewhere where we can walk in the sunlight together—where we can be seen kissing.…"

"Is this what's been bothering you?" she asked, as she put a staying hand on his sleeve.

"Oh, Erin," he sighed, holding her at arm's length and letting his eyes search her face. "There are so many things that are bothering me," he admitted, and a tortured look twisted his features.

"Can we talk about them?" she asked quietly.

"That's exactly what I have in mind. But I thought a change of scenery might do us both some good."

"You know that I can't leave at the drop of a hat."

"Why not?"

"My tenants… I've got an advertisement in the paper to rent the apartment downstairs."

"The apartment on the first floor, across the hall from Milly?" he asked.

"That's the one—how did you get on a first-name basis with Mrs. Cavenaugh?" Erin asked, a suspicious black eyebrow arching heavenward.

"That little old lady has excellent taste," he laughed. "She likes me."

"And she told you about the vacant apartment?" Erin guessed.

"That's right," he agreed with a smile that any Cheshire cat would envy.

"Then you understand why I have to stay here..."

"Don't worry about the apartment," he said dismissively. "I'll rent it until I find a more permanent residence. Does it have two bedrooms?"

"Of course, but—"

"Then it will be perfect!" he exclaimed.

"Perfect? For what?"

"Krista and myself."

"I don't know..."

His eyes grew dark. "It's the perfect solution to our problem."

Her breath caught in her throat. "I didn't know that we had a problem," she returned, and began to place her undergarments in the open suitcase on the bed. Was he actually going to tell her what had been bothering him, why he had been so wary of her?

He came up behind her and let his arms encircle her waist. His words fanned her hair and the sensitive skin at the back of her neck. He captured the black silk and entwined it in his fingers. Burying his face in her hair, he groaned. "The problem is that I want to be near you... always!" The confession was a tortured, unwonted admission.

"What are you saying?" she asked, and a tightness constricted her breath.

"I want to live with you!"

Her voice was unsteady. "And what about Krista? What would she think about her father and his busi-

ness associate living together? What kind of example
would we set? No, Kane…" She shook her head sadly.
"It wouldn't work!"

"Lots of people…"

"I'm not 'lots of people,'" she interrupted.

"So I noticed," he agreed, and his hands slowly kneaded
the softness of her abdomen. Warm curling sensations
grew to life within her. Slowly he stopped his seductive
movements. "I'm sorry," he whispered. "I'm pushing you
too quickly. Let's forget the entire suggestion—for the
time being. But, please come and spend the weekend with
me…"

Pulling herself away from him, she planted a fist
firmly against her hip and forced back a smile that flirted
with her lips. "I'll come with you—on one condition!"

Kane crossed his arms over his chest and leaned
against the dresser. The sweater strained across his shoulders. "Okay. I'm game. What's the condition?"

"That for once you tell me where you plan on taking me!"

"Spoilsport!"

"Kane!"

"Where's that girl who loves mystery and old movies?" he inquired, a twinkle coming to his eyes.

"You're not going to tell me, are you?"

"Not unless you think of some wildly erotic torture
that will force me into submission."

"Dreamer," she shot back at him, before turning to
pack.

The small motorboat churned through the cold gray
waters of Puget Sound and out toward the Pacific Ocean.
When Erin had stepped into the tiny vessel, she had
guessed that Kane was taking her to San Juan Island,

but he had preferred to keep the destination and his secret to himself. Now, as the frigid salt spray tickled her nose and clung to her hair, she was grateful that she had had the foresight to bring her down jacket with her. She drew the warm collar closer to her neck in an effort to keep the moisture-laden air off her skin.

By the time they reached Orcas Island the sun had set, and only a long orange glow remained along the horizon. Night was closing in, and the lights of Deer Harbor winked like silvery diamonds against the black island as the launch continued on its journey around the small piece of land.

Erin rubbed her hands together, and then pushed them deep into her pockets in an effort to warm herself. At that moment the rhythmic rumble of the small craft's engine slowed, and Kane maneuvered the boat inland. It was difficult to see clearly in the evening light, but Erin made out a small cove with a relatively private beach and a ramshackle cabin.

Kane cut the engine and jumped out onto the private dock. He secured the craft and helped Erin out of the boat. Her eyes swept the beach until she spotted the cabin. A slow smile spread over her features.

"Well, what do you think?" Kane asked, his arm draped possessively over her slim shoulders.

"I think this all looks suspiciously like a set from one of those 1940s, black-and-white, slice-of-life movies," she commented as her eyes studied the small cozy cabin and its state of apparent neglect.

"I knew you'd like it," Kane replied with a self-satisfied smile. "Come on. Let's take a look inside…"

The cabin was, if nothing else, rustic. A broad, sagging front porch protected the front door. The cabin was constructed of cedar, and to Erin's discriminating eye,

had never been painted. It bore the weathered look of
exposed gray wood blanched by the salt of the sea. At
one end of the porch a worn rope hammock swung in the
breeze coming off the ocean. The front door groaned as
it was opened, and the interior of the cabin had a musty,
unused odor. There was no electricity, but running water
was pumped into the kitchen. A woodstove in the kitchen
and a massive stone fireplace at one end of the living area
provided the only sources of heat in the building. Erin
surveyed the cabin with a skeptical eye. She had never
been much of a believer in "roughing it" when modern
conveniences were the available alternative.

Kane unpacked the boat and started searching for fire-
wood, while Erin lit the rose-colored kerosene lamps and
removed the dustcovers from the furniture. To air out the
interior, she opened all the windows, heedless of the chill
in the air, and felt the tickle of salt air burn in her lungs.

The cabin was rather barren, and what little furniture
there was appeared threadbare. But she had to admit
that once she had swept the dust from the floor, and the
fire was lit, the warm scent of burning wood mingled
with the fresh fragrance of the salt sea air, and the cabin
seemed bearable, if not cheerfully inviting. Fortunately
Kane had the foresight to stop off at a delicatessen in
Seattle before picking up Erin, and he had purchased
sandwiches and a bottle of wine. Erin rummaged in the
old-fashioned kitchen and was able to find an unopened
package of paper cups along with a tarnished but necessary corkscrew for the wine.

Pleased with her discoveries, she retraced her footsteps back into the living area. Brandishing the corkscrew
dramatically in the air, she captured Kane's attention.
"Voilà!" she announced theatrically, and placed the cups
on the floor next to the couch.

Because of the chill of the evening sea breeze, Kane was closing the final window in an effort to retain the heat from the fireplace when Erin reentered the room. He snapped the window latch closed and turned to face Erin, who wondered aloud, "How in the world did you ever find this place?"

"It's not exactly moonlight and roses, is it?" he asked, crossing the room to the fireplace. He squatted near the golden flames and warmed his palms against the heat that the fire offered.

"Who needs moonlight and roses?" she asked rhetorically, and shrugged.

"Don't you?" Gray eyes searched her face as if she were a puzzle to him.

"I'm a little too much of a realist to think that the world revolves around silver moonlight, cut flowers and soft music," she admitted dryly.

"Are you?" A smile of disbelief tugged at the corners of his mouth.

"Does it matter?" she asked, and unwrapped the sandwiches. "Anyway, you're avoiding my question—how did you come to find this private little hideaway?"

After dusting his hands on his jeans, Kane sat down next to her on the floor, allowing the slightly weathered couch to support his head and shoulders. His long legs stretched in front of him, and nearly reached the warm red coals of the fire. Erin silently offered him a sandwich, which he gratefully accepted, and between bites he explained.

"As you already know, I'm looking for a permanent residence for Krista and myself in Seattle. I read the classified ads every day, hoping to find something suitable." He paused to open the wine and poured the cool clear liquid into the paper cups. The light from the fire reflected and danced against the deep green bottle and in his clear gray eyes.

"Anyway—" he shrugged, as if it wasn't all that important "—I came across an ad for this place. I've always had a fascination for the sea and the wilderness, not to mention rustic old cabins. And I thought it would be good for Krista. This place sounded perfect."

Erin nearly choked on the wine that she had been sipping. She eyed the interior of the cabin speculatively. "You're not telling me that you bought this place sight unseen?" she gasped, unable to shake the astounded look from her face. It hardly seemed "perfect" for anyone, much less an eleven-year-old girl bound to a wheelchair! Erin surveyed the living quarters more closely. The old cabin needed a lot of work. The cleaning alone would take several days, and the varnish on the pine walls was cracking and beginning to peel. There was no hot water, the floors needed to be refinished, and the furniture—all of it needed to be replaced or repaired. The list of jobs seemed endless to her practiced eye.

Kane watched Erin with obvious amusement. The deep-timbred tones of his laughter drew her attention back to him. "No," he laughed, "I haven't bought this place. In fact, this weekend is just a trial run. A widow owns the place, but she hasn't been up here since her husband died a couple of years ago. She knows that I'm interested in buying it, but she agreed to rent it to me for the weekend—to look around for myself."

"You're really serious about buying it?" Erin gasped. "It doesn't even have electricity!"

"Part of its charm, wouldn't you say?" He grinned at her obvious dismay.

"It's your money," she conceded with a dismissive shrug, and took another sip of her wine. The bright embers from the fire and the heady effect of the wine lured her into a serene sense of complacency. She watched Kane over the rim of her cup, and noticed the mood swing that seemed to come over him.

At her offhand comment about money, Kane stiffened. "That it is," he agreed almost inaudibly. He set the remains of his uneaten dinner aside, and stared into the orange and black coals of the fire. His mood had indeed shifted, and Erin, even in her peaceful state, could sense that the tension was coiling within him again.

The fire crackled and popped as it burned the pitch-darkened wood. The movements of the flames reflected in menacing shadows over the angular structure of Kane's masculine face. His question surprised Erin.

"Did you know that Mitchell Cameron's arraignment hearing is scheduled for late this week?" he asked in an accusatory voice. Gray eyes slid sideways, trying to catch her reaction. His pose was relaxed, his hands crossed comfortably over his chest, but Erin could sense the strain due to the twist in the conversation, and saw the tense rigidity of the muscles in his face.

"I read about it in the paper," she replied unevenly. Carefully, with nervous hands, she set aside the rest of her suddenly unappetizing sandwich and took another drink from her cup. The cool wine felt smooth against the rough texture of her throat. Mitchell Cameron had become a taboo subject between Erin and Kane, a topic that was never brought out into the open. It was as if, by silent agreement, neither person would chance the subject of Mitch. For reasons Erin didn't understand, the subject of Mitch was a potential powder keg. Why then, tonight, would Kane turn the conversation in Mitch's direction?

Kane's voice broke into her fragmented thoughts.

"There's a chance that I'll be out of town at the time of the hearing."

"But don't you have to testify?"

"I've already signed a sworn deposition," was the clipped reply. "I'm sure it will satisfy the court."

"Oh, Kane." Erin sighed, suddenly feeling very tired and unnerved. "Are you sure that you want to prosecute Mitch?" she asked, her hand reaching out to touch his shoulder.

He withdrew as quickly as if he had been seared by her touch. Twisting his head to meet her startled gaze, he drew his lips into a thin and menacingly grim line. "Is that what this is all about?" he demanded, and grabbed her wrist harshly.

"What—I don't understand!"

"Is that what you want, for me to drop the charges against your ex-employer? Is that why you've been so willing?" Steely eyes swept over her body and charged her with a crime she couldn't understand.

"Why, you...bastard!" she gasped, suddenly understanding at least a part of his vicious accusation. Involuntarily she drew her free hand backward in an effort to slap him. But she stopped in midswing as the same tortured look that she had seen so often in the past softened the severity of his dark gaze.

He dropped her wrist and closed his eyes for a second. "I'm sorry," he whispered huskily.

"You should be!"

"All right!" He reached a hesitant hand to her cheek and caressed its regal lines with exploring and sensitive fingers. "I have no choice," he assured her. "I have to prosecute Cameron. The board of directors would insist upon it, the bonding insurance company...."

"But if you did have a choice?" Liquid violet eyes

melted into his, and he drew his caressing hand away from her face.

"Nothing would change! I would still prosecute!" He stood up and put some distance between her body and his. He found it difficult to think when he looked at her or touched her. She was too close to him and to the truth. Perhaps, even now, she knew that he suspected her of involvement in the embezzlement. He had to be cautious with her—or did he? Damn it! Never in his life had he let a woman come between him and his purpose in life. Never had a woman been so intimately involved in his private thoughts. Dear God, why did it have to be this woman who attracted him so achingly? His thoughts weighed heavily on him, and he leaned against the broad mantel of the fireplace and let his head rest against the worn wood. He needed time to think, time alone, to put his life in perspective. It was a mistake bringing her to this isolated haven; he should have realized that before he insisted that she accompany him. How could he have been such a fool? Where was his common sense? His voice, a throaty whisper, crept across the thick silence that separated them.

"Can't you understand, Erin?" he pleaded. "Mitchell Cameron is a crook, and he has to pay."

"But surely, as president of the bank, with your influence..."

His gray eyes held hers frozen. "Oh, God, Erin. My influence has nothing to do with my *responsibility*!"

"Why is the subject of Mitch always so difficult?"

"You tell me!"

"I don't know!" she admitted honestly.

The silence was an electric current that seemed to bind them together and yet sever whatever peace they had shared. Kane eyed Erin with a haunted wariness that seemed to tire him, and Erin watched him with eyes naked in love and confusion. What was he trying to say?

He leaned against the mantel and rubbed the base of his head with his palm. He closed his eyes and gritted his teeth, as if he were trying to rid his body of tension. Slowly he seemed to relax; his tight muscles lengthened. With the effort his weight sagged wearily against the fireplace. "I think," he managed to say, "that you and I should drop the subject of Mitchell Cameron until after the arraignment hearing."

Erin let out a steadying breath. "Do you really suppose that I can just ignore the fact that Mitch's fate depends on your decision?"

"Correction," he cautioned sharply. "His fate depends upon his decision, one that was made quite some time ago. Not mine! I had nothing to do with it except unfortunately to catch a thief."

"I don't know that I can just erase it from my mind— as if we've never had this conversation."

"Just for the weekend?" he suggested, and bent near to her. He took both of her hands in his and forced her to look deeply into his eyes. "I'm sorry for the outburst. The past two weeks have been a strain on both of us," he said in an effort at apology. "But let's just spend this time together and get to know each other a little better." Deep lines of intense thought creased his forehead. "I—well, I need some time with you. Alone. Apart from Mitchell Cameron and the rest of the world." His voice was a reluctant plea, and before she could answer him, he buried his head between her breasts and held her close to him. "Oh, Erin," he whispered, his hot breath tantalizing her skin and arousing her breasts to an aching tautness. "Why do you tempt me so?"

Ignoring the doubts and warnings that still crowded

her mind, she felt herself surrender to him, and her hands wound themselves in the thick strands of his burnished hair. Feeling her reaction, he slowly pulled his head away from the softness of her body and looked longingly into her eyes. Her breath came in short gasps, and she felt the warmth of desire curling upward in her body. A nearly wicked grin stole over his face as his fingers played with the buttons of her blouse. She made no move to stop him, and when the blouse finally parted, his gaze sought and found the swollen ripeness of her breasts.

She longed to be touched by him, to feel the heat of his body capture her soul and the essence of her being. Red and orange flames were reflected in the burning passion of his gaze.

"Do you know, do you have any idea, just how much I need you?" he asked, before covering her lips with his and seeking the open invitation of her warm, moist mouth. She couldn't get enough of him. The delicious scent and tantalizing taste of his body, in kisses flavored by the wine, lingered upon her lips and teased her senses into a yearning ache that she couldn't control. His lips explored the length of her body, all of her, gently nuzzling the hollow of her shoulder, rimming her ear, searching out the soft flat contour of her abdomen. "Dear God, how I want you," he admitted.

"Then love me, Kane, love me," she pleaded.

"I will, Erin," he vowed, and moved over her, gently probing the most intimate part of her. Even in her drugged sense of well-being, she realized that he was speaking only of physical love, not the eternal love that she had requested. But for the moment it was enough.

Chapter 9

The two days that they spent together on the island were carefree and warm. After a light cover of morning fog, the late-autumn sun would warm the sand, and for the most part the days were crisply cool and invigoratingly clear.

Erin taught Kane how to dig for razor clams along the edge of the tide, and after a few hesitant tries, he became rather adept at kneeling in the wet sand and furiously shoveling after the escaping mollusks. Once, when a particularly large wave caught him off guard and sent him sprawling headlong into the bitter, cold surf, Erin laughed, only to find herself dragged down into the icy water by Kane.

"That will teach you not to make sport of me," he quipped, before kissing her soundly on her bluish lips. Another cold wave climbed over them, and they both hurried indoors to escape the frigid water and the cool air of autumn. They stripped off the wet, sandy clothes in front of the fire, while warming hot water to clean up the grit from the beach that had clung to their skin.

For most of the two short days, they spent their time beachcombing or taking the boat into nearby Deer Harbor for sightseeing and browsing in the various antiques stores. It was a wonderful time to be together, and by the end of the weekend, Erin found herself more in love with Kane than she ever imagined possible. She hated the thought of leaving the island and dreaded returning to the city, the job and the pressures that always seemed to build between them at home. She enjoyed the freedom that the island provided and loved being alone with Kane, loved touching him whenever she had the desire, and loved kissing him in the light of day, unafraid of what others might think. Disturbingly she wondered if it was such a fairy-tale existence that it could never be re-created, only remembered. All too soon it would end.

During the nights they spread a large sleeping bag on the floor in front of the fire, rather than chancing the well-worn and musty bed in the attached bedroom. They spent hours in front of the fire, talking, laughing and making love until dawn.

It was a glorious, heady experience. The entire weekend was too good to last.

When, finally, after what seemed a short afternoon, the sun began to set against the cold gray sea, Erin found Kane standing studiously on the porch. She had packed together all of her things, and she knew that it was well past the hour that Kane had planned to leave. And still he lingered. He half stood, half leaned against the railing and stared endlessly out toward the broad expanse of the ocean and into the beckoning twilight.

Quietly Erin watched him. She knew that he, too, was

hesitant to leave the solitude of the romantic haven that this otherwise miserable excuse for a cabin had provided for them. She lowered her body into the rope hammock, which sagged and groaned against her weight. The noise distracted Kane, and he slowly turned to face her. His eyes were distant; his mind was light-years away. Lazily he leaned against the post that supported the roof of the porch and let his eyes slide caressingly over her body.

"I'm...ready to go," she stated. It was a poor attempt at conversation.

"Are you?" he drawled.

"Everything's packed. We really should get going."

"I know," he agreed reluctantly, and looked longingly once more at the ceaseless gray tide. He spoke softly, as if to himself. "It surprises me that I'm not itching to get back to the office. Usually I'm anxious and just can't wait to get back behind my desk. But tonight—I don't know—it all seems so pointless."

When he faced her once again, his gray eyes moved over her face, as if he were memorizing every contour of her creamy skin. He made a simple statement with measured slowness. "I'm going to buy this cabin. We'll come back together."

"I hope so," she breathed, and wondered why it was so important to her. Unconsciously she clung to the first promise that hinted of a future that they might somehow share together.

The week that followed was a dismal and lonely time for Erin. As Kane had promised, he refused to keep their affair quiet or in the dark. Although he didn't actually make an announcement of the fact, his cold indifference in the office had disappeared, and it was with difficulty that Erin had managed to keep up appearances during working hours. His eyes caressed her, and his affection was never hidden. Although inwardly Erin was pleased, she couldn't help but notice the reaction of the other employees of the bank, the expressively uplifted eyebrows whenever she was with Kane and the accusatory glances that were cast her way when she wasn't with him. She tried to ignore the gossip that was blazing through the bank, but she couldn't calm the churning of her stomach.

When Kane had to leave on Wednesday for California, Erin was slightly relieved that the pressure of keeping him at arm's length at the office would be relieved for a while.

It was on Friday morning when everything seemed to happen at once. Kane's absence, as expected, had created a little extra work for Erin as well as the rest of the staff, but what she hadn't anticipated was an outbreak of the flu, leaving the office very shorthanded. Nor had she expected that the bank's main computer would break down, slowing the month-end posting to a snail's pace. It was a hectic, frustrating day, and when the telephone rang for what seemed to be the twentieth time within the span of five minutes, Erin couldn't keep the tight strain of anxiety out of her normally composed voice.

"Miss O'Toole," she nearly shouted into the mouthpiece.

"Erin?" a familiar voice inquired.

"Mitch? Is that you? I've been trying to reach you for weeks," she exclaimed, and felt a pang of regret that she had answered the phone so harshly. "How are you?" she asked with genuine interest.

"I've been better," was the matter-of-fact reply.

"Oh, Mitch. I'm so sorry," she began, suddenly at a loss for words. What could she say to him? Any condolence sounded foolish.

"I know, Erin," he replied as if he really did understand that she still cared for him and considered him her friend.

There was an uncomfortable pause in the conversation, before Mitch cleared his throat indecisively and stated the reason for his call. "I was wondering if you would like to go to lunch with me today?" he inquired.

"Oh, Mitch, I'd love to, but I'm absolutely swamped," Erin replied as she gazed at the stack of unanswered telephone messages that had been growing on the corner of her desk.

"Too busy for lunch with an old friend?" he joked, but the humor fell flat.

"Of course not. It's just that…well, Kane is out of town, and everyone here is down with the flu—including the computer."

There was a harsh laugh on the other end of the line. "Yeah, well, I get the message" was the curt retort. "Some other time…"

Indecision tore at Erin. She knew that today was the day of Mitch's arraignment hearing, and she also knew that if the judgment was turned against him, it was unlikely that she would see him again for an indefinite period of time. Kane wouldn't approve of a meeting with Mitch; Erin was sure of it, and yet he had no control over her friendship with Mitch. For once her reason was cast aside as she thought about the lonely man on the other end of the telephone line.

"Oh, Mitch," she said suddenly. "I'm sure I can meet with you today," she choked out. "I'll just have to make some room."

"Good!" Was there excessive relief in his voice? "How about Shorty's at one-thirty?"

"Perfect," she agreed lamely, and felt herself something of a traitor.

The few short hours until her agreed rendezvous with Mitch flew by, and with an uneasy feeling in the pit of her stomach, Erin set out on the short walk to a local pub known for its specialty: barbecued spareribs. Located in an older hotel in Pioneer Square, Shorty's had become a favorite with some of the employees of the bank, as much for its earthy San Francisco atmosphere as its flavorful food. Erin had been to the restaurant bar with Mitch several times in the past, but today, under the shroud of the allegations against him and the twisted set of circumstances surrounding them, she felt apprehensive about the lunch. *Don't be silly,* she chided herself. *This is the same old Gay Nineties restaurant, and he's the same old Mitch. Don't let any of this talk of embezzlement go to your head.* But still her stomach knotted, and without thinking, she pulled her pewter raincoat more closely around her throat and shook off a chill that ran up her spine.

She swung the heavy wooden door inward, and stepped into the dimly lit and secluded restaurant. The tangy odor of honey and tomato sauce assailed her nostrils, and she felt herself relax a little with the familiar aroma. It was forced, but she even managed a smile for the blond hostess who led Erin to a table where Mitch was already seated. She hadn't seen her ex-boss for over three weeks, and it was difficult to hide her surprise and embarrassment for the shell of a man that Mitch had become. Although more sober than the last time she had faced him, he carried with him a haunted look that destroyed the pleasantness of his face. His features, once bold, appeared gaunt, and his once-bright eyes had faded to a watery blue. A small, thin cigar was burning unattended in the ashtray.

At the sight of Erin, Mitch visibly brightened. His smile,

though slightly strained at the corners, appeared genuine as he rose from the table while she was being seated. After she was comfortably settled in her chair, Mitch reached across the small table for her hand and clasped it warmly. "Erin," he shook his graying head in wonderment. "If possible, you're looking lovelier than ever!"

"Thank you," she murmured, and nervously pulled the napkin from the table in an effort to steady her hands. It wasn't like Mitch to gush, at least not the Mitch she remembered, and his bubbling enthusiasm seemed somehow phony and out of character. The uneasy feeling grew in the pit of her stomach. Perhaps it was the way he didn't quite meet her gaze, or the way he played with his cigar, but something about him made Erin definitely uncomfortable.

"So," he said with forced joviality, "how's it going at the old salt mine? Still as busy as ever?"

He had asked the question, but Erin had the distinct impression that he was totally uninterested in the topic that he had introduced.

"We're busy—all the time," she admitted, and when he didn't immediately respond, she continued chattering to break the uncomfortable silence that was building. "Kane—that is, Mr. Webster, has been out of town for a few days, and well, that just tends to make things all the more hectic for everyone else...." Why did she feel compelled to rattle on about the bank, and why did she feel so nervous around a friend whom she had once respected? She wiped her damp palms on the napkin in her lap.

The waiter deposited two platters of ribs on the table, and Erin turned her attention to the saucy food, hoping to dream up a polite way of excusing herself at the earliest possible moment. She knew now that it was a mistake to have met with Mitch; she wasn't ready to deal with him or any of the problems in his life. Loathing herself for her turn of feelings, she managed to continue to feign interest in her ribs, wondering why Mitchell Cameron had changed so much, and how she could manage an escape from the uncomfortable and intimate lunch.

It was then that Mitch brought up the subject of his courtroom hearing. "I suppose you know that the arraignment hearing is this afternoon?" he began slowly, and lit another cigar. His faded eyes waited to study her response.

"Oh, Mitch... I wish that all of this—problem—could be avoided," Erin claimed, and he could read the honesty in her eyes.

"Yes, well, it's a little too late for that now, isn't it?"

"I suppose so," she sighed, touching her napkin to her lips and pushing the uneaten ribs aside. Her appetite had diminished. "If there's anything I can do to help you, just let me know."

Blue eyes lighted. "There is something." His voice was bitter cold.

"Oh? What?"

Mitch shifted uncomfortably in his chair. "Nothing much." He shrugged his shoulders and reached inside of his jacket for a neatly folded piece of paper. "I was hoping that you could borrow a little information from the bank...."

"What?" she asked, perplexed, and ran a shaky hand through her sleekly restrained hair. "Information? What information?"

Mitch waved off her questions dismissively with the clean white envelope. "Well, it's really not all that important, except that I can't get my hands on the records, as I'm no longer employed with the bank." He puffed furiously on his cigar, cloaking his head in a thin veil of blue smoke as he offered her the envelope.

Reluctantly she reached for the paper, as her uneasy stomach began to churn. "This information—what do you need it for?"

"I know it's rather sudden," Mitch rattled on, "but I need documents that would help clear my name. Bank records, trust documents, computer printouts on the dividend accounts, stock certificate registrations...nothing all that important...."

"You're not serious!"

"Of course I'm serious. Everything I need is listed in there." He pointed dramatically to the envelope that Erin was holding. She dropped it onto the table.

"Mitch!" Erin's cool voice was tightly formal. "Are you suggesting that I confiscate private bank records and give them to you?"

"Not give... I just want to borrow the stuff, until I can get this embezzlement fiasco straightened out."

"But you know that I can't do that," Erin exclaimed. "For one thing it's against the law. All that information is confidential!"

"Erin!" Mitch interrupted her. "This is my life that we're talking about. I face more years in prison than you'd want to count!" His eyes beseeched her, but she didn't waver. She spread her hands against the linen-clad table, and looked him directly in the eyes.

"Mitch, you know I'd love to help you out, but you can't expect me to do anything illegal, for God's sake!"

He chewed on his cigar and rolled it from one side of his mouth to the other. All the while, his watery blue eyes impaled her.

"Can't your attorney subpoena the information that you need? Why come to me?"

"It would be better for me this way, Erin. Otherwise I'd never put you on the spot. You know that. But any information that my attorney subpoenas will be sifted through by the prosecution. If they don't know about the information until the time of the hearing, I could get the jump on them. You know, surprise the court, confuse the D.A., perhaps avoid the indictment!"

Erin began to shake her head in a negative sweep. "You're just putting off the inevitable. You can't expect me to take such a chance. I...can't..."

"And I counted on you as a friend," Mitch spat out with a bitterness that chilled the air.

"I—we are friends."

"No, you've got that one wrong, Erin, dead wrong!" he snapped, waving an angry accusatory finger and his cigar within inches of her face. "We were friends when it was convenient for you—when I was your boss, and I could help you. Especially when that jerk of a husband dumped on you and you needed a shoulder to cry on. But now, when the tables have turned, our friendship seems to be wearing a little thin, doesn't it?"

Erin drew in an unsteady and disbelieving breath. "You can't possibly mean what you're implying. You know that I care for you—I always have—but you're asking the impossible!"

"Ha!"

"Mitch...don't..."

"Don't what, Erin?" he taunted, all of his hatred coming to the surface. "Don't overextend your friendship? Don't ask you to help me, after I helped pull you back together during your divorce? Don't ask you to do anything that might endanger your fragile relationship with your new boss?"

"What?" she gasped, but the meaning of his words was clear.

"Don't give me that wide-eyed shocked virgin routine, Erin. It won't work. Besides, it's demeaning. I know that you're Kane Webster's mistress, and that you've been hopping in and out of bed with him since he first set foot in this town!"

All of the color in Erin's face washed away with Mitch's cruel words, and little protesting, choking noises came from somewhere in her throat. But Mitch's vicious tirade wasn't finished.

"You're surprised, aren't you. Well, let me tell you this—it's all over town!"

"No!"

His eyes narrowed evilly. "I never thought you would stoop so low as to sleep with such despicable scum as Webster. But then you've never had very good taste when it came to men, have you?"

"That's enough," she gasped, finding her voice and her purse at the same moment. "I'm leaving!"

"What's the trouble, Erin? Am I getting too close to the truth? I should never have promoted you over Olivia Parsons eight years ago. That's where I made my mistake."

Erin's lilac eyes flashed fire. "I'm sure she would agree with you." She stood and hurriedly pulled on her coat. "I don't know what it is that's making you so bitter...."

"The prospect of prison, Erin. It can be very frightening!"

"I'm sorry, Mitch, but there's absolutely nothing I can do." Her poise was beginning to come back to her. She sighed heavily. "But no matter what, if it's any consolation, I do wish you luck today."

"Sure you do," he echoed sarcastically. "Thanks but

no thanks. I don't need your good wishes, Erin. Not now, not ever!"

Erin turned on her heels and didn't bother to say good-bye. Her back was rigidly straight as she marched to the door and never looked over her shoulder. She felt tears begin to pool in her eyes, but she determinedly pushed them backward. She refused to cry over Mitch, not after the way that he had treated her today. She knew that she was trembling and weak-kneed by the time she reached the rain-dampened streets, but she ignored her weakness and the drizzle that collected on her hair and ran down the back of her neck. A queasy, nervous feeling of desperation was churning in her stomach.

How had Mitch changed so much, she wondered. What had happened to the kind and caring man she had once known and respected? And how—how had he guessed about her affair with Kane? Erin's mind was spinning in circles, and her face, now covered with drops of rain, had lost all of its color. Her sleek ebony hair had begun to curl in the rain, and tiny tendrils began to spring out of the tidy black knot at the base of her head. She walked along the rain-puddled streets, absorbed in her own distant thoughts for over an hour. With her head bent against the wind, her small fists thrust into the pockets of her raincoat and her jaw clenched at an angle, she hardly looked her pert businesslike self. She felt a burning sense of betrayal that Mitch would stoop so low as to ask her to confiscate bank records secretly for his personal use. How far did friendship reach? How much would he ask of her? Again, she was reminded of Mitch's initials on the chart showing that Erin had possession of a key that she had never seen. Had Mitch, somehow, tried to implicate her in his crime? Was it possible that she had been wrong about Mitch all this time? She stamped her booted foot impatiently on the sidewalk.

Suddenly aware of the passing time, she hurried back to the bank. She was oblivious to the fact that her usually neat appearance was disheveled from the wind and the rain and that her normally clear eyes were clouded and preoccupied. As she rushed into her office, she paused only to pick up her messages and remind her secretary more curtly than she had intended that under no circumstances, other than a telephone call from Kane, was she to be disturbed.

For the remainder of the afternoon Erin holed up behind her desk, and tried to immerse herself in paperwork. But all her concentration seemed to shift to Mitch, and she found it impossible to forget the hollow look of despair on his face or the nervousness of his hands or his eyes, once clear and blue, now gray and pasty. Erin's stomach twisted violently as she remembered him and realized just how suspicious she had become of a man she had once trusted completely. Was she being paranoid, or had she been a fool to trust him in the past? She let her forehead drop to her hand, and hoped to God that the afternoon would slide by without any further complications.

The little yellow car couldn't hurry home fast enough for Erin, and the snail's pace of the late-afternoon traffic as it snarled in the rain only added to her frustration. Maneuvering the Rabbit through the hilly streets of the downtown area of Seattle, she made it to the freeway, but to no avail. Tonight, even the freeways were choked with commuters anxious to get home, semis on their assigned routes and recreational vehicles hoping to get a head start on the wet weekend. As the windshield wipers danced rhythmically before her eyes, Erin sighed, realizing that because she usually worked much later than six o'clock, she had forgotten how difficult and frustrating rush hour could be.

It took her nearly an hour to get home. As she guided her car to a halt she jerked on the emergency brake before racing up the sidewalk and taking the steps to her third-floor apartment two at a time. With unsteady fingers she unlocked the door, hurried into the apartment and switched on the local news. She was too preoccupied to bother shaking the rain from her coat or umbrella.

The sullen-faced newscaster was already making predictions about the upcoming statewide elections as the television snapped on. From habit Erin began to unbutton her coat, but she never let her eyes waver from the small black and white screen that held her attention. At the next commercial break, she managed to slip out of her coat and toss it next to her on the couch just as the dark-haired newsman began to recount the story that was uppermost on her mind: an alleged case of embezzlement at a downtown Seattle bank.

Erin's eyes were riveted to the set, and nervously she began to bite at her lower lip. As the scene on the television changed to the district courthouse, the eye of the camera sought Mitch and caught him hurrying out of the double doors of the marble courthouse. He was accompanied by a rather short and balding attorney who attempted to protect his client by fending off persistent questions from the group of anxious reporters clustered at the courthouse doors. Mitch, shielding his face with his hands, rushed to a waiting car. Erin only caught a glimpse of her former boss, and she felt a rush of pity for the man as his watery blue eyes darted anxiously back to the attorney before he climbed into the waiting automobile and sped away from the newsmen.

"Yes," the mustached anchorman was stating, "Mitch-

ell Cameron, once considered one of Seattle's most prestigious and trusted bankers, was indicted today on seven
counts of embezzlement. If Cameron is found guilty, the
maximum sentence..." Erin couldn't listen to the rest of
the broadcast. She was too numbed by the chilling real-
ization that Mitch actually had been indicted! Rubbing
her temples with her slender fingers, she tried to think
rationally—indicted, what exactly did that mean? It took
her a few minutes to understand that Mitch hadn't been
found guilty of a crime, at least not yet. But apparently
there was enough evidence against him to warrant a serious investigation and a trial. Erin sunk onto the sofa,
mindless of the water that had started to collect around
her boots on the Persian rug.

The TV continued to talk to her. A picture of the bank
building, looking somehow more foreboding in the var-
iegated gray tones of the set, flashed onto the screen.
Consolidated First Bank stood out in bold letters, while
a reporter recounted the bank's recent history along with
the fact that, within the last month, the ownership of the
prestigious building had changed hands. The smug newsman noted that when the president of Consolidated, Mr.
Kane Webster, was summoned by the television station
to remark on the alleged embezzlement, Mr. Webster
declined. He was, of course, unavailable for comment—
supposedly out of the state.

Erin had heard enough, and she clicked off the television with cold, numb fingers. Drawing her knees beneath her chin, she wrapped her arms about her legs
and sat on the couch, staring at the black Seattle evening through the window. A loneliness settled upon her
and she thought about Kane, thousands of miles away
in southern California. The smoky gray drizzle and the
heavy purple cloud cover that cloaked the city only added

to her gloom. Unconsciously she began to take the pins from her hair, and shake loose the tight, confining chignon. She ran her fingers through her black tresses and rubbed her scalp, hoping to deter the headache that was starting to throb against her temples. If only Kane were here now—perhaps the lonely desperation that was closing in on her would fade....

She must have been staring into the oncoming darkness for quite a while, but she was too lost in her own black thoughts to realize that time had escaped her. The urgent ringing of the telephone startled Erin back to the present, and she rushed into the kitchen to answer its incessant call. As she spoke, she tried to conceal the note of depression that had crept into her voice.

"Hello?"

"Erin?" a concerned voice inquired.

"Oh, Kane!" She sighed, and let her knees give way in relief. Resting against the counter, she found herself overwhelmingly grateful for the thin wire that stretched the length of the West Coast and tied her to Kane.

"Are you okay?" he asked, and she recognized a tremor of concern in his voice.

"I'm fine," she assured him. "It's been a long, hectic week without you. I'm just a little tired, that's all."

There was a weighty pause in the conversation before Kane spoke again. "Have you heard about the indictment?" he asked, and his voice seemed to have become suddenly reserved.

"Yes... I saw the evening news...." She hesitated a moment. Should she tell him about her meeting with Mitch this afternoon and his proposition? Erin knew that Kane would be angry and upset when he found out about it, and she reasoned it would be better to tell him face-to-face. A long-distance call was too short and too impersonal. Too many misunderstandings could occur.

"I know that you care a lot about Cameron," Kane began, wondering to himself why he continued to pursue a subject that only incensed him.

"I did, and I suppose I still do...but, really, it's okay. This is the way it had to be, didn't it?"

Why did he feel that there was a trace of hesitation in her voice? His fist involuntarily balled at his side, and his grip on the telephone receiver tightened until his knuckles showed white. It had been a difficult week for him also. Dealing with his strong-willed daughter had proven to be nearly impossible. And the fact that Erin was alone and over fifteen hundred miles away only added to his irritation and short temper.

"Krista and I will be home late Sunday afternoon," he was saying. "Probably around six. And the moving company has promised to have the bulk of our belongings in Seattle by Monday—or so they claim. What won't fit into the apartment, I'll have stored. Will the apartment be ready for us?"

Erin couldn't hide the disappointment that swallowed her. She had hoped that Kane would be home this evening or, at the very latest, Saturday.

"What? Oh, yes," she agreed distractedly. "Mr. Jefferies moved out at the beginning of the week, and the cleaning people were here earlier today. I'm sure it will be ready by Sunday evening...."

"Good—I'll see you then."

"Good night, Kane," Erin whispered, not wanting to hang up the phone and sever the frail connection that bound her so distantly to him.

"Erin?"

"Yes..."

A pause. "Good night."

Erin felt an incredible loneliness as she hung up the phone.

"Oh, darling!" Kane murmured to himself as he heard her ring off. He slammed the receiver down in mindless frustration and rubbed his hands together anxiously, all the while leaning against the wall and staring at the clean, white telephone in his sister's apartment. How was he going to handle his emotions for Erin? God, had it only been four days since he had last seen—or touched—her?

Somehow he had expected and silently hoped that once he had put some distance between himself and her, the miles would erase the goddesslike image of her body and that her likeness in his mind would fade, cooling his hot-blooded need for her. But he had been mistaken, grievously mistaken, and just the reverse had occurred. Instead of forgetting her, the image of her body was burned savagely on his mind and achingly in his loins. He felt an urgency, a driving *need*, warm and molten, that throbbed against his temples and fired his blood. He had to see her again, and he had to see her soon, or he would surely go out of his mind!

And the lies! Oh, God, how he hated his lies. The duplicity of his situation was eating at him, tearing at him from the inside out. He slammed a powerful fist against the wall. How could he lie to her and to himself? How long could the tense charade continue?

Kane had convinced himself that it would be a good idea to live near Erin, in the same building, in order that he might watch her more closely. But now, as he stood staring at the phone, he knew that it was only his mind playing games with him again. Another lie to justify his urgent need to be near her and protect her.

Protect her? He laughed mirthlessly at himself and

reached for the tall glass of Scotch that he had poured before placing the long-distance call. Erin needed to be protected all right, from Kane Webster, from himself! *He* was the one who continued relentlessly and mercilessly to track her down, stalking her like some wild, criminal creature. He was suspicious of her and too much of a coward to admit it for fear of losing her. A damned hypocritical bastard, that's what he was, he conceded to himself.

Kane's hands were shaking from the turbulent emotions that were battling cruelly within his mind. He took a long drink, and groaned as the Scotch hit the empty bottom of his stomach. His thoughts were black and excruciating as he strode into the living room and levered himself down on his sister's uncomfortable floral couch.

Why couldn't he just forget about Erin O'Toole and her crazy connection with the embezzling scam? Why did he continue to torture himself with the memory of the gentle curve of her neck, the slim, feminine contour of her legs or the longing way that her near-violet eyes could reach out and touch him?

Damn it, Webster, his persistent mind scolded, *control yourself! For all you know that woman is just another two-bit thief, and you're letting her rip you to shreds! She's destroying your objectivity! Erin's a witch,* his mind warned, *the less you have to do with her, the better!*

Kane shifted his weight uncomfortably on the prim blue cushions of the couch and took another long dissatisfying swallow of the potent warm liquor. He needed to break away from Erin and the spell she was casting over him, he reasoned.

Then, why the hell couldn't he convince himself to leave her alone?

Chapter 10

Sunday morning dawned as gloomy as the rest of the Seattle weekend had, but Erin felt somewhat lighthearted at the prospect of seeing Kane again. It seemed like forever since he'd been gone. She stretched out on the bed, and discovered that she ached all over. The muscles in her arms and legs seemed to be all knotted and twisted this morning, but she smiled to herself in spite of the pain. In order to keep her mind off Mitch's indictment and Kane's absence, Erin had run out on Friday night and purchased several gallons of paint. That night and all day Saturday she had spent repainting Mr. Jefferies's old apartment and the massive entry hall. This morning her aching muscles rebelled.

Against the silent protests of her body Erin got up and showered. The new paint job had been such an improvement to the building that she had decided to continue the project. She had almost finished with the entry hall, and

today she planned to tackle Mrs. Cavenaugh's apartment.
Ever since the repairmen had insulated the flooring and
the windows, parts of the little old lady's apartment had
suffered, and a new coat of paint would hide the dirt and
chips of paint that had been loosened during the repairs.
Erin shuddered when she realized that she had nearly de-
pleted her savings with the insulation and painting proj-
ects. But it just had to be done!

Mrs. Cavenaugh had embraced the idea of repainting
her apartment, and by the time Erin had swallowed a cup
of coffee, looked over the headlines and nibbled on a bit
of toast, it was only eight-thirty. Yet Mrs. Cavenaugh was
already up and ready to help Erin with the task at hand.

For as long as Erin could remember, she had never
seen Mrs. Cavenaugh in anything other than a prim
housedress and a single strand of pearls. But this morning the half-bent figure of Mrs. Cavenaugh sported a
garishly loud green-and-purple scarf that was wound
tightly over her hair, oversize trousers and tennis shoes
that were presumably antiques. She was a comical sight
in the outlandish outfit, but her blue eyes sparkled with
eagerness, and against Erin's protests, the elderly woman
grabbed a brush and began to tackle the job at hand, only
pausing to grumble about working on the Sabbath. Erin
ignored her complaints and to her amazement found that
Mrs. Cavenaugh was handy with the brush and had the
endurance of a woman half her age.

"This is a wonderful idea," Mrs. Cavenaugh exclaimed,
"even if we are working on the Lord's day." Her blue eyes
were carefully checking over some of Erin's work with
a practiced eye. Not able to complain about Erin's painting, she continued, "Adds a lot to this apartment, don't
you think?" A pleased smile crept over her features. "You
really are a dear. You know that, don't you?"

"Keeping up the place comes with being a landlord, especially when I can get some free labor from my tenants," Erin laughed, and smiled at the little old lady's compliment.

"Is the apartment across the hall ready for the new renters? When are they moving in?"

Erin slid a suspicious glance at the old woman, who seemed intent on trimming the windowsill. "As a matter of fact I expect them this afternoon."

"Young couple?" Mrs. Cavenaugh asked, a mischievous twinkle lighting her eyes.

"No…it's my boss… Mr. Webster. I believe you've met?" Erin watched Mrs. Cavenaugh carefully.

"Charming man," the older woman agreed, and paid even more attention to the windowsill. "So he's moving in today?"

"Why do I get the feeling that I'm giving you yesterday's news?" Erin asked suspiciously. "You've already talked to Kane about this, haven't you?"

A smile spread across the wrinkled face. "Someone's got to look out for your best interests."

"And so you just appointed yourself guardian angel. Is that it?"

"Close enough," the little old lady averred. "Now don't you go jumping off the deep end, Erin," Mrs. Cavenaugh cautioned, and wagged a warning finger at Erin. "I just happened to mention in passing that there was an apartment available…."

"In passing! When did you see him?"

Mrs. Cavenaugh's face puckered for a moment. "Now listen here, young lady. I may not be as young as I used to be, but I have a pretty good idea of what goes on around here. I've seen Kane come and go, and I've also got it figured out that, for some reason, the good Lord only knows why—" she threw her hands heavenward in supplication "—you keep running away from him."

Erin began to protest, but the gray-haired lady would have none of it. "It's a mistake, pure and simple, for you to run from him. That man is hopelessly in love with you, Erin. Only a fool would let him slip through her fingers!"

"Oh, Mrs. Cavenaugh," Erin sighed, smiling wistfully. "If it were only that simple."

"It's as simple as you want to make it!" The old lady eyed Erin speculatively, and noticed the resigned droop of her shoulders. "Why don't you call it a day—the apartment looks fine. You go and get ready for your Kane and his daughter. They'll be here this evening, won't they?"

"Just where do you get all of your information?"

"Like I said before, I know what's going on around here!" Before Erin could voice any further questions or objections, the little bent figure hustled her out the door. "And don't you dare accuse me of snooping," she cautioned. "It's just that I care."

"I know you do," Erin replied thoughtfully, "but you do seem to have an uncanny sense about some things...."

"Comes with age, don't you know? My eyesight isn't what it used to be, and my hearing's, well, you know, a little less than it should be. But I can still see love when it stares me in the face. Now you hurry up and change into something pretty and make that man something to eat. I bet he'll be starved by the time that he gets home—the girl, too."

Erin started to protest, but Mrs. Cavenaugh pursed her lips, and balanced the wet paintbrush on one of her hips. "Scoot," she ordered authoritatively, and slammed the door tightly shut.

Several hours had passed, and somewhat reluctantly Erin had taken Mrs. Cavenaugh's well-meant advice, although she doubted that the little old lady downstairs would consider her slim designer jeans and print cotton blouse as "something pretty." But Erin had made dinner for Kane and his daughter, and then, realizing that Krista probably wouldn't be able to manage the two flights of stairs to Erin's loft, Erin had moved the meal downstairs to Kane's new apartment.

She paced nervously while waiting for Kane and glanced at her watch for the sixth time in the space of two minutes. The trying weekend without Kane had made Erin anxious and tired, and she found that her nerves were stretched as tightly as a piano string. How would she react to Kane's daughter, and how would Krista take to Erin? she wondered.

Erin had attempted to bring as much warmth as possible to the small first-floor apartment by bringing down a few pieces of her own furniture. To her credit, the interior did look a little less stark and more comfortable for all her efforts. The creamy new coat of vanilla paint gleamed against the walls, and the few small pieces of furniture, though sparse, added a homey familiarity to the otherwise vacant rooms. Erin had even managed to cover the card table with a linen cloth and centered a basket of freshly cut flowers on it. All in all, she had done a decent job of making the tiny apartment attractive, but she found it impossible to shake the feeling of apprehension that shrouded her.

The sound of feet shuffling in the hall snapped her attention to the doorway. She knew in an instant that Kane and Krista had made it home. Nervously she wiped her suddenly wet palms against her jeans and pasted what she hoped appeared to be a pleasant smile upon her face. The door swung open, and father and daughter entered the room. At the sight of Kane, Erin's heart turned over.

How, in less than a week's time, could anyone change so dramatically? He was dressed casually in jeans and a dove-gray sport shirt, but that's where the casual part of his image stopped. Erin could sense the signs of strain that hardened his features, the thin light lines of worry that crowded his forehead, and the somber tilt of his dark eyebrows that were drawn thoughtfully together. His eyes met hers for an instant, and a small flicker of relief and affection lessened the severity of his gaze.

At the whirring sound of the electric wheelchair, Erin's attention shifted from Kane to his daughter. Krista was beautiful in the classical sense: a small, evenly featured madonnalike face was surrounded by thick sun-kissed curls, and her deep-set, perfectly round icy blue eyes held a sparkle and a vibrancy of youth. Krista's cheekbones were high and noble-looking with just a hint of pink on her otherwise cream-colored skin. Even in the awkward stage of adolescence, it was apparent that Krista was an uncommonly beautiful girl. Only the mechanical apparatus of the wheelchair detracted from her wholesome, California-fresh appearance. The presence of the chair served to remind Erin just how difficult the past year of Krista's life must have been for the girl. Krista was much too young to have lived through the trauma of witnessing the death of her mother. Erin felt her heart go out to the attractive young girl in the mechanical beast.

There was a tense, uncomfortable moment as Kane dropped a bundle of blankets that he had carried into the apartment and shoved them into the corner of the room. For a split second Erin faced Krista alone and was surprised at the frigidity in the pale blue eyes of the girl. Uncontrollably Erin shuddered and hoped that she could somehow warm the cool look that hardened Krista's gaze.

After unsuccessfully arranging the pillows and blankets on the floor, Kane gave up and turned his attention to Erin and his daughter. He seemed to appraise the uncomfortable situation with knowing eyes, and in a minute, he stood near to Erin. He was smiling, but the grin was tight, forced as if it had been slapped on his face out of courtesy. He showed Erin no outward signs of affection, but his stormy gray eyes reached out for hers, and Erin realized that he was asking her indulgence with Krista. It was as if he had expected a confrontation.

"Krista," Kane said softly, and Krista's blue eyes sparked upward to him. "This is Erin. You remember, I told you all about her. She works with me at the bank, and she'll be our landlord until we can find a house of our own."

Krista's eyes skimmed over the interior of the apartment, and from the bored expression on her face, Erin sensed that Krista disapproved of her new, temporary home. The girl remained silent, and for a moment Erin wondered if the child had even heard the introduction. Kane's dark eyebrows melted together at Krista's rudeness, but for the moment, he chose not to reprimand her.

Continuing the stilted introduction, he said more firmly, "Erin, this is Krista."

Erin ventured a sincere smile for Kane's daughter and wondered if the young girl in the wheelchair was just being shy, or if she was purposely giving Erin the cold shoulder.

"Hello, Krista. It's nice to meet you. I hope you like it here." Erin offered her outstretched hand to the girl.

Krista didn't immediately respond to Erin's attempts at warmth or friendliness. In fact, Erin was sure that if Kane hadn't been in the room, the blue-eyed girl would have ignored the greeting altogether. As it was, Krista hesitated and then gave Kane an accusatory glare before

finding her manners and answering. "Hello," Krista muttered, almost to herself, and reached for Erin's open hand.
Her eyes never met Erin's puzzled gaze.

There wasn't time for a proper handshake. The instant
that Krista's smaller fingers touched Erin's open palm,
Krista withdrew her hand as rapidly as if Erin's touch
were white-hot. Erin found herself standing with her open
palm suspended in midair and an astonished expression
of disbelief disturbing her features. Was the girl always
so rude, or did she just dislike Erin?

Rather than commenting on Krista's complete lack of
courtesy, or asking about Krista's negative reaction to
her, Erin forced herself to remain calm and hang on to
the dwindling amount of control she had left. Excusing
herself, she turned her attention back to the kitchen and
preparation of the meal. She could hear the quiet reprimand that Kane was giving his daughter, but Erin tried to
ignore the tension between father and daughter—tension
that she somehow felt guilty about. Perhaps she shouldn't
have intruded on the homecoming. It was obvious that
Krista would have preferred that she had never met Erin.

As Erin extracted the platter of warm rolls from the
oven, she tried to convince herself that she was overreacting to Krista's indifference. After all, the girl was disabled
and probably extremely self-conscious about her condition. Aside from the obvious, it couldn't be easy moving away from the only family and friends she had ever
known to start a new life with a father she barely knew
in an unfamiliar city. It was no wonder that the child was
frightened and misbehaving. *Give the girl a chance,* Erin
told herself. *It's barely been a year since the young girl
witnessed her mother's death.* Armed with a new sense
of conviction, Erin decided to ignore Krista's coolness.

As she carried the meal to the table, Erin forced herself to smile and say, "Let's get started. I bet you're both hungry!"

"We ate on the plane!" Krista announced, and Kane threw his daughter a grim reproving glance. Krista ignored it.

"That we did," Kane acknowledged, "but that was several hours ago, and it wasn't particularly good." His steely eyes never left his daughter—it was as if he dared her to act up again. "As I recall, you didn't eat much." The muscle cords in his neck stood out clearly against the collar of his shirt, and Erin could tell that he was holding on to the rags of his patience. He was about to explode. Erin hoped that Krista realized how dangerous the situation was becoming.

Erin tried to steady her rapidly disintegrating nerves as she went back to the kitchen for the rest of the food. She couldn't gloss over it, not even to herself. For some reason Krista was determined to hate her. Erin mentally counted to ten, took several deep breaths, and once again poised, returned to face father and daughter. It took a lot of determination, but she was able to hide her discomfort and take some pleasure in serving the dishes that she had so meticulously prepared, although Krista's discriminating eye took a little of the satisfaction away from her. Though the aroma of the food was tantalizing, and the marmalade-glazed game hens looked delicious as they sat on a platter of steaming wild rice and mushrooms, the meal was tense and uncomfortable. Everything seemed to have soured slightly under Krista's disapproving blue-eyed gaze.

"This looks great!" Kane exclaimed a little too heartily as he helped Erin to her chair. His fingers brushed against her arm, and startled by the intimate gesture, Erin turned her eyes away from the meal to look more

closely at him. He seemed more than tired—he seemed
weary. She could tell his jovial words were just a cloak
for the tension coiling rigidly within him. Although his
voice was cheerful, the lines on his forehead, the muscle
cords strung tightly at his neck, and the darkness of his
gaze betrayed his calm exterior.

"Doesn't this look delicious, honey?" he asked his
daughter as he took his seat. Krista remained silent. Kane
cleared his throat and rubbed his hands together. "I'm
famished!" He looked at Krista with concern. Her large,
liquid eyes met his, but still she didn't speak.

Finally she broke her gaze from that of her father, and
stared instead at the napkin in her lap. Kane's forced
smile disappeared into a frown. He was obviously distressed by Krista's coolness and lack of manners, but
he wisely said nothing, preferring to wait until he was
alone with his daughter before having the argument that
he knew was brewing between them.

The meal began in silence, and Erin thought that she
would scream if some of the icy tension in the air didn't
melt. Fortunately the telephone rang, and Kane excused
himself to answer it. The conversation was extremely
one-sided and uncomfortable.

"Not tonight," Kane argued but was apparently interrupted. "No—it's absolutely impossible! I just got in
from California with my daughter. You'll have to handle
it yourself!" A pause, and the muscle in Kane's rigid face
tightened again. "Can't Jones handle it? No—how about
Martin?" Another long pause. "For God's sake, Jim,
doesn't anyone down there know what they're doing?"
Kane was shaking his head, raking his fingers through
the burnished copper of his hair and pacing the length of
the telephone cord. "All right, all right! I get the picture.
I'll be there in—" he checked his watch "—about twenty

minutes!" He slammed the receiver down viciously and uttered a curse under his breath.

"I'm sorry," he apologized sincerely, once he had subdued his temper. His gray eyes pleaded with Erin to understand. "It seems that there are major problems in the computer center tonight. I have to go to the bank for a little while...."

"No..." Krista began to wail, looking frantically from her father to Erin and back again. "Don't go...."

"I'm sorry, honey," Kane responded with a fond pat on her silky blond curls. "But, really, I have to go—just for a little while..."

"No...no..." Krista pleaded, clinging to her father's shirtsleeve.

"I'll be back in a couple of hours. You can stay here with Erin."

"Daddy! No!"

Kane's expression became confused, and for a moment Erin thought that he might reconsider. She fervently hoped so, but when his dark brows straightened again, she knew that the decision had been made. He was leaving Erin with the adolescent girl who obviously hated her.

"Erin, do you mind?" he asked, ignoring Krista's pleading eyes.

"Not at all," Erin agreed, as kindly as she could, and rained a warm smile on Krista. "We'll get along just fine!" Kane's gray gaze was dubious.

"Daddy, *please*, don't go!" Krista cried in a shaky voice. Her frightened blue eyes skittered over to Erin and back to her father.

"Look, honey," Kane answered, taking both of Krista's hands in his. He squatted next to the chair, so that the child could look him squarely in the eyes. "You know I don't want to go, so let's not make it any harder than it already is. I'll be back soon. I promise." He planted a loving kiss on the top of her forehead as if to ward off any further protests. His silvery eyes locked with Erin's for a moment, begging her to understand, but there was something more—the same old sense of wariness seemed to flicker across his face for an instant as he grabbed his jacket and walked to the door. Krista stared at her plate, unable to watch her father leave, but Erin followed him.

Kane stretched into his coat, took Erin's hand in his and gently guided her out into the semiprivacy of the hallway. "Thank you," he stated and his eyes held hers. Erin could see a question in their steely depths.

"It's no problem," she replied, doubting her own words as she thought about the headstrong blond girl.

Kane looked at her and seemed unconvinced. "You don't have to mince words with me. I know that Krista's a handful!"

"I can handle her," Erin insisted.

"I know." Still he hesitated, and in the dimly lit hallway Erin could sense an uneasiness creep over both of them. It was the same feeling that seemed to keep them from completely trusting each other. He began to reach for her and then let his hand drop. "I'll be back as soon as I can...."

"I'm sure it won't be long," she agreed, knowing that her voice sounded feeble. What was it that was bothering her? Something didn't seem right. "I thought that the repairmen fixed the computer on Friday," she puzzled, shaking her head in an effort to remember the details of Friday afternoon. "Yes, I'm sure that we got a call around five o'clock, stating that all systems were go."

Kane's jaw flexed. "Apparently there have been additional problems." His voice was strangely devoid of emotion—cold.

"Odd, isn't it?" she murmured. "Oh, well." She lifted her shoulders and managed a sincere smile. "Try to hurry home…."

His sudden and powerful embrace surprised and baffled her. His arms held her closely, tightly, as if he were afraid she might disappear. His strength imprisoned her, and she could hear the hammering of his heart, belying his calm exterior of a few moments before. His breathing was labored and uneven. She couldn't see his eyes as her face was crushed, almost savagely, against his chest. There was anger in his strength and passion in his words. They were torn from him as if his admission were painfully traitorous.

"God, but I've missed you, Erin," he breathed, and the pressure against the curve of her spine increased. "I've had dreams about you, ached for you…"

"Shhh…" Before he could utter another word, Erin checked his speech by placing a trembling finger against the warmth of his lips. "Later," she whispered, cocking her head toward the open doorway to his apartment. "I'd better go inside and check on Krista." Erin knew that she was shaking from the intensity of his passion, but she controlled the urge to reach up and trace the angled contour of his cheeks with her fingers.

Kane reluctantly let his embrace loosen and an unreadable, agonized expression passed over his face. "I won't be gone long—it should only take a minute…."

"Don't be too sure," she laughed hollowly as she stepped back toward the apartment. "Computer problems tend to be complicated…."

"That they do," he whispered cryptically, and let his eyes rove over her face searchingly. What did he expect to find? Finally he tore his gaze away from her and threw open the door before stepping into the night. If only Erin could guess the *real* reason that he had been summoned to the bank on this black, rain-drenched night, Kane thought sardonically. If only she knew that he was aware of the fact that another three thousand dollars had slipped out of the dividend account during his absence. *Oh, Erin,* he thought as he drove toward the winking lights of Seattle. His grip tightened on the steering wheel, and the tires of the black sports car screamed against the pressure of a corner taken too recklessly. *Why,* he wondered—*oh, God, why?*

Erin straightened her shoulders before she entered the tiny apartment and let the door whisper shut behind her. At the sound of the soft noise Krista stirred and looked longingly at the door with cold disbelieving eyes.

Mentally Erin fortified herself. She could tell that the upcoming evening was going to be a test of will between herself and Kane's stubborn daughter. And although Erin was an adult, and the old Victorian house was "her turf," she felt at a distinct disadvantage to the blond girl who had folded her arms defiantly over her small chest. Erin dreaded the argument that she knew was simmering in the air. Forcing herself to appear more collected than she felt, she walked back to the table and ignored Krista's wounded look as she spoke softly to the child. Erin's voice was friendly but firm.

"Is there anything else I can get you?" she asked the girl, and motioned to a basket of sourdough rolls at her end of the table.

Silence.

Erin gritted her teeth together in frustration and noticed that Krista hadn't touched any of the food on her plate. Once again Erin attempted to communicate. "How about a glass of milk?"

Nothing.

"Krista," Erin said, commanding the girl's attention, and bracing herself for the inevitable confrontation. "I'd like it very much if we could be friends."

Cold fearful blue eyes surveyed Erin as if seeing her for the first time. Pouty pink lips pressed into an insolent line. "I don't like you!" Krista hissed in a trembling voice.

Erin sucked in her breath but bravely continued the stilted conversation. "Why? Why don't you like me? Is it because I'm a friend of your father's?"

"I don't want to like you—and I won't!" Defiance and anger were evident in the tilt of Krista's finely shaped chin.

Erin sighed wearily and sat down in the chair opposite the rebellious girl with the fearful eyes. Their gazes locked and Erin found herself folding and refolding the napkin in her lap, while contemplating a way to bridge the gap that existed between her and Kane's daughter. She took in the challenging look on the girl's face, the proud carriage of Krista's head, and then Erin's gaze touched upon the empty wheelchair. Compassion washed over Erin. Krista was bearing a heavy cross.

"You don't have to like me," Erin stated simply, and a look of astonishment softened Krista's defiant features. "It's up to you."

Once again Erin paid full attention to her meal and hoped it seemed that she was enjoying her food, while all the time her stomach was twisting into knots of revulsion against the meal. It took all of Erin's will to finish the cold and suddenly tasteless meal.

It was several minutes before the silence was broken. Krista's small voice trembled and Erin politely looked at the girl. "They were getting back together, you know!" Krista announced, and toyed with the food on her plate.

"Pardon me?"

"Mother and Daddy. They were going to get married again. Mother told me so!" Krista's face was set for the denial she expected from Erin.

"Were they?" Erin asked calmly.

"You bet!" the girl nearly shouted. "And it would have been soon, too. And…and…we were all going to be a family again!"

Erin listened intently, not knowing exactly how to respond to Krista's outburst. She studied Krista and saw the turbulent play of emotions that was contorting the beautiful child's face.

"We were going to be together again. We were!" she proclaimed, tears glistening in her round eyes. "If only Mama hadn't died… I know we would!" Her frail voice caught and tears began to flow freely down her cheeks.

Erin's heart bled for the small girl at the other end of the table. Dropping her fork onto the plate, she got up and hurried to Krista's side. She let her hand touch the sobbing shoulders.

"I'm so sorry," Erin whispered.

"No, you're not!" the child sniffed. "If Mama was alive, then you couldn't have Daddy. He loved her! He did!" By this time Krista's body was racked with her uncontrolled weeping, and Erin let her arm reach tentatively around the slim shoulders.

"Don't touch me," Krista screamed. "Don't you dare touch me!" She pushed her chair back from the table and attempted to reach for the wheelchair. Erin knew that the situation was getting dangerously out of control, and she tried to help Krista by pushing the wheelchair in the girl's direction.

"I can do it myself!" Krista declared, and to Erin's surprise, the slender girl braced herself on the table's edge and took a few hesitant steps before falling into her mechanical chair.

They faced each other as if they were opponents on a battlefield. Each one eyed the other distrustfully. Hesitantly Erin drew herself up to her full height, and her lilac gaze rested on her ward for the evening. How was it possible to handle Krista? There was no answer but the obvious.

"Krista," Erin said, and offered the girl a tissue to dry her eyes. "I want you to know that there's no rule stating that you have to like me. All I ask is that you give me a chance, an honest chance. And, for your father's sake, I'm asking you to be, at least, civil to me. Is that so much to ask?"

"I don't want a new mother!" the girl cried, nearly hysterical.

"I understand that, and...I respect it," Erin agreed, still holding the tissue out to the child. "No one has the right to step into someone else's shoes, unless they're asked. I'm sure that your mother was a very wonderful woman, and that she loved you very much, but, unfortunately, I can't bring her back to you. Nobody can." Erin's eyes had begun to fill with tears as she looked into a face that was much too young to understand death. "I hope you know that whatever happens between your father and me, that I would *never* attempt to take the place of your mother—that's a promise!"

Krista stared silently at Erin for what seemed an eternity before taking the tissue and wiping the stain of tears from her cheeks. Assured that the girl was poised again, Erin turned toward the kitchen and hastily wiped her own tears with the cuff of her blouse. She hoped that Krista hadn't seen her tears or her weakness.

For the rest of the evening, while Erin cleared the

table and cleaned the dishes, Krista brooded in a corner of the room, pretending interest in the empty fireplace. Erin offered to build a fire, but Krista had withdrawn back into her shell and didn't respond to the invitation. Therefore, Erin shrugged her shoulders and acted as if it didn't matter in the least to her, one way or the other, before turning back to the task of straightening the kitchen. But she sensed that beneath Krista's cold exterior, the girl had begun to thaw.

Whenever Krista didn't think that Erin would notice, she studied the black-haired woman with interest. So this was the lady that her father was falling to pieces over. Although this Erin creature was very unlike her mother, Krista couldn't help but admire Erin's mettle. Maybe Seattle wouldn't be quite as bad as she had imagined.

It was late when Kane returned to the apartment house. He parked the car and sat motionless for several minutes, just staring into the darkness of the night. He was emotionally drained to the point of exhaustion, and he had the urge to restart the car and head to the closest tavern. He wanted a drink—make that several drinks—and then he wanted to fall into bed and sleep for days. He didn't want to face Krista and endure another fight, and he couldn't face Erin, not now.

He groaned when he thought about the scene at the bank: the evidence, the fear and the anger as Jim Haney explained about the latest development in the embezzling operation. Not only was three thousand dollars missing, but Jim had learned from Olivia Parsons that Erin had met with Mitchell Cameron on the day of his arraignment hearing—the very day the money was transferred from the dividend account. The only good news was that Jim had traced the money's path and it would only be a matter of days before he had sifted through all of the departmental checks to find one that was out of balance with the general ledger. At last the torture of the unknown would end, and Kane realized bitterly that Erin would be caught.

Erin was sitting in a chair, engrossed in a mystery novel, when Kane let himself into the apartment. Her black hair was wound into a loose ponytail, her glasses were perched on the end of her nose, and her legs were curled comfortably beneath her. As Kane saw her he was reminded of the first time he had seen her, dressed much the same and crouched in a pile of legal documents at the bank. He felt the same, now-familiar male response that he had several weeks ago. He wanted to run to her, to scoop her up in his arms, to crush her against him and to bury his head in the soft warmth of her breasts. Even now, suspecting what he did about her and knowing he was deathly close to the truth, he wanted her as he had never wanted another woman.

"Hi," Erin greeted him, and pulled her glasses off her face. She laid the book and the glasses on an upturned box that she was using as a table, stood up and stretched. It was an unconscious and provocative gesture that made Kane's blood heat as he watched the fabric of her clothes mold tightly to her body. Her eyes found his. "Can I get you anything? There's quite a few leftovers...."

He stood in the doorway, his shoulders drooped in resignation. Though she could tell that he, in his own way, was glad to see her, there was a strange look on his face.

"Are you well?" she asked.

"What? Oh, yeah. I'm fine," he responded, and rubbed the back of his neck.

"Were the computer problems that difficult?"

"The what? Oh, no, the computer is fine. But you

know how it is, one problem seems to lead to another, and before you know it, the half-hour that you planned to be gone has stretched into three." His voice was vague, distant, and Erin wondered if he was trying to tell her something.

"How's Krista?" Kane asked, and dropped to the floor. He grabbed a loose pillow for his head and patted the floor next to him, inviting Erin to sit next to him on the floor.

"We got along fine," Erin replied, and leaned against Kane, who cocked a dubious eyebrow. "Well, it wasn't easy—not at first," she admitted hesitantly. "But we worked things out."

"Did you?"

"Well, somehow we managed to get by...." Erin's voice drifted off. Kane seemed remote this evening, and she could see the evidence of exhaustion on his face. She hated to add to his problems, but she thought that he should know about Krista. "Did you know that she can walk?" Erin asked in a near whisper.

Kane stiffened. "What do you mean? Did she actually walk while I was gone?" His voice had lost all of its distance, and his fingers dug into her upper arm.

"Not exactly..."

"But you said..."

"I know what I said. Just listen a minute. Krista and I had an argument. It wasn't serious," Erin added hastily, and felt guilty for the lie. "And when I tried to help her to the wheelchair, she wouldn't stand for it. She braced herself on the table and took two—three—possibly four steps until she made it to her chair."

"You're certain?"

"Kane! I was right there—only inches from her! She walked."

"Oh, God," he murmured, and covered his face in his hands. "If only I could believe that she would be able to walk again. If only…"

"Have you spoken to a doctor in Seattle?"

"Not yet… I thought I'd wait until she was settled into a routine." He rubbed his chin thoughtfully. "The tutor comes on Tuesday for her evaluation, and then I thought I'd call the doctors that were referred to me by Krista's doctor in L.A."

"Good." Kane was weary, and now disturbed. It had been a long, tiring day for both of them. Erin stood up and tightened the thong around her hair. "Krista went to bed at ten. She wanted to wait up for you, but the poor thing was exhausted. Maybe you should go in and let her know that you're back…." Had he even heard her suggestion? He was looking at Erin intently, but for some reason, she felt that he was light-years away from her. "Well…I'd better be getting upstairs," she said, and then added more lightly, "Work tomorrow, you know. And my boss is a very punctual person."

"Don't go," Kane breathed, ignoring her joke and reaching for her wrist. "Stay with me tonight…." His face seemed so earnest, his gray eyes so intent, that Erin had trouble resisting him.

"I'd like to stay, you know that." She hesitated. "But I can't…"

"Why not? Erin, I need you."

"Oh, Kane. You know the reason why I can't stay with you—she's sleeping in the next room. You're the one who said she needed a more normal family existence," she reminded him, and lovingly touched his forehead. "What do you think she would do if she knew that you and I were sleeping together? You said yourself that her paralysis is psychosomatic, and now we know for sure—because she

walked tonight!" Erin was on her knees, placing both of
her hands on his cheeks. "Oh, Kane—perhaps the doctors were right, maybe she did need a change to get her
motivated to walk. But…we, you and I, we mustn't do
anything to blow it with her. We can't take the chance
and set her back, don't you see?"

Kane's eyes agreed with her, although he cursed his
frustration.

"Damn!" he spat. "You're right," he conceded, "but
just how long do you expect me to keep my hands off
you?"

"It's not what I want, and you know it. But I think
that we, both of us, need to give Krista some time for
adjustment."

"You're right," he sighed, and taking her hands in
his, pulled the two of them upright. The passion in his
eyes simmered for a minute, and he dropped her hands.
"Thanks for staying with Krista. I'll see you tomorrow
at work." He seemed calm, only his clenched fists gave
any indication of the restraint he was placing upon himself. "I'll be in late, because of Krista and the moving
company, but when I get to the office, I…I think that we
should have a talk."

"Oh?"

"You and I have a lot to discuss."

She smiled up at him and tried to ignore the unreadable expression in his eyes. "I'm glad you're back," she
whispered. "I missed you."

He started to respond, but stopped and closed his eyes
for a second before rubbing his temple. "I'm glad to be
back," he admitted, trying to rub away the deep ridges
of concern that were creasing his forehead. Erin thought
that he had finished speaking.

"Good night," she called over her shoulder, but his

voice whispered to her and stopped her as she started to ascend the steps.

"Erin?" he beckoned.

"Yes?" Her face turned to him, and even in the semi-darkness he knew it was the most beautiful face he had ever seen, the most incredible woman he had ever made love to.

"You would tell me, wouldn't you? I mean, if you were in any trouble, you would tell me about it so that I could help you?"

"Of course I would. Honestly! Don't you know that?" She couldn't hide the smile that played on her lips.

"Sure," he agreed absently, as if totally unconvinced.

"Good! Then trust me!" She laughed, and shook her hair loose from the ponytail as she sprinted up the two flights of stairs. What was Kane talking about so seriously? Sometimes, she admitted to herself, he was a bit overly dramatic.

As Kane closed the door to his apartment, he leaned heavily against the cool hard wood. Erin's final words echoed and reechoed in his ears. "Then just trust me... trust me..."

Chapter 11

Several days had passed, and Erin found it nearly impossible to spend any time alone with Kane. Even the meeting at work had to be postponed indefinitely. During the days at work, whenever their paths would cross, it seemed that there wasn't any time for the lengthy discussion that Kane had alluded to on Sunday evening. Most of the staff was still out with the flu, the computer was working erratically, and the general disorganization of the office kept Erin from seeing Kane. Also, Kane was in and out of the office, dividing his time between the office and home, hoping to get Krista settled. Fortunately for him, Mrs. Cavenaugh had been more than willing to be with his daughter when it was impossible for him to be at home. But the strain of the situation was wearing on him; Erin could see it in his eyes.

In the evenings, although Erin would eat with Krista and Kane, there wasn't much time spent relaxing. Kane's things had made it up to Seattle Tuesday afternoon, and after dinner each night for the next four days, Erin would help him and Krista get the apartment organized. It was a nearly impossible task. Although Kane had most of his belongings in storage, it still seemed to Erin that he had overstuffed the apartment with furniture, books, clothes and whatever else he could imagine. For the first time she realized how different Kane's lifestyle in California must have been. The expensive leather furniture, an endless wardrobe of clothes, everything he owned spoke of money.

Although Kane seemed to become more tense with each passing day, Erin decided it had to do with the added responsibilities of being a full-time father. All in all, Krista seemed to be adjusting better than Kane to their new life together in Seattle. Slowly Krista was coming out of her shell. She adored Mrs. Cavenaugh and had even accepted Erin. It was difficult, but the girl had begun to take hesitant steps in her father's presence, and at those times, all of the tension would drain from Kane and he would relax. The brooding sense of distrust in his eyes would die, and he would seem to enjoy life again.

The hectic week passed quickly, and Erin let a sigh of relief escape from her lips at six o'clock on Friday when she could forget about the flu, the computer, and the inheritance tax auditors. She grabbed her coat and hurried out of the bank building. Knowing that Kane was working late this evening, she hadn't even bothered to knock on his office door to let him know she was leaving. Tonight she had special plans.

She hurried along on foot for several blocks before locating the pet shop that she had found just this week. As promised, the owner had kept his store open the extra ten minutes that Erin needed.

Erin entered the little building and tried to keep her nose from wrinkling at the pungent odor within. Several fat puppies yipped to get her attention, and longingly she patted a black fluff of fur with sparkling eyes. The puppy's entire rear end was set in motion and a long pink tongue licked Erin's fingers.

"Oh, Miss O'Toole," the bearded shopkeeper smiled. "Have you changed your mind and decided on a dog?" He held up the fat black puppy, who responded by washing the shopkeeper's broad face.

"No, unfortunately, I don't have the space for a puppy." She wavered a moment, and then shook her head resolutely. "No, I think a kitten is a better choice. It's a gift for a friend."

The round shopkeeper held his hands out helplessly and shrugged his broad shoulders. "If you're sure. Just give me a couple of minutes. I know which one you picked out earlier." He hurried to the back of his store and came back with a tiny black and white kitten that couldn't have been more than six weeks old. "This is the one, right?" he asked.

Erin held out her hands and petted the warm powder puff of black fur. The kitten began to purr noisily and scratched its tiny paws against Erin's jacket. "She's perfect!" Erin breathed, raising the kitten to eye level and inspecting it.

The shopkeeper tugged on his beard. "That one's a male—is that acceptable?"

"It doesn't matter. This is the one I want!"

Erin couldn't hide her excitement as she tapped lightly on the door to Kane's apartment. The little cat was perched contentedly on her arm as she called through the door. "Krista? Mrs. Cavenaugh?"

"Where have you been?" Mrs. Cavenaugh scolded as

she opened the door. "Kane's already called twice. Finally decided to leave a message with me...say, what's that you've got there?"

Erin breezed into the room, looking for Krista. "What does it look like, Mrs. Cavenaugh?" Erin asked in a whisper. "He's a surprise for Krista."

"Oh-ho," Mrs. Cavenaugh said, shaking her head, but reaching a tentative hand out to pat the kitten's soft, downy fur.

The whir of the electric wheelchair caught Erin's attention as Krista came into the room. The defiant look of rebellion had left her features several days ago, and for the first time since their meeting, Erin was sure that Krista was glad to see her.

"Oh, there you are. Look!" Erin announced with a wide, infectious grin as she proudly held up the black and white kitten for Krista's inspection. The blond girl let out a squeal of delighted excitement at the sight of the small cat. "I brought him home for you—you do like cats, don't you?"

"Oh, Erin," Krista stammered, wheeling more closely to the object of her delight. Erin placed the black ball of fur on Krista's lap. The kitten stretched and curled into a sleepy ball, purring contentedly. "He's...beautiful...." Krista's sparkling blue eyes swept from the drowsy kitten to Erin. "Thank you."

Erin smiled back at the girl and was surprised to feel a lump in her throat. "You're welcome, Krista," she murmured, and for a moment her breath caught. Erin kneeled next to the wheelchair and stroked the dozing kitten. "Now, if you decide to keep him, you'll have to take care of him. Feed him, take him outside...."

"I will," Krista agreed hurriedly. "Does he have a name?"

Erin shook her head. "That's for you to decide, unless Mrs. Cavenaugh has any suggestions...." Erin looked at the elderly lady and caught the gray-haired woman taking in the scene before her with teary eyes.

"What? Me?" Mrs. Cavenaugh coughed back her tears. "Oh, no. I've never been much of a cat person myself."

"Then it's up to you, Krista," Erin said. She cocked her head and stroked her thumb against her chin as she studied the cat with feigned thoughtfulness. "What do you think?"

"How about—Figaro. You know, like the cat in Pinocchio?" the bright-eyed girl asked, and Erin realized that for the first time since they had met, Krista had asked for and needed her opinion.

"I think Figaro's a great name," Erin agreed. "Now," she said as she stood up and adjusted her skirt, "I'll hurry upstairs and change my clothes before I cook us all some dinner."

Mrs. Cavenaugh and Krista exchanged knowing, conspiratorial glances. "Don't bother," Mrs. Cavenaugh suggested. "Krista and I are going to eat a pizza and watch *The Late Show*. I suppose the cat will, too. Remember I told you that Kane called earlier. He wants the two of you to go out alone."

"I don't know...." Erin looked pensively at the blond girl in the wheelchair and the cat nestled comfortably in her lap. "Are you sure that Kane wanted only me? I thought he wanted to spend some time with Krista."

"It's already been decided," Mrs. Cavenaugh stated firmly. "He called a few minutes ago. It was his idea. You're supposed to meet him at a place called The Tattered Sail or some such nonsense. I think he said that it's on the waterfront."

"Are you sure?" Erin still wasn't convinced. "He didn't say anything to me about dinner...."

Mrs. Cavenaugh clucked her tongue and interrupted, "That's why he called. He missed you. He'd been in some sort of a meeting with a fellow from California, a Mr...."

"Haney," Erin supplied.

"That was it. Anyway, by the time he got out of the meeting, you had already gone." Mrs. Cavenaugh noted the puzzled expression on Erin's face. "Now, don't ask me any more questions, because I don't know anything else."

Erin turned her attention to Kane's daughter. The girl had managed to take a few steps on her own and flop down on the couch with the cat. Krista's progress was encouraging. "Krista, wouldn't you like to join us?"

The girl rolled her head negatively against the back of the couch and playfully scratched the kitten's belly. "Naw—not tonight. I think I'd rather stay here with Figaro. Besides, we've already ordered the pizza, and the movie is going to be great!"

Erin glanced at Mrs. Cavenaugh, who lifted her shoulders. A tiny hint of a smile pulled at the corner of the wrinkled mouth. "Well, if you're sure, but somehow I feel that I'm the innocent victim of a conspiracy."

"No one could accuse you of a lack of imagination. Conspiracy, ha!" Mrs. Cavenaugh rejoined, but her wise old eyes brightened. "Now, you'd better get going. You don't want to be late. Kane said he'd meet you at about eight o'clock."

Convinced that both Mrs. Cavenaugh and Krista were satisfied with their plans for the evening, Erin made her way up the stairs and began changing for her dinner date with Kane. She couldn't hide the feeling of excitement that surged within her. It seemed like an eternity since she had spent some time alone with him. It wasn't that she begrudged him the time he shared with his daughter, it was just that Erin missed the intimate and quiet times she had shared with him in the past. He had seemed so remote lately.

The cool amethyst silk dress that she chose for the date slid easily over her body. It was simple, smart and understated with its modest V-neck and long sleeves. The slit that parted the hem added just the right amount of flair to be called sexy in a discreet manner. Erin eyed herself speculatively in the mirror and was pleased with her reflection. Her ebony hair cascaded in loose curls to her shoulders and brushed against the neckline of the dress. Her skin was already rosy with the blush of excitement and only a few touches of makeup were necessary to add to the effect. She reached for her coat and purse and headed out the door.

Just as she had closed the door, the telephone began to ring insistently. Erin was late already, and she considered letting the maddening instrument ring, but she couldn't. It might be something important, possibly Kane rearranging their hastily made plans. Reluctantly she threw her coat over the arm of the couch and hurried to the kitchen to answer the relentless ringing.

"Hello?"

"Erin! I can't believe that I finally got through to you. I've been trying to get in touch with you for days. You never called me, you know," the male voice accused, and Erin could picture the pouting lips and hurt expression in Lee's boyish blue eyes.

"I'm sorry, Lee. I did try, but there wasn't any answer."

"You could have tried again."

"I…I decided that it probably wouldn't be wise."

"What if it had been an emergency?"

Her conscience felt a twinge. "It wasn't, was it?"

"No...but it could have been!"

Erin leaned heavily against the wall, and let her head fall backward. Why tonight? Why was Lee calling again? "Look, Lee," she whispered. "I'm in a hurry for an appointment. Was there something that you wanted?"

There was a heavy pause in the conversation before he replied. "I just...wanted to see you again...."

Erin bit at her fingernail. "Bull!"

"I need to talk to you," he pleaded, and his image flashed in her mind's eye: wavy blond hair, cut-off jeans, old tennis shoes, a grass-stained football jersey that she had given him for Christmas one year.

"So talk," she managed, her voice unsteady.

"Can we meet?"

"I told you I've got a date...." She glanced at her watch.

There was silence, then a deep, theatrical sigh. "Is he someone special?"

"Yes, Lee. He is. Very special. But what do you care, after all these years?" She blinked back the tears that threatened to spill.

"Believe it or not, babe, I've always cared about you."

"Don't lie to me, Lee. I've heard it all before. I don't think this is the time to go into all that. Not now."

"When?" he demanded.

"Oh, Lee, don't you understand? It's over for us. It's been over for a long time—probably before you met Olivia."

"Okay, Erin," he retorted testily. "I deserved that. I was a louse and I admit it. But can't you believe that I want to see you again?"

"No."

"Erin, I have to."

The tears she was choking back began to slide down her cheeks. "No!"

"But, babe..."

"And don't call me that! Just what is it you want, Lee? Money?"

Silence. Incriminating silence.

"Look, Lee, do us both a favor and don't call back— ever! We've been through this scene too many times, and I for one won't repeat it ever again. It's too hard on me and it's too hard on you."

"Erin, baby, listen to me…"

He was still talking when she hung up the phone. Hastily she brushed back the tears and attempted to recapture the sense of exhilaration she had felt before she answered the phone. Why did he insist on calling? There was only one reason, the same one that she'd heard in the past: money. Damn! How could she get him out of her life once and for all?

Erin pushed her wayward thoughts aside and dashed out to her car. Soon she would be with Kane alone. Soon everything would be all right, as it should be, and she would be able to forget about Lee, the telephone call, the past.

The Tattered Sail had a reputation for being one of the best restaurants in the Northwest for fresh seafood, and tonight Erin found the rumor to be true. Once in the intimate old, barnlike structure, Erin could feel herself beginning to relax. The atmosphere was smoky and dark, and Erin was sure that if she listened closely, above the light contemporary music and the quiet chatter of the patrons, she would be able to hear the waters of the Sound lapping quietly against the pier that supported the restaurant.

The succulent house specialty, fresh Dungeness crab in a tangy sauce, was superb, and the sparkling bottle of chilled champagne that Kane had ordered added just the right touch of elegance to the otherwise casual Pacific Coast cuisine. The dimmed lanterns, the massive ship's rigging that covered the walls and ceilings and the view of the inky water of Puget Sound all served to enhance the romance and intimacy of the evening. Erin ate quietly, entranced by the setting and her powerful feelings for Kane. His eyes, two dark silver orbs, never left her face, and the smile on his face spoke more clearly than words of the depths of his feelings for her.

Somehow he seemed to have shaken off the tension that had been boiling within him for the past few days. All the heavy undercurrents that were usually evident in his eyes had disappeared, at least for the night. The dinner was a thoroughly enjoyable experience, and Erin found herself unwinding as she hadn't since the weekend in the San Juans. They talked little and spoke mostly with their eyes, but Erin did mention that she had brought Krista the kitten, and Kane seemed more than pleased when he heard about his daughter's affection for the little black cat. The tender light that illuminated his face when he spoke of Krista touched Erin's heart.

The romance of the evening extended past dinner, and as they drove home together in her small car, Erin was overwhelmed by just how desperately she had grown to love the man sitting next to her. She couldn't deny to herself that she loved him with an unspoken passion that was consuming in its intensity. For the first time in weeks she wondered if, indeed, she and Kane and Krista might have a future together. Everything seemed to be falling into place. Perhaps someday, given enough time and affection, Kane could learn to love her. The little car climbed the hill that supported the Victorian apartment house. Its broad-paned windows winked cheerfully in the night.

As she shut off the engine, Erin felt the warmth of Kane's hand when it covered hers. "Let's not go in, not just yet," he suggested in a husky voice.

"But Krista…" The protest was feeble. Already she could feel the heat of desire beginning to warm her.

"She's fine," Kane assured her, and pushed a wayward wisp of her hair back into place. "She and Mrs. Cavenaugh planned to sit up and watch old movies all night long."

"But don't you think we should check on her?"

"In a minute," he insisted, and his face moved closer to hers. The warmth of his breath, laced with the clinging vapors of champagne, whispered over her face. "I'd just like to spend a few more minutes alone with you…" His fingers reached out and traced the curve of her cheek, the length of her throat, the neckline of the dress. Erin's breath began to constrict in her chest, it became ragged as she breathed. His hand found the slit in her dress and moved gently, heatedly against her inner thigh.

"Kane," she gulped, seeing the undying passion in his gaze. "I…we…can't possibly, not here…."

"Shhh…" he commanded, and rimmed her lips with his tongue. She was melting in his embrace, feeling herself begin to blend with him. "Walk with me," he suggested intimately. "The night's warm, and so am I."

His lips found hers, and he nibbled at them gently, persuasively. His hand moved in sensuous circles against her thigh. "Well," she agreed, her eyes closing, "a walk…a short one…"

He was right, she thought raggedly as they walked together in the clear October evening. Was it the night itself or Kane's presence that made it seem so special, so eternal? The cool nip of fall was in the air, and yet, under the stars winking in the ethereal moon glow, Erin was warm despite the season. Even in the half light, she could see the spiraling vapor of Kane's breath as it mingled with the chilly night air.

He held her hand tightly, as if he were afraid that his grasp would slip and that he might lose her in the shadows. It was a wonderful, exotic feeling; his magnetic touch and the magic of the night wound together. Erin felt drugged as together they made their way to the gazebo in the backyard. It was old and in sad disrepair. But against the backdrop of the clear night, its flaws hidden by the darkness and the stand of fir trees near the worn steps, it seemed intimate and regal with its undisturbed beauty of another era. Silently Kane helped her up the two weathered steps, and she felt herself begin to tremble.

"From the first time I saw this place, I knew that I wanted to make love to you here," he stated. The silver moon glow was reflected in the intensity of his gaze, and his head bent down slowly and seductively to find her chilled lips. He crushed her against his chest with a savage urgency that seemed to be ripping him apart. "Make love to me, Erin," he pleaded. "I don't think I can stand another moment of this agony. Touch me, love me!" His lips wet a trail of desire leading from her lips down her throat, to nestle hotly against her partially exposed breast. Once there he paused to moan, "God, I want you!" Her breathing began to come in short, uneven breaths in the cold night air. Kane fell to his knees and continued to press the warmth of his face against the frail fabric that covered her abdomen. "Love me," he commanded as his hands moved in circular seductive movements against her hips, and she felt the smooth fabric of the silk dress sweep gently upward to brush against her thighs.

"I want you, too," she whispered huskily, and her hands wound themselves in the thick strands of his hair. "Oh, Kane. I need you so much!" she confessed.

"I know," he murmured. Erin felt the cold shudder of autumn pierce her skin as the zipper of her dress was lowered and the silky fabric parted to expose her back and shoulders. The dress slipped to the floor of the gazebo, and Kane's gentle hands and mouth caressed her exposed skin, raining hot moist kisses against her flesh. He dragged her down to lie beside him and tentatively touched one rounded breast with the delicacy of a sculptor. An animal growl escaped from his throat as he watched her, and in wet, heated strokes, his tongue found the ripeness of her nipples.

His mouth seared against her skin, and his tongue licked and pressed hot moistness against her body. She felt the warmth of her desire spread from her innermost core through all of her body. Rivers of passion ran in her veins, and desire, hot and molten, pounded against her temples. She felt tides of feverish passion wash over her until she wanted to drown in its molten embrace. Despite the cool of the evening, a dusting of perspiration covered her body. On their own, without conscious thought, her fingers found the buttons of his shirt, the zipper to his slacks, the proud hardness of his desire. She arched her body heatedly against his, aware only of her agonizing love for him.

His lips teased and satisfied her, toying with her until she thought she would go mad, only to arouse her to still-untouched heights. His eyes, smoldering in the night, took in all of her: the look of yearning in her large luminous eyes, the way her provocative tongue continued to flick against her lips, the full, rounded breasts with nipples proudly erect, and her soft, sensuous hips, inviting him to explore her more intimately. He thought he would lose all control in the instant she arched against him, and he wanted to give in to his virile male urge to take her. God, he'd waited so long, and he felt a need, strong and inflexible, to make love to her, but he forced himself to wait, somewhat impatiently, caught up in the heat of his lovemaking, until he was certain she was ready for him.

Erin wondered if she would fall apart and crumble into fiery bursts of passion as Kane lowered himself onto her. With a sigh of long-denied pleasure, she wound her arms and legs around him, entrapping him and tempting him to make love to her. He could resist no longer.

"Oh, God, Erin. You're so beautiful, I need you..."

His words trailed off into the night in an unspoken confession as he found his way to her. In the shadow of the gazebo, his hot pulse at war with the cool night, he watched her as he loved her, and he saw the heat of desire blossom into the ecstasy of satisfaction. Together they found a love so exquisite that he knew it could never be recaptured. Only his own traitorous duplicity marred the perfect enchantment that he knew as he fell against her and felt the warmth of her breasts flatten against his weight.

It was several minutes before he spoke, as if he were unable to break the peaceful spell of enchantment that covered them. When at last he broke the silence, it was to murmur her name over and over in the night, as if trying to impress her memory upon his lips. It was so difficult to say all the things that he wanted so urgently for her to know. And the questions that had to be asked plagued him. He knew that it was time for explanation and discussion. Too much was at stake to continue to hide behind the truth. He needed her so desperately, yet his duplicity was eating at him. The fear of losing her gripped him more savagely each day. It was time for something to be done.

"What is it?" Erin asked suddenly, staring at the dread in his eyes. Once again she sensed the wariness had appeared, and the knowledge frightened her. She had hoped that all Kane's reservations had melted away. Shivering more from Kane's obvious apprehension than from the coolness of the night, she felt the same cold doubts crawl up her spine. He noticed the chill, rolled off her and pulled his jacket lightly over her shoulders.

His hands trembled as they pressed against her face. "Marry me, darling," he whispered in a voice dry with emotion. For a moment Erin's heart turned over. Her first impulse was to throw her arms around his neck and confess the depth of her love, but something in his face made her pull the reins in on her excitement.

"What?" she asked quietly, looking deeply into his eyes for the trace of love she hoped to find.

"I'm asking you to marry me. Now—as soon as possible," he clarified, and pressed her fingers against his lips. "We need to be together."

She wanted to accept his proposal, to take part in the elation that was beginning to burst in her veins. But there was the strong scent of accusation that hung between them and made her pause.

"I would love to marry you," Erin breathed, trying to think rationally. The stars, the moon, the wind of the night were all closing in on her, and she found it difficult to concentrate on anything but the feelings of love that were swelling in her veins. "You must know that...."

"Then, get packed. We'll fly to Reno tonight—or early in the morning. The sooner the better." He began to slide into his pants in his urgency to persuade her.

"We have time...."

"No!" he nearly shouted. And then, in a somewhat calmer voice, he continued, "No—we don't have any time."

"But, Kane," she argued, fearing the continuation of the discussion, but unable to stop herself. "You have to put certain things into perspective. We have to take Krista's feelings into consideration—surely you can understand that. And the bank—"

"Erin!" He grabbed her shoulders roughly, and forced her to look up at him. His grip tightened on her forearms, and his face was a harsh mask of determination. "It's got to be soon. You know that."

"Why? We have the rest of our lives…"

"No, we don't!" he snapped. "Don't you understand?" His eyes were shadowed by the darkness of the gazebo, but Erin could feel the pain and torture of his words without being able to probe his desperate gaze. Why was he so insistent? A cold strange feeling passed over her, transferred from him by the urgency of his forceful grasp on her upper arms.

With an unsteady voice, she asked, "Kane, just what is it that you're trying to say?"

"I'm asking you to be my wife, pure and simple. Is that so difficult to understand?"

She wasn't convinced. "There's more, isn't there? Has it got something to do with Krista, because she's already made it plain to me that she doesn't have room in her life for a 'new mother.'" In the blackness Erin tried to read the expression on Kane's face. Hoping to find love, she was disappointed. A cloud passed over the moon, and once the pale light was restored, she found his eyes torn with an emotion she couldn't understand. She tried to draw away from him but still he held her desperately, passionately.

Slowly the grip on her forearms relaxed, and resignation covered Kane's features. "Get dressed," he commanded softly. "And then I promise you we'll talk."

Hurriedly she did as he instructed her, running her pantyhose in her hasty efforts. Was it the chill of the night that made her shudder, or the cold look of determination heightening the masculine angles of Kane's face that cooled her blood?

As she was smoothing the silk dress over her hips, he began to speak in a distant voice that was dry with dread.

"When I was in California," he started, stepping away from her and pacing the length of the gazebo, "some more money was embezzled from the dividend account…three thousand dollars to be exact." He whirled to face her, and his guarded eyes found hers. The expression on her face was one of confusion.

"I don't understand—I thought that Mitch was the suspect…."

He cut off her conjecture. "Of course he's the prime suspect, but it's become apparent that he has an accomplice in the department!"

"No!" she gasped.

"Yes!"

Her voice was faint, barely a whisper. "But who?"

"Why don't you tell me?" he suggested, his voice taking on the quality of a smooth courtroom lawyer.

"But I don't know."

"Don't you?" Accusation singed his words.

"No… I can't imagine…." She was so taken aback by his supposition of an accomplice for Mitch that she hadn't noticed the suspicion in his eyes, the way his arms crossed over his chest, the grim hard angle of his jaw. But now, after the shock of his statement had dissipated, she knew what he was thinking.

"You're not…you couldn't be," she was stammering, but she couldn't control herself. Slowly she stood up and watched the play of emotions that rampaged over his face. "I don't believe that you would think I could somehow be involved. You wouldn't be suggesting anything like that…would you?" Before the anger took hold of her, disbelief and agony tortured her eyes.

"Why don't you explain…"

"No!" She stamped a bare foot on the thin floor of the gazebo. "I don't have to explain anything to you.…" Tears burned in her eyes, but she tilted her head defiantly in spite of them. As they began to flow slowly down her face, they caught the moonlight in tiny rivers of outrage. "Are you accusing me of embezzlement?" Her voice was as chilling as the wind that rustled the leaves overhead.

"Erin," he said in a calm voice devoid of emotion. "I just want to know the reason for certain facts.…"

"Facts? You mean evidence? I don't believe it. You don't have any evidence—you couldn't, just an overactive and suspicious imagination!"

He tried to interrupt, but she wouldn't let him. "I wondered, from the beginning, why all the questions about Mitch, why all the vague insinuations and especially why you would look at me the way you did. But I must have been a fool, a damned idiot, not to have put two and two together." She took a gasp of cold autumn air, only to find that her entire body was quivering with rage and betrayal. "How can you stand there and accuse me, after all that we've shared together? Oh, Kane—why?"

"If you could just be reasonable."

"Reasonable?" she shrieked, and then laughed from the tension that was capturing her in its angry claws. "Reasonable? How can you expect me to be 'reasonable' after you ask me to marry you and accuse me of a crime I didn't commit?"

"Erin, don't make this any harder than it already is," he pleaded, and leaned against a beam that supported the roof. "I can't ignore the facts, as much as I'd like to.

I know that you need money—the employee loan application states as much—"

A protesting sound gurgled in her throat, but he ignored it.

"And your ex-husband, Lee Sinclair—" the name came out in a snarl of disapproval "—you loaned him money once, and he's back in town."

"How?"

"It doesn't matter." He shook his head, and continued in a flat, dry voice. "And there was the securities key discrepancy. You were one of the people who had access to the bearer bonds that were taken, and suddenly, somehow, you find the money to paint the apartment house and fix it up for the winter. An odd set of circumstances, wouldn't you say?"

"Exactly that, circumstances," she commented indignantly.

"That first morning in the bank I found you alone in your office. You had the perfect opportunity...."

"Enough!" she stammered, and started down the two weathered steps of the gazebo. "I've heard enough." She paused for a minute, her hands supporting her weight on the railing. "What I don't understand is why, if you suspected me from the start, you didn't tell me—or ask me? Didn't you have the decency to respect my innocence and ask me about all those 'facts'?"

"It doesn't matter, not now," he said with a rush of enthusiasm. "We can get married, and I'll find a way to replace the money." He strode over to her and captured her wrist. "Don't you see, no more money will be taken, and all the cash that's missing since Mitch left the bank will be replaced."

"Just like that?" she asked incredulously. Her eyes narrowed and she surveyed the hand on her wrist suspiciously. "You really think that I was a part of this, don't you?"

"Erin," he sighed disconsolately as he tilted her face with his thumb. "I know that you met Mitch on the day of his arraignment. I also know that the money was taken on that day...."

"You bastard!" Before she could think, her free hand arched upward and slapped Kane's cheek. The loud smack echoed in the night, and Kane's eyes grew black with suppressed fury. His jaw clenched, and for a moment Erin wondered if he was going to retaliate and hit her.

His voice, suddenly soft, reached out to her. "Erin..."

"Don't! I don't want to hear anything more! Not ever again. I'll...I'll hand in my resignation tomorrow...and I think it would be best for all of us if you would move out of the apartment as soon as possible. You...you can... have two weeks...." The sobs that she was quietly withholding began to rack her body, and she felt as if she were about to be torn in half by his betrayal. At the pressure from Kane's hand on her shoulder, she drew away as if wounded and started stumbling toward the house.

"Erin, wait!" Kane ordered, but she ignored his plea. "You can't resign. If you're innocent, you can't resign. It will appear more incriminating!"

Whirling to face him, nearly tripping on the exposed root from a nearby fir tree, she replied bitingly, "I'm quitting. I...I don't want anything more to do with you...or your bank!"

"Erin, don't!" He was beside her in a minute, and his features had softened. "Don't you understand? I need you, I want you... I love you!"

"Love? You don't have any idea what the word means. And, as for *needing* and *wanting*, I think you're getting them confused with *using*. Because that's what you did to me, wasn't it? You used me—tried to get close to me so that you could 'look into my darker, private side.' Isn't that how you phrased it? I didn't know what you meant, not at the time, but I know now, don't I? You wanted to get inside my head and find a way to incriminate me for a crime that I had no part of...."

"Please try and understand...."

"Just leave me alone!" Her eyes met his, and even though they were filled with tears, he could see that she meant every word she was speaking.

"I don't want it to end this way."

"There isn't any alternative. You took care of that!"

"I'm sorry."

"Not good enough, Kane, not good enough." Her words were colder than the autumn wind that pushed her black hair away from her face, and highlighted the proud, near-perfect oval with its fine cheekbones and luminous violet eyes.

"All right, Erin. If that's the way you want it."

"That's the way it has to be," she sighed, and stepped aside to let him pass. She watched him silently as he walked toward the front of the house and disappeared around the corner. When he was finally out of her range of vision, she let herself slump against the tall fir tree near the gazebo. "You are a fool," she muttered under her breath. "And he is a bastard!" The tears started to flow again. How could he even think that she would stoop so low? How could he have misjudged her so? And how, in God's name, how could he be so gentle and caring one minute and so ruthless the next?

It was past midnight when Erin found the strength to return to the loft that she had once shared with the man she still loved.

Chapter 12

An insistent, impatient knocking awoke Erin from a night whose fitful sleep had been interrupted by dismal nightmares. The dull ache in her head increased with each knock on her front door. "I'm coming," she groaned, running her fingers through her tangled hair and hoping that her response would stop whoever it was from making any further racket.

Jerking on her peach-colored terry robe, she cinched the belt tightly around her waist and glanced haphazardly into the mirror over the bureau. The reflection that stared back at her was disheartening—the long, anxious night had taken its toll on her face. Large blue circles under her eyes intensified the pale, washed-out complexion of her face. The large eyes that had always sparkled seemed lifeless, and her black hair hung in tangled curls against her neck.

The pounding started up again. "I'm coming," Erin repeated loudly, and wondered who would be calling so insistently at seven in the morning. The knocking subsided for a minute. Erin half expected to see Kane when she opened the door and braced herself for whatever confrontation might occur when she came face-to-face with him. "Just a minute," she called through the wood panels, and tugged the door open.

What she hadn't expected to see on her doorstep—not in a million years—was Lee. His blond hair was meticulously combed and his blue eyes were as brilliant as ever, perhaps even more so. He was perched atop the polished wood railing of the landing. One arm was bent around a carved banister to aid his balance. His casual slouch, accented by faded jeans and a lightweight sport shirt was a theatrical display of relaxation by design, belied only by the tiny muscle that worked constantly near the back of his jaw.

"Hi, babe." He greeted her with a wink and gave her a long, suggestive head-to-toe appraisal. "Rough night?" A smile, boyish yet sinister, curved his thin lips.

After the initial shock of seeing him, Erin regained her composure and propped her shoulder against the doorjamb, keeping a careful distance between them. Without conscious thought, she tugged on the belt of her robe and pulled it more tightly around her slim waist.

"I'll ignore your insinuations for now," she replied with a plastic copy of his smirk pasted on her face. "What are you doing here?"

Hopping off the railing in a lithe movement, he responded, "I couldn't seem to get through to you on the phone. So I decided if Mohammed wouldn't come to the mountain...."

"I get the gist," she retorted coldly. She could feel an uneasy caution tighten the muscles of her back. "That doesn't explain why you're here, banging on my door loudly enough to wake up the entire neighborhood at seven in the morning. What do you want?"

"How about a cup of your coffee, for starters. From there, who knows how far our relationship can progress?" There was another long, suggestive look.

"I'm sorry, Lee, but as you already guessed, I did have a rough night last night. I'm tired and I'm not up to playing word games with you. Why don't you just tell me what it is you want? Then you can leave." She crossed her arms over her breasts to shield herself from his gaze. Lee made her uncomfortable, but she did her best to hide her apprehension.

"Why are you always so suspicious of me?" he asked in a low voice that was meant to be hypnotic.

"Because I know you."

"Erin, baby," he cooed, coming more closely to her. Involuntarily she shrank back. "What's happened to you? Let me make you feel better."

"And just how do you think you could do that?" she asked wryly, a grim smile twisting her lips and her black brows cocking nervously.

"We used to get along just fine," he suggested smoothly, and his hand reached out to trace the neckline of her robe.

Jerking away from him, Erin glared at his bemused face. "Look, Lee, just say whatever it is you think you have to say to me and then leave." She paused for a moment, and then continued. "What is it? Do you need money again?"

Sandy-blond eyebrows shot up with undisguised interest. "Ah, well, that's not the main reason that I came over here, but now that you mention it, I could use a few bucks." He smiled his most winning smile and shrugged his shoulders. Erin was surprised at her reaction, total disinterest in his most becoming grin. "You know how it is—I had a run of bad luck."

"Haven't we all?" she muttered under her breath, and raked her fingers through her tangled black curls.

"Ah, come on, Erin. Don't give me that. The way I hear it, you're loaded."

"Is that the way you hear it?" She laughed tightly, despite the headache that was pounding relentlessly in her ears. "I guess you've got the wrong information."

"What do you mean?" he asked, a sudden seriousness killing his smile. *He looks old,* Erin thought to herself. The sunny college-boy looks only survived when he smiled.

"What I mean, Lee, is that I'm out of a job," she explained, her words a little less caustic than they had been. "I'm sorry. I can't loan you any money. I just don't have it."

"You? You've got to be kidding!"

"I'm not!" She shook her head to emphasize her point.

"You must have a savings account—*something!*"

"Not much," she admitted. "And anyway, I don't feel that I owe you any favors. That might sound a little cold-blooded, but it's the way I feel."

Lee began to bite his lower lip, and his eyes darted around the landing. "Look, babe, I'm desperate. I need to get my hands on some bread, and fast!"

"Why don't you get a job?" she asked, and hated herself for the acidic sound of the sarcasm.

A stricken expression covered Lee's face. "A job? I've been looking for a job night and day. It's…just that the right…opportunity hasn't presented itself."

Erin rubbed her hands against her temples and gave Lee a final sorrowful expression. "I'm sorry about that, too," she said honestly, "but if you don't mind, I'm tired, and I'm going back to bed." He must have misinterpreted her feelings, because as she reached for the handle of the door, Lee was against her, his body molding tightly to hers. She tried to wriggle out of his embrace, but there was no escape.

"Erin, baby," he growled. "Why do you enjoy teasing me?"

"What? Lee, let go of me. What are you doing?" She felt the power of his body push against her and force her rigidly against the cold, hard wood. His hands reached for the knotted belt of her robe, and she could feel his long, cold fingers probe against the flimsy fabric of her nightgown. A shudder of fear stiffened her spine.

"Let me go," she hissed, but his lips, dispassionately cool, descended on her open mouth. A sinking sensation of fear swept over her as his tongue pressed ruthlessly against her gums. With all the strength she could gather, she lifted her bare foot and hoisted her knee sharply upward, but Lee had anticipated the move and dodged the misplaced blow.

"So you want to play rough," he growled, and pulled her hands over her head to pin them cruelly against the door frame.

"Lee! Stop this. You're acting like a lunatic," she asserted, but the command in her voice was diminished by the fact that her words were trembling.

"Let her go!" Kane's voice commanded from the lower landing. At the sound Lee turned.

"What?" Lee studied the source of the noise. The man, tall and dark, was stripped to the waist, wearing only faded jeans as he began to slowly ascend the stairs. "Hey, look, mister," Lee said guardedly. "Why don't you mind your own business? This is my wife…." Lee jerked his head in Erin's direction. "We're just having a little disagreement…."

"I don't think so." Kane mounted the stairs and stood only a few feet from Lee. His gray eyes glinted like steel, and though his voice was outwardly calm and solicitous, his clenched fists and hardened jaw reinforced his words.

"Do you have a hearing problem?" he asked. "I told you to let her go!"

Reluctantly Lee stepped away from Erin and glowered menacingly at Kane. "Just who the hell do you think you are?" he snapped, while Erin crumpled in the doorway. The smell of a fight was in the air.

"I was just about to ask you that same question," Kane's calm, hard voice rejoined.

"I'm her husband!" Lee snarled, tossing a look of red-hot anger and rage toward Erin.

"Ex-husband," Kane corrected. "And what sort of power does that title give you? The right to rough up the lady?"

"I wasn't…"

Kane's fury snapped and his eyes sparked disgusted fire. "Don't bother with any of your explanations. Just get out before I throw you over this railing!" Kane's voice had risen with his anger, and Erin saw Lee gulp and hesitate, casting a final threatening glance in her direction.

"I'd just like to see you try," Lee warned back to Kane. A light of grim satisfaction warmed Kane's face. Lee saw the reaction and slowly, carefully backed down the stairs.

"And just one more thing, Sinclair," Kane cautioned with an evil smile. "If I ever so much as hear that you've been bothering Erin again, I won't wait for you to show up. I'll come looking for you!"

Lee hastened down the remainder of the stairs, the front door crashed closed, and for a few seconds there was silence. Only the feeling of electricity crackling in the air disturbed the tranquillity of the moment until the noise of a racing engine split the silence as it roared angrily down the hill. Erin sighed as she realized that Lee was finally gone.

"I can't say much for your taste in husbands," Kane commented dryly. The grim set of his jaw hadn't relaxed.

"He's not so bad," Erin replied uneasily, as if convincing herself. "Not really, he's just had a run of bad luck...."

"Bad luck?" Kane threw his hands over his head in exasperation. "That gives him the right to come in here and force himself on you?" He regarded her ruefully, since she looked so small and vulnerable this morning. "Erin, you are incredibly naive! What is it with you anyway?"

"What do you mean?" she asked, feeling herself start to bristle, partially because she knew that he was close to the truth.

"I mean, first, Mitchell Cameron—you defend him to the hilt when he's an A-1 jackass—"

"Now, wait a minute," Erin gasped.

"No, you wait a minute! And now your husband, pardon me, your unfortunate ex-husband who's had 'a run of bad luck,' so he takes it out on you by almost..." His pause was effective, and Erin's face flooded with color. "Erin, don't you see? Sinclair's a bastard, a loser. You should know that better than anyone. As far as I can see, so far you've had a pretty poor track record of picking male companions!"

"Is that a fact?" she fired back at him, her temper sparking. "Does that include the latest man in my life? You remember him—a wonderful guy. I trusted him completely only to discover that he thinks I'm a crook!" Sarcasm flavored her words with bitterness.

Kane looked as if he'd been slapped. The stunned expression on his face and the sudden dead look in his eyes tore at Erin's heart, but she proudly held her ground. It would be too easy to forgive him, too easy to let him back into her heart.

His shoulders relaxed, the firm muscles slackening. "So that's how it stands, does it? You won't let me help you?"

"I don't need any help. I'm innocent," she maintained defiantly.

"Would it make you feel better to know that I believe you?"

"Ha! Then why did you accuse me of thievery last night? Why did you wait all this time? Why didn't you just ask me what I knew about the embezzlement and the fact that there is supposedly an accomplice? Why did you wait," she asked, her voice quaking, and her eyes meeting his with accusation, "all the while silently condemning me with your eyes!"

"Oh, God, Erin," he groaned. "I'm so sorry—I was hoping that maybe you had changed your mind...."

"No!" She shook her head firmly, but her voice softened. "Look." She reached out to touch his arm, but he jerked away from her. "I want to thank you for helping me with Lee. He...was...getting a little out of hand."

"Erin," Kane's voice was steady and low. He stood half-supported by the railing, his head drooping down and facing the lobby two stories below him. "I want you to marry me. I need you to be my wife, and Krista needs a mother. Perhaps I judged you too quickly, but it was only because I was afraid of the truth. I wanted to talk to you about it earlier." His eyes rolled heavenward and his voice became husky. "God, how many times did I try?" He shook his head disconsolately and continued to stare blankly ahead of him. "But I just couldn't."

"Because you didn't trust me. You couldn't find it in your heart to accept my innocence," Erin added in a flat, dead voice.

"There are other possibilities. The accomplice has to be in the legal department...."

"But I was the most convenient choice. The easiest target, right?"

His silence was as condemning as the pained droop of his shoulders. "Oh, God, Erin. Just believe that I love you!" he pleaded.

"I guess you and I have a different meaning for the word," she replied, her voice broken by emotion. "Goodbye, Kane," she whispered as she slipped through the door and listened to the sound of his footsteps retreating heavily down the stairs. Biting back the tears that were struggling to fill her eyes, she hurried to the bedroom and pulled out her worn leather suitcase. She tossed it recklessly on the bed. "You're a coward," she snipped at herself, "running from the truth that you love him, and no matter what he's done, the one thing that you want most in life is to be his wife." Her tiny fist balled up and crashed down on the suitcase. *Damn! Why am I such a fool?* For an instant she thought about running after him and throwing herself into his arms, but her pride forced her to restrain herself. He thinks you're a thief, she reminded herself, and the feeling of cold betrayal once again settled upon her. Hurriedly she tossed the rest of her things haphazardly into the suitcase and snapped it shut. She looked around the bedroom to see if she needed anything else but found that she had to get out of the room. It was too crowded with memories, gloriously happy memories of making love to Kane in her bed.

With shaking, unsteady hands she dialed the phone and made reservations for the week. Then, as calmly as possible, she wrote down the phone number and address of the hotel and placed it in an envelope before sitting down near the window and waiting. It wasn't long, maybe only ten minutes, but it felt like an eternity to Erin before she saw Kane walk out toward his car. Fortunately Krista was with him. Erin managed a smile through her tears as she saw that Krista was able to walk to the car with her father's assistance. Although she leaned heavily on Kane, the girl stumbled only once and he was able to catch her. The playful little kitten followed along. There appeared to be a slight argument of some sort, and Erin guessed that it had to do with the cat. Kane was shaking his head, but in the end, the black ball of fur was allowed to tag along for the ride.

After Kane's car was out of sight, Erin hurried out of her apartment and sprinted down the stairs to knock on Mrs. Cavenaugh's door. Erin tapped lightly against the wood, and the door was opened in an instant. The little old woman was up and dressed, as if she were expecting company.

"Good morning," the gray-haired lady said cheerily, her wise blue eyes flicking from Erin's distressed face to the suitcase in her hand. "Good morning, Mrs. Cavenaugh," Erin replied. "I…I've got to leave town for a while…."

Mrs. Cavenaugh's gray eyebrows shot upward and her mouth pursed into an expression of distaste. Erin continued. "Urgent business… I'll be gone for a week, maybe longer. In this envelope is the telephone number and address of the hotel where I can be reached in case of an emergency…."

"Erin," Mrs. Cavenaugh's calm voice broke into her chatter. "You know that I hate to pry, but what's the matter? Did something happen between you and Kane?" Kind, concerned blue eyes probed Erin's rigid face.

"What…what do you mean?"

"I mean 'leaving town because of urgent business' is a trifle overused." A wry smile twisted the wrinkled face. "Honestly I would have expected something with a little more imagination."

"Well, it's the truth," Erin maintained.

"And you're a terrible liar."

"Mrs. Cavenaugh, I'm not lying, honestly. Something has come up, something I can't deal with. I need a little time and distance in order to sort things out."

Mrs. Cavenaugh's knowing smile broadened. "Well, at least you're opening up a little. I understand that you might need a little space, isn't that what they say these days? I can't argue with that, but..."

"What?"

"Well, don't let your pride come between you and something you really want."

Erin sucked in her breath. "You mean Kane, don't you?" she sighed dismally and broke eye contact with her elderly tenant.

"He's a man who loves you dearly. And his daughter!" The old lady threw up her hands and shook her head at the incredulity of the situation.

"Krista? What about Krista?" Erin asked, her voice full of concern.

"Oh, nothing other than the fact that she worships the ground you walk on."

"Be serious!"

"I am—I've never seen the likes of it! Oh, at first, I'll grant you she was determined to hate you. But can you blame the child—losing a mother the way she did? All she had left was her father, and she didn't want to share him. But now—" Mrs. Cavenaugh moved her head thoughtfully "—that poor girl can talk of nothing but you—except for the kitten of course."

The lump in Erin's throat began to swell, and some of her firm resolve began to be chipped at. Mrs. Cavenaugh was working on her; Erin knew it, but she couldn't help but hope that there was just a sliver of truth in the sweet old woman's words.

"I'm sorry, Mrs. Cavenaugh," Erin managed, looking hastily at her watch, "but I've really got to run. Now, promise me that under no circumstances will you tell Kane where I am!"

"I don't know if I can do that," the older woman replied honestly.

"You have to! I *need* time to myself."

"Well, if you're so dead set against it, I'll give you my word," Mrs. Cavenaugh unwillingly agreed.

"Thanks," Erin sighed, kissing her friend lightly on the cheek. "I'll see you soon."

"Dear," Mrs. Cavenaugh said, placing a bony hand on Erin's sleeve. "Do be careful."

"I will," Erin promised, and turned to leave the apartment building. She could feel Mrs. Cavenaugh's kind eyes boring into her back as she walked to her car, but she didn't have the heart to turn and wave. It took all her strength to hoist her suitcase into the car, start the engine and race down the hill toward the city and the waterfront.

Once back in Deer Harbor on Orcas Island in the San Juans, Erin realized what a disastrous mistake she had made in returning to the island where she had had such a carefree and loving existence with Kane only a few weeks earlier. Although she was far removed from the rustic cabin that they had shared together, memories of the small town still burned in her brain, and it seemed that she couldn't walk anywhere without coming face-to-face with memories of Kane. The pain in her heart didn't disappear.

The seasons had changed in the past weeks, and each day was as gray and cold as the Pacific Ocean. Wind and rain deluged the coastal town, and although Erin tried several kinds of outdoor amusements, she found that most of her days were spent inside her tiny hotel room staring

vacantly at the television or brooding about the turn of
events in her life. Knowing that her attitude was as dis-
couraging as the somber, gray rain-washed days, she attempted to pull herself out of her depression, but found
it impossible. Nothing seemed to work. And thoughts of
Krista and the fact that she hadn't even bothered to say
goodbye to the lonely girl only made Erin more miserable
and guilt-ridden. While the island had once been a haven,
now it seemed like a prison, but Erin elected to continue
her confinement until she could no longer afford it. How
could she possibly go home to an empty house and no job?

It had been over a week, and the depression still clung
to her like a heavy shroud when she picked up the Seattle newspaper to look through the classified advertise-
ments in search of employment. As usual, the openings
for legal assistants were few, and Erin faced the fact that
it would be more difficult than she had first imagined to
find a decent position. Disinterestedly she perused the
rest of the paper and stopped at the financial section.
A photograph of the bank building with a caption concerning the embezzlement caught her eye. With more
interest than she had felt for days, she began to read the
article. As the meaning of each sentence in the column
became clear to her, Erin began to feel her stomach
churn with emotions of rage and disgust. According to
the article, Mitchell Cameron had in fact worked with
an accomplice—a woman with whom he had shared
responsibility for years—Miss Olivia Parsons. The article explained the scam more fully and the fact that the
scheme was so elaborate that it had taken the auditing
staff and the president of the bank a lengthy amount of
time to prove the guilt of the parties involved.

Erin felt a growing nausea as she read the article, and
when she had finished, she tossed the newspaper into the

wastebasket near her bed. Never would she have suspected Olivia of doing anything illegal. Just like Mitch, Olivia seemed far too professional to stoop to thievery. The delight that Erin should have experienced as she realized that she was no longer under suspicion of the crime seemed to have soured as she thought of Mitch and Olivia, two respected members of the banking industry who had tossed away their careers and possibly their lives for greed. Erin wondered what could have caused their joint journey into crime.

Two days later Erin began preparing for her trip home to Seattle. She had been gone far too long already, and her money was running out. She realized that she couldn't run away from Kane and her love for him, and there was really no reason to linger on the island.

Just as Erin began to pack her things, the telephone jarred the stillness of the hotel room. For several seconds Erin just stared at the telephone, wondering who would be calling her. Kane? Unlikely. A wrong number? Perhaps. Her heart began to thud wildly in her chest as she reached for the receiver.

"Hello?" she inquired, and felt a welling sense of dread when she recognized Mrs. Cavenaugh's unsteady voice.

"Erin—Erin, is that you?" the old lady demanded.

"Yes, it's I... What happened?" Erin asked, convinced that Mrs. Cavenaugh wouldn't call unless there was an emergency of some sort. Nervously she bit at her thumbnail.

"Oh—I know that he told me not to call, but I knew that you would want to know. It's just awful—I really don't know what to do. Dear Lord in heaven!" The little old lady continued to ramble in endless circles of words and phrases that meant nothing to Erin. Apprehensively Erin interrupted.

"Mrs. Cavenaugh! What's wrong? Try and pull yourself together and just tell me what's the matter." The hairs on the back of Erin's neck began to stand on end.

"It's Krista," Mrs. Cavenaugh moaned in a voice so low that Erin thought perhaps she had misunderstood.

"Krista?" Erin echoed. "Oh, God, what's happened to her?" Erin's heart leaped to her throat and her pulse began to race. Tiny droplets of perspiration moistened her skin, and she felt her knees give way as she sank against the bed.

"Oh, Erin, it's so awful. Ever since you've been gone, Kane, well, he hasn't been himself—in a terribly foul mood." Erin swallowed hard and tried to press back the feelings of guilt that assailed her. "And Krista, well, she didn't fare any better. She...withdrew. You know. You remember what she was like when she first arrived in Seattle...." Erin gasped, and the little lady reassured her. "It wasn't nearly that bad, you understand, but still she just wasn't her cheery self. I'm afraid that she's missed you terribly."

Erin closed her eyes and leaned her head against the headboard of the bed for support. "She didn't stop walking, did she?" Erin held her breath.

"Thank goodness—no." Erin let the air escape from her lungs in a rush. "However, she was distracted, wouldn't eat, was thoroughly depressed." Erin felt as if a knife were being slowly twisted in her stomach. How could she have been so heartless as to have left Krista without explaining anything? Mrs. Cavenaugh continued. "And then, late this morning...well, Krista was chasing that little kitten of hers, and it scrambled up the stairs. She tried to follow it but fell. She hit her head on the bottom step."

"Oh, no," Erin gasped, the color draining from her face. "Is—is she seriously injured?"

"Well, that's just it. No one seems to know for sure. She's still in the hospital for observation, been there all day as far as I know. I think she regained consciousness, but I'm not really certain." The elderly woman's voice had begun to quake, and Erin felt herself shiver.

"Mrs. Cavenaugh, where is Krista?"

"Virginia Mason Hospital on First Hill, but you shouldn't go there. Kane's there and he specifically instructed me not to tell you."

Erin stifled the sob that threatened to belie her calm words. "Don't worry about Kane. I can handle him—I'm leaving as soon as possible. I'll see you when I get home."

"Good."

"Oh, and Mrs. Cavenaugh?"

"Yes?"

"Thanks for calling."

"I knew that you'd want to know," came the somber reply.

Erin stripped her things out of the closet and dresser. As hastily as possible she threw them into her case, paid the hotel bill and rented a small boat back to the mainland. It wasn't easy to find someone who was willing to take her out in the stormy weather, but fortunately she found a young sailor with a sense of adventure who loved to make a quick buck.

The rain washed down in torrents and the small craft rocked and lurched against the rough whitecapped waters of the Sound. Several times the boat rocked so crazily that Erin was sure that they would capsize, but the steady hand of the dark-complexioned young man kept the tiny craft miraculously on course. The wind tore at Erin's face, pelting it with cold rain, and whipping her long black hair away from her neck. But she continued to watch the shoreline and prayed that Mrs. Cavenaugh had exaggerated Krista's condition.

"Hey, lady," her companion called to her over the roar of the boat's engine and the howl of the wind. "Would you like something to drink? I've got a thermos of coffee, or...something stronger, if you like rye whisky."

Erin shook her head. The thought of something in her already-knotted stomach made her want to gag. "No... thank you. I'm fine."

"You sure?" he asked, not convinced. The young woman was pale and scared, and deep lines of concern creased her otherwise beautiful face.

"Yes, really," Erin asserted, and managed a wan smile. The young man lifted his shoulders and turned his attention back to the sea. The remainder of the trip was made in silence. It seemed an eternity before Erin was on solid ground once again.

Virginia Mason Hospital stood out starkly white against a threatening charcoal-gray sky. Inside, the corridors were hushed, and the white walls were only made more severe by the garish splotches of color in the modern-art prints that hung on the walls. The bustling, white-uniformed staff, the mechanical groans of the elevators, and the overall oppressive silence gave Erin a strange sense of impending doom.

Room 538 was easy enough to find, and Erin braced herself to enter the white cubicle just as a portly nurse in a neatly starched uniform approached her.

"Looking for someone?" the nurse asked in a professional voice. There was a calm smile on the broad face that spoke of authority and efficiency. "Can I help you?"

"I hope so. I'm a close friend of Krista Webster. I just found out about the accident today, and I hurried over here as quickly as I could." The disapproving brown eyes of the nurse studied Erin, and for the first time she realized what she must look like in her rain-drenched clothing and wet hair.

"You're not a member of the family?"

"No...not exactly." Erin shook her head.

The nurse placed a friendly hand on Erin's arm. "I'm sorry, but only family members are allowed to visit Miss Webster. Perhaps you would like to wait in the lobby? There's a coffee machine and some magazines...."

Erin refused to be brushed off. "Can you at least tell me how she is? Will she be all right? I...I have to know!"

"I understand," the nurse replied, and Erin felt that those wide, brown eyes and large, kindly face wouldn't lie. "Krista had a very bad fall and suffered a concussion, but Dr. Sampson is caring for her and the prognosis is very hopeful."

"But...what does that mean, exactly? Will she recover? Will she be able to walk again?"

The nurse was steering Erin toward the waiting room. "Don't worry. Dr. Sampson is a very capable doctor, and he has the entire staff of the hospital to support him." With that, the nurse excused herself to answer another patient's call, and Erin found herself alone in the clinically clean waiting room with its ancient magazines and battered plastic furniture. She waited impatiently, staring out the window at the gloomy city, and ignored the stacks of outdated magazines that cluttered the table, while she sipped bitter coffee from a machine that looked as old as the hospital.

The sound of a familiar voice startled her, and she pulled her gaze from the dismal gray sky and the gathering dusk into the direction of the deep-timbred sound that made her heart leap. For several seconds she found it impossible to move or to speak as she studied Kane, his face lined with concern. He was speaking in low tones to a short, balding man with heavy glasses. The identification tag indicated that he was Dr. Sampson. The conversation was short and one-sided, with Dr. Sampson explaining Krista's condition in medical terms. Although the doctor seemed optimistic, Kane's entire bearing was a slouch of resignation and grim defeat. Erin felt her eyes burn with tears as she saw the pain and confusion in Kane's normally clear gaze. *He loves Krista so much,* Erin thought, *and he is hurting so badly.* She felt the urge to run to him, to comfort him, to love him, but she restrained herself.

Dr. Sampson excused himself, and Kane stood transfixed in the waiting area. He hadn't noticed Erin yet; he was too preoccupied with his own black thoughts. Suddenly she felt very out of place, an intruder. How would he feel when he finally saw her? How could she explain how she felt about him and his daughter, the love that was smothering her in its encompassing grasp? He had instructed Mrs. Cavenaugh not to call Erin. Perhaps he truly didn't want to see her. What would he do?

Her conjecture was cut short as Kane whirled to face her. It was as if he had sensed her presence and her uncertainty. His expression was cold, guarded, and Erin felt her heart stop as her eyes clashed with his brittle gray gaze.

"Erin?" His dark brows drew together. "How did you know?"

"Mrs. Cavenaugh told me."

"That woman can't keep a secret to save her soul!" He bit out the words and Erin wondered once again if she had made a grave mistake by intruding into his private grief. She took a step toward him and stopped. There was so much to say, so great a misunderstanding to bridge, and she wondered if it was at all possible.

"I'm sorry about Krista," she whispered, and the pain in her eyes was undeniable.

She saw him hesitate for a moment. He closed his eyes and seemed to give into the pressure that was battering against him. When he opened his eyes, they were clear once again, and in swift strides, he was by her side.

"I'm glad you came," he admitted, his voice rough from the strain of the day.

"Didn't you know that I would?"

"Erin, I don't know anything, not anymore!" His confession was a sigh of disgust.

"How—how is Krista?"

Lowering himself onto the edge of the plastic orange couch, he rubbed the tension from the back of his neck and ground his jaws together. When he spoke, it was in a monotone. "Dr. Sampson seems to think that she'll be fine, even taking into consideration her previous problem. She's got a concussion, but supposedly it's not serious, or at least not too serious. She was unconscious for a while, but she came to. Now she's resting. They gave her something—a sedative. The doctor thinks she'll wake up soon and that I can see her. God, I hope so. This waiting and not knowing is driving me up a wall." His long fingers raked deep gorges in his thick chestnut hair.

Erin sat next to him, not knowing the comforting words that would soothe him. They sat only inches apart, and yet Erin felt as if it might have been miles. Kane's eyes remained closed as if he were frighteningly weary and unable to face the trauma that was in store for him.

At the sound of Dr. Sampson's clipped footsteps Kane's eyelids flew open, and he was on his feet in a moment. "How is she?" he asked.

The pudgy doctor smiled. "You worry too much, Mr. Webster. Krista is going to be just fine. As a matter of fact, she's coming around now. You can see her if you like."

Erin couldn't keep up with Kane's swift strides as he

nearly ran back to Krista's room. The frail figure in the hospital bed brought back Erin's earlier feelings of apprehension and dread. Krista's complexion was nearly as white as the stark bedsheets that draped her, and the bandage on her head only seemed to add to her fragile appearance. A colorless fluid dripped into Krista's arm from a suspended I.V. bottle positioned near the bed. The tiny arm was secured to the bedrail by a strip of gauze.

Krista's eyes fluttered open after what seemed like hours, and a look of utter confusion and fear crossed her small face as she called to her father.

"Daddy?"

Kane's voice cracked with emotion as he responded. "Krista, honey, I'm right here." His fingers reached out and touched her cheek. "Oh, sweetheart, you don't know how good it is to hear your voice," he sighed.

Krista tried to lift her head, but her small face cringed in pain. "Oooh, where am I?"

"You're in the hospital, honey. Remember you hit your head while chasing the kitten?"

"Figaro? Where is he?" she asked with childish concern.

Kane smiled despite his tension. "Don't worry about him, honey. He's in good hands. Mrs. Cavenaugh promised to take care of him until you get home."

Krista's eyes moved around the room until she spotted Erin. A smile brought back a little of the color to her face. "You're back!" Krista's enthusiasm shined in her eyes. "I knew that you'd come back!"

"You were right," Erin choked out, stepping nearer to the bed. "You should have known better than to think that I'd ever leave you."

"I did. I knew you wouldn't go without saying goodbye. See, Dad, I told ya she'd be back!"

"That you did," Kane whispered, and his eyes locked with Erin's questioning gaze.

Dr. Sampson came back into the room with his usual quick, short stride. "Well, little lady—so you did decide to wake up after all. About time, I might add! Your father here, he was beginning to worry." The little man's expert fingers probed Krista, and his knowing eyes studied her as he talked.

"That's okay. Dad always worries."

"Is that so? Well, maybe next time you'll be more careful on those stairs," the doctor reprimanded teasingly. When his examination was over, he studied Krista with feigned concern. "I think you should get some rest, young lady, before I send down for a special dinner for you. I'm going to send your dad home for a while, but he can come back and visit you later—what do you say?"

Disappointment crowded Krista's fine features, but she gave in. "All right," she agreed, and turned her attention back to her father. "But you will come back tonight, won't you?"

"You can count on it, pumpkin," Kane said huskily.

"And you, Erin?" Krista asked, her sky-blue eyes searching Erin's face.

Erin cast a quick glance at Kane and then smiled tenderly down at the child. "Sure, Krista. I'll be back," she promised.

As they stepped out of the room, Dr. Sampson gave Kane a quick report on Krista, assuring him that the little girl was responding well to treatment, and Erin felt a tide of relief wash over her. Kane, too, seemed visibly encouraged by the news. They walked out of the hospital together, and Erin wondered what their futures would be—together or apart. Kane was lost in his own thoughts but shook his head when Erin offered him a lift home.

"No, thanks," he said, "I've got my own car." Disappointment shattered Erin, but she tried not to show her feelings. "I have to stop off and talk to Mrs. Cavenaugh. I know she's worried about Krista."

"Will…will I see you later?" Erin blurted, unable to restrain herself.

"Do you want to?"

"Of course I do!" She shook her head in frustration. "I've missed you so badly."

"Shhh," he held her close to him for a moment, and she could hear the clamoring of his heart. "I'll meet you back at your place in an hour," he promised. "It's important that I speak to Mrs. Cavenaugh—you understand that, don't you?"

"Of course," she whispered as he walked away from her.

The hour stretched out to two, and Erin found herself nervously pacing the floor of her apartment. Where could he be? Was he even coming at all? She had tried to fill the time by taking a hasty shower, unpacking and finally brewing a strong cup of tea. The minutes ticked slowly by. What was he doing?

When at last he arrived, she steeled herself for the rejection that she knew was coming. Too much had happened—too many bitter words had been lashed out— it was just too damned late.

She didn't bother to get up when he opened the door and came into her antiques-filled loft.

"I'm sorry I'm late," he apologized, but didn't move to take off his jacket. "I've spent the last two hours driving in circles, wondering how on earth I can say the things that have to be said."

"I know," she whispered.

"I appreciate the fact that you came to the hospital."

A wry smile curved her lips. "You don't have to thank me. I had to come. Krista means a great deal to me."

"Erin." She let her eyes melt into his as he spoke her name. "I feel as if I owe you this incredibly large apology about the embezzling."

"Oh, Kane, not tonight, not after everything that's happened to Krista. It…doesn't matter."

"Damn it, Erin! The least you could do is let me explain. Then, if you want to throw me out of here, I'll go." Kane walked into the living room and sat on the small antique coffee table, positioning himself directly in front of Erin. She found it impossible to take her gaze from his. She was compelled to listen to him.

"After our last fight, I began thinking about alternate suspects in the embezzlement. You were right and I feel like a fool admitting it, but I was so blinded by my love for you, so afraid that you were the culprit, that I couldn't see the facts correctly. It was an unforgivable injustice to you."

Erin started to protest but he ignored her. "Just let me finish," he commanded. "I started putting some of the pieces together and discovered that Mitch was having an affair with Olivia. It really wasn't all that difficult to see, once I knew you were innocent. Olivia was the one person who seemed to know too much—everything about you, the securities key, the meeting with Mitch on the day of the arraignment. She was clever and subtle, but she took great pains to mention that you and Mitch had always been friendly, and Cameron, the bastard, didn't deny it."

Erin shook her head in disbelief as Kane continued. "At the point that I began to suspect Olivia, I was inhibited because of Krista's depression. I'm sorry, Erin, if you can only guess how really sorry I am that I thought, even for a moment…"

"It's okay," she whispered, and reached to touch his arm.

"No, it's not!" He closed his eyes and shook his head. "And what makes it worse is the fact that I fell in love with you the moment I saw you sitting in the office on the floor with all those books spread around you, and still I thought that you were involved with Cameron. I must have been out of my mind."

Erin's head was reeling with the magnitude of Kane's confession. He had said it over and over—that he loved her. Was it really possible?

"I want you to know that it doesn't matter, not anymore. When I heard about Krista from Mrs. Cavenaugh, I realized that nothing matters—nothing except for you and Krista," she admitted, smiling into his face.

His eyes opened slowly. "Erin, just what are you saying?" he asked quietly.

"I'm saying that I love you, and the only reason that I wouldn't marry you before was because I didn't think that you loved me."

"How could you have been so blind?" he asked, reaching for her and crushing her to him. "It was so evident!" He didn't wait for an answer. His lips came crashing down on hers with a fiery passion that was soon exploding in her veins. "I'll never let you get away again," he vowed. "We're getting married as soon as Krista is out of the hospital."

"You haven't heard any disagreements from me, have you?" she asked.

"Thank God for small favors!" He sighed, and let the weight of his body fall against hers.

* * * * *

Elle James, a *New York Times* bestselling author, started writing when her sister challenged her to write a romance novel. She has managed a full-time job and raised three wonderful children, and she and her husband even tried ranching exotic birds (ostriches, emus and rheas). Ask her, and she'll tell you what it's like to go toe-to-toe with an angry 350-pound bird! Elle loves to hear from fans at ellejames@earthlink.net or ellejames.com.

Books by Elle James

Harlequin Intrigue

Mission: Six

One Intrepid SEAL
Two Dauntless Hearts
Three Courageous Words
Four Relentless Days

Ballistic Cowboys

Hot Combat
Hot Target
Hot Zone
Hot Velocity

SEAL of My Own

Navy SEAL Survival
Navy SEAL Captive
Navy SEAL to Die For
Navy SEAL Six Pack

Visit the Author Profile page at Harlequin.com.

DEADLY FALL

Elle James

This book is dedicated to my readers,
who buy my books and let me live the dream of writing
full-time. Without you, I'd still be commuting to work
wearing business clothes and tight shoes instead of
working at my desk in my yoga pants, barefoot.

Also to my family, who puts up with my late-night writing,
taking my laptop on vacations, and letting the
cooking and cleaning go when I'm on deadline.
They know I'm working and try to get along without me.

I also dedicate this book to my little dogs,
who remind me to get out of my chair and take them
outside. They keep me company during the day when
I'm writing and are just happy to be with me. Okay! Okay!
I'm getting up. Sheesh! You could at least have
let me finish my dedication...

Chapter 1

"Leigha?" Andrew Stratford called out.

The old mansion had been quiet for too long.

"Leigha?" he said a little louder.

He glanced up from the computer terminal, having spent the last three hours day-trading, buying as the prices on several of the stocks he had his eye on dipped to an all-time low.

He'd made his fortune on Wall Street. Since the accident, he'd left it all behind and moved to Cape Churn, Oregon. Giving up the high-stress job of managing the fortunes of other people to only managing his own portfolio had been a decision he'd never regret.

Not that he'd had much of a choice. With the scars he'd acquired, his high-powered, beautiful clients would be less likely to come to entrust their money to him. So intent on being the wealthiest, most beautiful people money could buy, they wouldn't have the courage to face a man with a wicked scar running from the base of his jaw up to his eye. The burn scars on his right hand would be a deal breaker in a society where a good handshake was a measure of a man's character.

But the main reason he'd come back to Oregon was the reason he rose from his desk.

"Leigha," he called out.

Now that he had a daughter to look after, he couldn't live the fast-paced, late-night lifestyle he'd been living for the past ten years as one of the most eligible bachelors in New York City. And, frankly, he didn't want to. He'd burned the candle at both ends with a high-powered job and a jet-setter lifestyle. Sure, he'd amassed a fortune, but what else did he have to show for it?

Andrew stretched. He needed to get up and move. His housekeeper, Mrs. Dottie Purdy, had ducked in an hour ago saying she needed to stock the pantry and Leigha preferred to stay and play.

Normally, Leigha played in the big mansion with Brewer, her black Labrador retriever. Andrew could count on the reassuring sound of little feet and canine toe-nails clicking across wooden floors. For the past fifteen minutes there had been nothing. No sounds, no squeals of delight or soft-spoken tea parties in the salon two doors down from Andrew's office.

Silence used to be calming when he was a bachelor without a care in the world. Now that he had Leigha, silence was disconcerting.

The little girl was always into something. Though she was abnormally solemn, she was a natural-born explorer and adventurer. She reminded Andrew of himself at that age. His nanny had despaired of keeping up with him. Unfortunately, Stratford House perched on the edge of a three-hundred-foot cliff. If she wandered too far from the house, Leigha could fall to a very grisly death on the jagged rocks below.

On that thought, Andrew hurried from his office and out into the mansion's huge entry hall. "Leigha!"

He listened, hoping to hear an answering call in the little girl's high-pitched voice.

More silence greeted him.

The mansion had three living areas: a massive formal dining room, fifteen bedrooms and a full basement complete with a wine cellar. The child could be anywhere inside.

Andrew went room to room on the main floor and then stood at the base of the sweeping staircase. "Leigha!"

Again, no answering call.

Had she gone outside without telling him? Andrew's pulse quickened. A glance through the window made his chest tighten. While he'd been busy working at his desk in the study, a cold, gray fog had crept in from the Pacific cloaking Cape Churn in what the locals called the Devil's Shroud.

"Damn," Andrew muttered and hurried for the door. If Leigha had gone out when it was clear, she might now be lost in the fog.

Andrew burst through the massive front door and ran out onto the marble portico. "Leigha! Brewer!"

A dog barked in the distance, the sound coming from the back of the house, farther along the coastline, sounding too near to the edge of the cliff for Andrew's comfort.

Andrew broke into a sprint, trying to remember just how many steps past the garden led to the cliff's edge. He'd contracted a local handyman to erect a decorative wrought-iron fence, but he had to wait for the man to finish renovations on another home before he had time to start the work on the fence and other repairs around Strat-

ford House. In the meantime, Andrew worried Leigha or
guests might walk off the cliff in a dense fog, such as the
one now hiding the treacherous shoreline.

"Leigha? Brewer?"

Again the dog barked.

Andrew slowed, knowing he was close to the edge of
the cliff. He would be of no use to Leigha if he fell off.
But the thought of the child being out there in the damp
fog, her foot slipping on a wet rock, made him hurry as
quickly as he could.

Andrew nearly walked into a tree trunk clinging to
the ledge.

As he stepped around it, something moved. A shad-
owy figure detached from the tree and slammed into him.

Andrew's forward momentum shifted sideways, sending him over the edge of the cliff. He dropped ten feet, hit
a jutting boulder, his arms wind-milling the air, grasping at the fog for purchase to keep him from falling three
hundred feet to the rocky shoreline. His hand tangled in a
tree root. Closing his fingers around it, he held on. Damp
with the mist, the root slid through his hand. He grabbed
with his other hand and held on tightly. When his body
fell below his hands, his arms felt as though they were
being ripped out of their sockets. But he managed to arrest his downward plunge.

Andrew clung to the root, his breath caught in his
throat as he held on, his hands wrapped around the root,
his feet dangling in the air.

For a long moment he hung in midair, thankful for
the stalwart tree and its tenacious hold on the rocky cliff.
Then he raised his legs, kicking out his feet, searching
for ground to dig his toes into. Using the tree roots, he
inched his way up the side of the cliff until he was back
where he'd started before he'd fallen over the edge.

Or rather, before he was *pushed*. No tree in the span of Andrew's lifetime had ever managed to shove him over a cliff.

As he dragged himself up onto the path, he braced himself, prepared to fight for the ground he could stand on. Fog swirled around him but nothing jumped out.

Staggering to his feet, Andrew pressed on, more afraid than ever for Leigha.

Brewer barked again, closer to him and far too close to the cliff's edge for Andrew's liking.

"Mr. Stratford?" a tiny voice called out.

"Leigha?" Andrew's heart pounded against his ribs and he strained to see through the thick fog.

"I'm here. I got lost," she said, her voice wobbling.

"Stop," Andrew ordered. "Stay right where you are. But keep talking to me so that I can find you." Andrew moved forward, careful not to get too close to the ledge.

"I'm scared," Leigha said, her voice thin and shaky.

The Labrador materialized out of the fog and walked toward him.

Holding on to the dog's tail was the little girl Andrew obviously had no clue how to care for. He swept her up into his arms and hugged her tightly. "Thank God."

Leigha wrapped her arms around his neck. "Brewer and I were playing with my friend. Then the clouds came in and I couldn't see my way back home."

"You have *me* now. I'll make sure you get back," he assured her.

"I held on to Brewer's tail," Leigha said. "He knows the way. He was leading me home when we found you."

The big Lab leaned into his leg. His tongue lolled and his tail thumped against the hard ground.

Andrew glanced down at the dog. He'd never had a pet. As a child growing up in New York City, his parents refused to have an animal in their apartment. When he was old enough to make his own decisions, he got caught up in making a living, and then powered on to make a fortune. A pet didn't have a place in his intensely busy life.

Now he stared down at the dog that seemed to be smiling up at him, daring him to smile back.

"Brewer is happy to see you," Leigha said. She placed both of her small palms against Andrew's cheeks and turned his face toward hers, undaunted by his scars. "Mr. Stratford, why are you bleeding?"

"I tripped and fell." Andrew swept a damp strand of blond hair out of Leigha's eyes, leaving a streak of blood across her forehead.

Leigha captured his hand. "You have a boo-boo on your hand, too. You need to go to the doctor."

For the first time since his fall over the cliff, Andrew felt the pain of a cut on his hand. The way it was bleeding couldn't be good.

"I'll take care of it when we get back to the house," he assured her.

Leigha leaned her head against his shoulder, her pretty little brow puckering. "Mr. Stratford, are you going to die?"

He snorted. "Not today, Leigha. Not today."

"Tomorrow?" Her fingers curled into his shirt and held on as he walked in what he hoped was the direction of the mansion, his attention focused on sounds and any movement. Holding Leigha in his arms, he was doubly aware of his responsibilities toward the child.

Someone had pushed him over the cliff. But who? And why?

When Stratford House finally appeared in front of him, he sighed and hurried through the back entrance, into the large kitchen.

"There you are." Mrs. Purdy stopped in the middle of unloading a bag of groceries and set the can in her hand on the counter. "What happened to you?" she cried. Grabbing a kitchen towel, she rushed over to him.

Andrew lowered Leigha to the ground in time for Mrs. Purdy to grab his hand.

"Good Lord, you look like you got into a fight," the older woman said.

"It's nothing," he said, trying to calm his housekeeper.

"Nothing?" She frowned and led him by the hand to the kitchen sink. "That cut is deep enough it might require stitches. And I don't know how they go about stitching over burn scars."

"A bandage will do." He let her drag his hand under running water and winced as pain shot up his arm. He jerked his hand back, but the woman stubbornly held on.

"You need to have a doctor look at this. I'll wrap it up, but you'll continue to bleed if you don't have it stitched."

"Please, Mr. Stratford. Please go to the doctor." Leigha touched his arm and stared up at him. "I don't want you to die."

"I'm not going to die," he insisted. "And I'm not going to bleed to death."

Mrs. Purdy crossed her arms over her chest and stared him down. Then she tipped her head toward Leigha. "If not for yourself, do it for Leigha."

Outnumbered, Andrew sighed. "Okay. I'll let a doctor look at it. I'll make an appointment for tomorrow."

"Today," Leigha said.

"We'll go to the ER in Cape Churn." Mrs. Purdy wrapped a clean kitchen towel around his hand. "I'll drive."

"I'm perfectly capable of driving myself to Cape Churn."

"You're bleeding like a stuck pig. You might get dizzy." She held up her hand. "I won't take no for an answer."

"I'm going with you." Leigha clutched his sleeve.

"And I'm driving," Mrs. Purdy insisted.

"Do I have a choice in this matter?" Andrew asked.

"No!" Mrs. Purdy and Leigha answered as one.

Thus outmaneuvered, Andrew found himself loaded into the passenger seat of Mrs. Purdy's minivan and driven all the way to the Cape Churn Hospital emergency room.

Once inside, he was whisked back to an examination room. Mrs. Purdy and Leigha waited in the ER lobby. As the door closed between them, Andrew noted Leigha burying her face into Mrs. Purdy's sleeve, her eyes clouding with tears. The child appeared terrified for him.

He had to admit, he was terrified for her. After nearly falling to his own death, he realized how easily it could have been Leigha. The thought of finding her body smashed against the boulders made him sick to his stomach. He sat on the edge of the hospital examination bed, pain throbbing through his hand with each beat of his heart.

A nurse carrying a clipboard stepped into the room. "Hi, Mr. Stratford. I'm Emma Jenkins. I'll be your nurse. What brings you here today?" She set the clipboard on the bed beside him and took his injured hand in hers, unwrapping the dish towel. "How'd you get this cut?"

Andrew's first instinct was to retract his scarred hand. Instead he stared at the gash. "I was pushed over a cliff."

Emma blinked. "Say again? Someone pushed you over a cliff?"

He nodded, more certain than ever it hadn't been a

ghost or a blast of wind in the fog. "Someone pushed me over the cliff behind my house."

"Do you want me to notify the sheriff? He can send a deputy out to take your statement while we stitch the wound."

Though he didn't like anyone invading his privacy, Andrew nodded. If someone had pushed him, he couldn't ignore it. What if that someone tried to push Leigha? "I think that would be best."

Emma waited until the doctor appeared before she slipped out to make that call. Within minutes, a sheriff's deputy appeared.

"Hi, I'm Gabe McGregor. I believe we've met once before."

Andrew nodded, his lips thinning. "You came to my house when you were looking for a murderer, several months ago." They'd questioned him as a suspect. "I'm glad you caught him."

"You and me both," Gabe said. "I'm sorry I had to question you on that case."

"Don't be. I understand. I was the new guy in town." Andrew gritted his teeth as the doctor stuck a needle in his hand to deaden the area around the cut.

"So tell me what happened." Gabe pulled a notepad and pen out of his front pocket.

While the doctor and Emma cleaned and stitched the wound, Andrew recounted what had happened.

"And you didn't see a face?" Deputy McGregor asked.

Andrew shook his head. "It happened so fast. I stepped around the tree, and the next thing I knew, I was clinging to a tree root, thankful for that tree and the root, or I wouldn't be here to tell you the story."

The deputy's brows drew together. "I'm sorry it happened to you. I'll follow you home and have a look around the area. Maybe there will be some footprints."

"It's not safe in the fog. Besides, the cliff edge is primarily rock and moss. That tree on the edge is the only one there. How it found enough soil to grow as big as it is still astounds me."

"Any idea who might want to hurt you?" McGregor asked.

"No. And it's got me concerned. I found a loose board on the outside step yesterday. At first I didn't think anything of it. I just got out a hammer and fixed it. But when I did, I noticed the board wasn't old or weatherworn. It looked like someone loosened it. I brushed it off as an overactive imagination. But after being shoved off a cliff, I'm rethinking it."

"I knew your grandfather." Emma used a wad of sterile gauze to sop up the excess blood from around the wound as the doctor sewed another stitch. "Though the ME ruled his death as accidental, I thought it pretty strange the old man who'd walked two or three miles a day, and had a healthy heart the last time I could get him in for a checkup, should fall over dead on one of his walks. The ME said his heart was fine. He'd died from the fall. Hit his head on a rock."

Andrew leaned forward. "Are you saying someone murdered him?"

Emma raised both of her hands, wad of bloody cotton and all. "I'm not saying anything. Just the facts."

"Look, all I know is I came to Cape Churn because I thought it would be a safer, quieter place to raise Leigha. I didn't want her to grow up in the concrete jungle where I grew up. She deserves a place where she can run and play." Not a park with a nanny and polluted air.

Andrew knew he was far from the father Leigha deserved, but he wanted her to have a normal childhood, where she could play outdoors, have a pet and be happy.

"Cape Churn can be all of that," Emma said. "I've lived here all my life and love all the cape has to offer. The community is supportive and the summer activities are what most kids dream of. I'd love to teach Leigha how to scuba dive, when she's a little older."

Andrew's heart warmed at the offer. "I want all of that for her, too."

"I feel a 'but' coming," Deputy McGregor said.

"But, after what happened today, I'm rethinking my decision to bring her here. After I nearly fell to my death, Leigha told me she and the dog were playing with her friend. A man. When I asked her about him, she said he's been visiting her every day."

Emma, the deputy and the doctor all frowned.

"Have you had a talk with Leigha about stranger danger?" the doctor asked.

"I have." Andrew snorted. "She said he's not a stranger. He's her friend."

The doctor completed the last stitch and held the strand out straight.

Emma used a pair of scissors to snip it close to the knot.

The doctor set his tools on the tray. "I'll leave you in Emma's capable hands. I have other patients I need to attend." He peeled off his gloves and gave Andrew a stern glance. "Try not to fall off any more cliffs."

After the doctor left, Emma cleaned the area around the wound. "Have you considered hiring protection?"

Andrew frowned. "I've never hired a bodyguard. Where would I start?"

Emma shrugged. "I don't know."

"What about the people Creed, Nicole and Nova work with?" Deputy McGregor asked. "Could they help?"

"Normally they work bigger issues," Emma said. "You know, save-the-world kind of problems." She glanced across Andrew's head at the deputy. "But maybe they have someone who could help while Mr. Stratford goes through the interviewing and hiring process." She turned her attention back to Andrew. "Do you want me to ask?"

"Do you trust them?" Andrew asked.

Emma nodded. "With my life."

"How about with the life of your child?" He captured Emma's gaze and held it.

She nodded. "Absolutely."

"Then yes. If I could get someone on a temporary basis that is trustworthy, it will give me time to look for a full-time bodyguard."

Deputy McGregor closed his notepad and slid it into his pocket. "Tell you what... We're having dinner at McGregor Manor tomorrow night. Why don't you and Leigha come? You can discuss it with some of the members of the SOS team then."

Andrew frowned. "SOS?"

"Stealth Operations Specialists," Emma clarified. "They're like the FBI and CIA, only better. Somehow they've opened a branch here in Cape Churn. You should come. You can meet all of them, and maybe by tomorrow night they'll have an answer for you. Or they might have a suggestion of who to hire for the job of bodyguard to you and Leigha." Emma wrapped a bandage around his hand. "Keep that out of water for a couple of days. In a week you can come in and I'll remove the stitches. Otherwise, I'll see you tomorrow night."

Emma gave him the routine discharge instructions and a prescription for antibiotics and sent him out to the lobby, where Leigha and Mrs. Purdy waited.

Leigha ran to him and hugged him around the legs. "I was so scared."

"I'm fine." He patted the child's head and lifted her up on his uninjured arm. "Since we're in town, why don't we get some ice cream at the Seaside Café?"

Leigha clapped her hands together. "Yes, please."

The smile on Leigha's face made warmth spread across Andrew's chest. He never ceased to be amazed at how much one little human being could make him feel more important than an entire office building of employees.

He vowed to keep this little girl safe, no matter the cost. If it meant hiring a bodyguard, he'd do it. But it had to be someone special. Someone he could trust completely. There weren't many people he knew who fit that bill. How was he going to trust a stranger to fill that role?

Chapter 2

Dixie Reeves pulled into the parking lot of McGregor Manor. The lovely old home perched on the edge of a cliff outside the small community of Cape Churn, Oregon. In just under twenty-four hours she'd gone from being unemployed to having a job, to getting her first assignment.

What she was supposed to do as a bodyguard to a rich man was beyond her. As a squad leader in the Army, she'd been responsible for her soldiers, the first all-female squad of Airborne Rangers.

She'd done her best as a leader among her peers until one of their special operations had gone bad. They'd been caught in the middle of a firefight. Dix, manning a .60-caliber submachine gun, had remained behind, laying down cover fire for her squad, allowing them to escape. When she'd run out of bullets, she hadn't had time to put her handgun to her head before she was captured.

Dix shook off the memory of the week she'd spent in

hell in an enemy camp where she'd been humiliated, tortured and beaten repeatedly until the Navy SEALs were sent in to extract her.

That was over three years ago. Her life had changed dramatically. Processed out of the Army, she'd spent two of those years as a member of the Mixed Martial Arts fighting community. But the nightmares still lingered.

Dix stared at the lush landscape damp from the previous night's mist, so foreign to the deserts of Afghanistan and Las Vegas she might as well have been on another planet.

From what she'd been told, the building in front of her had once been a rich man's home, but had been turned into a bed-and-breakfast by the remaining members of the family. As a home, it was larger than anything Dix had ever lived in. As a bed-and-breakfast, it was quaint and had a heck of a view of Cape Churn.

Her new boss, Royce Fontaine, had tracked her down to her small apartment in Las Vegas, where she'd been sorting through what was left of her belongings after donating most of them to a local women's shelter. He'd said he'd been following her career. At first, she'd assumed he'd meant her career as an MMA fighter. She'd done pretty well, winning one championship after another, focusing all of her anger and frustration into her fists.

Her opponents didn't have a chance. The women she'd fought had never been through the intense training she'd survived as one of the first women to pass the Army Ranger training program. Nor had they been tortured in an enemy camp. The anger had fueled her fists until one day she'd gone too far and left an opponent comatose with a very slim chance of recovery.

Royce thought she'd be a good fit for his team. Dix wasn't so sure. But with no other skills to add to her résumé, what else was she fit for? She might have gotten a job as a security guard at one of the casinos, but the noise bothered her, making her head ache and the tensions multiply.

So, now she was going to be a member of the SOS team. What exactly did an agent with the Stealth Operations Specialists do? Royce had told her, *Anything that needed to be done.*

Then he'd gotten word from one of his other agents that a wealthy man needed bodyguard services on a temporary basis while he interviewed and hired one he could trust.

"But what does a bodyguard do?" she'd asked Fontaine.

And he'd answered, "Whatever needs to be done."

"Not helping," she muttered as she walked toward the bed-and-breakfast. Hopefully the other members of the SOS team could shed light on her responsibilities. She couldn't afford to lose this job. It might be the only offer she got, and the pay was good. As far as she could tell, all she had to do was keep a rich dude alive.

How hard could that be in the States? They didn't have Taliban or Islamic State fighters…at least, not that she knew of.

"Hello. May I help you?" a female voice called out from the front door of the manor.

Dix shaded her eyes and squinted. "Is this the Mc-Gregor Bed-and-Breakfast?"

"It is." An auburn-haired woman stepped out onto the porch and smiled. "I'm Molly McGregor, one of the owners. Do you need a place to stay tonight?"

"I don't think so," Dix said. "I'm supposed to meet someone here."

The woman frowned. "Meet someone? Anyone in particular?" she asked, her smile warm and welcoming.

"Royce Fontaine sent me. Does that name ring a bell?"

Ms. McGregor's eyes widened. "You're D. Reeves?"

Dix nodded. "Dixie Reeves."

The bed-and-breakfast owner clapped a hand over her mouth, smothering what sounded suspiciously like a giggle. She dropped her hand, a sparkle dancing in her eyes. "We've been expecting you."

"We?" Dix didn't like the sound of that. A single contact was all she'd been led to believe would be waiting for her in Cape Churn.

"Yes," Molly continued, cheerful and happy, something Dix couldn't begin to relate to. "The gang's all here. We thought you'd be here an hour ago."

"My plane was delayed by weather over Vegas or I would have been here sooner."

"No worries. I kept your dinner warm." She waved a hand. "Come inside. Everyone is waiting for you."

"Everyone?" Dix halted with one foot on the bottom step. "I was told to meet my contact here." After quitting the MMA circuit, Dix had no desire to step in front of a crowd of people ever again. Whether it was a throng of three thousand or a party of five, she wouldn't perform like a trained monkey to the delight of others. In her mind, being a bodyguard was being invisible until she needed to step forward to protect her client. She'd actually looked forward to being invisible. No celebrity status. No paparazzi. After dropping out of the MMA, she never wanted to be in the public eye again.

"The entire West Coast office of SOS agents is in attendance tonight. You'll get a chance to meet all of them." Molly grinned. "Don't worry—they won't bite. Unless you try to take their clam chowder. I managed to save a bowl for you."

"If it's all the same to you, I'd prefer to meet my contact out here, get my marching orders and go on to my client."

Molly's smile slipped. "Oh, okay. But your client is inside, as well. He's having clam chowder, too." The woman's smile returned. "You might as well have dinner with us. I think your client gave his housekeeper the night off from cooking."

Dix squared her shoulders and continued up the steps. She wasn't getting out of the dog and pony show. "I don't mean to be rude, but I'm here to work, not socialize."

"Is that our newest SOS agent?" A dark-skinned man, with brown-black eyes, a full, sensual mouth and a slight Hispanic accent, stepped through the front door behind Molly and slipped his arm around the redhead's waist. He frowned, his head tilting to one side. "Dix Reeves? *The* Dix Reeves?" His face split into a wide smile. "Are you a guest of the bed-and-breakfast?"

So much for being invisible. Dix sighed. "No, I'm not here to stay. I'm here on work-related business."

"Dix, this is Casanova Valdez. Or Nova for short." Molly turned to the man. "Nova, this is the agent Royce sent."

Nova's frown deepened. "I don't understand." He flicked a hand toward Dix. "That's Dix Reeves, one of the most talented MMA fighters ever."

"MMA?" Molly asked, her brows rising. "I'm sorry— is that another one of your military acronyms?"

Nova laughed out loud. "No. It stands for Mixed Martial Arts. Dix, here, is at the top of her game." He reached out a hand. "It's an honor to meet you."

Dix held out her hand and, with a firm grip, shook Nova's.

"Wait—what did you say?" Nova didn't release her hand. "You're the agent Fontaine sent?"

With a nod, Dix extracted her hand. "That's me."

"But you're with the MMA."

"Not anymore. I quit a week ago."

"That's a shame. I watched your last fight against Peggy Pounder. You threw some wicked punches and kicks. I don't think I've seen anything quite that intense."

Her lips thinned. *Intense* was one way to describe the fight. *Insane* was closer to the truth. She'd had a particularly bad night's sleep, plagued by nightmares from her time as a guest of the Taliban. She'd gone into the ring, not to claim a championship, but to beat the demons out of her head.

She'd nearly killed her opponent.

Molly touched Nova's arm. "Was that the fight you were watching last weekend?"

Nova nodded. "Incredible."

Molly's brows knit, her smile fading. "Didn't that woman end up in the hospital?"

Dix's belly clenched. "Yes. She's still in a coma. It's not one of my prouder moments." Dix stared at Nova. "Are you one of Fontaine's agents?"

With a grave nod, Nova answered, "I am. But I'm not your contact. That would be Tazer. She's inside."

"Good. I'd like to get on to my assignment."

"Well, that's the place to start." Nova held open the door. "Just follow Molly. And don't forget to try her amazing clam chowder. It's *muy bueno*."

Molly entered the manor first. "Everyone is in the dining room."

Dix followed, bracing herself for more questions than

she was ready to answer. If Nova recognized her, she hadn't done a good job of blending in. She'd have to buy some hair dye and go from blonde to brunette to hide her identity. In the meantime, she squared her shoulders and turned toward the sea of faces in front of her.

The men pushed back from the table and stood.

Molly turned to her. "Everyone, this is D. Reeves. Otherwise known as Dixie Reeves or—"

"I'll be damned." A woman sitting at the other end of the table stood. "Dix Reeves. Mixed Martial Arts World Champion." The woman had long blond hair, combed straight and hanging in a soft curtain down her back. In tan slacks and a cool, white-cotton blouse, she could have been a model for one of the fashion magazines. She stepped away from her seat and rounded the table, a smile quirking the corners of her lips. "Fontaine sure knows how to pick them." She stopped in front of Dix and held out her hand. "Nicole Steele. But my friends call me Tazer."

Dix shook the woman's hand, surprised at the firmness of her grip. "Sounds like an MMA call sign."

Tazer shrugged. "Suits me. I guess you could say I earned it." She raked her gaze over Dix. "So, you're going to be Andrew Stratford's bodyguard." She let the smile spread a little wider. "Makes sense."

Dix pulled her hand free of Tazer's grip. "I'd like to get on to my assigned duties, if that's possible."

Tazer grinned. "More than possible."

Dix glanced around at the faces all staring at her. Which one was the rich man she was supposed to protect?

Tazer chuckled. "It's none of the men at the table. Mr. Stratford stepped out to take a call. He'll be back in a minute. As far as I know, you start your assignment immediately."

"In the meantime—" Molly pulled out a chair "—have a seat and a bowl of chowder. I won't take no for an answer."

The pretty redhead might be smiling and sunny, but Dix suspected she was as tough as the muscular men seated around the table. "Yes, ma'am." Before she could sink into the chair, a deep, resonant voice spoke from behind her.

"I'm sorry. I need to leave. Leigha isn't feeling well. If you could send the bodyguard over when he gets here, I'd appreciate it."

"As a matter of fact, your bodyguard is here." Tazer hooked Dix's elbow and turned her around.

Dix stared at the most beautiful man she'd ever laid eyes on. He stood half turned toward the exit, only one side of his face visible. While all the other men in the room were dressed in jeans or khaki slacks, this man wore a dark suit that appeared to be tailor-made to fit his body to perfection. His dark hair was shortly cropped, showing a bit of a wave. And those ice-blue eyes...

Then he squared off, spinning to fully face the room of people. A jagged scar ran from the edge of his jaw all the way up to the corner of his eye.

Dix drew in a sharp breath. She hadn't expected such a magnificent man to have such a wicked scar.

His dark brows drew together into a V over his nose. "Where is he?"

"Not *he*," Tazer said in a slow, deliberate voice. "*She* is here and ready to go to work." She shoved Dix forward a step.

The gentleman shook his head, his eyes tapering into little more than a slit. "I don't understand. I asked for someone who could protect me and my family." His gaze raked over her. "I don't need another female in my household. I need someone strong and capable of protecting Leigha."

Her shock at the rugged scar on his face morphed into anger roiling deep in her belly. Dix let it bubble up to the surface. Yeah, she was probably overreacting, but she'd put up with more gender discrimination than most women, and had to fight and claw her way through every leg of the journey that had brought her this far. "Just because I'm female doesn't mean I can't defend myself, or take care of you and your family." She planted her fists on her hips and lifted her chin. "Go ahead. Try to take me down."

"Uh, Dix, I'm not so sure that's a good idea," Nova said. "He's the client."

Andrew Stratford raised a hand. "It's okay. I don't think she's the right person for the job. If she can prove she is, I might reconsider." He gave her a narrow-eyed, assessing glance. "I don't want to hurt you."

She snorted. "Oh, sweetheart, you're not going to hurt me." *I might hurt you*, she thought, but kept the comment from coming out. "Aren't you afraid I'll wrinkle your suit?"

Tazer's lips tilted upward. "Mr. Stratford, you might be biting off a little more than you can chew. My boss wouldn't send someone who couldn't do the job, and Dix is more than qualified. I've seen her dossier."

"I can't trust her with my family until I know she can handle the job."

Tazer shook back her beautifully groomed hair. "Okay, but take it out in the yard. You don't want to damage Molly's dining room."

Molly bit her lip. "I don't want you to damage yourselves."

Another man stood and clapped his hands together. "I've gotta see this."

"Creed, don't encourage them." A sandy-blond-haired woman stood.

He shook his head, a smile spreading across his face. "You're a nurse. If someone gets hurt, you can stop the bleeding until the ambulance gets here."

"That's right," Nova said. "We have Emma. She can stabilize the loser until the ambulance gets here."

Mr. Stratford waved a hand toward the door. "Ladies first."

Dix fumed at his condescension, but swallowed her anger and focused on teaching this man not to judge a book by its cover, or a woman by the color of her hair or the size of her body. With her head held high, she marched through the living area and out the front door, letting it close in the man's face.

She didn't stop until she was standing on the ground in front of the manor.

Footsteps behind her indicated Stratford had followed her.

Before she could turn to face him, strong arms circled her, clamping her own arms to the side.

Used to facing her opponents in the MMA, the sudden attack brought back memories of being held in captivity, bound tightly, unable to fight her way out. Panic almost set in. Two years of therapy came to her rescue. She breathed in and out, forced the bad thoughts to the back of her mind and shut the door on them. Then her thoughts flashed to the best way to extricate herself from the man's strong hold.

"If you can't defend yourself," he whispered against her ear, "you can't defend me or my family."

Dix drew in another calming breath and let her body go limp, a complete deadweight in his arms.

Stratford staggered backward.

She slipped downward, bunched her legs beneath her and planted her feet in the dirt. Then she twisted her body, taking his with hers, flinging them both to the ground.

As they fell, his grip loosened to break his fall.

Dix rolled over, grabbed his arm and jerked it up and behind his back, forcing Stratford onto his belly. She straddled his hips, sat on his back and leaned over to whisper in his ear. "Sorry I wrinkled your suit, Mr. Stratford. I'm also sorry I wasted your time. And, for the record, I'm not interested in protecting someone who doesn't trust my ability to do the job. Thank you for the opportunity but no thanks. I'll find another job."

Dix released his arm and stood, stepping over his prone body. She turned back to the people gathered on the porch, clapping and cheering for her. She shook her head and repeated, "Thanks, but I don't want the job."

The cheering died down. Tazer descended the stairs, her brow furrowing. "What do you mean you don't want the job?"

"I don't. Mr. Stratford obviously doesn't think a woman will suffice. I've fought my share of gender discrimination. I'm done." She started toward the rental car, wondering how long her savings would last after she paid Fontaine back for the flight and the car rental.

Before she'd gone four steps, a leg shot out and swept her off her feet. She landed hard on her back, the air knocked from her lungs.

Stratford straddled her hips, grabbed her wrists and yanked them above her head, pinning them to the dirt.

"Sorry I messed up your hair and smudged your makeup, but you can't quit until I fire you."

Dix gasped, her lungs remembering how to inhale. "I'm not wearing makeup. And it's too late. I already quit."

He shook his head. "I don't accept your resignation."

"You don't have to." She shoved at him and lifted her leg sharply, attempting to knee him in the back. "It's not negotiable." She grunted.

"I need someone to protect my family." He scooted back on her thighs, trapping her legs on the ground. "Despite your bad temper, I want you to do it."

She opened her mouth to protest.

He released one of her wrists and pressed a finger to her lips. "I don't have anyone else. I need someone temporarily until I can hire a full-time replacement. At least give me that."

"I'm not your *man*," she bit out.

"Call me crazy." For the first time since she'd met the man, his lips twitched in something akin to a smile. "I don't want a *man*. I want *you*."

Chapter 3

Andrew wasn't sure what made him tackle the female. Not only had he pinned her to the ground, he'd insisted she take the job. He told himself it was her stubborn determination to prove herself that had pushed him past his concerns. The heat of her thighs straddling his hips and the way she'd pressed her breasts against his back had nothing whatsoever to do with his decision. Though his skin still tingled and the warmth of her breath on the side of his neck lingered in the cool night air.

The plain facts were that he needed someone to keep track of Leigha and keep her safe from whoever was trying to hurt him. What worried him more was the secret friend Leigha went on and on about. Should the person actually exist, he had no business hanging around a six-year-old without her father's permission. Until Andrew had a permanent fix for the situation, Dix Reeves would have to do.

And even if she were as attractive as she was tough,

he wouldn't hold that against her. He rose to his feet and extended his hand to the woman on the ground.

She shoved it aside, easily rolled to her feet and brushed the dust from her jeans. She moved like an athlete, with a spring in her step. Fast and strong, the woman could be an asset. At the very least, she'd be a good temporary solution to his needs. Tomorrow he'd log on to the internet and search for reputable bodyguard services. "If you're ready to leave, I need to get home. As I mentioned, Leigha isn't feeling well and I don't like leaving her for very long with only Mrs. Purdy to protect her."

Dix crossed her arms over her chest. "What part of 'no thanks' did you not understand?"

Ignoring her refusal, he walked to his SUV and climbed in. "Follow me. The road can be hard to find in the dark. And by the looks of it, the Devil's Shroud is moving in."

Dix shot a glance from Andrew to Tazer. "What's he talking about?"

Tazer nodded. "He's right. By the time you get back to his place, the Devil's Shroud will make it very difficult to find your way." Her lips twisted. "The folks around here have a flair for the dramatic. The Devil's Shroud is what they call a thicker-than-pea-soup fog that blinds anyone trying to find their way through it. If you live here long enough, you will undoubtedly experience it firsthand. Probably tonight."

Molly stepped forward. "They say that when the Devil's Shroud rolls in, you can count on evil coming along with it."

Dix snorted. "Well, I should be able to find my way to town and a hotel before it gets that thick."

With a shrug, Molly glanced toward Andrew. "You might try saying 'please.'"

Andrew pressed his lips together. As one of the most powerful traders on Wall Street, he'd been used to giving orders and having people follow them without question. Since *the accident*, he'd left that world behind. But that world hadn't completely left him. He swallowed the desire to tell everyone to go to hell and forced out, "Please."

Dix's brows puckered and a smile curled the corners of her mouth. "Wow. That's the best you can do?"

He growled before he could stop himself. "Take it or leave it."

She hesitated, her gaze sweeping him from head to toe. As he expected, her perusal slowed on the scars he'd acquired in *the accident*.

Andrew fought the urge to turn his face away as well as to hide his hand from her all-seeing eyes. But he stood fast, refusing to back down. She'd see the scars on a daily basis; she might as well get used to them now.

When her gaze reached his toes, she looked up and nodded curtly. "I'll take it. But only on a temporary basis." She pointed a finger at him. "And not for you, but for your daughter. Hopefully she doesn't have her father's bad temper."

Andrew slipped into the SUV without saying another word. He didn't wait to see if she would follow, but pulled out of the gravel driveway and onto the paved highway.

Lights shone into his rearview mirror.

He let go of the breath he hadn't realized he'd been holding and focused on driving through the increasingly thick fog along the curvy coastal highway leading toward his estate.

When she got too far behind, he slowed and waited. By the time he reached the turnoff to his driveway, the fog had completely taken over. Andrew waited for Dix to turn in behind him before he hit the button to activate the automatic gate opener. The gate remained open long enough for both cars to pass through. Then he was leading the way along the twisting drive to Stratford House, the mansion his grandfather had left to him.

Not until he was right in front of the structure could he see the lights glowing a hazy yellow from the main living room and one of the upstairs bedrooms. The rest of the house lay in shrouded darkness.

In the fog, the house resembled one of those Gothic buildings in a horror movie. Andrew wondered what Dix was thinking. Would she turn around and leave? Or would she accept the challenge, creepy house and all?

He got out and waited for her rental car to pull to a stop next to his SUV.

Dix climbed out of the vehicle and stared up at the three-story mansion. "This is where you live?" she asked. Her gaze shot to him.

"It's my home," he said.

"It's big enough to be a hotel. No wonder you need help keeping track of your daughter. Someone could easily get lost in that house."

"It was my grandfather's," he said, surprised at the defensiveness in his tone.

"Did he have a large, extended family, aunts, uncles and cousins who moved in with him?"

A smile pulled at the corners of Andrew's lips. "No. He built it for his wife, whom he loved dearly."

Dix shook her head. "Why?"

"Some say they had hoped to fill each room with children. Others think my grandfather and my grandmother liked making love in a different room every night. It gave them a multitude of options."

Dix's cheeks blossomed into a pretty shade of pink and she turned toward her rental car. "I'll have a look around the house. As big as it is, it has to have multiple entry and exit points."

"It does."

She lifted a gym bag from the backseat of the car and straightened. "Do you check each one of them every night?"

"I do. It takes approximately fifteen minutes to check and secure all of them." He held out his hand. "I can take that for you."

She shook her head. "I can manage."

"Where are the rest of your things?"

She lifted the bag. "This is it. I travel light."

Andrew stared at her. She didn't wear makeup and her blond hair was straight and neatly brushed. Jeans, a powder blue T-shirt and a slightly worn pair of running shoes made up Dix's outfit. She looked like the girl next door. No. More like the tomboy next door. So completely different from his ex-lovers. Some of them had to have a new pair of shoes for every outfit. Several families could be supported for a year on the amount they'd spent on footwear alone.

He strode to the front door, inserted a key and threw open one side of the massive double-door entrance. Andrew waved his hand. "Ladies first."

Dix's eyes narrowed but she stepped past him into the three-story foyer.

"Wow, it's as massive on the inside as it is on the outside." Even though Dix spoke softly, her words echoed against the walls and marble floors.

Andrew closed the door behind him and twisted the dead bolt. "My grandfather and grandmother had a flair for the dramatic."

"No kidding." Dix spun in a circle. "Yeah, I can see where you could lose a kid in this."

Andrew had been coming to his grandfather's house since he was a small child. He was used to the grandeur. Seeing it through Dix's eyes, he could understand how overwhelming it could be. Especially if you were tasked with protecting the occupants of such a large building.

"Oh, good. You're home." Mrs. Purdy, his housekeeper, hurried down the sweeping staircase. "Leigha was asking for you."

"Any improvement?"

Mrs. Purdy's lips pressed together. "None. She's still running a temperature despite the anti-inflammatories and cool compresses. I think she's a bit delirious, as well. When you didn't come after she called, she asked for her imaginary friend."

In the months Andrew had taken over the care of his daughter, he'd only had to contend with a case of the sniffles and an odd nightmare or two. Never a fever and delirium. "Should I call the doctor or take her to the emergency room?"

Mrs. Purdy shook her head. "Her fever has only been up to 102 degrees. If it goes higher, you should take her to the hospital. For now, she needs to sweat it out." The older woman glanced back up the stairs. "I'd stay, but Mr. Purdy wasn't feeling on top of the weather himself." For the first time, the woman noticed Dix. "I'm sorry. I didn't see you back there." She held out her hand. "I'm Dottie Purdy. And you are?"

Dix held out her hand and opened her mouth to reply.

Before she could, Andrew cut in. "Mrs. Purdy, this is Dix Reeves. She's an old friend who will be staying with us for the next couple of weeks."

Mrs. Purdy smiled and shook Dix's hand. "Oh, that's just lovely. This big old place needs more people to fill it up. I'll be sure to add a plate to the dinner table tomorrow. Anything in particular you prefer to eat, or allergies to anything?"

"I'm pretty open to anything," Dix said. "No allergies."

"Great." Mrs. Purdy beamed. "Then I'll see you two tomorrow. Call if you have any questions about Leigha. My children all went through fevers and upset stomachs a number of times. They all came through just fine." She waved her hand. "Cool compress. Her next dose of Tylenol should be in four hours. Rub a little mentholated cream on her chest if she gets stuffy. Other than that, stay with her. She seemed a little sad and frightened tonight."

Andrew almost stepped in front of Mrs. Purdy to block her from leaving. "Are you sure I'm qualified for this? Should I call a nurse, anyone with more experience?"

Mrs. Purdy patted his scarred cheek. "You have as much experience as most new parents. You'll do fine. And I'm sure Miss Reeves will help."

"Me?" Dix touched a hand to her chest. "I don't know anything about sick children."

"All you have to do is stay with her. Check her temp and keep her calm." Mrs. Purdy glanced at her watch. "I really must go. It will take me quite a while to get home in the fog."

Panic threatened to overwhelm Andrew. He'd had a nanny for Leigha in New York City. And Mrs. Purdy did most everything for him since he'd arrived in Cape Churn and secured her services. He was completely unqualified to deal with a sick little girl.

Mrs. Purdy didn't stay to argue. She was through the door and gone before Andrew could order her to stay. Not that she would. Mrs. Purdy wasn't one of the Wall Street interns he could order around. She did things when she was good and ready, on her own schedule, in her own way. And she kept his house in order.

Dix crossed to the door and twisted the lock behind Mrs. Purdy. "If you'll tell me where I can drop my things, I'll start my inspection of the house."

"I'd like you to start your inspection in Leigha's room," Andrew said.

"Oh, no, you don't. You just want me to take care of your kid." Dix held up her hands. "Just because I'm female doesn't mean I know what to do with a sick child. She's your little girl. *You* fix her."

A weak cry came from above. "Mrs. Purdy? Mr. Stratford? I don't feel good." Sobs followed.

Andrew's gut knotted. So, he didn't know how to take care of a sick little girl. He'd wing it. Leaving Dix standing in the entryway, he took the steps upward, two at a time, and entered the third doorway on the right. The room closest to the master suite.

Leigha lay in the queen-size bed, a small figure swallowed by puffy, cotton-candy-pink blankets. Her long blond hair fanned across the pillow and her face was even paler than normal. Brewer lay at her feet, his chin between his paws, his tail thumping against the comforter.

"Hey, Leigha. Mrs. Purdy had to go home."

She stared up at him, her eyes wide. "Who's going to take care of me?"

Andrew sat on the edge of the bed and brushed a strand of hair out of her face. His hands felt so big and clumsy next to her delicate features. God, he wished Mrs. Purdy hadn't left. "I guess you're stuck with me."

Footsteps sounded outside the bedroom door.

Andrew shot a glance over his shoulder.

Dix peeked in and added, "And me."

Leigha's eyes widened. She reached for Andrew's hand and whispered, "Who's she?"

Andrew waved his hand behind him, urging Dix forward. "Leigha, this is Dix. Dix, this is Leigha."

Leigha's brows lowered. "What is she doing here?"

Andrew hated lying to the child, but he needed her

to trust Dix. "Dix is my friend, and she's come to stay with us for a little while. I'm counting on you to show her around. This place is so big, she might get lost."

"I don't feel like showing her around. My tummy hurts."

"You don't have to show me around today, sweetie." Dix entered the room and came to stand beside Andrew. "Maybe when you get better?" She reached out her hand to the dog. "Is this your dog?"

Leigha nodded.

"What's his name?" Dix asked.

"Brewer."

Dix scratched behind Brewer's ears. "Does Brewer like to listen to stories?"

Leigha frowned up at Dix. "Brewer's a dog. He doesn't always understand people."

Andrew hid a grin. His daughter wasn't going to give Dix an inch. She'd have to work for a connection.

His new bodyguard walked over to a shelf and thumbed through the colorful books. "I bet he likes it when you talk to him, doesn't he?" Dix lifted a book off of a shelf. "Do you think he would like it if I read to him?"

The little girl closed her eyes. "He might." She reached for Andrew's hand and squeezed it, uncaring that it had burn scars and didn't feel like a normal hand. She didn't mind that he wasn't perfect. She always seemed glad that he was just himself. His heart swelled. This little girl he hadn't known he had until a year ago was his.

"What would he like to listen to?" Dix asked.

"He likes the book about the island and the blue dolphins."

Andrew almost laughed out loud. From claiming Brewer was just a dog to admitting the animal would like to listen to the book *Island of the Blue Dolphins*, Leigha had come full circle.

Score one for Dix. Despite her claim that she didn't

know anything about children, she'd gotten Leigha to come around to her way of thinking without having to order her to do so.

Andrew nodded. "I'll let you three get to it." He started to rise but was stopped by the little hand holding his.

"Please stay, Mr. Stratford." Leigha stared up at him with glassy blue eyes, her face flushed and her body hot.

"Tell you what…" Dix handed the book to Andrew. "Let your father start the story, while I get a fresh cloth to cool your face."

"But Brewer wants to hear *you* read," Leigha said.

"And I will. After I get something to cool you down." Dix drew an X across her chest. "Cross my heart."

"Okay." Leigha turned to her father.

Outmaneuvered by the woman, Andrew opened the book. "Where should I start?"

"At the beginning." Leigha closed her eyes and lay back against the pillow.

Andrew started reading.

Dix disappeared into the room's adjoining bathroom and returned with a damp cloth. She folded it several times and laid it across Leigha's forehead.

Andrew couldn't help noting how gentle Dix was with his little girl. The woman was a natural with kids. While he read, Andrew studied Dix out of the corner of his eye.

Without makeup and her hair hanging loose around her shoulders, she wasn't a classic beauty. Her shoulders and arm muscles were well-defined and taut. She didn't have an ounce of fat on her body. Whatever she'd done before going to work for Fontaine, she'd kept physically fit. No, she wasn't like Tazer, a woman who could pose for a fashion magazine. Nor was she bone-thin, like so many runway models who looked like they could use a big hamburger or treatment for an eating disorder.

No, Dix was what Andrew would call a healthy, granola girl, adept at hiking up hills without breaking into a sweat. She might even be capable of scaling cliffs with her bare hands.

But at that moment she was showing a side of herself she probably didn't know she had. A side that made Andrew look at her in a whole new way.

The tenderness with which she applied the cool cloth to Leigha's brow and cheeks was nothing short of maternal. She moved slowly, carefully patting Leigha's face as she smiled down at the child.

So engrossed in watching Dix's movements, at one point, Andrew forgot to read.

"I'm not asleep yet." Leigha opened her eyes. "Please keep reading."

"Sorry," Andrew said, shaking aside his obsessive desire to watch Dix's every move.

Dix chuckled low in her chest.

The sound made Andrew warm all over and he wanted her to do it again. He jerked his attention back to the book and read each word, without really seeing them or absorbing the story.

As he ended the first chapter, Andrew realized two things.

Leigha had fallen asleep and Dix had chinked away a piece of the wall he'd erected around himself.

That would not do. The woman was a hired hand. A temporary one at that.

The sooner he found a replacement bodyguard, the better.

Chapter 4

Dix smiled down at the little girl with the spun-gold hair splayed out on the pillow. She remembered a picture of herself at about Leigha's age. Her hair had been long and wavy, and she'd been full of curiosity and mischief. Her mother had never been able to keep up with her. Looking back, she was surprised she'd lived through some of her more dangerous escapades.

If her mother had known where she'd been exploring, she would have had more gray hair. To the young Dix, life had been one big adventure.

Joining the military had been a logical choice for Dix. She related better with men than with women, and she'd always liked getting dirty and shooting guns with her father. In fact, she liked fishing, hunting, yard work and anything her father had liked. Housekeeping, cooking and laundry had been her least favorite things to do growing up. She'd been happiest outdoors in the sunshine.

So why did her heart skip several beats and then tighten in her chest when she stared down at the little girl lying against the cool sheets, her body warm from fever?

Something she'd never felt before welled up inside. A fierce desire to protect this small creature so dependent on adults to keep her well and alive. Was this how parents felt about their children? While her mother had wanted to hold her back, she'd done it out of a desire to keep her safe. Her father, on the other hand, had wanted to share his love of the outdoors with her, to show her some of what she could do if she broadened her mind beyond the walls of their little house in the country.

The deep, resonant tone of Mr. Stratford's voice filled the room, making it seem smaller, more intimate. The soft glow of the lamp on the nightstand brought them closer together. They probably looked like a family.

Dix jerked upright. She hadn't come to Stratford's mansion to become part of his family. She'd come to protect this family.

She glanced around, wondering where Leigha's mother was and why she wasn't there, taking care of her child.

Fontaine had told her she would be the bodyguard for the Stratford family. From what she could tell, that family consisted of two. Father and daughter. And the daughter called her father "Mr. Stratford."

Why?

As her father read, Leigha's eyes closed. Dix backed away from the bed, her hand clenching around the damp cloth. Her goal was to leave the room and perform the search of the giant house for any weaknesses in entry and exit points.

She'd almost made it to the door when a little voice said, "Please, don't go."

Dix turned to find Leigha staring across the room at her, her cheeks flushed, her eyes glassy.

"Your father will stay with you," Dix pointed out, hating to disappoint the girl but feeling the need to escape. This sweet little family scene threatened to choke her. After all she'd been through, she doubted seriously she'd ever have children of her own or be the mother they needed.

"But I want you to stay, too," she said, her voice trailing off, a single tear slipping from the corner of her eye. "I don't feel good." She raised her little hand, reaching for Dix.

Mr. Stratford stopped reading and turned to add his gaze to his daughter's.

Her heart contracting, Dix couldn't step through the door and leave when the little girl had asked her so sweetly to stay.

She sighed. "I'm only going to wet the cloth again and make it cooler. I'll be right back." Dix changed direction and headed into the bathroom. There she turned on the cold water and dipped the cloth beneath. While she soaked and squeezed the excess out, she stared at her reflection in the mirror.

I can't do this.

Fighting in the MMA had given her an outlet for her anger and sorrow. Without it, she had no way to channel the energy or to push aside the pain.

This father and daughter pair already had her gut tied into a very twisted knot and she hadn't been there for even a day.

Dix's parents had died in a helicopter crash while touring the Grand Canyon. She'd been deep in Army Ranger training on the field training exercise when it had happened. The training officers hadn't told her until she'd completed the most challenging portion of the exercise.

No one had been there when she'd graduated, nor had she had the opportunity to celebrate because she'd gotten right onto a plane and flown to her home state of Texas to attend her mother and father's funeral.

Going home had been the hardest thing she'd ever done in her life. The house hadn't been the same without her mother and father in it. She'd listed it with a Realtor, packed a few photo albums, her great-grandmother's antique candy dish and given the rest of the furnishings and clothing to a local charity.

She hadn't had much time to manage it all before she'd had to report back to her new unit only to ship out within two weeks to the war zone.

All of those memories were still raw, even though it had been years.

Dix glanced down at the cloth she'd squeezed so much it barely retained any water. She dampened it and started over. A minute later she returned to Leigha's bedroom and draped the cloth over the girl's forehead.

"You came back," she whispered and reached for Dix's hand. She pulled her closer until Dix was forced to sit on the side of the bed.

The little fingers in hers were too warm. She wondered how long it would take for the fever to break. If it didn't, they might be making an emergency trip to the hospital before the night was over.

Mr. Stratford glanced up, his gaze connecting with Dix's.

A sharp stab of awareness coursed through Dix's veins. She averted her gaze and stared down at the little hand resting in hers.

Stratford started another chapter of the book, his voice droning on until Leigha finally slept.

Dix slipped her hand free of Leigha's and stood.

"You can go. I'll take it from here," Mr. Stratford said.

With a nod, Dix left the room. Once in the hallway, she dragged in several deep breaths before she started down the stairs and took her time going through each room on the ground floor, checking windows and doors to ensure they were all secured.

All the while, she thought of the little girl and her father in the room upstairs. Other than a housekeeper and a dog, they seemed incredibly alone in the huge old mansion. How sad. Even if the mansion was a family inheritance, she would have converted it into the hotel it seemed more suited for or she'd have sold it. The McGregors had the right idea converting their big old house into a bed-and-breakfast. At least it was full of people, not dark and lonely.

All of the doors and windows on the first floor were secured. In the kitchen, she found a door leading into the basement. She flipped the light switch. A yellowed bulb gave an eerie glow that barely lit the stairs halfway down. Hollywood had given basements a bad reputation. Everyone knew a lone female going into the basement by herself was a bad idea. It never ended well.

Dix snorted. Having trained in snake-infested swamps as well as having significant experience in hand-to-hand combat and mixed martial arts, she didn't consider a basement a threat. But she wasn't stupid. Dix grabbed a butcher knife from a drawer and descended the stairs. At the bottom, she found another switch. When she flipped it, bulbs lit at different locations. Some appeared burned out.

The space below the mansion was almost as exten-

sive as the first floor, broken up by thick posts, crates,
old furniture, a room set up as a wine cellar and stacks
of cardboard boxes. A veritable maze. Scattered around
the outer walls were tiny windows and one exit leading
to a trapdoor that probably opened out into a garden. She
pushed against the door. It held firm, no matter how hard
she tried to open it. In the morning she'd check it from
the outside. She suspected it had a padlock holding it in
place. The small windows were locked and, other than a
creepy feeling, the basement appeared secure.

As she started for the stairs, something moved in the
shadows with a scuffling sound. As big as the house was,
it might have a mouse or rat problem.

A shiver slipped down Dix's spine and her hand tightened around the handle of the butcher knife. She inched
forward, her ears straining to pick up the sound again.
If she could pinpoint the direction, she might actually
find the culprit.

There it was again. Only this time it sounded more
like a footstep. Dix ducked behind a stack of boxes and
waited. Whoever it was shouldn't be sneaking around
the basement. If it was Mr. Stratford, he would have announced his presence, wouldn't he?

Or was he like her, wondering who would be sneaking around a basement so late at night? Dix opened her
mouth to say something, announcing her presence. She
didn't want to startle the man. He could be carrying a gun
and react by shooting first, asking questions later. Before
she said anything, she shut her mouth and remained silent. The footsteps faded away into silence.

Dix waited several minutes before moving again. Why
hadn't Stratford said something? If he'd come down to
the wine cellar, he would have passed her stack of boxes.
But no one had walked past her hiding place.

Shrugging the tension from her shoulders, she stepped out from behind the boxes, calling herself every kind of fool. She knew better than to let a creepy old mansion scare her. It was just a building. She'd performed sweeps of many buildings in her Army career. The difference being she'd carried an M4A1 rifle, worn protective gear and had a trained team backing her.

She had just placed her first foot on the bottom step leading up to the kitchen when the lights blinked out.

The darkness in the basement was so complete, Dix couldn't see anything but the sliver of light beneath the door to the kitchen at the top of the stairs. But, wait— how could the light be on in the kitchen and not in the basement? Someone had to have turned out the lights or a breaker had tripped to cut the electricity to the lights where she stood.

The sound of wood crashing against the concrete floor made Dix jump. She stumbled against the riser, nearly stabbing herself with the butcher knife as she scrambled for a handhold. She found her footing and raced up the steps toward the slim bit of light finding its way beneath the door.

At the top, Dix held her breath, twisted the knob, flung open the door and burst into the kitchen, running into a solid wall of muscles.

A strong hand wrapped around her wrist, holding it and the butcher knife at a distance.

"Didn't your mother ever tell you not to run with a knife in your hand?"

At the sound of Stratford's voice, Dix sagged against him, at once relieved, quickly followed by chagrin that he'd found her running out of a scary basement because of a noise. Some bodyguard she'd prove to be if his house gave her the willies.

She pushed her free hand against his chest, inhaling the faint yet tantalizing scent of aftershave. "Thank you, but I was doing fine until you stepped in my way."

He chuckled. "Where were you going, brandishing that butcher knife?"

She pulled her hand free and tilted her chin. "I was headed to the drawer to put it away." As if to prove out her lie, she walked to the drawer where she'd found the knife and slipped it in. Gathering her wits, she turned to face him, her brows rising. "I have a question."

"Try me. I might have an answer."

"Where's the breaker box?"

His brows dipped. "Why do you ask?"

"The lights went out in the basement while I was down there checking windows and doors."

His frown deepened. "The breaker box is in the basement. I had the wiring upgraded several years ago. Since then, I can't recall having issues with breakers being thrown." He walked to the door Dix had stormed through a moment before and flipped the light switch. The light came on. "Seems to be working now."

Dix's face heated. Could she have hit the switches by accident?

"I'll check the breaker box, just to make sure. But if this light is on, the others will come on, as well. The basement is all wired to the same breaker."

Dix nodded. "I'd feel better if you did check. Perhaps there's a short in one of the wires."

Mr. Stratford descended the steps.

Dix followed, wishing she'd brought the butcher knife.

A wooden chair that had been stacked on top of an old table lay on the ground, its legs broken and splintered. She could have brushed by, dislodging it from its perch. But that still didn't explain the lights extinguishing when they did.

She followed Stratford to a metal box mounted in the wall. He opened it, ran his finger down through the labels until he stopped on the one marked Basement. He flipped the switch and the lights went out.

The breath caught in Dix's lungs and she strained to hear the sound of footsteps, like she had a few minutes before. Silence stretched until another loud click heralded the lights coming back on.

Stratford turned to her. "Seems to be working fine."

Great. She looked like an idiot. But that didn't bother her as much as the memory of shuffling footsteps when she'd been hiding behind the cardboard boxes.

She didn't believe there was a real problem with the electricity. The problem was that something or someone had to have flipped the breaker to make all of the lights in the basement go out at once.

"Besides you, me and Leigha, are there any other people who live in this house?"

Stratford shook his head. "No. Mrs. Purdy comes in every day to cook and clean for us. But that's it."

Dix nodded. She'd be sure to carry a gun with her whenever she entered the basement. If for nothing else, to shoot at the rats.

"Any more questions?" he asked.

"Yes." She stared up into his eyes. "Where will I sleep?"

Stratford cupped her elbow in his hand and led her toward the stairs. "I have Leigha in the room next to mine with an adjoining door. I'd like for you to sleep in the bedroom beside hers."

Dix nodded, her skin tingling where his hand rested on her arm. In a structure the size of Stratford House, she could have been assigned a room in a completely different wing. She was glad he put her close to Leigha for the child's sake. But being close to the man added an entirely different dimension to this task. "One more question."

His lips quirked on the corners, making the wicked scar less menacing. "Shoot."

"Where's Leigha's mother?"

The hint of a smile vanished, replaced by a fierce frown. "Why do you need to know?"

"I was sent to protect the family. I assumed husband, wife and child. If I'm to protect the entire family, I need to know who that consists of."

"All you need to be worried about is making sure Leigha is safe. I can take care of myself."

Dix persisted. Stratford wasn't happy about something and he was avoiding a direct response. "Your wife?" She held her breath, part of her hoping there wasn't a wife. The other part of her wondering why she cared. She'd just met the man.

"Leigha's mother is dead."

Andrew turned away from Dix and marched up the steps to the kitchen. He didn't wait for her to follow. The sooner he got away from her, the better. All the old rage roiled up in his belly, threatening to take him to that dark place he'd lived in when he'd been in the hospital suffering the pain of skin grafts. All because of Jeannette and her horrible, hateful revenge.

A hand on his arm slowed him to a stop. He breathed in and out like a bull preparing for the charge, but he refused to face Dix.

"As a bodyguard, I feel like the more I know about you, Leigha and this place, the better equipped I'll be to take care of all of you. I'm sorry. I didn't mean to step over the line. I didn't know."

"I told you—I don't need anyone to take care of me. Focus on Leigha. She's the one who needs you. Not me." He shrugged her hand off his arm.

"I'm sorry. Losing your wife is hard enough without someone dragging up the memory. You must have loved her a lot."

Fury surged upward. Andrew was powerless to hold back. He spun, gripped Dix's arms and shook her. "Jeannette wasn't my wife, and I can honestly say that I hated her with every fiber of my being. Any mother who could willfully set fire to the apartment she shares with her daughter, and then stand by watching it burn with her daughter inside, is a monster. I'm glad she's dead." He shook her again. "Do you hear me? I might rot in hell, but I'm glad she's dead."

Chapter 5

Dix lay in the bed one door down from Leigha, her arms sore from where Andrew had squeezed so hard he'd left bruises. Yeah, they hurt, but nothing like whatever it was Andrew had gone through. She assumed the scars on his face and hand were caused by the fire Leigha's mother had set.

Though he'd answered the question about a wife, he'd left so many more unanswered. Was Leigha his daughter? If so, why did she call him "Mr. Stratford"? Question after question spun through Dix's mind to the point she couldn't go to sleep.

She rose from the bed and padded barefoot down the hall to Leigha's room. Pushing open the door, she entered. A night-light shone in a corner, giving just enough light for Dix to see everything in the room, including the little girl in the middle of the big bed.

Leigha stopped beside the bed and laid her hand on Leigha's forehead. Thankfully, the fever seemed to have broken and the child appeared to be resting comfortably.

Grateful Leigha was better, Dix turned toward the door.

"Stay with me." The little girl's voice stopped her before she could take a single step.

Dix smiled down at her and brushed a strand of golden-blond hair away from Leigha's brow. "Why aren't you sleeping?"

"Sometimes I get scared," she said, taking Dix's hand in hers.

"Are you scared now?"

She pressed Dix's hand to her cheek. "Not when you're here with me."

Dix's heart melted a little at the girl's puppy-dog eyes. "Sweetie, you don't even know me."

"My friend said I could trust you."

Dix's hand tightened around the child's. "Your friend?"

The child nodded. "He said you're one of the good guys."

Dix perched on the side of the bed, wishing she'd stopped long enough to pull on a pair of jeans. The extra-large T-shirt didn't seem fully adequate should Leigha's father choose to come in and check on his girl. But then, Leigha had Dix's hand and didn't seem willing to relinquish it anytime soon. "How does he know I won't hurt you?"

She shrugged. "He just does." Leigha scooted to the far side of the bed and threw back the blanket. "You can lie down, too. I won't kick."

With her legs cooling in the night air and Leigha still holding tightly to her hand, Dix caved. She slid between the sheets and laid her head on the pillow beside Leigha.

The child immediately rolled into her side and rested her head in the crook of Dix's arm. "You smell like flowers."

Dix smiled. "It's probably the soap from the bathroom."

"I think it smells good on you." Leigha snuggled into Dix's side and laid her arm over Dix's stomach.

Dix sniffed the girl's hair. It had that soft, clean smell of baby shampoo. "You smell pretty good yourself."

Leigha hugged her. "My friend thinks you're pretty."

Dix stiffened momentarily and then relaxed. She supposed many children had imaginary friends to keep them company when they were lonely. "Does your friend have a name?"

She nodded, her eyelids drooping. "Bennet."

"Do you play with your friend often?" Dix asked.

"Every day," she whispered, her voice fading as her breathing grew deeper.

For a long time, Dix lay with the little girl nestling against her. She listened to the sounds the mansion made, creaking like an old lady's knees as she settled in for the night.

A few days on the Oregon coast keeping track of one little girl who could very easily steal her heart wasn't bad for her first gig as a Stealth Operations Specialist. She would ease into her role and learn more about the man who'd engaged her and his expectations of the bodyguard he'd hired.

The black Lab, lying at the end of the bed, rolled over onto her foot, completely relaxed. Acceptance by two of her clients had been accomplished. Now all she needed was to win the approval of the head of the family, one darkly brooding, deeply scarred man who didn't mince words or waste time. But he did read to his daughter when she wasn't feeling good, and he cared enough to hire someone to keep her safe from an unknown threat.

Tomorrow, Dix would ask him who might have it in for him and the exact nature of the inciting incidents that had set him on the course to finding a bodyguard for his daughter. In the meantime, her charge was to protect

Leigha. With the little girl sleeping soundly against her side, Dix let her eyes slide closed.

Just as she was about to drift into sleep, a waft of cool air caressed her skin. Her eyelids fluttered open and she stared up at a man with black hair and dancing blue eyes, a smile curling his lips. His clothes appeared to be from another era. Wearing a dark suit and a fedora, he could have been a gangster from the early nineteen hundreds.

Was she dreaming? She blinked and the image was gone.

Dix gasped and jackknifed into a sitting position, her heartbeat thundering against her ribs.

Leigha lay with one hand tucked beneath her cheek and the other reaching out to Dix. Brewer lifted his head as if to question her for waking in the middle of the night. Then, as if his head were too heavy to hold up, he let it drop back to the blanket and sighed.

Had an intruder been in the room, surely the dog would have let her know or at the least been agitated.

Convinced the man she'd seen was nothing more than the beginning of a dream, Dix lay back on the pillow and willed her pulse to slow. Dreams of bygone eras had to be the norm for guests of Stratford House. The structure and the furnishings conjured ghosts of the past. If not real aberrations, then those dreamed up in the minds of present-day inhabitants. No wonder Leigha had an imaginary friend.

Dix finally relaxed. The day had been full of revelations and tomorrow she'd learn more about her new assignment. For now, sleep claimed her, sweeping her into a dream that spanned a continent and swept her out to sea in a mobster's yacht.

Andrew lay in his bed, tossing and turning, drifting in and out of sleep. He fought the lure of the recurring nightmare that had plagued him for almost a year. But every time he closed his eyes to sleep, the dream returned, filling his night with memories of that awful day. Pulling him back into that flaming inferno of Jeannette's apartment building—an image he could never erase from his mind. He'd go into the blaze to rescue the daughter he hadn't known he had until that day he'd gone into hell to bring her out.

Jeannette had been a willing partner, but she'd failed to tell him she was married when they'd met in a bar in New York City. He'd been drunk, celebrating a Yankees win, when she'd invited him to her hotel room.

One night of sex he couldn't even remember, and six years later he'd gotten a call from a woman he couldn't recall, claiming he had a daughter.

When he'd called her bluff, Jeannette had told him she couldn't afford to keep the brat since her husband had left her. If he didn't take her, she'd leave her in the apartment where she couldn't afford to pay rent.

At first Andrew chose to ignore the call. After all, he was a wealthy man. The woman could be scamming him.

When she'd called a second and third time, more desperate than the first, she described a tattoo Andrew had on his right butt cheek. She claimed the child had his blue eyes. She couldn't keep her. Her landlord had threatened to evict them. With nowhere to go and no way to support a child, she had no other choice but to end it for both of them.

At that point, Andrew couldn't ignore the woman. A child's life could be at stake. He coaxed an address out of her and, in the middle of the night, he'd raced to the apartment building in a ramshackle section of the Bronx. When he arrived, smoke billowed from a window on the third floor of an eight-story building.

Women in bathrobes and men in boxer shorts herded small children from the building as Andrew ran inside and up the stairs to the third floor. Alarms blared but the sprinkler system never came on.

Choking on the acrid smoke, Andrew pulled his T-shirt up over his mouth and nose and pressed on, arriving at the door to the apartment where most of the smoke seemed to be coming from. He tried the handle. The door was locked. With the potential of a child being trapped inside, Andrew threw his shoulder into the door. It didn't budge. He kicked and kicked until the door frame splintered around the dead bolt and the door swung open, emitting a cloud of black smoke.

Andrew crouched low and ran inside. His eyes had stung and his lungs had burned. He found Jeannette throwing a burning blanket over a couch.

When she saw him, she screamed and tried to run past him. "You didn't want her. Nobody wanted her."

Andrew grabbed her by the arms. He didn't recognize the woman like she was, her hair tangled, her face streaked with soot. He didn't care if the child was his or not—she didn't deserve to die in a fire lit by a crazy woman. "Where is she?" he shouted.

"You can't have her. No one can have her!" The woman kicked him hard in the shins.

His grip loosened and she flung herself away from him. Before he could catch her, she ran screaming into one of the two bedrooms and slammed the door.

The other bedroom was completely consumed in flames. Andrew prayed the child hadn't been in there. He focused his attention on the room into which Jeannette had run.

This door didn't take long to breach. Two hard kicks

and it crashed open. Andrew searched through the thickening smoke and couldn't find the woman or the child.

Then he heard a whimper from beneath the bed. He crouched below the curtain of smoke and spied Jeannette holding on to a little girl. The child coughed and cried, "I'm scared, Mama!"

"Shut up!" Jeannette yelled. "Shut up!" She pulled her deeper beneath the bed.

Andrew reached in to grab the girl, but Jeannette lashed out with clawlike fingernails, scratching his arm. He pulled his hand back, but the heat of the blaze behind him pushed him to try harder. "Don't do this to her, Jeannette. Let's get out of here. I'll make sure you're all taken care of."

She spit at him and clutched the child closer. "No! You can't take her from me."

"You wanted me to get her. I'm here now. Let me take her."

"No one wanted her. No one cared about me. We're leaving this world and taking this stinking apartment building with us."

Andrew couldn't stand by and let that happen. He grabbed what he could. His finger wrapped in the woman's hair and he dragged her out into the open. She let go of the little girl and fought like a wildcat.

The child slipped back beneath the bed. Andrew couldn't take care of her until he subdued the animal Jeannette had become.

He grabbed her around the middle and held on.

She freed one of her hands and raked her nails down the side of his face.

Pain seared through him, but he didn't let go. He carried her to the apartment door and shoved her out into the hallway, peeling her claws off of his arms. She had been like an octopus, clinging to him, refusing to let him return to rescue the girl.

Finally, he freed himself, slammed the door in her face and ran back into the thick smoke. He staggered into the bedroom, his eyes burning so badly he could barely see.

Dropping to his hands and knees, he crawled under the bed, grabbed the girl by her leg and dragged her out.

She cried, coughed and wrapped her arms around his neck, burying her face in his shirt. "Help me!"

When he turned toward the exit, the flames leaped. By then the blaze was so hot, Andrew felt as if he and the child would be cooked alive if he took a step back into the living room. He closed the bedroom door, grabbed a chair and flung it through a window. Smoke poured out into the night. He kicked the jagged shards out of the way and leaned out, hoping for a breath of fresh air.

Several emergency vehicles were parked on the street below, lights flashing, and the first responders were unloading equipment. Some ran toward the burning building.

People huddled in small groups, pointing upward to the window through which Andrew leaned. He wished he and the girl could be counted among them. Instead of hanging out a window, uncertain of their fate.

An explosion behind him nearly knocked him and the child over the ledge.

Two firefighters leaned an extension ladder against the wall of the building and one man started up. When he neared the top, he reached for the child.

The little girl refused to let go. Andrew finally peeled her arms from around his neck and handed her to the firefighter. Step by step, he eased back down the ladder, careful not to drop the girl.

The door exploded behind him and Jeannette ran in,

carrying a flaming blanket. She tried to throw it at Andrew, but it tangled in her arms and caught her hair on fire.

Screaming, she ran around in circles, trying to pat the fire out with the blazing blanket.

Andrew tackled her, slapping at the flames with his bare hands. Pain seared through his skin. Jeannette pushed him off, ran for the window, hiked herself up over the sill and flung herself out.

Numb from pain and the smoke filling his lungs, Andrew dragged himself back to the window and over the ledge. One hand had been burned so badly he couldn't use it to hold on to the metal ladder. One rung at a time, he eased himself downward. Ten feet from the ground, his body and lungs gave up the fight. He fell the rest of the way, landing beside the limp body of the woman who'd condemned her daughter to death. Then he passed out.

A sound woke Andrew from the nightmare. He sat up, drenched in sweat, and pushed his hand through his hair. Why couldn't time heal his mind? Surely a year was enough to push the horrible event from his memories.

Another noise penetrated the lingering haze of his dream and he tilted his head, straining to pinpoint the direction. It was coming from Leigha's bedroom.

He flung back the covers, leaped from the bed and ran through the connecting door, skidding to a halt at the foot of her bed.

Leigha lay sleeping peacefully, her body curled into the side of Dix's.

Dix's eyes were open and she had a finger pressed to her lips. "She's fine, just wanted someone to hold her," she whispered.

Andrew let go of the breath he'd been holding and relaxed. Seeing the two of them lying there so close made him realize just how similar they were. Leigha had golden-blond hair. So did Dix. Leigha had blue eyes like him, that clear ice blue. Though Dix had moss green eyes, on first impression, she could pass as Leigha's mother.

Andrew's chest tightened and he squeezed his fists, the pull on his scars a painful reminder he wasn't the man he used to be. Scarred and besieged by horrific nightmares, he wasn't fit to be anything to anybody. Leigha was his only concern. Making her life better, giving her the happiness she deserved after what she'd been through, was his number one priority. Andrew was surprised the child didn't have more nightmares than she did.

Andrew backed up a step, determined to return to his room and forget how different he'd pictured his life. Then he remembered why he'd come into the room in the first place. "I heard a noise. Did you?"

Dix's cheeks flushed with color and her gaze darted to a corner. "Sorry. I was having a bad dream. I might have called out."

With a nod, Andrew took another step backward. "I know how it feels," he muttered. A little louder he said, "Sleep well." And he left the room, almost running back to his own.

For a long time, he lay in the bed, unwilling to go back to sleep, knowing the nightmare would return. Instead he filled his mind with the image of Leigha and Dix holding each other. It warmed his heart and eventually allowed him to drift into a deep, dreamless sleep. Deep down, he knew it was a mistake to frame that image in his mind. Dix was a temporary solution, not to be confused with a permanent relationship. That could never happen.

Chapter 6

"Dix?" a tiny voice whispered in her ear.

Dix tried to brush the sound away with her hand.

Little fingers caught her hand and held on. "Dix, are you awake?"

"No," Dix answered, trying to pull her hand free. She opened her eyes and closed them immediately as sunlight assaulted them with cheerful brightness. "Please tell me it's not morning."

A little giggle sounded beside her and a warm, soft body squirmed against her side. "Okay, I won't tell you. But you have to get up soon. My tummy is rumbling and I smell bacon."

Dix inhaled the mouthwatering scent and the rest of her body came alive. "Wow, that does smell like bacon." She rolled over to face Leigha. "What are we waiting for?"

"Last one to the kitchen is a rotten egg." Leigha leaped out of bed and ran for the door.

"Last one *dressed* and down to the kitchen is a rotten egg." Dix rolled out of the bed, onto her feet, and raced for the bedroom door. She ran out into the hall and smacked into a wall of muscles.

She staggered back but a hand on her arm kept her from falling. She glanced up into the twinkling blue eyes of Andrew Stratford. For a moment he looked familiar. Then she remembered the more rakish image of a man with similar hair color and those sparkling blue eyes. She rubbed her hand over her eyes and looked again. No, it was her client, Mr. Stratford. Perhaps her mind had played tricks on her with the ghostly image of a mobster Andrew Stratford.

"Are you all right, Miss Reeves?" His hands on her arms tightened.

"I am. And I can stand on my own."

Immediately he released her and dropped his arms to his sides. Then his brows rose into the tuft of hair that fell over his forehead. "Do you always run around half dressed?"

Heat burned in her cheeks as Dix remembered she'd gone to bed in an oversize T-shirt and not much more. The hem more than covered all of the important parts, but it only came down to just below her bottom, with a long expanse of legs left bare. "I was just headed to my room to dress."

A whirl of pink flashed by her, long curls flying out behind as Leigha darted between them and ran for the staircase. "I'm not going to be a rotten egg!" Her little feet moved in double time as she descended the staircase.

"Slow down!" Stratford yelled.

"Can't," Leigha responded. "You wouldn't want me to be a rotten egg, would you?"

Dix chuckled.

Her client frowned. "What is she talking about?"

"I told her the last one dressed and down to the kitchen would be a rotten egg." Dix shrugged. "I guess that will be me. If you'll excuse me, I'll put on something more presentable."

His frown deepened. "Do that."

Dix turned and started for the door down the hall, but something made her turn back to her client. "You know, you look a lot more approachable when you smile." She held up her hand to stop him from saying anything. "Just saying." Then she ducked through the door and closed it behind her. She didn't require a response, and she knew it wasn't her place to tell the client he had a grumpy face. But, boy, it transformed when he smiled. That smile practically made her heart flutter and her knees grow weak.

Hmm. Maybe it was better if he continued to frown. She didn't need the distraction of his smile muddying her perspective.

She threw on a clean, if wrinkled, T-shirt and a pair of blue jeans, slipped into her brogan boots and pulled her hair back in a ponytail. Satisfied she was ready to work, she eased open the door to the hallway. Thankfully, Stratford wasn't there for her to crash into again. She found standing so close to him to be very unnerving. The breadth of his shoulders and the incredible blue of his eyes made her feel a little off balance, not quite on her game.

Dix followed the smell of bacon to the kitchen.

Mrs. Purdy stood at the stove, ladling a spoonful of scrambled eggs onto a plate. "Oh, there you are. Miss Leigha has been talking nonstop about you."

Dix drew in a long, deep sniff. "Is that bacon I smell?"

"No, it's rotten eggs," Leigha piped in and giggled. "I beat you down."

"And so you did." Dix rubbed her hand over the little girl's hair. "I'll be smelling like rotten eggs for a week."

"Don't be silly. That's only pretend." She smiled up at her. "Are you staying here forever?" Leigha's gaze shone up at Dix, her brows high and her expression hopeful.

"I don't know about that, but I'm here now and I'm going to be with you all day." Dix patted the child's cheek. "How does that sound?"

"Great!" Leigha said, bouncing in her seat.

Dix turned toward the housekeeper. "Is there anything I can do to help?"

"No, ma'am. You just sit there and keep Leigha company while I serve up your breakfast." Mrs. Purdy leaned toward Dix. "I'm just glad the little sweetheart is feeling better this morning."

Dix snorted. "You'd never know she'd been sick last night."

Mrs. Purdy sighed. "Oh, to be so young and resilient again." She handed Dix a plate piled with fluffy scrambled eggs, bacon and biscuits. "Enjoy."

"This isn't all for me, is it?"

"Honey, you'll need all the energy you can get to keep up with that one." Mrs. Purdy tipped her head toward Leigha.

"Surely one little girl won't be that much trouble."

"Not at all, but she's constant motion. If you try to keep up with her, you'll be going from the time she leaves that table until the time her head hits the pillow." Mrs. Purdy turned back to the skillet. "Trust me. I speak from experience."

Dix sat across the table from Leigha. "Is she right? Are you constantly on the go?"

Leigha looked up, wide-eyed. "Who, me?"

"Are there any other little girls in this room?" Dix asked.

Leigha glanced around and shrugged. "No."

"Then that would mean you."

Her brows dipped and she puffed out her chest. "I don't get into trouble."

"But I imagine sometimes you disappear?" Dix queried.

Leigha's frown deepened. "No, I don't." She held up her arm. "I can see me." She stared up at Dix. "Can't you?"

"Yes, but—"

The little girl didn't wait for Dix to explain. She looked past Dix and asked, "Can you see me, Mr. Stratford?"

"I certainly can."

The deep voice behind Dix made her jump.

Footsteps brought the man around the table to ruffle his daughter's hair.

Dix tensed with a forkful of eggs remaining poised halfway to her mouth. The air around her seemed to sizzle with Stratford's presence.

"I see Mrs. Purdy has been busy this morning. She's the best cook on the entire Oregon coast."

Mrs. Purdy laughed. "I wouldn't say that. I can stir a pan of eggs and make a mean lasagna, but I'm not quite as good as Nora Taggert."

"Mrs. Taggert's got nothing on you," Stratford insisted.

"You know best." Mrs. Purdy shifted her spatula in the pan full of eggs. "Speaking of which… You remember I'm leaving at noon today. I'm taking my husband in to Portland for a doctor's appointment. I won't be back until tomorrow. You'll have to fend for yourself for dinner tonight."

"No worries, Mrs. P.," Stratford said. "I can open a can of beans."

"I can burn toast on a good day," Dix offered. She really was terrible in the kitchen. "I can make a decent salad. Basically, I'm hopeless at anything that requires an oven or stove."

Mrs. Purdy turned to face Dix. "You three should go out to the Seaside Café and sample some of Nora's fine cooking. Then you can judge for yourself who's the better cook."

Dix noted the frown descending on Stratford's face. Already he was shaking his head.

Leigha bounced in her chair. "Mrs. Taggert has ice-cream cones. Please, Mr. Stratford. Please can we go?"

"I don't know," Stratford said.

"It's been months since you got out of this old monstrosity of a house," Mrs. Purdy pointed out. "It would do you good." She turned to Dix. "And you need to show Miss Reeves around town. If she's staying for a while, she needs to know where to find things."

Dix glanced up at Stratford and almost grinned at his discomfort. She found the fact interesting that a man as strong and handsome as he was didn't like leaving the house.

He lifted a hand to his scarred cheek, his lips pressing into a line. "Miss Reeves can take Leigha. I'll stay home. I have work to do."

"Oh, pooh. That's your code for 'I don't want to.' Your friend needs someone to show her around the town. As her host, you have a responsibility to do that. No, you should have the decency to give her a tour of Cape Churn. Show her where to find groceries, the drugstore, library, sheriff's office and anywhere else she might need at a moment's notice."

The more Mrs. Purdy pushed, the deeper Stratford's frown grew.

"If she ends up watching out for Leigha, she needs to know these things." Mrs. Purdy crossed her arms over her chest.

"Okay. I'll do it." He pointed at the stove. "You're burning my eggs."

Mrs. Purdy threw her hands in the air and spun back to the stove to rescue the eggs, muttering, "Wouldn't have burned them if my boss wasn't so darned stubborn."

"I heard that," Stratford said. "I'm in the same room."

The housekeeper scraped the eggs onto a plate loaded with bacon and carried it to the table. "Good. I wanted you to hear it. You're a stubborn man, Andrew Stratford. As stubborn as your grandfather."

"And my father," he added, taking his seat at the head of the table. "I'd rather be stubborn than a pushover."

Mrs. Purdy snorted. "You only need to be smart enough to know when to use that quality and when to let it go."

Dix fought the chuckle threatening to rise up her throat. Watching the big, strong Andrew Stratford battle it out with a five-foot-nothing housekeeper and lose was highly entertaining.

"I'm done eating. Are you?" Leigha glanced across the table at Dix.

"Almost." Dix really didn't want to leave the table while Stratford and Mrs. Purdy were going at it, but she had a job to do, and her name was Leigha.

Shoving the last bite of eggs into her mouth, she carried her plate to the sink, grabbed the two pieces of bacon from it and hurried after Leigha. To stir the pot, she paused on her way past Stratford. "I'll have Leigha dressed and ready by five thirty this afternoon."

Stratford had just lifted his fork when he glanced up. "Ready?"

"Seaside Café? Dinner?" She shook her head. "You wouldn't disappoint your daughter, would you?" Dix didn't wait for his answer. The fact that his brows met in the middle was what she had hoped for.

Mrs. Purdy smothered a chuckle by the sink.

Brewer trotted after Leigha, leaving the temptation of bacon in the kitchen. If Dix wasn't mistaken, the dog stayed with Leigha to protect her as much as Dix would. Which reminded her... She needed to talk to Stratford about the expected threats before they ventured too far out of the house. She needed to know what to be on the lookout for. Otherwise, she'd be more or less walking into the Devil's Shroud blindfolded.

Andrew's gaze followed Dix out of the kitchen. The woman might be tomboyish, but the sway of her hips was purely feminine.

"I like her," Mrs. Purdy said. "I think it will be good for Leigha to have another woman around her."

He pushed back from the table. "Don't say it."

"What? That the girl needs a mother?" Mrs. Purdy smiled. "Okay. I won't. But it's true."

"She has me."

Mrs. Purdy's brows rose. "A girl needs a mother to show her the ropes of being *female*."

"Not the mother she had."

"Agreed. But someone who's strong and independent and can show compassion." Mrs. Purdy nodded. "Sounds like Dix, doesn't it?"

"You just met her," he said, carrying his plate to the sink.

"I have a good sense of who people are. Dix is the real deal. She seems honest, open and a good influence for Leigha."

"As long as she keeps a close eye on her. I don't want her getting lost in the woods again."

Mrs. Purdy wiped the counter clean and nodded. "If anyone can keep up with Leigha, Dix can."

"I hope so. I have work to do this morning and can't hold her hand while she makes sense of the estate."

Mrs. Purdy raised her hand. "Leigha's the expert there. She'll show Miss Reeves all of her hiding places."

"I hope so. She hasn't shown them to me."

"Because you don't spend enough time with her. She needs a father as much as she needs a mother." She raised her hands. "Not that I'm telling you how to raise your daughter. You're the boss. You know best." She waved her hands at him. "Now, out of the kitchen so I can finish cleaning up. I have a few more chores to tend to before I leave for Portland, and you have a business to run."

If he was the boss, then why did he feel he didn't have any control over his housekeeper? His employees on Wall Street would never have spoken as frankly as Mrs. Purdy telling him how to run his household. But then, he had all the experience on Wall Street and none raising a little girl.

Shaking off the sense he wasn't doing it right, he marched to his office and went to work. So, he wasn't as attentive as usual. He could still put in a good bit of day-trading and increase the value of his portfolio for the hundredth time.

His thoughts strayed to Leigha and Dix, wondering where they were and what they were up to. By noon, he hoped to have his work squared away. Perhaps then he could ask his daughter to show him where all the hiding places were. If she refused to show him, he could demand that Dix take him there.

He almost laughed at himself. Dix? Taking commands

from him? Well, she had to have followed orders some-where in her military career, or she wouldn't have made it as far as she had. The dossier Tazer had shown him indicated Dix had been an Army Ranger, as well as a Medal of Honor and Purple Heart recipient. He wondered what wounds she'd sustained to receive a Purple Heart. The thought of her being wounded made his fists clench. And when he clenched his scarred and now rein-jured hand, the pain reminded him to quit thinking about Dix and get to work.

An hour later he pushed his chair back from the desk and went in search of his daughter and the bodyguard. If he couldn't keep his mind on task, he might as well join them in their exploration of the property.

He wandered through the halls, listening for the sounds of female voices. The vacuum whirred in the upstairs bedrooms, but that was the only sound he could hear. Where had they gone?

He stepped out of the front door and looked around. He didn't see any sign of Leigha, Dix or Brewer. Andrew frowned. What was the good of having someone watch over Leigha if she disappeared with the child?

A sheriff's vehicle rumbled up the sweeping, paved drive and pulled to a stop in front of the house. Gabe McGregor and an older man emerged.

"Good morning, Mr. Stratford. I'm Sheriff Taggert." He climbed the steps and held out his hand. "How are you feeling today?"

"Fine." *If I could find my child and the woman who is supposed to be looking out for her.* Andrew held up his hand, displaying the stitches. "I hope you don't mind if we don't shake."

"Not at all," the sheriff responded.

Andrew glanced to the right and left, hoping to catch a glimpse of his daughter and Miss Reeves.

"I read through McGregor's report about the attack on you two nights ago. We'd like to look at the area in the daylight. Perhaps there is some evidence we could have missed in the density of the fog from last night."

Andrew nodded, unable to ignore the two men. The sooner he helped them, the sooner he could find the ladies. "I'll take you to the exact location." He turned and walked around the house, through the garden and out to the edge of the rugged cliff.

McGregor and Taggert followed.

"Any more incidents since two nights ago?" the sheriff asked.

"No." The lights going out on Dix in the basement could have been anything. Since she hadn't been attacked, she'd probably suffered through a freak short. He'd have an electrician come check the panel and the wiring.

Once he led the lawmen to the spot where he'd been attacked, he got a good look at it with a different perspective—looking down at what he'd gone over and had to climb up. A chill rippled down his spine. He was lucky to be alive.

They checked around the tree, enlarging the circle a little at a time, staring at the ground. The rocky ledge didn't give them much of a chance to find footprints. Thirty feet out from the tree, they entered the forest where the ground was covered in evergreen needles and moss. Again, not good for finding footprints. But then, maybe they weren't looking for footprints.

A bark sounded from the direction of the house.

Andrew glanced around to see Brewer bounding his

way. Leigha and Dix hung back, moving toward them at a more sedate pace.

Before he reached Andrew, Brewer slowed, his tail wagging.

Andrew bent to scratch behind the dog's ears.

Brewer then moved on to the sheriff and his deputy, sniffing hands and wagging his tail.

Sheriff Taggert and Deputy McGregor crossed the ground and rejoined Andrew.

"Didn't find anything, did you?" Andrew asked.

Taggert shook his head. "I didn't expect we would. But we have to look in case the perpetrator left a calling card, a scrap of cloth, some DNA…anything."

"Unfortunately, he didn't leave a trace," McGregor confirmed.

"Gentlemen, I'm sorry to waste your time." Andrew herded them toward the house.

"Investigating a crime is not a waste of our time," Taggert argued. "We wish we could be of more help. Gabe said you didn't know of anyone who might be mad at you or want you off the property. No disputes over property lines, no ex-wives looking to take you to the cleaners, former business partners who might have a gripe?"

Andrew shook his head. "I'm the sole heir to the Stratford estate. Never been married. No ex-girlfriends stalking me and no former business partners with a complaint."

Taggert sighed. "For the time being, you might want to stay away from the cliff's edge at night or in the fog and grow eyes in the back of your head. Wish we could help more."

"Thank you for taking the time to come out to investigate," Andrew said.

By then they'd reached Dix and Leigha.

Andrew's daughter held tightly to Dix's hand and stared up at the sheriff and his deputy. Brewer sat at her feet, leaning into her body. She reached out to run her hand over the animal's fur, stroking it slowly.

"Hi, Leigha." Deputy McGregor squatted beside her and scratched Brewer's ears. "Do you remember me?"

Leigha nodded, her eyes wide and wary.

Brewer nudged McGregor's hand and then rolled over, exposing his belly.

The deputy laughed and scratched the dog's belly. "I like a dog that knows what he wants."

"Brewer likes to have his belly and ears scratched," Leigha said.

"I'll remember that the next time I visit." The deputy smiled at the little girl and stood. "Miss Reeves, my sister Molly had good things to say about her meeting with you last night. I wish I had been there." His lips turned upward on the corners and he cast a sideways glance at Andrew. "I hear I missed a show."

"You didn't miss anything," she said.

"Well, I'm glad you're here to help Mr. Stratford and his daughter."

"It's my pleasure." She smiled, and the few floating clouds that had been blocking the sun cleared, leaving the big blue sky wide open and the sun shining brightly.

Something woke inside Andrew he thought long dead. Something he didn't expect or want to wake. But now that it had, he couldn't make it go away. His heart swelled and his chest tightened.

Dix smiling hit him like a ray of sunshine.

Damn the woman to hell.

Chapter 7

After the sheriff and his deputy left the estate, Dix followed Leigha back into the house, fully aware of the man two steps behind her. Every nerve ending shivered in anticipation of him touching her arm, her back, somewhere on her body.

But he didn't. Instead he opened the back door to the house and held it for his daughter and Dix.

She swung as widely as she could to get around him without actually bumping into him. Why she went to such lengths she couldn't guess, but somewhere deep inside she knew that if they touched, all kinds of electric impulses would zing through her body and confuse her more than she already was about this man.

Leigha skipped ahead to the kitchen, giving Dix time to confront Stratford about what had happened to bring him to hire a bodyguard. Royce had said something about being pushed off a cliff. After having been out to the cliff

Stratford had been showing the lawmen, Dix could see why that was such a big deal. How he'd survived was beyond comprehension. The three-hundred-foot drop to the boulder-strewn shore would have killed a lesser being.

She stopped in the hallway and faced the man.

His head was down and he didn't notice she'd stopped until he ran into her. He reached out to grab her arms and held her steady.

"Sorry. I should have let you know I was stopping."

He slowly lowered his hands, removing them from her arms. "I should have been watching."

"So, tell me what happened to make you think you needed a bodyguard." She tipped her head toward the door. "You don't strike me as someone who would call the law unless it was the last resort."

"Someone pushed me over the cliff two nights ago during a really thick fog."

"Are you sure it wasn't an accident?"

"If someone barreled into you like a lineman on a football field, would you consider it an accident?"

Dix shook her head. "Did you see his face?"

"No." He hooked her elbow and led her toward the kitchen. "I'm not worried for myself. I worry for Leigha. She's an innocent. She can't tell who is friend or foe."

"Understandable. She's a great kid."

"Did she show you all of her hiding places?"

"Not yet. I think she's still trying to decide how far she can trust me. We did the tour of the third floor. This place is huge. Have you considered transforming it into a hotel?"

"Absolutely not."

"But it would be incredi—"

"No." He stopped at the entrance to the kitchen. "I

value my privacy. Opening it to other people will put my daughter at too great a risk."

"This place needs to be full of people. It's too big for just the two of you."

"It's my home now. I brought Leigha here so that she could grow up in a small community, not the big city. Cape Churn is a nice little town."

"I wouldn't know. All I know about it is what I saw when I drove through yesterday and straight out to the McGregor B and B."

"You'll see more this afternoon when we go into town for dinner."

Dix hid a smile as she stepped through the kitchen door.

Leigha carried a plate full of sandwiches to the table. "Mrs. Purdy made lunch. But she's leaving now, so we have to clean up."

Dix hurried to take over for the housekeeper. "We've got this. I might not be a cook, but I can make a pretty decent sandwich."

"They're already made. All you need to do is come up with your drinks. Chips are in the pantry." Mrs. Purdy removed her apron, hung it on a hook near the back door and then looped her purse over her arm. "I'll see you tomorrow. Enjoy dinner at Nora's café." She dropped a kiss on Leigha's head and breezed out the door, leaving the kitchen silent in her wake.

Dix filled glasses with ice and water from the tap, setting them on the table.

Stratford grabbed an assortment of bags of potato chips from the pantry and laid them on the table.

Leigha grinned. "This is almost like a picnic." Her smile faded a little. "I've never been on a picnic. But this is nice."

Dix stared at the little girl, her eyes wide. "No picnic?" She glanced at Leigha's father. "Well, Dad, how can we remedy this serious lack in her upbringing?"

The man stood beside his daughter, his brows twisting. "What do you mean?"

"I mean we're going on a picnic." She took a sandwich out of Leigha's grip and wrapped it in a napkin. "Show your father where he can find a blanket you don't mind getting dirty while I pack this food into something we can carry."

Leigha leaped from her seat, grabbed her father's hand and practically dragged him out of the kitchen. "Hurry! We're going on a picnic!"

Minutes later Dix had found a basket in the pantry, packed the sandwiches inside, a few water bottles, two bags of chips and napkins. By the time Stratford and Leigha returned with a blanket, she was ready.

"Are you coming with us?" Dix asked her client.

Leigha looked up at her father, her eyes big...hopeful.

He nodded. "Of course. You have my sandwich, and I'm starving."

Leigha clapped her hands and grinned from ear to ear.

Dix's heart filled with some of the joy Leigha was experiencing. She'd gone on quite a few picnics with her parents. It was one of the many things she missed about them.

By dying young, her parents would never know their grandchildren. And Dix's children would never know their grandparents. Shoving aside the sad thoughts, Dix fought to recapture Leigha's joy and led the way out of the house, checking right and left for any threats.

Stratford locked the door behind him and quickly caught up. "I know just the place."

The three of them marched into the woods. Brewer ran ahead, chasing birds and small animals.

Stratford seemed to know the woods better than Dix expected.

"I used to spend my summers here with my grandfather. We explored, he took me fishing, and we even camped in these woods. Sometimes we'd pretend to be treasure hunters and search for pirates' gold in the caves among the cliffs." He shook his head. "I loved doing all the activities I couldn't do from our apartment in New York City."

"You grew up in the city?" Dix asked.

"I did. My parents both worked for large corporations that had home offices in Manhattan."

Dix could imagine the adventurous little boy trapped in a concrete jungle. No wonder he'd chosen to bring Leigha to Oregon.

They ventured deeper into the woods until they came to an open glen with a burbling stream running through the middle.

Dix couldn't have found a better spot. The three of them spread the blanket and anchored it with the basket and a couple of rocks. A gentle breeze blew in from the Pacific, keeping the air cool and the sky clear.

Leigha took charge of the basket and passed food to them, while Stratford held Brewer back from stealing all of their sandwiches.

When they'd had their fill, Dix closed the basket and stretched out on the blanket, staring up at the sky between the branches of the trees.

Leigha and Brewer ran off to play on the edge of the creek.

"This place is beautiful. I don't know how anyone

would want to leave it for the city," Dix said in a reverent voice, caught up in the beauty of the Pacific Northwest.

Stratford lay on the opposite side of the blanket, his hands linked behind his head. "My father and grandfather had their differences. I contend they were too much alike—both very stubborn."

"What about your mother? Didn't she like living in Cape Churn?"

"My parents left shortly after their wedding and never looked back. I didn't know I had a grandfather until he showed up one day and asked to see me."

"What?" Dix turned to face him.

"Like I said, my father and grandfather didn't always get along. My grandfather knew my father wouldn't come back and settle at his estate in Oregon and he needed to have someone to leave Stratford House to. The need for an heir, and a promise to my grandmother, made him swallow his pride and fly all the way to New York City. The man hated to fly. He did it to ask my father to let me come spend my summers in Oregon."

"So you ended up coming to live here." Dix faced the sky again.

"Not right away."

"Not until Leigha." Dix watched the little girl playing with the dog. Her hair shone brightly in the afternoon sun.

"I remembered how much fun it was to explore and have free rein to do what I wanted at my grandfather's house. I also remembered what a big deal it was to go to a park for what they called fresh air in Manhattan." He leaned up on an elbow, his gaze following Leigha. "I couldn't do that to her. She deserved better."

Dix enjoyed the quiet conversation so different from the cold, stony silences the man had subjected her to in the beginning. "Why does Leigha call you 'Mr. Stratford' instead of Father or Daddy?" And with that one question, the warmth left the air and quiet, like a deep, deep chasm, stretched between them. "You don't have to answer that." She sat up and slipped the water bottles into the basket. "We should head back before it gets too dark. Besides, Leigha will need a bath before we go out to dinner. *If* you still want to go." Dix was rattling on, and she knew it, but she didn't know how to stop until Stratford laid a hand on her arm.

"I don't mind answering," he said. "I didn't know Leigha existed until she was already five years old."

"A year ago."

He nodded. "And she didn't know she had a father."

"Her mother kept her from you?"

"Leigha is the result of too much liquor and a one-night stand. Not one of my prouder moments." He sighed. "But I can't regret it."

Dix nodded toward the little girl laughing at the dog. "You have Leigha because of it. Five years is a long time for her mother to keep her from you. Are you sure she's your daughter?"

His lips thinned and a fierce frown pushed his eyebrows downward. "My name is on the birth certificate."

"Her mother could have lied. They have DNA tests they could conduct to prove lineage."

Stratford pushed to his feet, placed the basket on the ground and waited for Dix to move to the side.

She rose and lifted one end of the blanket while her client took the other, and they met across the hems, their hands touching, an electric shock running up Dix's arms into her chest. Her gaze captured his and she knew. "You don't want to know for certain, do you?"

"My name is on the birth certificate," he repeated firmly. "That's all I need to know."

A glance at Leigha reinforced his conviction. That would be all she'd need to know, too. The little girl was what was important. Making certain she had a loving, happy, healthy environment to grow up in was all that mattered.

But that niggle of doubt crept into Dix's thoughts. Holy hell. What if Leigha wasn't even Stratford's daughter?

Andrew had enjoyed the picnic up to the point where Dix had challenged Leigha's lineage. After what Jeannette had tried to do to the child, Leigha had been in the hospital for a week, recovering from smoke inhalation and the trauma of being caught in a horrific apartment fire.

He'd insisted on the best care and treatment money could buy. Moving her to a private room in one of the most reputable children's hospitals in the city was only a fraction of what he'd done for her. He'd been there every day that he could, putting off his own surgery until Leigha was in the clear. With his hand and face bandaged, he'd probably scared her more than reassured her. But someone had to be there when she'd cried for her mother, unable to understand why she wasn't there.

His heart had broken into a million pieces when tears fell from her eyes, soaking the sheets. He'd wanted to take all of the pain from her and make her life better. When she'd asked who he was, he didn't feel like he'd earned the right to tell her he was her daddy. So he'd said he was Mr. Stratford, her friend.

Leigha had accepted it and calmed down. She looked forward to his visits with her every day. In the meantime, Andrew had had his lawyers do whatever it took to transfer guardianship of the little girl to him. Whether it was through lawful or criminal channels, they were able to produce a birth certificate bearing Jeannette's name as Leigha's mother and Andrew Stratford as her father.

Everything else was a formality. With an overburdened foster care system, the judge had ruled in favor of granting custody to the biological father who had proved he could afford to support the child.

He'd hired a nanny to care for Leigha while he'd gone through several surgeries on his hand. When he could get away, he'd packed up what he wanted from his apartment, loaded Leigha onto a chartered plane, and the two of them had left New York City behind to start a new life together.

They'd been in Oregon for over eight months. Andrew hadn't known what to expect, but he was no closer to building a good relationship with his daughter. He didn't know how. They'd lived in the same house and shared meals, but Leigha had withdrawn into a very quiet, reserved child. Until Andrew had brought a wiggly black puppy home from town.

Brewer had helped Leigha out of her shell a little, and she'd transferred all of her love and attention to the dog.

By then, enough people had called her his daughter that she had to know he was her father. But still, she hadn't called him Daddy.

And he hadn't been much of a father to her. Sure, he'd given her a better place to live than in that ratty apartment in the Bronx, but he hadn't shown her the love he knew she needed.

He didn't know how to. His parents hadn't been the demonstrative type. Hugging was almost a painful necessity on rare occasions.

Watching Dix gather their things, he felt a little stab

of jealousy at how easily she'd fit into Leigha's life. See-ing them lying in the same bed the night before had been bittersweet. They'd looked like they were mother and child. It had warmed his heart and left him cold at the same time.

Leigha needed a strong female influence in her life. Dix, with her background in the military and her MMA fighting, would make an excellent role model. She could even teach her how to defend herself should someone at-tack her.

What left him cold was the possibility Leigha wasn't his child. If not his, whose was she? Some deadbeat who wouldn't want her anyway? Wasn't that what Jeannette had screamed at him? Nobody wanted Leigha.

Jeannette had been wrong. Andrew wanted her more than anything he'd ever wanted in his life. More than that, he wanted her to be happy. Rather than risk losing her after what they'd survived together, Andrew preferred to live with the burning question. Was she his biologi-cal daughter?

Chapter 8

Andrew carried the basket and the blanket and led the way back through the woods to Stratford House, more somber than when they'd set out on their little adventure. As they neared the path leading past the high cliffs, he glanced down at the water below. Had he died, what would have become of Leigha?

He'd had his attorney set up a trust for Leigha. Everything he owned would go into that trust to be paid out to his daughter over her lifetime. No matter if she was his or not, she'd get everything he owned as it was spelled out in his will. But if he died, he had no one to leave her with. He hadn't made any friends since he'd been back in Oregon, rarely leaving his house to go into town.

For Leigha's sake, he needed to remedy that oversight and find someone he felt confident could raise Leigha with the love and kindness she needed. After being pushed over the edge of the cliff, he couldn't guarantee he'd be alive to see her all the way to maturity.

Dinner out in Cape Churn might give him the opportunity to work toward finding godparents for his daughter. He needed a backup plan to ensure Leigha's future happiness.

They returned to the house without incident.

Andrew left Leigha and Dix in the kitchen unloading the leftovers from the basket into the refrigerator. He checked his email and phone messages and then headed upstairs to his bedroom, where he showered and slipped into black slacks, a silver button-down dress shirt and the black leather shoes he used to wear when he went out to the nightclubs in Manhattan. Though most folks dressed more casually in Cape Churn, Andrew wanted to look good. He skipped the tie, leaving the top button undone.

He was surprised at how nervous he felt at going out in public. Before "the accident" he'd gone out practically every night of the week. He really had no reason to feel nervous. So he had a scar slashing across his face and his hand was mangled with burn grafts and now stitches. At least he still had his life and that grafted hand had helped save him from falling to his death.

He squared his shoulders and stepped into the hall.

Leigha came out of her room a second later, smiling. She wore a pretty powder blue sundress and white sandals. Her hair was pulled back on both sides with a yellow barrette. She spotted Andrew and her eyes widened. "You look like a handsome prince," she exclaimed and ran to wrap her arms around his waist.

"Then you must be my princess." He lifted her up into his arms, trying not to wince when he disturbed the stitches. "May I have this dance?"

She giggled and laid her hand in his damaged one.

Andrew danced around the corridor with his daughter in his arms. It might be silly to onlookers, but it felt right to him. And the smile on Leigha's face was worth looking like a fool.

When he made another turn, he caught a glimpse of someone standing in the hallway and he came to a halt, his mouth falling open and his pulse slamming through his veins. "Miss Reeves?"

"Dix!" Leigha squirmed out of Andrew's arms and ran to Dix. "You're like a beautiful fairy princess."

Dix's face flushed a pretty pink, complimenting the flowing white-fabric dress that draped off her shoulders, hugged her waist and fell in soft layers that floated down to her knees. Every time she moved the skirt swayed around her like wisps of clouds. "You must be my fairy princess sister, then. You're adorable." She bent to kiss the top of Leigha's head.

"Come see Mr. Stratford. He's our prince." Leigha grabbed Dix's hand and pulled her toward Andrew.

Dix stopped in front of him and smiled. "Well, aren't we dressed up for a night on the town?"

"Indeed we are." He offered his arm to Dix and his hand to Leigha. "Shall we?"

Dix nodded and placed her hand in the crook of his arm.

They descended the grand staircase like royalty.

While the ladies waited in the foyer, Andrew went out to the garage and brought out his black SUV and swung around the front of the house.

He and Dix buckled Leigha into a booster chair in the backseat. Then Andrew followed Dix to the passenger side of the SUV and held the door for her.

She hesitated getting in. "Just so you know, I'm armed, should anyone try to hurt you or Leigha."

"Armed?" His gaze swept over her body, his brow rising. He couldn't see any sign of a handgun on her.

She slid her skirt up her thigh, exposing a strap around her leg with a holster and an H&K .40-caliber pistol. Some men might consider her carrying a weapon some-what intimidating. Andrew found it sexy as hell. He wanted to slide his hand up the inside of her thigh and touch the cold, hard weapon lying against her warm, soft skin.

He held the door while she climbed in, her dress hik-ing up as she settled in her seat. Once again, Andrew had a clear view of her legs. Tanned and smooth, with well-defined muscles and narrow ankles, they would wrap nicely around his waist. He resisted the urge to reach out to trace his fingers along the length of those sexy legs. She was his employee. He was her client. He risked los-ing her as a bodyguard if he crossed the line.

His body tense, his groin tight, Andrew closed the passenger door, rounded to the driver's side and got in.

The trip to town took only fifteen minutes. The sun was setting as they pulled into the parking lot of the Sea-side Café. The sun's rays glittered like amethysts across the bay, turning gentle waves into sparkling jewels.

Many cars filled the parking spaces. He had to search for an empty one. Which meant the café would be busy and full of people. For a moment he considered turning around and going back to the house. After spending the past year as a recluse, he didn't look forward to enter-ing a crowded room full of people who would stare at his face and hand.

"I want chocolate ice cream," Leigha said, bouncing in her booster seat. "Please."

One glance at his daughter's shining eyes and Andrew knew he couldn't disappoint her. He unbuckled his seat belt, sucked in a deep breath and got out of the SUV.

Dix was out and already unbuckling Leigha's belt by the time Andrew made it around to the passenger side.

Leigha took Dix's hand and grabbed Andrew's un-injured hand and swung between them all the way into the café.

"Welcome to the Seaside Café," a friendly voice called out. A woman with gray hair, wearing a soft yellow summer dress and a crisp white apron, hurried toward them, carrying menus. "Three?" She glanced behind them.

"Just three," Andrew said.

The woman's smile widened. "Three it is. I'm Nora Taggert. Are you all new in town?"

Andrew swallowed a groan.

Dix chuckled and hid it with a cough.

"Nora, honey, this is Andrew Stratford." Sheriff Taggert disengaged himself from a seat at a counter and joined Andrew and Dix. "He's the owner of Stratford House." The sheriff held out his left hand to Andrew. "So glad you came to town. My wife makes the best meat loaf in the state."

Andrew shook the sheriff's hand with his uninjured one and released it.

Nora swatted playfully at her husband. "Oh, go on. It might not be the best in the state, but everyone tells me it's the best around *here*."

The sheriff nodded to Dix. "Miss Reeves is here to help look out for little Miss Leigha." He squatted on his haunches and grinned at Andrew's daughter. "Isn't that right?"

Leigha stepped closer to Dix, nodding.

Dix dropped a hand to Leigha's shoulder and squeezed. "We're getting to know each other."

"We went on a picnic today," Leigha offered softly, her eyes lighting up.

"A picnic?" Nora beamed. "I love picnics. Did you take sandwiches or fried chicken?" She held out a hand to Leigha, who took it and let her lead her away to a table in the corner. Dix followed close behind.

"Sandwiches," Leigha responded.

Andrew realized by keeping to his house, he was depriving Leigha of company and social interaction. He resolved to fix that, as well.

"Everything okay out at the house?" Sheriff Taggert asked.

Andrew nodded. "No further incidents."

"Glad to hear it." The sheriff's mouth firmed into a straight line. "But don't let your guard down."

"I won't." Andrew stepped around the sheriff and joined the ladies at the table.

"Six years old!" Nora exclaimed. "Such a grown-up little lady. Are you excited about going to school next fall?"

Leigha glanced up at Andrew. "I don't know."

"We've been home-schooling," Andrew said. "Mrs. Purdy has been very helpful."

"I should think so." Nora smoothed her hand over Leigha's hair. "As a retired teacher, she's an excellent choice." She laid menus on the table and stepped back. "What would you like to drink?"

They gave their orders.

Nora returned with their drinks and took their orders. "While you're waiting, why don't you show Leigha the koi pond we installed on the back patio?"

"Would you like that?" Dix asked.

Leigha's brows dipped. "What's a koi pond?"

"They're like really big goldfish."

Leigha's eyes widened and she clapped her hands. "May I?"

Dix glanced across at Andrew. "Care to join us?"

He shook his head. "I'll stay and hold the table."

Leigha slipped out of her chair and let Dix take her hand as she led her to the back of the café.

Andrew sat back and looked around at the people gathered at the café. Some appeared to be tourists, early for the summer season. Others looked like regulars, there for coffee and pie.

At the table beside him, two young men leaned over a map, talking excitedly. Andrew couldn't help overhearing their conversation.

"The dive boat captain is ours for the week. We have to make this venture count."

"No kidding," the other young man agreed. "I'm spending the rest of my college money on this. If we don't find something soon, I'll be working at my father's machine shop for the rest of my life."

"The data is all there. We just have to spend some time in the water to locate the ship."

"What if they got the jewels to shore before they scuttled the yacht?"

"Then it has to be somewhere nearby. I'm not giving up. We've spent too much time and money researching this."

Andrew's curiosity was captured. He wanted to know what boat they were searching for and what jewels they expected to find.

The front door opened and a couple entered with a blast of cool air.

A slip of paper blew over to land at Andrew's foot. He lifted it and studied the drawing. It was a detailed sketch of Cape Churn. Other landmarks were noted ringing the coastline, including Cape Churn Marina, McGregor

B and B and Stratford House. An *X* marked a spot in the water just off the coast from Stratford House.

"Sir, do you mind?" The sandy-blond-haired young man from the table beside Andrew stood beside him. "That's my drawing."

Andrew handed the drawing to him. "Treasure hunting?"

The young man shot a glance at his partner, who looked enough like him they could be twins.

The other guy shrugged and answered, "Trying."

"You from around here?" the guy standing asked.

Andrew nodded.

The young man stuck out his hand. "I'm Jared Kessler." He jabbed a thumb over his shoulder at his partner. "He's Joe, my brother."

Andrew raised his bandaged right hand. "Are you two related?"

Jared dropped his arm, his lips twisting. "Yeah, we're twins."

Joe scooted his chair closer to Andrew. "Do you know if anyone lives in the big mansion on the cliff?" He pointed to Stratford House.

Andrew choked back his laughter. "Yes. Someone lives there."

"We want to call and ask him if he'd mind if we looked around the caves along the shoreline," Jared said.

"Yeah," Joe added. "We don't want some trigger-happy landowner shooting us for trespassing."

Andrew dipped his head to hide his smile.

Jared dropped into his seat and pulled it closer. "We've been studying the history of Cape Churn and the Oregon coastline for the past two years as a project for our major."

Andrew's grandfather had read a lot about the early inhabitants of Cape Churn. He'd told Andrew stories about pirates of the Pacific Northwest and the rumrunners of the early twentieth century. "The West Coast is said to have been a pirates' haven back in the seventeenth century."

Jared shook his head. "Oh, we aren't going back that far."

"We've concentrated our research on a pair of thieves and rumrunners known as the Bonnie and Clyde of the Pacific Northwest—Peg and Percy Malone."

Andrew stiffened. His grandfather had told him stories of the antics of the pair with whom the Stratfords were rumored to be related. "What exactly are you looking for?"

"News articles dating back to the late 1920s followed the exploits of the Malones. They were crafty rumrunners who transported kegs of whiskey from British Columbia to San Francisco."

"And you're looking for a lost shipment of whiskey kegs?" Andrew shook his head. "That's a lot of research for old barrels."

Joe shared a grin with his brother. "That's not all they did."

Andrew knew the stories. His grandfather had repeated them time and again as they'd sat on the back patio watching the sun set on Cape Churn. But he let the twins tell their version, their eyes bright, their bodies tense with excitement.

Jared leaned closer, his voice dropping lower. "The Malones were also jewel thieves. One shipment of whiskey was supposed to be delivered to a wealthy San Franciscan, Willard Jameson, who owned a number of speakeasies and jewelry stores."

Joe picked up the story. "Rumor had it the man paid off the local law enforcement. They seized the shipment as soon as the Malones pulled into port. The Malones escaped, learned of Jameson's betrayal and vowed to get their revenge."

Jared glanced around the room and spoke in a hushed voice. "They broke into one of Jameson's jewelry stores, took all of the most precious of gems, including the Star of Nairobi, a special diamond Jameson had imported to make a wedding ring for his fiancée."

Joe jumped in with, "They stole one of Jameson's fastest yachts and headed north in the middle of the night. Reports from the coast guard indicated a light flashing by during the night as far north as the southern tip of Oregon, but the authorities never spotted the yacht during the daytime."

"A friend of a friend of the Malones wrote a fictional account of the couple and published it."

"Fictional?" Andrew asked.

Jared nodded. "Only we think it was based on the truth. It was published years after the theft occurred. The Malones disappeared after that last run, never to run rum again."

"The newspaper from that time reported that Jameson offered a reward for anyone with any information leading to their arrest." Joe shuffled through a file and pointed to a photocopy of an old newspaper report. "In the editorial comments, an anonymous writer said Jameson had put a price on their heads for anyone who would assassinate them."

"Others say Peg got pregnant and they went into hiding, changed their names and started over." Jared sat back. "But the Star of Nairobi never surfaced."

"And how did you end up in Cape Churn searching for the Malones?" Andrew asked.

"In the book, the author referred to the Malones as Margaret and Percival. We researched court and church records and went online with ancestry sites looking for people who fit the age and description of the Malones."

"And?" Andrew prompted.

"And we found Margaret and Percival Mason. Here in Cape Churn. They had one daughter, Rowena Mason, who married Thomas Stratford."

"Of the Stratford mansion on the cliff," Jared finished.

"And you think Stratford might know where the Star of Nairobi can be found?" Andrew asked.

Jared shook his head at the same time as his brother. "We think they hid the jewels and forgot about them. The Masons died in a car crash when Rowena was twelve years old. She was raised by members of the church."

Dix and Leigha emerged from the back of the café and started toward them.

Andrew wrote his phone number on a napkin and passed it to the Kessler twins. "You can reach Stratford at that number. He doesn't like trespassers, so be sure to call ahead before you enter his property."

"Thank you," Jared said. "But what is your name?"

"Andrew." A smile tugged at his lips. "Andrew Stratford."

Dix and Leigha arrived at that exact time. The twins scooted their chairs back to their table, grinning and talking quietly.

"Did we interrupt something?" Dix asked.

Andrew shook his head. "No. How was the fishpond?"

"Great!" Leigha said and then told him all about the different colored koi she'd spotted.

Dix's eyes narrowed and her gaze alternated between Andrew and the two men sitting at the table beside them.

He'd fill her in later on the treasure hunters. He wanted her take on them. Would she think they were dangerous?

Could one of them have been the one to push Andrew over the cliff?

He didn't think so, but then, he really had no idea who might have done it. He didn't know many people in the area, as evidenced by Nora Taggert's mistaken assumption that he was new to town. He had to fix that, for Leigha's sake. And as soon as they caught the man responsible for pushing him off the cliff, he might consider letting Leigha go to the public school in Cape Churn. She needed friends to play with. Andrew felt like a fish out of water when it came to parenting.

He would ask Dix if she knew of a manual that could help him figure out what he was supposed to be doing.

Chapter 9

Dix polished off a healthy slice of Nora's famous meat loaf and would have had a beer, but felt she needed to have all of her wits about her, so she'd opted for ice cream instead. Being a bodyguard to a little girl was a huge responsibility she couldn't take lightly. The nudge of the handgun strapped to her thigh reminded her to stay alert.

The two young men who'd been talking with Stratford eventually packed up their maps and left the café, waving to her client as they walked out the door.

Now that they were gone and Leigha was happily licking her cone, Dix posed the question. "What were you talking to those two guys about?"

Stratford sat back in his chair and studied the rounded mound of ice cream on his cone. "Treasure."

Dix frowned. "Your ice cream as treasure, or are those guys searching for treasure?"

"Both." He licked the cone and sighed. "We need to come have dinner here more often."

"Yes, please." Leigha licked her cone, getting a spot of chocolate on the tip of her nose.

Dix's attention latched on to the way Stratford attacked his cone, studying it carefully before licking it in just the right spot. That look of intense concentration from his incredibly blue eyes and the long, deliberate stroking of his tongue on the creamy dessert made a tingle ripple through her body and pool low in her belly. She licked her own suddenly dry lips and cleared her throat. "Care to explain what you mean?"

He shook his head and tilted it slightly toward Leigha. "I'll tell you about it later."

Her curiosity and everything else in her body piqued, Dix worked her way through the rest of that chocolate cone, anxious to get back to Stratford House to get to the bottom of that tongue—er, story.

Her cheeks heated. Even though she hadn't spoken her slipup aloud, she'd thought it. Was she insane? Daydreaming about a client's tongue couldn't possibly be one of the duties of a good bodyguard. She averted her gaze, staring out at all of the patrons of the café, wondering if one of them was the person who'd pushed Stratford off the cliff.

At that thought, she went from hot all over to a cold chill. She shivered.

"Cold?"

She gave him a weak smile. "Maybe a little. Must be the ice cream." Or a creepy feeling the culprit was watching them as they enjoyed their dessert.

Leigha finished her cone and licked her fingertips. "I'm sleepy," she announced and leaned back in her chair. "Can we go home now?"

"You bet." Stratford finished the last bite of his cone and waited at the cash register while Dix took Leigha to the ladies' room to wash the chocolate off her fingers.

"Andrew Stratford?" a deep voice called out behind him.

Andrew tensed as he turned. "Yes."

A gray-haired man stood behind him, wearing nice trousers and a button-down, long-sleeved shirt. He held out his hand. "Nelson Clayton. I grew up with your mother."

Andrew held his hand up, displaying his bandages. "Nice to meet you, Mr. Nelson."

"Mr. Clayton," he corrected.

"My apologies." Andrew dropped his hand to his side. "How can I help you?"

"Heard you were back in town. Just wondered for how long. Seems you only ever came for the summers."

Andrew nodded. "You are correct. I came to spend summer vacations with my grandfather. When I was a child." He started to tell Nelson he was there for good, but Nora Taggert hurried over, wiping her hands on her apron.

"Mr. Stratford, I hope you enjoyed the meal."

He smiled at the woman. "We all did. And the meat loaf was excellent."

She beamed, took his credit card, ran it through the machine and handed him the slip to sign. "I hope you won't be such a stranger. We'd love for you to come back."

"You can count on it."

"Good." She handed him the receipt with a smile. "So, are you staying for the summer? Or are you here for good?"

"We're here for good, Mrs. Taggert. Thank you for dinner." He turned to Mr. Clayton. "Nice meeting you, Mr. Clayton."

The older man nodded. "Your mother is a special woman. We hated to see her leave Cape Churn."

Andrew didn't know how to respond to the man's remark and was saved from doing so by the sight of Leigha and Dix walking toward him. "Excuse me."

Clayton stepped aside, allowing him to pass.

He walked to the door and waited for Dix and Leigha to catch up. "Ready?"

"Yes, sir," Dix said.

He opened the door for her and Leigha. As Dix passed, he leaned close and said, "Please don't call me 'sir.' My name is Andrew."

"Yes, sir," she said automatically and then added, "Andrew."

He shook his head, his heart lighter than it had been in a very long time. What was it about Dix that made him feel things he hadn't felt for years? He touched his hand to her back, a shock of electricity running up his arm. He tried to ignore it, but he couldn't. "That's the military in you," he said, reminding himself she was a tough woman who was there to work.

"Hard to beat it out of a person," Dix said.

He stared at her, wondering what she meant by her remark. He started to ask, but he didn't get the opportunity.

Dix pushed her shoulders back and marched to the SUV like a good soldier.

"Dix, you're hurting my hand," Leigha said, pulling her out of her musings and back to the present.

Dix released the little girl's hand. "I'm sorry, sweetie." She bent to the child's level and rubbed her little fingers. "Better?"

Leigha nodded and raised her arms to Dix.

Scooping her up, she carried her the rest of the way to the SUV. After she'd buckled Leigha into the SUV, Dix straightened.

"Dix?" Leigha called from inside the vehicle.

Dix bent to look at the little girl.

Leigha patted the seat beside her. "Will you sit with me? Please?"

Andrew could imagine the look Leigha was giving her, with those big blue eyes that could melt the hardest heart. He gave Dix two seconds to think about it before she caved to Leigha's strong suit—mental manipulation. She could guilt anyone into doing exactly what she wanted.

Only one second had passed when Dix straightened again and captured Stratford's glance.

He nodded, pressing his lips together tightly to keep from grinning.

Score for Leigha.

Dix climbed into the backseat, next to Leigha, and took her hand.

Andrew slipped behind the wheel, started the engine and shifted into Reverse. He glanced in the rearview mirror to see two blond heads tipping toward each other. Again, he was reminded of how much they looked alike. He checked through the rear window and shifted his foot off the brake and onto the accelerator. No sooner had he started moving than a big white pickup darted behind him and stopped.

Andrew slammed on the brakes, bracing himself for the impact. When he didn't hear the sound of metal crunching into metal, he checked his side mirror and released the breath he'd caught and held. Then he pulled forward again, shifted into Park and got out of the SUV, anger burning through his veins.

The truck driver pulled into an empty parking space and got out.

Andrew walked up to him, fists clenched. "What the hell do you think you were doing?"

The man wasn't as tall as Andrew, but he made up

for it in size. He had to be at least two hundred and fifty pounds or more. He puffed out his chest and snorted like a bull in a ring. "It's a free country. I have as much right to be in this parking lot as you rich folks."

"Not at the speed you were going."

The jerk made a show of looking around. "Don't see no speed limits posted."

"You don't need speed limits in a parking lot—you need common sense. People bring their children here. You could have run over one."

The man stepped around Andrew and shouted over his shoulder, "Then those people should keep their brats on a leash." He pushed the door to the Seaside Café open so hard Andrew was surprised the glass didn't break.

Sheriff Taggert and his wife stood just inside the door. The sheriff put out his hand and stopped the belligerent man as he entered. "Slow it down, Clayton, before someone gets hurt."

"You gonna give me a ticket for walking fast?" Clayton demanded.

"No, but keep it up and I will give you a ticket for destruction of property."

Clayton shook the sheriff's hand off his arm. "Either give me a ticket or leave me alone."

Andrew was halfway to the door, prepared to come to the sheriff's defense.

Taggert started to say something but Nora leaned close and whispered in his ear. The sheriff snapped shut his mouth, his eyes narrowing as Clayton stepped past him and walked into the café.

As Andrew reached the door, he asked, "Are you two okay?"

The sheriff nodded. "Yeah, but I got a real itchin' to take that fool down a notch."

"Tom," Nora warned. "I can handle him."

The sheriff turned to his wife and brought her hand to his lips. "If he gives you even a hint of a hard time, don't serve him, and call me."

She smiled. "I will. Now go on and let me do my job."

The sheriff glanced once more at the man he'd called Clayton and stepped out onto the sidewalk in front of the café. "I don't know what's wrong with that boy."

"That boy" had to be at least thirty years old and he was bigger than a defensive football player. "Who is he?" Andrew wanted to make friends in Cape Churn, but not with that one. He needed to know whom to watch and avoid.

"That's Dwayne Clayton. His father is your neighbor, Nelson Clayton. They live on the other side of the ridge from you. Saw Nelson talking to you inside."

"My neighbors?" Andrew hadn't known that. With Stratford House surrounded by forty acres of forest and rocky shoreline, he hadn't run into anyone other than the man who'd pushed him over the cliff. He stopped to think about the size of his attacker. It had been so foggy, and happened so quickly, he couldn't be sure, but he didn't think the man had been as big as the younger Mr. Clayton. Though he wouldn't put it past Dwayne Clayton to push a stranger off a cliff. He'd have to make sure Leigha didn't stray onto Clayton property. The young Mr. Clayton had no love of children.

After her heartbeat settled to normal, Dix sat in the backseat of Andrew's SUV, holding one of Leigha's hands and resting her other hand on her full belly. Nora's meat loaf had been the best she'd ever had, and she'd loved her own mother's meat loaf. Up until that rude redneck nearly caused an accident, she hadn't felt that relaxed since before she'd gone to Ranger training.

Not long after they left town, Leigha nodded off, her head lolling to the side. She was a beautiful child with a sweet disposition. How anyone could hurt someone so precious was beyond Dix's comprehension. Every protective instinct inside her stood at the ready to defend this little bit of sunshine.

Dix leaned back and stared out at the sparkling night sky. She hadn't seen many stars in Vegas. The multitude of neon lights eclipsed nature's beauty. Here, along the Oregon coast, big, fluffy clouds chased the stars around the moonlit sky as a breeze blew in from the west, stirring up tiny white-capped waves in the cape.

"What a huge change from the city that never sleeps to a sleepy town on the West Coast," Dix said.

Andrew snorted softly. "Sometimes it can be too quiet. In New York City, all the noise drowns out the little things. Here, you can hear yourself breathe, and sometimes you think the house is alive with all the creaks and groans."

Dix smiled. "Vegas was like New York City. Noise and light all night long." She sighed. "You must love living here."

Andrew nodded. "I didn't realize how much I missed my summers with my grandfather until I came back. I wish I'd spent more time as an adult visiting him. He was an interesting man."

"What about your grandmother?"

"I never got to know her. She passed before I started coming to Oregon to visit my grandfather. I think she made him promise to get to know his grandson. My grandfather didn't talk much about her. I got the impression he missed her terribly. He never remarried. I went with him once to visit my grandmother's grave. He laid a single red rose on it and stood for a very long time."

Dix's heart squeezed hard in her chest. "He must have loved her so much. How did she die?"

"My grandfather told me she died of a broken heart. But my father said she died of a very aggressive breast cancer. By the time they found it, it had metastasized and spread throughout her body. She only lived two weeks after the diagnosis. My father flew out to be with her the last few days of her life. I remember him coming home looking much older and sad."

"I'm so sorry."

Andrew shrugged. "Now they're both gone."

"What about your parents?"

"Still alive. Still working for large corporations, living the fast-paced life in New York."

"What did they think about you having a daughter?"

His jaw hardened. "They asked for DNA results."

Dix drew in a long breath and let it out. After her conversation about the same thing, she understood Andrew's aversion to finding out if Leigha was really his.

Now that Dix had spent some time with the little girl, she understood. She'd hate to see her go into a state-run foster care system that was already overloaded with children. Andrew had sufficient money and a good home for her. Why tempt fate by checking her lineage? She had a father who loved her enough to provide a beautiful home and anything she could possibly want.

Before she knew it, they'd pulled through the gate of Stratford House and she'd gotten more out of Andrew Stratford that evening than she'd ever thought possible.

One thing was very clear: he would do anything for Leigha. Including risk his life for her. He had the scars to prove it.

Andrew parked the SUV and came around to the passenger side.

Dix had loosened the buckle around Leigha, but she stood back for Andrew to carry the child into the house.

Before he reached in for Leigha, he handed the key to the house to Dix.

Reminding herself she had the duty to protect, Dix glanced around the exterior of the mansion. Andrew had left the light burning on the front porch. Everything appeared too peaceful and untouched.

Dix unlocked the front door. As soon as she did, she could hear Brewer barking from somewhere in the house. They'd left him running loose. He would have been waiting at the door.

The hairs on the back of her neck rose. "Take Leigha back to the car," she ordered.

"What's wrong?" Andrew held Leigha close.

"Something isn't right," she said softly. "I need you to take Leigha back to the car and get inside. Let me check the house before you bring her in."

Andrew hesitated. "Maybe you should stay with Leigha and let me check the house. Or let me call the sheriff."

"Let's not waste time arguing about this. I have a gun. I'm trained on how to use it and I'm experienced in urban warfare." She slipped her hand beneath her skirt and pulled out the handgun. "Go."

She waited for him to leave the front porch and then she pushed open the front door with the tip of her gun, standing to the side to avoid being the target of whoever might be on the other side.

Dix looked first then slipped through the doorway. Staying away from the moonlight shining through the windows, she moved from room to room, working her way to the back of the house to the kitchen. The back door stood ajar, as if someone had left in a hurry. From a quick inspection, Dix couldn't see any sign of a forced entry. She closed the door and locked it.

Brewer barked again, the sound coming from behind the basement door. Dix twisted the knob, pushed open the door and switched on the light over the stairs. Having been in the basement before, she wasn't sure she trusted the lights to stay on. Retreating to the kitchen, she pulled the rechargeable flashlight out of its charger on the wall by the back door. Armed with the flashlight and the gun, she inched her way down the stairs.

When she reached the bottom, she flipped the switch and illuminated the floor of the basement.

Brewer was tied to a beam in the middle of the basement, with a length of thin rope. He jumped and strained at the lead, his tail wagging.

For the moment Dix left him tied as he was while she made a complete search of the basement. When she was certain they were alone, she untied the dog.

He jumped up on her, planting sloppy kisses on her chin.

Her hands full of flashlight and a gun, Dix couldn't fend off the dog. When he'd greeted her to his own satisfaction, he raced up the steps to the kitchen.

Dix hurried up after him. One by one, she and Brewer searched the rooms until she was certain no one else was in the house.

Finally, she exited the front door and waved to Andrew. "All clear. Let's get Leigha in her bed. Then you can tell me what the hell's going on."

He got out of the car, gathered his daughter and carried her up the steps. Andrew brushed past her and hurried up the staircase.

Dix secured the front door and climbed the stairs.

He'd laid Leigha on her bed, pulled off her shoes and tucked the blankets around her. For a moment he stared down at his daughter, and then he bent and kissed her forehead.

When he straightened, his gaze met Dix's. "Let's talk," he said and led the way out of the bedroom.

Brewer started to follow.

Andrew pointed to the bedroom. "Stay."

The dog didn't cross the threshold of Leigha's room. After a moment he turned back and trotted toward Leigha's bed.

Her heartbeat fluttering, Dix followed Andrew to the first floor.

"Where do you want to talk?" Dix asked.

"On the back porch. I need some air."

"You sure that's a good idea?" Dix asked. "What if the intruder is out there? He could have a gun."

"I refuse to be confined to my house," he said. "If someone wanted me dead badly enough to shoot me, he'd have done it already." Andrew gripped her arm and guided her through what appeared to be a study toward a French door that led out onto a large patio with a view of the ocean.

"Here, let me have that." He took the flashlight from her and switched off the beam. Then he glanced at the gun in her hand. "Do you have to carry that?"

"If you want me to protect you and your daughter, I might need it." Her hand tightened on the grip.

He stared at her for a moment, his gaze slipping over her bare shoulders and down to the gun in her hand and lower. "Seems a little incongruous. You, looking beautiful in that white dress, carrying a gun that could kill a man."

Dix tilted her chin upward. "Don't judge a woman by her clothes."

He raised his hands in surrender. "Oh, I know that now. You can take down a full-grown man. I have the bruises to prove it." He waved toward the door. "Ladies with guns go first."

She stepped through the door, calling back over her shoulder, "I'm no lady."

His chuckle warmed her. "From where I'm standing, you're one-hundred-percent female."

Dix stood on the patio, peering into the shadows, wondering who had been in the house and had gone to the trouble of tying Brewer to a post.

A hand touched her shoulder. "Is everything all right?" Andrew asked. "What made you think something wasn't right?"

"My first clue was that Brewer didn't greet us at the door. I could hear him barking from the other side of the house."

"He could have gotten himself caught in a room and couldn't get out."

She shook her head, her lips pressing into a thin line as she stared up at Andrew. "I found him in the basement, tied to a post."

Chapter 10

Andrew's heartbeat stopped for a full three seconds and then rushed to catch up, thundering against his ribs. "I didn't leave him that way," he said.

"I didn't think you did. Does Mrs. Purdy ever tie Brewer in the basement?"

"Never."

"That's what I thought." She shook her head and descended two of the stone steps leading down to the garden and then sat on the top one. "The dog was in the basement tied up, and the back door was open, no sign of forced entry on any of the exterior doors. And, as far as I could tell, nothing appeared disturbed." She set the gun down beside her.

Andrew dropped to sit on the step, his thoughts roiling through his mind, searching for a reason. "Why?"

"Someone came into your house while you were gone and didn't take anything that I could tell." She shrugged.

"If you have a safe or a stash of jewelry, you might want to check those."

"Hold that thought." He rose and reentered the study. He kept important papers and valuables locked in a wall safe behind a portrait of Leigha. He stepped behind his desk and slid the portrait to the side, exposing the safe.

"That portrait of Leigha is completely captivating," Dix said from behind him.

"I commissioned Kayla Davies, Gabe McGregor's wife, to paint it."

"It's nothing less than breathtaking," Dix whispered as she lifted her skirt up her thigh to slide her pistol into the holster.

Andrew swallowed hard and fought to remember what she'd just said, when all he could think about was that smooth, sexy thigh. She'd mentioned something about the painting. "I love the artist's work," he said, twisting the tumbler on the lock. "Only I think Leigha appears too sad."

"The painting captures her. When I first met Leigha, I got that sense from her. She seemed sad."

Andrew's fingers twisted too hard and missed the number he was aiming for. Dix had hit the problem on the head. Leigha seemed too sad for a girl of six. "I've given her everything she needs. I just don't know how to make her happier." He started the pattern all over, his heart pinching inside his chest. He'd brought Leigha to Stratford House to give her the home she deserved, but he didn't know how to make the house a home to the little girl.

"I'm not a parent, so I don't know everything. But I would think most kids just want to be loved and to feel safe."

Andrew turned to the last number, grabbed the handle and pushed it down. The door swung open. "Yeah, well, I love the girl, and I have *you* now to help her with the safe part."

"Safe isn't all about having a bodyguard. It's about knowing the ones you love aren't going to disappear on you. Or, in her case, aren't going to leave her or try to kill her."

Andrew grabbed a stack of documents and turned toward Dix. Even though her skirt was down around her knees, he couldn't get the image of her thigh out of his mind. "You mean she might think I'll leave her or try to kill her?"

"I doubt she'd think you'd try to kill her after saving her from the fire. But she might be afraid to love you for fear of losing you."

"So she calls me Mr. Stratford, even though she knows I'm her father," he said.

"Maybe." Dix touched his arm. "Or maybe she's waiting for you to give her permission to call you Daddy. Or maybe I'm reading too much into it." She took the stack of papers and laid them on the desk. "Forget it. I'm not a psychologist. I'm just a grunt who shoots guns and fights. I can't even analyze my way out of my own hang-ups." Her shoulders slumped and she straightened the pile on the desk, her hands shaking slightly.

This was the first sign of weakness Andrew had seen in Dix. Up until then, she'd been ready to charge into any situation, take on any challenge and kick butt. This chink in her armor made him look at her differently. What did he know about this woman other than what it said on her dossier?

She squared her shoulders and looked back at the safe. "Can you tell if anything is missing?"

Andrew tore his gaze from her and glanced into the

safe. "I don't know. I never did an inventory on the contents. Most of my stocks and bond certificates I keep in a safe-deposit box in a Portland bank. I don't have any jewelry, other than a pair of diamond cuff links my parents gave me at my college graduation."

"So what is all of this?" She waved to the items on the desk.

"Things that meant something to my grandfather." Andrew sifted through the collection. There was a ledger his grandfather had kept to note expenses pertaining to the house, a bundle of letters tied with a string and a few large envelopes.

Dix lifted the bundle of letters that had yellowed with age. "The postmarks on these go all the way back to the 1930s."

"They do?" Andrew slipped the string off the bundle and took one of the letters.

Taking a couple of them off the top, Dix pulled them from their envelopes. "These letters all begin with *My Dearest Thom* and end with *All my love, Rowena.*"

"Thomas Stratford was my grandfather's name. Rowena was my grandmother."

Dix smiled. "These are love letters between them. How sweet."

Andrew dug into the pile again and found a small leather-bound book. He ran his fingers over the smooth surface and opened it. Each page had a date written on one corner and an account of what had happened on that date.

Third night at sea and thus far we've not run into the coast guard or any other privateers in the waters. The sea has been fairly calm with the wind out of the Northwest. Luckily, we've had no storms or fog with which to contend. At our current rate, it won't take long to get to San Francisco with our cargo.

Dix leaned over his shoulder. "What have you got?" Her nearness made him warm all over. "I believe it's a captain's log for a boat or ship." Andrew turned the book over and opened it to the inside cover, searching for the name of the author. None existed. He opened to another page and read.

My love and I had to abandon our vessel at the dock when revenuers descended on our decks. Thankfully, we were in town at the time. Fortunately, our first mate was able to escape and find us, giving us sufficient warning. We were able to get away, but had to leave behind all of our belongings. Our cargo was declared contraband and was confiscated. We had invested every penny we owned in those barrels and now we are destitute. True, we are without means, but not without our wits and love.

Andrew shook his head. He knew this story. His grandfather had told him the adventures of a certain pair of rumrunners who'd dodged the law so often they'd made quite the reputation for themselves. The book must have been where he'd gotten the stories.

He turned the page and read on.

After hiding in the roughest neighborhoods of the city and being constantly on the lookout for revenuers and lawmen, we got word our buyer had been the one to inform the police of our illicit activities. Not only had he turned us in, he was secretly given our cargo as payment for the tip. We will have our revenge!

"Turn the page. I want to know what happened next." Dix leaned over his arm, her body warm next to his.

Andrew's pulse quickened and his groin tightened. The woman had no idea what she was doing to him. In that dress, her bare arm touching his, she was stirring up so much lust inside him, he could hardly breathe, much less focus.

"Finished reading that page?" she asked.

He nodded.

She turned the page for him, her fingers brushing against his. His nerve endings lit like Fourth of July fireworks, sparking desire throughout his body. His vision blurred. Thankfully, Dix read the next passage aloud.

"Today, revenge is ours. We have recovered, in worth, all that has been taken from us. Now the race is on to escape SF before we are discovered, and make our way north. I have never met a more ingenious woman, or one who is as willing to embark on a dangerous mission as my love. She amazes me at her resilience and cunning. I have met my match and am blessed to call her my wife."

Andrew flipped to the next page but he was happy to let Dix continue to read the words in her throaty voice.

"It has been many months since my last entry. I thought I had lost this journal in our struggle toward a new life and a new home. Alas, I found it buried among the few items retained from our past. We have made many sacrifices and started over—

new names and a new home, in a beautiful town that has welcomed us with open arms. We live by the sea, which will always be a part of us, even if we don't traverse its waters anymore.

"My love is expecting a child and I cannot begin to describe how full is my heart. I know there is much to do to ensure a stable life for the baby and for my love, but I have work at the local mill and I'm climbing the ranks quickly. I hope to own a business of my own someday. Our secrets, with our treasure, are safely stowed until such a day as they might be needed. For now, we are happy and have all we could wish for…each other."

Again, turning the page, Andrew was disappointed to find the rest of the book empty. He could have gone all night listening to Dix.

"That's it?" Dix exclaimed. "I want to know what happened to them."

Andrew closed the book and laid it on top of the other documents, not ready to move away but sure it was the right thing to do. "I know what became of them."

Dix touched his arm again, sending a pulse of electric shocks through his system. "You know?"

He drew in a steadying breath and let it out before answering. "Yes."

"You mean you know who they are?"

"I'm pretty sure." Though the journal had no name written on it or inside, he knew who'd written it. "My grandfather used to tell me stories of a daring pair of rumrunners who risked it all to make their fortune."

"Who were they?"

He smiled. "My great-grandparents. To the people of Cape Churn they were known as Margaret and Percival

Mason. I suspect the journal was a family secret passed from their daughter, Rowena, to my grandfather, her husband, Thomas."

"A more modern-day Wild West?"

"Exactly. It was during the Prohibition era. You see, before Margaret and Percival came to Cape Churn, it would appear they had built a reputation as notorious rumrunners Peg and Percy Malone. On their last run from British Columbia to San Francisco, the man to whom they were to sell their whiskey double-crossed them. He turned them into the law. Their ship was confiscated and the rum disappeared."

"Into the cellar of their stool pigeon?" Dix offered.

Andrew nodded. "Peg and Percy were never caught. Two days after their ship was confiscated, the San Franciscan who'd turned them in reported a robbery at his jewelry store and claimed it had to be Peg and Percy Malone. Every town along the coast was alerted, and a reward was offered, but the authorities never caught the infamous pair."

"Because they no longer existed." Dix grinned. "Good for them. What happened to the jewels from the heist?"

Andrew shrugged. "You read it. They hid it until such a time as they needed it."

"You think they ever needed it?" Dix's eyes narrowed.

"If they had tried to sell the jewelry, they risked being caught. With a baby to think about, they couldn't take that risk."

"Are you sure that's all that was in the safe?" Dix walked over to peer inside. "No fancy jewelry? No treasure?"

Andrew paced across the room and back. "You think it's possible someone broke into the house looking for the jewels?"

"It's a valid motive."

"You have to remember, this house wasn't here when Peg and Percy hid their treasure. My grandfather built this house for his bride, Rowena."

"Could Rowena's parents have given her the treasure to hide in the house?"

"Maybe, but I doubt it. They died when she was twelve."

"Taking their secret to their graves." Dix sighed. "So somewhere in or around Cape Churn is a treasure."

"Theoretically." Andrew placed all the documents and the journal into the safe and closed the door. "The treasure could be in the bay. If they arrived to Cape Churn in a boat, they could have scuttled the boat at the bottom of the bay."

Dix's eyes widened. "Is that what those two guys in the café were doing with the maps?"

Andrew nodded. "Seems they found what was supposed to be a fictional account of Peg and Percival's escapades and they're convinced the boat is at the bottom of the bay."

"Do you think that's where they hid the treasure?"

"I really hadn't thought about it. As a kid, I thought the stories my grandfather told were really just stories to entertain me."

"And now?"

He frowned. "Now I think he might have been telling them to me for a reason."

"He wanted you to know there was a treasure out there. If not for you to find, then for your heirs." Dix tilted her head. "And you don't want to get to it first?"

"I have to admit, the twins sparked my curiosity. But what do I need with the money? I have all I can use."

"I contend that it's not about the money. It's about the legacy."

"If my great-grandparents had wanted that legacy to carry on, they would have told someone where the treasure was. They couldn't unearth the treasure without risking exposing themselves. But their heirs could."

"But you said they died when Rowena was twelve. Then their secret would have died with them."

"True."

"Here, let me play devil's advocate." Dix leaned her bottom against the desk and crossed her arms over her chest. "If you let someone else find it, that's a legacy you let pass you by that could have gone to Leigha or Leigha's children."

Sweet heaven. When Dix crossed her arms, it plumped her breasts and drew Andrew's attention to those two lovely mounds. He dragged his gaze up to her full, lush lips. "Did anyone ever tell you that you're beautiful when you're so intense?" Andrew couldn't resist tucking a strand of Dix's hair behind her ear.

She captured his finger in her hand.

For a moment Andrew thought she might break his finger in two.

"No one has ever told me I was beautiful." Her brows descended and her gaze met his. But she didn't let go of his hand.

"Someone should have."

She shook her head slowly. "What were we talking about?"

"Legacies." He raised his other hand and brushed his thumb along her cheek, careful not to bump his stitches.

"Legacies?" Her voice came out in little more than a whisper and her hand tightened on his.

"What I don't understand is why Fontaine sent me a beautiful bodyguard." He tipped Dix's face upward and slid his thumb across her lips.

"I'm not beautiful," she said, her voice so soft she could barely hear it herself.

Andrew ignored her protest. "Did he not realize how distracting it could be?"

Her lips puckered ever so slightly against his thumb, but she said, "We should concentrate on the issue at hand."

"If I weren't such a messed-up bastard, I'd kiss you right now."

Dix shook her head and raised her hand to cup his scarred cheek. "We all have our scars."

He circled her waist with his injured hand and the back of her neck with the other, bringing her closer until her belly pressed against the hard ridge beneath his trousers. "Some more so than others."

She tipped her head and stared into his eyes. "Some have deeper scars on the inside. Scars that can't be seen but still hurt."

Andrew bent to claim her lips in a long, slow kiss.

She wrapped her hands around the back of his neck and deepened the kiss, opening her mouth to him.

He slid his tongue along the length of hers, caressing it with long, slow thrusts. She tasted of chocolate ice cream, sweet and too tempting to pass up.

When he finally remembered to breathe, Andrew leaned his forehead against hers and whispered, "What happened to you, Dixie? What scars are hiding beneath that beautiful, tough exterior?"

As the words left his mouth Andrew felt Dix's body go from soft and receptive to stiff and resistant.

She pushed away from him and scrubbed a hand over her face. "Mr. Stratford, that should not have happened."

"But it did."

"And it won't happen again."

"No?" He reached for her.

She moved away. "Look, we're better off keeping our relationship on a professional level." Then in her coldest, most distant voice, she said, "It's been a long day. If you'll excuse me, I'd like to check on Leigha before I call it a night."

With those parting words, she left the study and walked up the stairs, her back straight, her head held high.

Andrew watched her until she disappeared. Then he sat at his desk and called himself every kind of fool in the book.

No matter how tempting her lips or how perfect the curves of her body felt against his.

You don't kiss the help.

Chapter 11

Dix held herself together all the way up the sweeping staircase, counting each step as she went to take her thoughts off the man in the study below. But each riser represented one step farther away from what she really wanted. And that was to run back down and throw herself into Andrew's arms and kiss him again like they might not see another tomorrow.

But she wasn't there to kiss the client. And she had too many hang-ups with her past to let herself dare to fall for a guy. Every time she thought she could settle down, she got that itchy feeling to move. The longer she stayed in one place, the more she wanted to leave. Ever since she'd been held captive, she couldn't stand to be confined. She'd barely spent any time in her apartment in Vegas. If she wasn't out on the street running, she was hiking in the hills or working out at the gym.

No. Just no.

She couldn't wish herself on anyone.

Stick to the job. Leave the emotions out of it.

Dix checked on Leigha. The little girl lay curled into the blankets, still wearing her sundress.

In keeping with her need for continuous motion, she strode to the child's dresser, rummaged around quietly and found a soft jersey nightgown. As carefully as possible, she undressed Leigha and slipped the nightgown over her head. Dix went to the bathroom, wet a cloth with warm water and returned to wash Leigha's face and hands. When she was done, she pulled the blanket up to the little girl's chin and bent to press a kiss to her forehead.

A smile curled the corners of Leigha's mouth and she tucked a hand beneath her cheek and slept on.

If only it were that simple to fall asleep. Dix turned to find Andrew standing in the doorway, his gaze on her.

"She should be okay for the night. I'll leave my door open and listen for sounds," Dix said.

"Thank you for taking care of her."

"It's not difficult. She's a wonderful person. Anyone would do the same."

Andrew's mouth tightened. "Not everyone."

Dix's gut burned.

He was right.

Jeannette had tried to kill her own daughter. And Dix thought *she* was messed up. Jeannette had been one deranged woman. Too bad she'd let her crazy loose on her daughter. How much had that damaged the child?

Dix shook her head. The three of them were so much alike in many ways. Each damaged by the actions of others. Each of them suffering some form of PTSD. Yeah, Dix didn't need to add to the Stratford family's problems with ones of her own.

She strode toward the door.

Andrew didn't move until the last minute, turning sideways to let her through.

Just when she thought she might make good her escape, he touched her arm and stopped her.

"Dix?"

She froze, unable to move. If she were honest with herself, she was *unwilling* to move, afraid that she would do something she would regret like throw herself into his arms. Flames ignited where his hand touched her bare skin and spread through her body like wildfire. She stared at that hand, willing it to release her.

"I'm sorry if I took advantage of you," he said. "But I'm not sorry I kissed you."

Her belly clenched and heat pooled at her core. "Damn you," she said between her teeth. "Why couldn't you leave it?" That unnamed "it" hung between them like something physical and alive.

"Tell me you didn't feel it and I'll leave you alone."

She dropped her chin to her chest to keep from looking at him. Her gaze fell to his scarred hand and she remembered the way the grafted skin felt against the back of her neck. Smooth, cool and so tender. "I didn't feel anything." She lied to him. To herself.

He raised his hand, cupped her chin and lifted her face, forcing her to see him. "Look me in the eye and tell me you didn't feel anything," he whispered, his breath warm on her cheek, tingling against her lips and smelling of chocolate ice cream.

She fell into his ice-blue gaze, her resolve crumbling with every breath. Dix, the MMA fighter, Army Ranger and all-around tough gal, melted into goo as she stared into Andrew's eyes.

That urge to move hit her like a freight train. She

popped up on her toes, grabbed his cheeks between her hands and kissed him hard, and then she ran. Down the stairs, through the study and out into the garden, her eyes burning from holding back the tears. Since her capture, she'd refused to cry. *Ever.* Nothing could be as bad as being tortured by the enemy, never knowing if you'd live to see another day. *Nothing.*

Not even this heart-pounding, gut-wrenching certainty that she could never love again. As a person, as a partner, she was too broken to allow someone else into her world for any length of time.

A few minutes stretched into fifteen as Dix stood in the chilled night air, her skin bathed blue in the moonlight, her face turned to the sky. She counted over three hundred stars before her pulse returned to normal and she could face going back into the house and its constrictive walls.

Up the stairs and into her room, she moved quietly, grabbing clean underwear and her soft sleep T-shirt. Then ducked into the bathroom.

During her years in the military she'd honed her bathing skills to make her movements swift and efficient in the shower. She made mental images of her problems, imagining them washing down the drain with the shampoo and soapsuds. When she rinsed clean she almost felt normal. Except for the hollowness in her chest.

She'd get over it. Having survived a lot worse, Dix knew she could get over anything, given enough time.

When she stepped into the hall, soft sobs caught her attention. They emanated from Leigha's room.

Wishing she'd brought a pair of shorts, Dix tiptoed down the corridor to Leigha's room.

The little girl lay on her side, curled in the fetal position, her hand on her face, tears slipping down her cheeks.

Dix could hear the shower going in the master suite through the open connecting door. Quickly, she slipped between the sheets and gathered the girl in her arms. "Shh, baby. Everything is going to be all right."

Leigha's sobs subsided as she snuggled against Dix. Soon she lay quiet and still, her breathing deep and restful.

For a long time Dix stared at the ceiling, her lips tingling and places farther south burning inside. All the while, the man who'd stirred the embers settled in the king-size bed in the connecting room, a short distance away.

What would he think if she walked into his room and slipped between the sheets of his bed?

She closed her eyes and tried not to let her thoughts stray in that direction. The last thing she needed was to sleepwalk into Andrew Stratford's room and climb into bed with him. She would be completely powerless to resist her body's desire.

Andrew lay for hours, staring out the window at the star-filled sky. He knew the minute Dix had returned to the house because he couldn't rest until she was safe inside the walls. He'd gone down to the kitchen on the pretext of getting a glass of water, when, in fact, he'd known he could see the garden from the kitchen window. He watched like a voyeur as Dix stood staring at the sky, her skin and the white dress turned a mystical blue in the moonlight.

He'd wanted to join her there, pull her into his arms and kiss away her doubts. But who was he to woo the woman? He was scarred, damaged and ugly.

Dix deserved a man who didn't frighten children with his face. A man who had a lot more to show for his life than a bank account and a huge mansion that was too big for a family. Like she said, it might as well be a hotel. And he also came with strings attached. Whoever loved him had to love his daughter, too. She'd also have to understand that no matter what, Leigha was his number one priority.

What would a former Army Ranger and MMA fighter want with a broken-down stockbroker, a mansion on the edge of nowhere and a little girl?

Yeah, that was Andrew's life and he wouldn't have it any other way. He'd earned his scars saving his daughter, and he'd do it all over again. Leigha was worth every bit of the pain he'd suffered through skin grafting. Physically, she'd come out of the incident with a mild case of smoke inhalation, which was better than he could have expected. Inside, she'd take a little longer to heal.

They had all their lives to heal together.

Eventually, Andrew fell into a fitful sleep where fires burned. This time, not only was Leigha's life at stake, Dix was trapped behind a wall of flame. Her pretty white dress caught fire and she writhed in pain. Only she didn't scream or cry. She looked at him and told him to save Leigha. Just save Leigha.

No.

He couldn't let Dix die in the fire. Burning to death would be the most painful way to die. Having burned his hand, he knew the amount of pain flames could inflict on a body. He couldn't leave her to die like that.

But first he had to find Leigha and get her to safety. He searched the room, even looking beneath the bed. Instead of Leigha, he found Jeannette, laughing at his desperation. She flung a flaming blanket at him. It covered his head and he couldn't see his way out of the flames.

"Andrew," someone called.

He struggled to open his eyes. If only he could see, he'd follow whoever was calling to him out of the fire. But no matter how hard he tried, they wouldn't open.

"Andrew. You're dreaming. Wake up." A hand touched his shoulder and stroked down his arm. "Wake up. You're dreaming."

He grabbed the hand in his and held on, pulling himself out of the flames and into his bedroom. With what felt like a mighty effort, he forced his eyes open and stared up into the moss green eyes of the woman who'd sacrificed herself in the dream fire so that he could save his daughter.

"No," he said, his voice hoarse. He sat up, swung his legs over the side of the bed and pulled her against him, holding her tight. She was safe. Thank God, she was safe.

"It's okay," she said, stroking his hair, talking in a soothing tone. "You were dreaming."

As he surfaced from the lingering effect of the dream, he realized she wore only a T-shirt.

She stood between his legs, her skin pressed against his.

His pulse, still racing from the terror of the dream, continued to pound through his veins now for an entirely different reason.

He ran his uninjured hand up her back and down to the swell of her bottom. Her curves were soft, but the muscles firm beneath her skin.

"Are you awake now?" she whispered.

"Sweetheart, I'm so awake, my body is on fire." He gripped her hips, careful not to disturb his stitches, and set her away from him. "You'd better go now. If you stay any longer, I don't know if I'll be able to keep my hands to myself."

Dix stood still, staring into his eyes, her hands resting on his shoulders, her bottom lip caught between her teeth.

Andrew wanted to suck that lip into his mouth so badly he groaned.

"Are you okay?" she asked, her hands rubbing circles on his shoulders.

"No, I'm not okay. You're standing in front of me in only a T-shirt, and I'm fighting an uncontrollable urge to rip it from your body, toss you in the bed and make love to you."

She continued to worry that bottom lip, until finally she let go of it and removed her hands from his shoulders.

Andrew resigned himself to the need for a very cold shower and watched as she backed out of the V of his legs.

Dix shot a glance toward the connecting door to Leigha's bedroom. Nothing stirred in that direction. Then she grabbed the hem of her T-shirt and yanked it up over her head.

She stood in front of him wearing nothing but a pair of lace panties that left very little to the imagination.

Andrew's heart stood still, his lungs seized. Blood rushed through his veins and he sucked in a ragged breath. "I never would have thought a former Ranger and MMA fighter would wear lace panties."

Dix chuckled. "I might be tough on the outside, but I'm all female on the inside." She held out her hand. "I'm not asking you to fight your urges. I'm finding I have a few of my own."

"I won't do anything you don't want me to," he said, pulling her to stand between his legs again.

"Just take it easy on me. I haven't done this in a long time."

He smoothed his hands over her hips and upward to

cup her breasts. "You're even more beautiful with your skin kissed by moonlight."

She wove her fingers through his hair and bent to press her lips to his. "You taste like chocolate ice cream."

He clamped his arms around her and lay back on the bed, pulling her with him. Then he rolled to his side, easing her onto the mattress. "Say the word and it all stops here."

She reached for his cheek, laying her hand across the ragged scar.

He fought his natural instinct to flinch, but held steady and let her trace the line from his temple to the corner of his mouth.

"This hurt, didn't it?" she asked.

"Not as much as it would have hurt if my daughter had died in that fire."

Her eyes narrowed. "This isn't a burn scar."

"No."

Dix's brows lowered. "*She* did that? Jeannette?"

He nodded. "She fought to keep me from saving Leigha."

Her finger slipped over his lips. "If she were still alive, I'd kill her."

"Even I didn't have that satisfaction."

"What happened to her?"

"She dove, headfirst, out of the eight-story building."

Dix shook her head and leaned up to press her lips to the corner of his mouth where the scar began. "Was that what you were dreaming about?"

"Some." Her mouth moving across his jaw scrambled his wits. "I was back in that apartment. I couldn't find Leigha. Jeannette was there...and you."

Her eyes widening, Dix stared up into his eyes. "Was I helping or hurting?"

"You told me to save Leigha."

"You should have let me fight off Jeannette."

"Enough about my dreams. Why were you awake?" He smoothed a strand of blond hair away from her eyes and kissed the tip of her nose.

"I have dreams of my own."

"About?"

She shrugged. "Doesn't matter. They were just dreams."

"Bad enough to wake you." He nodded. "When you're ready, I want to know what you dream about. I don't know enough about you." He brushed his thumb across her bottom lip where the thin line of a scar marred an otherwise beautiful face. "Like where did you get this little scar? In the fighting ring?"

She shook her head and pulled him closer to kiss his lips. "No. In a much darker place," she whispered against his mouth. Then she kissed him harder, thrusting her tongue through his teeth to connect with his.

Andrew tasted, twisted and stroked until he was forced to come up to breathe. He stared into her eyes, wondering what had caused the shadows in their green depths. There were so many unanswered questions about this fighting woman.

But for now, she wasn't willing to share her story. However, she *was* willing to share her body and she'd asked for him to be gentle.

Taking it slowly, he kissed a path from her lips along her jawline to the sensitive area beneath her earlobe.

Dix laced her fingers in his hair and guided him lower.

Andrew skimmed his mouth along the long line of her neck and pressed a kiss to the pulse beating at the base of her throat. Unable to stop there, he moved lower, at first kissing and then tonguing the swell of her breast until he reached the rosy nipple puckering beneath his touch.

Dix arched her back and pressed her hands against the back of his head, urging him to take more.

Flicking, licking and nipping at the beaded tip, he teased her until she writhed beneath him.

Then she took his head between her hands and dragged him to the other breast.

He treated that one to the same, until the tip beaded and Dix moaned.

With increasingly difficult restraint, he plied kisses and nips to each rib, working his way slowly down her torso to the thatch of curls covering her sex.

His body on fire, he fought to keep it slow, steady and controlled, when all he wanted to do was part her legs and thrust inside her.

As if she heard his thoughts, she spread her knees farther apart.

Andrew moved over her, positioning himself between her legs, slipping farther down her body until he hovered over the juncture of her thighs.

Dix pushed her panties over her hips.

Taking over from there, Andrew dragged them down to her ankles and off. Then he stroked the inside of her calves and thighs with the tip of his finger, drawing a line toward her glistening center.

Her chest rose as she dragged in a ragged breath. "I feel like I'm coming apart at the seams."

"Maybe you need to. Maybe we both need to." Andrew thumbed her entrance swirling around the inside, collecting the musky juices. From there, he dragged his wet digit up to that special place. Parting the curls and the folds, he stroked that little nubbin of flesh.

Dix moaned, lifted her knees, dug her heels into the mattress and pushed upward. "Oh, dear heaven, there!" she whispered.

He bent and tongued that very spot, flicking, licking and teasing.

Dix's back arched and her hips rose. "Yes!" she cried, her voice hushed but no less strident. Her body tensed beneath his and her fingers curled into his scalp. She stayed that way for a prolonged moment.

Andrew continued to caress her with his tongue until she fell back to the bed on a sigh, gripped his hair in her fingers and dragged him up her body.

"I need you inside me." She kissed his jaw and slid her hands over his shoulders and downward to slip beneath his boxers. Hooking her fingers into the elastic, she tugged the shorts downward.

He rolled off the bed, dropped his boxers and reached into the nightstand, praying he had at least one condom there. Since moving from New York City, he hadn't even thought about making love to a woman. After the horror of Jeannette, he wouldn't consider a one-night stand.

But the drawer had been packed and moved full. Thankfully, he found a string of packets and tore off one.

"Glad one of us is thinking." Dix took the packet from him, opened it and swung her legs over the side of the bed to face him. With deliberately slow movements she rolled the protection over him, her hands gliding down the length of him to the base. With a sassy half smile, she looked up. "Ready?"

Sweet heaven.

He growled deep in his throat, scooted her back on the bed and climbed up between her legs. Nudging her with the tip of his erection, he said, "You tell me if I'm ready."

"Mmm." She clutched his buttocks, widened her knees and guided him to her. "I'd say yes."

Gently he eased into her, careful not to hurt her. Her slick entrance made it easy and soon he was all the way inside. Her channel contracted around him, sending electric currents throughout his body. Going slowly would kill him. But she'd asked him to go easy. And he would.

"Can you go faster?" she asked, her voice tight, breathy.

"Are you sure?"

"Oh, yeah." She tightened her hold on his buttocks and pushed him, slamming him right back in. Again and again, setting the pace.

When Andrew took over, he plunged in and out, increasing the rhythm and intensity.

Dix let go of him and clutched the comforter in her fingers. She buried her heels in the mattress and raised her hips to meet his every thrust.

The tension built inside Andrew. The ripples of fulfillment started from where he touched her inside, spreading through his body and outward to the very tips of his fingers. He thrust one last time and buried himself deep.

Dix wrapped her legs around him, holding him as close as two people could get.

Waves of sensations washed over him and he shook from the force. When he finally came back to earth, he lowered himself on top of her and rolled to the side, taking her with him. "Wow. You are amazing."

Dix let go of a long breath and lay back against the pillow, a smile teasing the corners of her lips. "You're not so bad yourself."

He leaned up on his elbow and twirled a strand of her hair around his finger. "So where do we go from here?"

Dix stared up at him, her green eyes darkening. "I don't know that we go anywhere. I can't…" She rolled out of the bed and gathered her clothes.

Andrew's chest tightened. "Can't what?"

"I can't do this."

He shook his head. "Do what?"

"I don't know. Trust me. You don't want to start something with me. I'm damaged goods."

He frowned and sat up. "*You're* damaged goods?"

"Yes." She pulled her T-shirt over her head and down past her hips. "Can we just leave it at 'wow'?"

Andrew shook his head. "I don't think I can."

She walked around the room, staring at the floor. "Where are they?"

Andrew rose from the bed and plucked her panties from the floor. "Looking for these?"

She snatched at them.

He raised them out of her reach. "Talk to me, Dix."

"There's nothing to talk about. I'm not the girl for you." She tried again to reach the panties. When she couldn't get to them, she shook her head. "Keep them." And she spun, running out of the room and down the hall to her own.

Andrew stood with a pair of sexy panties in his hand, wondering what the heck he'd done wrong.

Chapter 12

Dix put on a pair of underwear and jogging shorts, and waited a few minutes before opening her door again. She wanted to listen for any sounds in Leigha's room. Then she lay on the bed, staring up at the ceiling, cursing the wickedly delicious ache between her legs. She wanted more than anything to go back into Andrew's room and tell him she wanted to be with him. But she was afraid.

Afraid she'd feel confined and need to bust free. Afraid her nightmares would make her lash out.

Andrew and Leigha had enough healing to do without having her add her own problems to the mix.

Stick to the job. Don't get involved. Don't fall in love.

Dix clapped a hand over her mouth to keep from crying out. No. She couldn't be falling for Andrew Stratford. He deserved someone who wasn't broken. He'd have no problem finding a wife who could love him and Leigha. The father and daughter were perfect, everything a woman could want in a husband and child.

Eventually she slept, waking with a start when she heard the sound of little footsteps padding down the hallway.

Leigha stood in the doorway to Dix's bedroom, wearing her nightgown.

"Hey, sweetie."

"Are you awake?" she asked.

Dix pushed back the covers and got out of bed. "I am. Are you hungry?"

Leigha nodded.

"Let's get dressed and brush our hair before we go downstairs." Dix went to her bag and unearthed a T-shirt and a pair of jeans.

Leigha entered the room and wandered around, touching the few toiletries Dix had brought with her. "Do you like it here?" she asked.

Dix put on her bra beneath her nightshirt. When it was in place, she shucked the shirt and dragged the T-shirt on before responding. "Yes, I do."

The little girl tilted her head to the side and stared at Dix with her big blue eyes. "Why?"

"For one, I like *you*." Dix kissed the top of the child's head.

Leigha smiled. "I like you, too."

Dix walked to the window and stared out at the incredible view. "I also like that you can see the ocean from here."

"Me, too." Leigha lifted Dix's brush and ran it through her hair. "Do you like Mr. Stratford?"

The girl's question caught Dix by surprise and she dropped the jeans she'd been holding. Where was Leigha going with her questions? "Of course I do. Your father is a good man."

"I know. I just wondered." She laid the brush back on

the dresser and skipped to the door. "I hope Mrs. Purdy is making pancakes this morning. I love pancakes." She left the room and ran back to her own.

Dix finished dressing and followed Leigha.

The child had dressed herself in jeans, a T-shirt and sneakers. She was brushing her hair, though she struggled with the tangles.

"May I?" Dix held out her hand.

Leigha laid the brush in it. "Did your mommy brush your hair?"

"Yes, she did."

She stared at her reflection in the mirror. "Mine didn't."

Stumped again, Dix didn't know if she should comment or let Leigha's announcement pass. "Would you like me to braid your hair?"

She smiled. "Yes, please."

Though never a girlie-girl, Dix could dress up and do her hair when she had to. As a female MMA fighter, the sponsors and television networks had certain expectations of the lady fighters. Though they were punching, kicking and knocking each other out, they had to look good in the process. Hair, makeup, athletic clothes and toned bodies.

Dix had just wanted to hit something, but she'd been forced to look good while she did it. She'd gotten good at French braiding her hair.

Leigha's long blond hair was easy to braid, and so very soft. When Dix finished twisting the strands, she secured the end with an elastic band. "Ready?"

The child nodded. "I'm hungry."

"Me, too."

As she stepped out into the corridor, Dix's breath caught and held until she realized the hallway was empty. What had she expected?

Even though Andrew lived there, she wasn't destined to run into him every time she came out of her room. She released the breath she'd held and willed her pulse to return to normal.

What was it about the man that made her heart beat faster? He was just a man. Her client. Hell, he was more than that. Tall, dark, incredibly attractive even with the scars. He made her stomach flip whenever they were in the same room. And after last night... Boy, was she in trouble. He was an excellent lover.

Dix's belly tightened and her sex ached from the night before. Though she knew it was wrong to have slept with her client, she couldn't help reliving it over and over in her mind.

Mrs. Purdy was in the kitchen stirring batter in a big bowl. She beamed at Dix and Leigha. "Anyone up for pancakes this morning?"

Leigha raised her hand and shouted, "I am! I am!"

"Well, then, if you two will set the table, I'll make them fresh and hot for you." Mrs. Purdy nodded toward an upper cabinet. "Plates are in there."

Leigha went for the flatware.

"How many do I plan for?" Dix asked, her belly knotting.

"Just you and Leigha. I ate breakfast at home with my husband, and Mr. Stratford ate an hour ago and left for Portland. He said he had some business to take care of."

Dix's heart slipped into her gut like a ten-pound weight.

Andrew had gone to Portland without telling her. Not that he was obligated to inform her of his movements, but after last night, she'd thought he would at least say something to her this morning.

Like what? *Great sex.* Or worse, being there and being

caught in a painful silence where neither could look the other in the eye.

Dix sighed. Andrew had chosen the right option. Leave and avoid an awkward moment altogether.

Mrs. Purdy served them blueberry pancakes and blueberry syrup.

Leigha dug in, smearing blueberry juice across her smiling lips.

Her appetite a bit curbed by Andrew's departure, Dix ate at a more sedate pace. The pancakes were light, fluffy and heavenly. Even her mood couldn't dampen her enthusiasm for her breakfast. The next thing she knew, her plate was empty and she was licking the sticky syrup off her lips.

Dix and Leigha cleared the table, taking their empty plates to the sink for Mrs. Purdy to wash.

"Let's brush our teeth and then we can decide what we want to do today," Dix suggested.

Leigha ran up the stairs ahead of Dix.

Dix followed close behind, finding the little girl's eagerness contagious. She could explore the house and the grounds more thoroughly without Andrew around. She wouldn't be tense about running into him at every turn.

A few minutes later Dix entered Leigha's bathroom, where the little girl was wiping toothpaste from her mouth.

"What do you want to do today?" Leigha asked.

"I'd like to explore the house and yard," Dix said. "I want to see all of the places you like to play."

Leigha's eyes brightened. "Bennet will be so excited. He doesn't get many visitors where he is."

Dix frowned. "Just where is Bennet?"

"I'll show you." Leigha led the way down the stairs

and through the beautiful entryway to what Dix would describe as an old-fashioned parlor or sitting room.

Brewer followed, his toenails tapping on the marble tiles.

Leigha aimed for the far side of the sitting room and a massive fireplace. Fresh logs were laid out on the hearth, but no signs of ash could be found. Dix doubted the fireplace had been used lately.

When Leigha didn't slow, Dix frowned. Where did she think she was going? It wasn't as though they would climb up the chimney.

Leigha walked right next to the stack of logs and turned to the side where she pressed on one of the bricks. A door big enough for Leigha opened inward.

Dix had been in that parlor before and hadn't noticed the secret door.

Leigha entered, pulled a string above her head and a light blinked on, illuminating a room or passageway beyond. She turned and waved for Dix to follow. "It gets bigger once you go through the door."

Before Dix could take a step forward, Brewer shot through the opening and past Leigha, disappearing into darkness beyond.

Feeling like Alice in Wonderland falling down the rabbit hole, Dix followed Leigha through.

She waited for Dix to clear the little door and straighten before she turned and led the way through a narrow tunnellike corridor.

"Does your father know about this place?" Dix asked.

Leigha shook her head. "No. Bennet didn't want anyone to know."

A shiver of apprehension slipped across Dix's skin. "Why?"

"He said it was our secret."

Alarm bells went off in Dix's head. Anyone asking a child to keep such a big secret had to have nefarious plans. "Then why are you showing it to me?"

"Bennet trusts you. He said I could bring you and it would be okay."

"But not your father?"

She stopped for a moment, her chin dropping to her chest. "Sometimes Mr. Stratford doesn't like me very much."

Dix dropped to her haunches in front of Leigha. "Oh, sweetie, he does like you a lot. He loves you so much, he brought you here to live. He wanted you to have a great place to run and play."

Leigha scuffed her foot on the wooden flooring. "I like it when he reads to me," she conceded.

"Then ask him to do it more."

"He always seems too busy."

Dix made a mental note to tell Stratford to spend more time getting to know his daughter and making her feel more comfortable around him.

"You really should tell your father about this. What if you fell and got hurt? He wouldn't know where to look for you."

Leigha's brows dipped. "Do you want to come or not?"

Dix nodded, knowing she'd pushed far enough. If Leigha didn't show her father the secret corridors, Dix could show him later. She hated to think of Leigha wandering around and possibly getting hurt and no one knowing how to find her.

As she followed Leigha through the narrow corridor, Dix caught occasional glimpses through peepholes in the walls. At one point, she could see into a study through a narrow slat in the wall. She memorized the angle of the view. Next time she was in the study, she'd look for the hole in the wall that allowed her to see into the room.

Dix would have loved to take her time and explore more thoroughly, but Leigha appeared to be a child on a mission. After a while, the wooden flooring ended at a door. Leigha opened the door and the path gave way to hard-packed earth beneath their feet. The tunnel no longer was the wooden slats of antique walls but carved-out rocks and dirt.

Leigha stopped long enough to retrieve a flashlight from a cubbyhole in the dirt wall. She flicked the switch and aimed it into the darkness of the tunnel.

"How did you find this place?"

"Bennet showed it to me."

Walking behind the child who held a flashlight, Dix stumbled several times over the rugged ground. Eventually the small tunnel emerged into a cavern the size of a school auditorium.

In the middle of the cavern was a clear stream, meandering its way through.

Leigha hopped across the narrow strip of water and kept walking.

"Sweetheart, I'm not so sure this is a good place for you to play."

"Why?"

"Rocks could fall on you. There could be an earthquake that shakes this hillside and blocks the entrance."

"There's another way out."

"Still, it's not the best place a little girl could play alone."

Leigha frowned. "But I'm not alone. I have Brewer and Bennet."

The child's declaration didn't make Dix feel any better. "Where is Bennet?"

"He's here." Leigha smiled and waved her hand toward the cave wall.

Dix stared in that direction, wondering what the girl was seeing that she couldn't. "I don't see him." Yes, the girl had an imaginary friend. But just for grins, Dix asked, "Could you take me to him?"

Leigha giggled and turned to Dix. "He's right next to you."

A chill rippled down Dix's spine. "May I have your flashlight?"

Leigha handed her the device.

Dix spun in a circle. Still, she couldn't see anyone beside her, behind her or anywhere else. Willing the gooseflesh rising on her arms to subside, she pulled herself together. "I take it only you can see Bennet?"

Leigha giggled. "He's right beside you."

Standing in a dark cave, with only the beam of the flashlight cutting through the darkness, Dix was ready to grab the child and run back to the lit corridor. The creep factor was really high.

Brewer trotted up to Dix and stopped a couple of steps away, tail wagging and tongue lolling. He didn't seem to be looking at Leigha or Dix. Instead he appeared to be staring at the empty space beside Dix.

Another chill rippled across Dix's skin. "He's here now?"

Leigha nodded. "He says you're a gorgeous dame." Leigha tilted her head and shifted her gaze to Dix. "What's a dame?"

"A woman." Dix bunched her fists. If she had to hit someone, who would it be? She had to be able to see the person to hit him. But then, if he were a ghost, what good would it do to take a swing at him? Hell, what was she thinking? Ghosts weren't real. Or were they?

"Wow, this is getting a little too weird, even for me." She took Leigha's hand. "We should probably go back to the house."

"But I haven't shown you the place I like to play."

Dix's brows rose. "This isn't it?"

Leigha shook her head. "Of course not. It's too dark."

Dix handed the child the flashlight with a resigned feeling of dread. "Show me. Then we're going right back to the house."

Leigha took the light and headed for another tunnel on the opposite side of the cave from the one leading toward the house.

Dix prayed she'd remember which one would get them back. All she needed was to get lost in a maze of tunnels and caves with the little girl she was supposed to be protecting. Call her crazy, but she followed Leigha. She couldn't wait in the cave for the little girl. Not in pitch black. Not with a ghost called Bennet calling her a gorgeous dame.

Brewer walked beside Leigha as she led the way through the tunnel. Soon a faint light appeared at the end of the tunnel and grew larger as they neared.

Dix closed the distance between her and Leigha. Having no idea where the tunnel came out, she didn't want Leigha to fall over a ledge or be captured by the unknown threat Dix was hired to protect her from.

Leigha held up her hand. "You have to go slow here," she said. With her back to the side of the tunnel, she slipped around the corner.

Dix stepped into the bright light streaming into the tunnel entrance and let her eyes adjust. Then her heart screeched to a halt and her breath hung in her lungs. "Holy sh—shenanigans!" she said and stepped back, her hand going to the cave wall. Before her was the ocean and a one-hundred-foot drop to the rocky shoreline below. One more step and she would have gone over the edge and crashed to her death on the rocks.

"Leigha!" she shouted, her voice rising. "Leigha!"

Leigha appeared around the corner, her pretty brow furrowed. "What's wrong?"

Dix clutched the little girl's hand. "That's a deadly fall."

"I know. That's why I go around the side." She smiled at Dix. "It's okay. There's a path you can follow all the way down to the beach. That's where I like to play."

Dix wasn't so sure about sliding around the edge of the cave. One misstep and she'd be free-falling to the ground.

Leigha laughed.

"It's not funny," Dix grumbled.

"Bennet thinks so. He's making me laugh." Leigha slipped around the corner with Dix's hand in hers.

Dix either had to follow or let go of Leigha.

She followed, hugging the cliff side with her body as she inched her way around the corner.

Once out of the cave and onto a path, the trail widened and led a few feet away from the sheer drop-off. Leigha clicked off the flashlight and skipped ahead with Brewer.

Dix glanced up and couldn't see the top of the cliff above. From what she could surmise, they had exited the cave halfway down the side of the cliff. Stratford House was another one hundred feet above them.

The trail wound along the face of the cliff with its own pockets of trees and grass. Before long, Leigha came to a set of steps leading downward. Carved out of stone, the steps were partly natural with a few obviously chipped out by man.

As they neared the bottom, the trail narrowed again but the drop-off was less frightening.

At last, Leigha hopped off the last stone step onto a thin strand of beach.

"The tide is out. If the tide was in, the beach would disappear beneath the water."

"And your father doesn't know about this place?" Dix glanced at the sixty feet of beach.

"No," Leigha called out and darted away, running along the sand, chasing Brewer.

Dix shook her head and stepped onto the sand. First thing when she got back and Andrew returned home, she would show him what Leigha had shown her today.

If he wasn't concerned, he had no business being a father to a curious little girl. The child shouldn't be coming to this little beach alone. Wandering through a cave and a couple of tunnels alone was bad. A beach that disappeared at high tide was equally bad.

Dix's mind went through all of the horrible situations that could have happened. But there was Leigha, alive and happy, running across her favorite place to play. She'd be mad at Dix for telling her father about her secret place, but someone needed to let Andrew know what his daughter was up to. He probably had no clue.

Since Leigha never left the house through any of the known doors, and Andrew hadn't found the hidden door himself, no one could have known what Leigha was up to without dogging her every step.

She would burst that bubble later. For now, Leigha was safe. Dix would make sure they got back to the house without mishap.

The sun shone down on the little beach. Leigha threw a stick for Brewer and he retrieved it twelve times before he got tired of the game and wandered along the sand, sniffing.

Dix found a boulder to sit on and watched the waves

roll up on the beach. The continuous ebb and flow mesmerized her. She could stare at the waves and the ocean for a very long time and never get bored.

A shout drew her attention. Only the shout wasn't the high-pitched call of a little girl. Instead it was a man's voice.

Dix dragged her attention away from the waves, Leigha and Brewer to locate the sound. Out in the bay, she spotted a dive boat. A man on the deck waved toward her. From the distance, she wasn't exactly sure who it was. Not wanting to appear unfriendly, she gave a little wave back.

The dive boat swung around. For a moment Dix thought it was pulling away from the shore, but it made a complete circle and slowly moved toward the spot where Leigha and Dix were.

Fifty yards from the shoreline the boat captain stopped the boat, dropped an anchor and stared down at the water. He wore a dark wet suit, unzipped and peeled down around his waist, exposing a thick, muscular chest. He glanced up and yelled, "Can you hear me?"

Dix nodded. She could just hear the captain's voice.

"There are two divers down there. They should have been up by now. I'm going down to find them. If I don't come back up in thirty minutes, could you send for help?"

Dix climbed down from the boulder. "Yes, of course."

The man quickly shoved his arms into his wet suit and zipped. In under a minute he had on his buoyancy control device, tanks, regulator, masks and fins. Shoving his regulator into his mouth and pulling his mask over his face, he gave Dix the okay sign and stepped off the back of the boat.

Leigha came to stand beside Dix. Brewer stood at the edge of the water, staring toward the boat.

Dix counted the minutes. Searching the surface of the bay for bubbles. Unfortunately, the bay had just enough wave action to keep her from spotting any.

"Where did that man go?" Leigha slipped her hand in Dix's.

Dix shifted her empty hand to feel for the small hand-gun she'd tucked beneath her lightweight jacket before she'd left her room that morning. If the man who'd gone under planned to stage an attack via the bay, he'd have a surprise waiting for him. A lone woman and a little girl might look like easy prey, but Dix could take care of her-self and the child.

Fifteen minutes passed and still the man in the wet suit hadn't surfaced.

Dix moved closer to the shore, Leigha at her side.

"Is that man going to drown?" Leigha whispered.

Dix slipped her arm around the child's shoulders. "No, sweetie. He knows what he's doing." At least, she hoped he knew what he was doing.

A second later a head popped up out of the water. Then another and another only ten feet from shore.

One of the three men gave an okay sign and pulled his regulator out of his mouth. "I'm sending these guys up with you. They're too tired to swim back to the boat and the boat can't get any closer to the shore. Too many submerged rocks in the area. Can you get them to a tele-phone?"

"Sure," Dix said, not too happy about the unexpected company on the beach. Especially considering there would be two of them against her and one little girl.

The two men swam toward the shore, the third man shoving them from behind. When they could stand, the third man trod water a little away from the shore. "Are you from the Stratford House?"

Dix nodded.

"I'm Dave Logsdon. I'll call to check on them later. Thanks for helping out. I'd stay and make sure they got back to Cape Churn, but I need to take my boat back to the marina before the fog rolls in."

Dix nodded and waved to Dave.

He slid his mask in place and turned toward the boat.

Dix rested her hand on the gun beneath her jacket and waited for the two men to emerge from the surf.

They sat in the shallow water, pulled off their fins and tossed them to the shore. Then they stood and walked toward her and Leigha.

"Thanks for letting us come ashore. I don't think I could have made it back to the boat." The diver's voice sounded familiar. When he pulled off his mask and wet-suit hat, he grinned. "Hey, you're the lady who was with Stratford last night at the café."

Dix recognized the guy as one of the twins who'd been at the table next to them.

Leigha slipped behind Dix's legs.

Reminded of her duty to protect, Dix smiled, but kept her hand on her H&K .40-caliber pistol. "What happened?"

"We got hung up in kelp," the young man closest to Dix said. "By the time the dive master found us, we were almost out of air."

His twin added, "Thank goodness he did find us. I was beginning to think we weren't going to make it."

Both men dropped to the thick sliver of sand and pulled off the gear they'd been wearing, leaving on the wet suits.

Leigha tugged her hand. "That man made it to his boat." She smiled up at Dix, the relief evident in her eyes.

"Yes, sweetie, he did." Dix turned to the two men.

"The tide is starting to come in. I know you're tired, but we need to move you and the gear to higher ground before the beach disappears beneath the water."

The two men lurched to their feet, gathered their tanks and other gear.

Dix nodded toward the path. "Follow the trail up the hill. You can drop your gear when you get to where the path widens. It should be well above the watermark and safe."

"We can retrieve it later, after we rest," one of the twins said. "Right now, I just want to lie down for a couple of hours."

"Me, too," the other twin said. "But I don't want to lose the gear. We don't have it in our budget to replace it."

"No, we don't."

They reached the widened area of the trail and set the gear up against the rising bluff, as far away from the drop-off as they could get it.

When his hands were free, the first twin stuck one of them out. "By the way, I'm Jared Kessler." He elbowed his brother. "He's my brother, Joe."

Dix released Leigha's hand and took Jared's cautiously, prepared to take him down if he tried anything. He shook her hand and let go.

Joe offered his and did the same.

Not letting her guard down for a moment, Dix said, "You two can lead the way up the trail. We'll follow. When you get to the top, you'll have to squeeze around the side of a cave entrance. Be careful. A fall could prove deadly."

The twins nodded in unison.

"Got it," Jared said. He took a deep breath and let it out, and then started up the hill.

Joe followed.

Dix fell into step behind them, holding Leigha's hand and balancing her other hand on her gun. Brewer brought up the rear.

The trip up the trail took longer and was more strenuous than the descent. Still in good shape from all of her training as an MMA fighter, Dix didn't even get winded.

The twins were slow, but steady, arriving at the cave entrance as the sun slipped behind a heavy bank of fog rolling into the cape.

After the two men eased around the corner of the cave entrance, Leigha pulled Dix to a stop and pointed to the fog creeping toward shore. "Bennet calls that the Devil's Shroud." She glanced up at Dix. "What's a shroud?"

"It's like a blanket or sheet they pull over dead people," Dix answered, her gaze on the fog closing in on them. She shivered and turned away. The sooner they returned to the house, the better. Her hand on the gun, she slipped into the tunnel.

Jared and Joe stood at the entrance staring out at what should have been a view of the bay.

"That's some wicked fog," Jared said.

"I've never seen anything like it move as fast or blanket everything so thickly," Joe added, his voice low, his eyes wide. "I hope Dave made it back to the marina before it got too bad."

"Yeah," Jared agreed.

Brewer ran ahead, disappearing into the dark tunnel. Dix put Leigha in the lead with the flashlight, positioning herself between the child and the two men. She didn't like being in front of them, but she wasn't going to hand them the flashlight.

She let Leigha get a few steps of a head start. Then she turned toward Jared and Joe and said in a low tone, "Just so you know, I'm a trained fighter. I can kill people with my hands. Try anything against me or that little girl and I won't hesitate to kill." She stared into their eyes in the limited light from the cave entrance. "Understand?"

The twins nodded.

Jared grinned. "What kind of fighting? Tae Kwon Do? Jujitsu? Boxing?"

"Army Ranger and MMA."

Joe smiled. "Bro, you don't want to mess with her. She means business."

Jared nodded. "We're not going to hurt you or the girl. We're just happy you were here to get us out of the water. I've never been more scared of drowning in my life." He nodded toward Leigha. "But we better get moving before we lose sight of the only one here who has a flashlight."

Dix gave them a hard stare.

Jared and Joe both raised their hands.

"Seriously," Joe said. "We're not here to hurt you."

Only slightly convinced they were telling the truth, Dix turned and hurried after Leigha, who'd reached a corner in the tunnel. As soon as she turned, the light became so dim Dix could barely see the walls and floor. She put her hand out and lightly skimmed the cool stone surface, moving as fast as she could to catch up to the girl.

Footsteps and muttered oaths behind her indicated the twins were doing their best to keep up.

When she turned the corner, she could see the light ahead.

"Leigha, wait up," she called, tired of tripping over rocks.

The little girl stopped and shone the light back into her eyes.

Dix held her hand up in front of her face. "Other way, sweetie. Turn the light the other way. You're blinding me."

"Sorry." Leigha pointed the light at the floor.

The two men behind Dix caught up and they continued, entering the cavern with the stream.

"Are you sure you know where you're going?" one of the men said from behind.

"No, but the girl does," Dix reassured him.

"Seriously?" the guy said.

Dix chuckled and stepped over the stream.

Leigha entered the tunnel Dix recognized as the one she'd come through earlier. Before long they came to the door to the hidden corridor inside the house. Leigha flipped a light switch and left the flashlight in a small hole in the dirt wall.

"Now we're talking," Jared said.

A few minutes later they ducked through the door in the fireplace and emerged into the formal sitting room.

Jared and Joe grinned and laughed out loud.

"I would never have guessed we'd come out in a place like this," Joe said.

"I thought we'd end up in an ancient torture chamber." Jared stared around the room. "Where are we?"

"Stratford House," a deep voice said from across the room.

Dix spun toward the sound and her body heated at the sight of Andrew standing with his arms crossed over his chest, glaring at her. "Please explain yourself, Miss Reeves."

Chapter 13

Andrew had left that morning for Portland to meet with his attorney and accountant. But the farther away he got from Stratford House, Leigha and Dix, the more his chest tightened and his hands gripped the steering wheel. He'd had the overwhelming urge to turn around and go back.

Someone had attacked him on the cliff. Dix might be a trained soldier and a former MMA fighter, but she was smaller than most men. She could be overpowered. Then she *and* Leigha would be in danger. And he'd be too far away to help.

An hour and a half out of Cape Churn, he'd made a U-turn in the middle of the highway and exceeded every speed limit to return to Stratford House.

"I've been all over this house from top to bottom looking for the two of you. I even called Sheriff Taggert. He's on his way out here now." He drew in a deep breath and demanded, "Where have you been? And what are these two men doing in my house?"

Leigha came out from behind Dix and faced her father. "It was my fault. I wanted to show Dix where I like to play. It took longer than I thought it would."

Dix placed her hands on the girl's shoulders. "It's okay, Leigha. You don't have to defend me." She lifted her chin and stared at him. "We were playing outside when these two men got into a bit of trouble." She turned toward them. "You remember them from last night?"

Jared held out his hand. "Mr. Stratford, we're sorry to drop in on you like this."

Andrew recognized Jared and Joe from the café the previous evening, but he wasn't in the mood to be nice. He ignored the outstretched hand. "I thought I told you I didn't like people to just show up at my house."

"Sir," Joe said, "we were diving in the bay off the nearby shoreline when we got caught up in kelp."

"It was all we could do to get to shore," Jared finished. "Our dive boat captain helped us ashore and then went back to his boat. He had to get to the marina before the fog set in."

Joe ran a hand through his hair, standing it on end. "Miss Reeves brought us up to the house to use the phone. As soon as we can call for a taxi, we'll be out of your hair."

"No one's going anywhere," Andrew said. "A taxi won't be able to get here and back to town before the fog gets too thick. You'll have to wait until it clears."

"That's fine. We can wait out on the road," Jared offered, inching toward the door.

Dix frowned at the twins. "Don't be ridiculous. You're exhausted and probably on the verge of hypothermia. We can get some dry clothes for you and you'll stay here until the fog clears." She faced Andrew, her mouth set in a thin line, her chin high, as if daring him to kick her out with the guys.

Andrew loved the fire in her green eyes and the way she stood with her feet slightly spread, her fists bunched tightly. Ready for a fight.

Now that he knew Dix and Leigha were all right, his heartbeat was well on its way to returning to normal, but he wasn't letting Dix off easy. He narrowed his eyes and glared at her. She needed to fear his ire so that she didn't run off to God knew where with his daughter. She'd scared several years off his life. "Don't run off again without telling anyone where you're going," he said, his tone low, as intense as he could get it. He didn't want to be that scared ever again. "Understood?"

She glared back at him, giving him as much guff as he gave her. Then her mouth loosened into those full lush lips he'd kissed the night before and she nodded. "Understood. I'm sorry we upset you. It won't happen again." She ran her hand over the top of Leigha's hair. "Right, Leigha? You won't disappear without telling someone where you're going, will you?"

Leigha glanced up at Dix and then turned her gaze to her father. "No, I won't." She raised a hand, curled her fingers and extended the last finger and took a step toward him. "Pinkie swear."

Andrew stared at her hand, not sure what she was talking about.

"You heard her," Dix said. "Pinkie swear." Her lips twitched at the corners.

"I don't know what you mean."

Dix dipped her head sharply toward Leigha. "Go on."

Leigha and Dix obviously knew what a pinkie swear was, but Andrew didn't have a clue. Not to be shamed by the bodyguard, Andrew dropped to his haunches. "Show me."

Leigha took his uninjured hand, curled his fingers into a fist and then pulled out the last one. Then she hooked her pinkie with his and smiled. "I pinkie swear that I will always tell someone where I'm going before I leave."

"That's it?" He glanced up at Dix.

Her lips had spread into a full-blown grin. "You've officially been graced with a pinkie swear. Leigha knows she can't break that promise."

Leigha nodded. "I won't."

"Okay, then." Andrew straightened and ruffled Leigha's hair. "Now, go tell Mrs. Purdy you're okay and you would like to have two beds made up in the west wing for our guests."

As his daughter started to pass him, Andrew scooped her up and hugged her tightly. "Don't scare me like that again." He held her away from him and stared into her face. "I was very worried."

Leigha caught his face between her palms and kissed him on the forehead, like he'd done putting her to bed. "I'm okay."

"Good." He set her on her feet and brushed the hair out of her face.

Leigha skipped out of the sitting room with Brewer keeping pace, leaving Dix, Jared and Joe for him to contend with.

Andrew waved a hand. "Dix, you can go."

Her brows dipped. She opened her mouth but snapped it shut instead and left the room.

A chuckle rose up his throat but he swallowed it back. He'd hear about that later. Frankly, he looked forward to it. But now he had a couple of men in his house for what appeared to be overnight. Once the Devil's Shroud moved in, it wouldn't recede until the following morning.

His eyes narrowed and he glared at Jared and Joe. "What are you really doing in my house?"

Both young men started talking at once.

Andrew held up his hand. "Jared."

Jared nodded. "We were searching for the ship Peg and Percy Malone scuttled when they arrived in Cape Churn. We thought we saw it when we got caught up in the kelp."

"And you thought it would be okay to waltz into my house and make yourself at home?"

"No, sir," Joe said. "We would have gone back out to the dive boat, but we'd used up all of our scuba air and just didn't have the strength to swim back out. Dave told us to stay on shore. We were lucky enough to find Miss Reeves and your daughter on the beach."

"On the beach?" Andrew stared at the men as if they'd grown horns. "What beach?" In all the years he'd visited Stratford House, he'd never known there to be a beach on the property. The cliffs were too rugged to climb down.

The twins exchanged glances.

Joe faced Andrew. "There was a little bit of a beach at the base of the cliffs and a trail leading up to a cave. Tunnels in the cave led to the house and this room." He shrugged. "You should ask your daughter. She led the way."

He couldn't believe what he was hearing. A dull ache started in his temples and radiated through his head and down into his shoulders. The drive toward Portland and his subsequent confrontation with Dix and these men had taken their toll. "You two can stay, but don't touch anything or go anywhere you're not invited. And if you so much as harm a single hair on my daughter's head, I'll kill you with my bare hands."

Jared and Joe backed up a step, raising their hands. "We really don't mind standing out by the road until the fog clears, Mr. Stratford."

Joe elbowed his brother. "Speak for yourself." He faced Andrew. "You don't have to worry, Mr. Stratford. We won't hurt your daughter. She's a smart little girl. I can't believe she led us through those tunnels and cave. What makes it more amazing is that she can't be more than seven years old."

"Six," Andrew said, his anger spiking at what the men were telling him. It meant Dix had allowed his daughter to wander around dangerous caves, cliffs and beaches while he'd been away. He would have a few choice words for Miss Reeves.

Dix followed Leigha to the kitchen, where Mrs. Purdy was pulling a roast out of the oven. "Thank goodness you two showed up when you did. I'll just call Sheriff Taggert and tell him it was a false alarm."

The older woman lifted a phone out of a receiver on the wall and dialed the sheriff's office. "Gabe? Good. I'm glad it's you. Could you put a call out to Sheriff Taggert that Miss Reeves and Mr. Stratford's daughter are home and safe? No, they weren't lost, just out exploring. Thank you, Gabe. How are Kayla and the baby? That's nice. Glad to hear it."

Mrs. Purdy hung up and turned to Dix. "I'm just finishing dinner preparations and need to get to town before the fog's too thick to see the road. Leigha can show you to the west wing. I have a couple of bedrooms I keep aired out in case we have guests. We just need to put sheets on the beds. Do you two mind helping?"

"Not at all," Dix said. The woman had her hands full

with pots on the stove and bread baking in the oven. "Where can I find sheets?"

"In the linen closet at the end of the hallway. Leigha will show you, won't you, darlin'?" Mrs. Purdy smiled at Leigha. "She knows where everything is in the house. I'll finish up here and be on my way."

Dix had to agree with the housekeeper on that statement. Leigha had shown her places Dix hadn't dreamed existed. She wondered if there were other secret passages that led in and out of the house. If so, there might be more entries and exits that could be used by bad guys hoping to pay a surprise visit to the Stratfords. While she had Leigha alone upstairs, she'd ask the child if she knew about other secrets.

Leigha, with Brewer, once again in the lead, took Dix up to the second floor of the huge house and turned right instead of left to their wing of bedchambers.

"Bennet said he used to sneak into the house when the owners were sleeping and smoke cigars in the study downstairs." Leigha glanced back at Dix. "What's a cigar?"

"It's like a big, fat brown cigarette, only it smells a lot worse." The child had no limit to her curiosity. "Leigha, are there other secret tunnels or corridors in the house?"

Leigha shrugged and opened a cabinet door. "I don't know." The little girl's face reddened. "Here are the sheets."

Dix took out two sets of sheets and followed Leigha to the bedrooms Mrs. Purdy had designated. Inside, the rooms were spacious with rich, mahogany furnishings and light, airy curtains and comforters.

Dix suspected Leigha knew more than she wanted to admit about other secrets in the huge old mansion. "Will you show me the others tomorrow?"

Leigha took one end of the sheet and dragged it across the mattress. "Okay."

Dix played down her enthusiasm. "Thank you, Leigha."

To protect the family, Dix needed to know everything about Stratford House and its surroundings. She might even take a trip to the local library to see if they had any history on the place that could warrant someone wanting to get rid of the Stratfords. Secret passages leading to caves and the sea had to have had some basis in smuggling.

Between the two of them, Dix and Leigha made the beds in the rooms and put fresh towels in the bathroom across the hallway.

Andrew joined them in the hallway, carrying a stack of clothing.

Dix leaned to look behind him and raised her brows.

"Mrs. Purdy is filling them full of hot cocoa to warm them up."

"The beds are made. I'll sleep with Leigha tonight."

Leigha smiled and clapped her hands. "Yay! We can have a slumber party. I've never had a slumber party."

Dix's heart squeezed in her chest. The little girl should have friends to play with instead of the imaginary one. She shivered. Or ghost.

Never having believed in anything she couldn't see for herself, Dix refused to start now. Leigha had a wonderful imagination and a sense of adventure. Why not an imaginary friend? Maybe if she had real friends, she wouldn't need to make up a friend named Bennet.

When the house settled in for the night, Dix would have a heart-to-heart with Andrew. He needed to know about the hidden passageway in order to close it off to keep others from entering the house.

Dix held out her hands for the stack of clothing.

As he handed the items to her, Andrew caught her gaze. "We need to talk."

A thrill of excitement slipped through her veins. "Yes. We do." Had nothing else happened that day, she might have thought they would talk about what they'd shared in his bed the night before. With the twins in the house and she and Leigha having been missing for a couple of hours, Dix was almost certain he had a more serious conversation in mind.

Andrew's eyes narrowed briefly and then he turned and walked to the staircase. His expression had been unreadable.

She handed half of the clothing to Leigha and pointed to a bedroom. "You can put these on the bed in that room." Dix entered the other room and set her stack on the bed.

She met Leigha in the hallway. "Do you think Mrs. Purdy would make cookies and popcorn for our slumber party?"

Leigha's blue eyes lit up. "I'll ask."

"Don't just ask, Leigha. Offer to help. Grown-ups love to have company and help when they're cooking."

"I love baking cookies with Mrs. Purdy. She makes the best!" Leigha and Brewer ran ahead and descended to the first floor.

Dix held her breath until the child made it to the bottom without tumbling all the way down in her rush to the kitchen.

"How do parents do it? I'll be a nervous wreck by the time this gig is up," Dix muttered.

"You do the best you can to protect them, but you have to let them have some freedom or you'll make them afraid to live."

Dix spun to face Andrew. He stood so close behind

her, she took a step back. Her foot met air and she would have fallen down the stairs if Andrew hadn't reached out and grabbed her, slamming her body against his.

Her breath caught in her throat. Dix couldn't breathe and didn't want to. She was in Andrew's arms. If she inhaled, she'd take in the heady scent of his aftershave.

She closed her eyes, recalling the feel of his skin on hers, as they lay naked in his bed. Sweet heaven, Dix wanted to drag him back to that bedroom and do it all again.

Wrong, wrong, wrong! her logical thoughts warned her even as her fingers curled into the fabric of his shirt.

Andrew dipped his head, his mouth skimming her temple. "Are you all right?"

No, she wasn't. She was in her client's arms, lusting after him when she should be downstairs looking after his daughter.

"I'm fine," she forced out through constricted vocal cords, with barely enough air to make a sound.

His hands splayed across her lower back, pressing her closer.

She could feel the hardness of the ridge beneath his fly nudging her belly. *Holy hotness.* How could she extricate herself when all she wanted was to be even closer?

"Mr. Stratford?" a male voice called from below.

Dix pushed against Andrew's chest and stepped away, careful not to fall down the stairs. She shoved her hair back from her face and resisted the urge to fan herself as heat radiated throughout her body.

"Up here," Andrew responded.

Jared started up the stairs with his brother, Joe, right behind him. "Mrs. Purdy said you would be able to show us to the rooms we'll occupy tonight."

"I can do that."

"I'll go check on Leigha." Dix turned away but was caught up short by a hand on her arm.

"I'm serious," Andrew said, his voice soft enough only Dix would hear. "We need to talk."

She nodded, her pulse hammering, electric currents racing from where his hand held her arm through her body, dropping low into her belly.

When Andrew released her, Dix ran down the steps as if the devil himself was chasing her. Not that Andrew was the devil. Her own lusty thoughts were sending her into a tailspin she wasn't sure she could recover from.

She had begun to wonder if she was really needed there. In the couple of days she'd been at Stratford House, nothing had happened to make her think Leigha and Andrew were in danger. In their talk, she'd ask him if he'd made any progress on finding a permanent bodyguard to replace her.

The thought made her chest tighten and her eyes sting. Already, she'd formed an attachment to Leigha. But the connection she had with Andrew wasn't good. Even though it felt really good when they'd been together in his bed.

Chapter 14

Dinner had been festive with their two guests. Jared and Joe were entertaining, talking of some of the adventures they'd been on during summer break from their studies at Washington State University.

Andrew wasn't ready to think they were harmless. Not with his daughter's welfare at stake, but he did get caught up in their tales of archaeological digs in Africa, where they'd unearthed remnants of ancient civilizations. And then there were the dinosaur bones they'd found in North Dakota.

By the time they'd finished the roast beef and mashed potatoes Mrs. Purdy had left for them, the two young men were ready to call it a night. They headed for their respective bedrooms.

Leigha yawned and rubbed her eyes. "Are we going to have a slumber party?"

"If you stay awake long enough," Dix said. She gathered the plates and cups from the table and laid them in the sink.

"We'll see how you feel after a bath." Andrew lifted her in his arms and started for the stairs.

She laid her head on his shoulder and snuggled into his strong arms. "Are you coming to my slumber party, Mr. Stratford?"

"If you want me to," he answered, his voice catching in his throat. This was the first time his daughter had wanted him to participate with her in any activity. He'd sleep on a bed of nails if she asked him. Anything for her smile, for her acceptance.

He carried her to her bedroom and set her on her feet. "I'll get your bath started. You grab the pajamas you want to sleep in."

"Okay."

Dix had followed them into the bedroom, but she stood by the door. "Want me to take it from here?"

"No need. I can manage a faucet." He entered the adjoining bathroom, started the water and checked the temperature, and when it was right, he filled the tub.

Leigha entered behind him, carrying her nightclothes.

Andrew turned off the water and straightened. "I'll be back to kiss you good-night."

"And to stay for my slumber party?" she asked, looking at him with expectant eyes.

He smiled and ruffled her hair. "And to stay for the slumber party." Andrew didn't think she'd make it fifteen minutes after her bath before her eyelids closed and sleep claimed her.

He left the room and walked down the hall to the master suite, where he stripped out of the trousers and white shirt he'd worn for his aborted trip to Portland. In minutes, he'd showered and changed into a pair of sweats and a T-shirt. He padded barefoot through the connecting door into Leigha's room.

His daughter had dressed in her favorite pajamas and was sitting in the bed. Brewer lay curled up next to her.

Dix sat behind her wearing that darned T-shirt and a pair of athletic shorts, braiding Leigha's hair. She glanced up, her gaze raking over him. Then she returned to the braid she was working, pink spots of color glowing in her cheeks.

Leigha patted the bed. "Sit here. You can read a story while Dix braids my hair."

"Shall we pick up where we left off with *Island of the Blue Dolphins*?"

Leigha smiled. "Yes, please."

Andrew plucked the book from the shelf and settled on the edge of the bed. He read and Dix braided. Between the two of them, they had Leigha yawning by the time Dix secured the braid and Andrew finished the chapter.

Leigha slipped between the sheets and tucked her hand under one cheek. "Don't stop reading," she whispered. "I'm awake, just resting my eyes."

Andrew hid his smile.

Before he'd read another paragraph, he could see his daughter had fallen asleep.

Dix scooted to the edge of the bed, dropped her feet to the floor and exited the bedroom.

Andrew waited a moment or two more before he rose and set the book back on the shelf. He pressed a kiss to his daughter's forehead and pointed at Brewer. "Stay." As if he needed to tell the dog to stay with Leigha. She was his human and he'd protect her at all costs. Andrew tiptoed out of the room, closing the door behind him.

Dix had disappeared.

Andrew frowned. He'd specifically told her they needed to talk. Well, they were going to have that conversation, even if he had to drag her out of bed to do it. The thought of Dix lying in bed in that unflattering T-shirt made his groin tighten and blood burn hot through his veins.

He raised his hand to knock on her door but it opened before he could.

Dix's eyes widened when she spotted him standing there with his fist raised to knock. She'd been pulling a sweater on over her T-shirt and she'd put on a pair of sneakers. "Oh, there you are. We should go downstairs to the study or out on the porch. Do you think Leigha will be okay with the Kessler twins on the same floor?"

Andrew nodded. "If they try anything, Brewer will raise a ruckus and we'll hear them."

Dix glanced down at his bare feet. "You might want to put on some shoes."

"Why?" Andrew asked.

"Just trust me on this."

Andrew returned to his room, slid into some boat shoes and returned to the hallway.

Dix studied his shoes, hesitated for another second, seemed semi-satisfied with his footwear choice and led the way down the stairs.

He hadn't noticed just how taut her calves were or how narrow her ankles. He could imagine how those legs would feel wrapped around his waist again. And there he went, diving into his imaginary fantasy with his lusty thoughts of Dix naked.

When she reached the bottom of the stairs, Dix turned and walked past the study. She led him to the sitting room he'd found all of them standing in earlier that day. It wasn't his choice of places to conduct a conversation, but it would suffice.

Dix stopped in the middle of the room and faced him. "Now that Leigha isn't here, you need to know what she showed me today. But, first, do you have a padlock?"

He frowned. "Padlock?"

Dix nodded.

He held up a finger. "Don't go anywhere. I'll be right back."

Andrew left the sitting room and returned a minute later with a combination padlock.

Dix was standing next to the fireplace when he returned. She held out her hand and he placed the lock in it. "Do you know the combination?"

He nodded.

"Good. We'll need it." Then she did something peculiar. She ducked low and stepped into the fireplace. Granted, the logs weren't burning, but her actions were perplexing.

Dix pushed a brick and frowned. She pushed another and another until the last brick she pushed slid inward and the rest of the wall of brick slid open.

Andrew swore softly. "I've been all over this house and never knew that was there. How did you find it?"

She raised her brows. "I asked Leigha to take me to her favorite place to play."

"And this was it?"

Dix shook her head. "You haven't seen anything yet. Hold on to your hat—I'm about to tell you what your daughter has been up to when you weren't watching her."

Andrew tensed, ready to tell Dix he didn't need an outsider telling him how to raise his daughter. But then she disappeared through the small door.

His pulse quickened and he leaned across the hearth, peering into what looked like a very narrow corridor. Andrew ducked through the door and stood up straight. The ceiling of the corridor was as high as the ceiling of the sitting room. "Well, I'll be damned."

Dix snorted. "Babe, you need to see the rest."

His heart sped at her use of the word *babe*. He tamped

down the urge to reach out and crush her against him. But she moved away.

"I don't feel comfortable leaving Leigha for any length of time, but we need to go to the end of this corridor and lock the door to keep Leigha from going out and strangers from coming in. The Kessler brothers know about the tunnel now, but we don't know who else could have found it or will find it."

"Thus the need for the lock," Andrew stated. "I don't like leaving Leigha, either. Go," he urged her.

Dix hurried along the wooden floor to the end where it dropped out of the house and into the hillside tunnel.

Andrew went a few steps farther, studying the solid walls of the tunnel. "I can't believe this has been here all along and I didn't know. Makes me wonder if my grandfather knew. If so, why didn't he tell me?" He stared back at Dix.

She shrugged. "You said you were a lot like Leigha. Maybe your grandfather knew it was dangerous for a small child to wander around the caves and tunnels. He probably didn't tell you to keep you from getting lost or falling off the cliff."

Andrew's heart skipped several beats. "I thought Leigha was safe as long as she played in the house." He shook his head. "I didn't know she'd found a way out. But how?"

Dix frowned. "When I asked her how she found the tunnels, she said her imaginary friend showed her."

Andrew pounded his hand into his fist. "Her and that damned imaginary friend."

"She might have dreamed him up because she's lonely. Kids need other kids to play with."

"I know. I'm going to fix that. But it takes time." Andrew scrubbed a hand over his face and turned back to the narrow corridor. "For now, we need to block this passageway."

"Tomorrow, you need to follow it to the beach."

"What beach?" Andrew's head spun with the discoveries he'd never expected. He thought he knew his own home.

"You'll see when you follow the tunnels all the way out to the ocean." Dix's lips twitched into a smile. "You might have to have Leigha show you the way to keep from getting lost." She moved backward as Andrew re-entered the corridor.

He turned and pulled shut the door, slipped the padlock through the hasp and closed the lock. Then he leaned on the door and swore. "My six-year-old daughter has been wandering around in caves and out on cliffs and I sat in my office as if she were in a padded playroom."

Dix laid a hand on his shoulder. "She needs attention, and she's a little afraid of you."

Andrew jerked his head up. "Afraid? Of what?"

"You are pretty intimidating when you raise your voice."

"Damn it! I'm not intimidating!" His voice echoed in the long passageway.

Dix raised her brows and stood with her arms crossed. "I'm an adult, but I can see where she's coming from." Her lips quirked upward. "You can be downright scary to a six-year-old."

Andrew wanted to wipe that smile off her face.

With a kiss.

He started to step past her in the tight confines. His body brushed against hers and he couldn't resist. He turned and grabbed her, smashing her against him, his lips crashing down on hers.

She gasped, her mouth opening enough to let him thrust his tongue past her teeth and sweep along the length of hers.

At first her hands pressed against his chest, pushing him away. But the longer he kissed her the less she resisted.

Soon Dix's hands slipped up his chest and wrapped

around his neck. Her body melted into his and her leg curved around the back of his.

Andrew moaned and leaned her against the wall, his hands slipping down her back, over her buttocks and lower still to cup her thighs. He lifted. And, oh, those legs wrapped around his waist and squeezed tight.

He broke the kiss and drew in a deep breath. "You drive me crazy."

She laughed. "I think you have that backward." She brushed her thumb along the scarred side of his face and leaned in to kiss him again.

All that stood between them was the stretchy clothing they wore. It wouldn't take much to remove them…

Dix sighed. "We can't leave Leigha for long. I don't feel comfortable with her all the way up the stairs and us in this corridor where we wouldn't hear her if she screamed."

"You're right." He lowered her legs and helped her straighten her shirt. Then he took her hand and led her to the door in the fireplace.

Once they were in the sitting room, Andrew tilted his head to the side and listened for any sounds of distress.

The house remained silent. But that didn't mean anything. Even silence was threatening when it came to his daughter.

He didn't wait for Dix. He strode out of the sitting room and climbed the stairs two at a time, his heart beating faster as he neared the top.

He couldn't relax until he pushed the door to Leigha's room open and saw the girl lying in her bed, her hand tucked beneath her chin and Brewer looking up at him as if to reassure him that he was on the job.

Dix touched his shoulder. "I'll stay with her tonight."

"No." He turned and rested his hands on her hips.

"You'll stay with me. We'll leave the door open between the two rooms."

She cocked her brows. "Is that an order?"

"That's a strongly worded invitation I hope you will accept."

She stared at him for a long moment, her head moving slowly in a negative.

His heartbeat slowed to a stop and he held his breath, wondering if he'd pushed her too far. He'd never been good at asking people to do his bidding. As a businessman, he'd told people what he wanted and they did it. Not Dix.

"Say 'please,'" she whispered, her hand rising to cup his face. "Say 'please' and I'll think about it."

He swallowed, his groin tightening so hard he was glad he'd worn the sweatpants. "Please," he said through gritted teeth. He wasn't sure how much longer he could hold back from unleashing his passion on her.

Dix touched her lips to his and said, "Okay."

Andrew swept her up in his arms and carried her toward his bedroom, pulse pounding and every nerve in his body on fire, ready to make love to this incredible woman.

As he reached for the doorknob, a small voice called out. "Mr. Stratford? Dix?"

With a groan, Andrew held tightly to Dix for a moment and waited to see if Leigha would go back to sleep.

"Dix?" she called out. "Mr. Stratford?"

"I'll check on her." Dix wiggled free of his grasp and dropped to her feet. She leaned close, kissed him and pressed her finger to the spot she'd warmed with her lips. "Hold that thought."

She disappeared into Leigha's room.

Andrew stood still, willing his body to calm before he entered his daughter's room.

Dix lay on the bed beside Leigha, holding the child.

"She's thirsty. Do you want to stay with her while I go down for a glass of water?"

"I want you to stay." Leigha clung to Dix, snuggling into the curve of her arm. "Please, Dix. Stay with me."

Andrew raised a hand. "Stay here. I'll go."

Dix frowned. "Are you sure?"

"Yes." He performed an about-face and walked along the dimly lit landing to the stairs. Perhaps Leigha's request was just what he needed to keep him from losing his head over Dix.

At the bottom of the steps, he turned toward the kitchen. Strategically located night-lights provided just enough light to see where he was going. When he arrived in the kitchen, he pulled a glass from the cabinet and filled it with cool water. He filled another for Dix and started back toward the stairs.

A sound in the sitting room caught his attention. His pulse quickened. What if someone had come through the secret corridor? He shook his head. Not possible. Not with a lock on the door.

Another sound made him stop and set the glasses of water on a side table. Had the twins come down to snoop around the house?

Anger burned in Andrew's gut. He'd invited the two young men into his home. If they'd wanted to look around, all they'd had to do was ask. With words poised on the tip of his tongue, Andrew marched into the sitting room and reached for the light switch.

Before his fingers touched it, something hit him in the back of the head. He yelled, pain blinded him, and he dropped to the floor, complete darkness blocking out the soft glow of night-lights.

Chapter 15

As soon as Andrew left the room, his daughter had fallen back to sleep.

Dix rose from the bed and paced the length of the little girl's room. The walls seemed too close, so Dix stepped out into the hallway. What was keeping Andrew?

What should she do about his request for her to stay in his room through the night? It was a recipe for disaster. The more time she spent with him, the harder it would be to leave. And she would leave. That itchy feeling she got when she stayed in one place too long would drive her away.

Dix leaned over the railing, searching the shadows below for signs of Andrew. As big as the house was, she doubted she'd hear the sound of him rustling around in the kitchen. Leaving Leigha again didn't seem like a good idea, but Dix was getting nervous.

A muffled shout sounded from somewhere below followed by a heavy thud. "Andrew?" Dix called out. He didn't answer. "Andrew!"

She ran back to her room for her gun and then raced for the stairs.

Two doors opened down the hall and the Kessler twins' heads popped out.

"What's wrong?" one of them asked.

"I don't know. I thought I heard someone yell." Dix dashed down the stairs, her heart pounding against her ribs. "Andrew?"

Footsteps sounded behind her as the two young men followed.

She hurried toward the kitchen, flipping light switches wherever she could find them.

The kitchen was empty with no sign of Andrew.

"I found him!" one of the twins yelled. "Call 9-1-1!"

Dix's heart sank to the bottom of her belly as she followed the sound of the young man's voice into the sitting room they'd all been in earlier.

Andrew lay on the floor, completely still.

Dix dropped down beside him, laid her gun on a table and carefully shook his arm. "Andrew."

Jared pressed a hand to the base of his throat. "He's got a pulse."

Joe pointed to the knot forming on the back of Andrew's head. "Looks like he was hit with something. Hit hard. That's a big goose egg."

Andrew groaned.

"Andrew?" Dix leaned close. "Can you hear me?"

"Shh," he said. "You don't have to shout. I've got a splitting headache." He pushed against the floor but only managed to roll onto his back and wince. "Sweet heaven. That hurt."

"You have a lump on the back of your head," Jared said. "What happened?"

Andrew pressed his fingers to the bridge of his nose. "I don't know. I got a couple glasses of water to take upstairs. Heard a noise in the sitting room. Then nothing." He sat up and swayed.

Jared and Dix slipped arms around his back and steadied him.

"We're calling an ambulance," Joe said.

"No." Andrew shook his head once and cringed. "I'm okay...just need to wait until the room quits spinning."

"We're calling 9-1-1," Dix seconded. "You could have a concussion or swelling on the brain."

A scream silenced all of their arguments.

"Leigha." Dix grabbed her gun, leaped to her feet and ran out of the room, calling back over her shoulder, "Don't let him get up."

"Like hell," Andrew said.

She glanced back to see him lurching to his feet.

Jared and Joe slipped Andrew's arms over their shoulders and ran with him.

Satisfied Andrew wouldn't run up the stairs on his own, Dix raced to the second floor and burst into Leigha's room. She sat up in bed, her eyes wide, tears streaming down her face.

"What's wrong?" Dix asked, hurrying to her bedside.

"Fire was all around me. I couldn't breathe because of the smoke. I was so afraid." Leigha bent over, sobbing.

Dix slid the gun onto a dresser and then sat beside the child, pulling her into her arms. "Oh, sweetheart, it was just a bad dream."

"No." She shook her head, her eyes squeezing shut. "It was real. I was there. I couldn't get out."

"You're okay now. Open your eyes. See? No smoke. No fire. Just your pretty bedroom."

"Where's my daddy?"

"I'm here." Andrew broke free of Jared and Joe's hold and walked slowly into the room. "I'm here, Leigha. I'll always be here for you."

She reached her arms up.

Andrew lifted her into his embrace.

Dix stood, ready to assist if Andrew passed out.

He didn't. He held Leigha close, talking soft, soothing words.

"You saved me. I know it was you. I remember," she said. "You saved me…" Leigha's voice faded and she laid her cheek against his chest.

"Is everything okay?" Jared asked from the door.

"Is the little girl all right?" Joe whispered.

Dix nodded, her eyes stinging. "She had a bad dream."

Jared stepped back. "We'll check the house and make sure whoever did this is gone."

Dix shot a glance at Andrew and Leigha and then walked over to the Kessler twins. "I'd rather you stayed to make sure Mr. Stratford doesn't fall down holding his daughter." She eased past them, snagging her gun from the top of the dresser. "I'll check the house."

Jared followed her out into the hallway and grabbed her arm. "You can't do that. You could be hurt, too."

Dix held up her gun. "I'll be okay. I know how to use this."

Jared raised his hands. "I believe you, but at least take one of us with you. Two sets of eyes are better than one."

She didn't need Joe or Jared getting in the way if she had to fire her weapon. But Jared was right. "Then *you* come with me. Joe can stay with Andrew and Leigha."

Jared nodded, whispered instructions to his twin and followed Dix down the stairs.

They moved from room to room, checking everywhere. They didn't find anyone or anything out of place.

Dix stood in the foyer, shaking her head. "After Leigha showed me the secret passage in the sitting room, I'm willing to bet there's one, maybe two, more. Mr. Stratford and I checked all the windows and door locks. Whoever hit him had another way into the building."

Jared stood with his back to Dix. "I don't like it. He could still be here, listening to us talking."

Dix didn't like it, either. She'd have to stand guard through the night to make sure no one else was hurt. In the meantime, Andrew needed someone to look at him. He could be suffering from concussion. He might feel all right now, but if he had any swelling on his brain, he could be dead in minutes.

She sent Jared up to check on his brother, Andrew and Leigha while she called Tazer.

The SOS operative answered immediately. "I hear you have houseguests. Dave told me what happened earlier in the bay."

"Dave?"

"My fiancé," Tazer clarified. "He's the dive boat captain who took the Kessler twins out today."

"Oh, was that him?" Having just met Tazer, she hadn't had the chance to meet her fiancé.

"Yeah," Tazer said. "He said he got really worried about them when they didn't come up on time. I can't believe they were caught in kelp."

"They're lucky Dave went in after them. I take it Dave got back all right?"

"The Devil's Shroud almost had him, but he made it back in time to see the marina."

"I'm glad." Dix drew in a deep breath and let it out before continuing. "I called because we had another attack here at Stratford House."

"Want me to send the team over?"

"No. I think we have it under control. But Mr. Stratford refused to go to the hospital. I'm afraid he might have a concussion from being hit in the back of the head."

"I'll send Creed's girl over. She's a nurse at the Cape Churn hospital. Maybe she can convince one of the doctors to make a house call. Either way, she can at least check him out. He might listen to her if she thinks he needs to go to the hospital."

"Thanks." Dix started to hang up.

"Are you sure you don't need reinforcements?" Tazer asked.

"No. I'll stand watch tonight."

"You need sleep, too," Tazer reminded her.

"I've pulled all-nighters before in worse places than this. Try standing knee-deep in a foxhole filled with freezing water, while a thunderstorm rages overhead. This will be a cakewalk."

Tazer snorted. "Must be all that Ranger training." She paused. "Okay, but I'll be over in the morning to give you a break. Even Rangers need to sleep. Be on the lookout for Emma Jenkins. If I can get her on the phone, she'll be out there within the next thirty minutes."

Dix ended the call and hurried back to Leigha's room.

Jared and Joe stood out in the hall, talking softly. When she approached, they straightened.

Jared stepped forward. "Mr. Stratford lay down with his daughter. We're not sure that's a good idea. Aren't you supposed to keep concussion victims awake for a couple hours?"

"I'll take care of it," Dix said. She smiled at them.

"You two can go back to bed. Lock your doors. I'll stand guard in the hallway until morning. No one else is getting hurt on my watch."

Jared nodded. "I'd offer to take the next shift, but I don't think you want me handling a gun. I'd probably shoot myself."

She shook her head. "Thanks, but I can handle it. I have a nurse coming to check Mr. Stratford. If she thinks he needs to go to the hospital, we might be packing up and heading into Cape Churn."

"Do you want us to stay and babysit Leigha?" Joe offered.

"No," Dix said. "She'd come with us."

"Let us know." Jared shot a glance at his brother. "We might go with you."

Dix's lips twisted. "I wouldn't blame you. Who wants to stay in a big house where the owner is attacked?"

"Exactly." The two men spoke in unison and laughed.

Dix returned to the bedroom.

Leigha lay curled against her father's side, her breathing slow and steady.

Andrew lay on his back.

Dix checked to see if his chest was moving up and down. When she couldn't tell, she leaned over him and listened for his heartbeat.

A hand smoothed over her hair. "Don't worry—I'm alive," he said, his voice rumbling against her ear.

She straightened. "How do you feel?"

"Got a headache. I don't suppose you'd get me a couple of pain relievers?" he asked, closing his eyes.

"I'd rather wait until the nurse gets here," she said, brushing a strand of his pitch-black hair back from his forehead.

"Should we move to a hotel?" he asked.

"Not tonight." She stood by the bed, smoothing Andrew's hair back from his forehead. When the clock on the nightstand indicated it had been twenty-five minutes, she bent to whisper in Andrew's ear, "I'm going to check on that nurse."

He caught her hand. "I don't need one. I need you."

She smiled. "I'm not a nurse."

"There's a phone in my room. Call from there."

Dix left his side and crossed through the connecting doors into Andrew's room. She called Tazer.

"I was just about to call you. I hate to tell you, but Emma couldn't make it out to you. The roads are socked in with the Devil's Shroud. She tried, but she almost ran off the road a couple times before she left town. If she could have made it, she would have. It's just not safe for anyone, including an ambulance, to drive out to you."

"Anything I should do to monitor him?"

"She said he should get plenty of rest. If he is nauseous, has trouble with balance, is dizzy or incoherent, you might have to get an ambulance out there."

Dix resolved to wake Andrew every two or three hours just to check to see if his condition was worsening. "Can I give him some pain relievers?"

"You can give him acetaminophen. Nothing else. You need to know if the pain is getting worse."

"Okay."

"I'd offer to come out and help, but I looked outside. Emma was right. It's really bad out there. The worst I've seen it since I've been here."

"I think we'll be okay. I'm going to keep an eye on Stratford through the night. If anything changes, I'll call."

"Thanks for keeping me informed," Tazer said. "I'll see you in the morning as soon as the fog clears."

Dix ended the call and returned to Leigha's bedroom.

Andrew raised his hand.

Dix captured it in hers. "How are you feeling?"

"Like I was hit by a train."

"I'll bet you don't feel better lying on your back. Do you need help turning onto your side?"

"No, but I could use a hand getting into my own bed."

"You're not going anywhere."

He stared up at her, his lips twisting. "I guess this means we're not making love tonight."

"Absolutely not. No contact sports for you until we know for sure you don't have any bleeding on the brain."

His grip tightened on her hand. "At the very least, why don't you join us?" He started to scoot over.

Dix bent to kiss his knuckles. "I'm not sleeping in here."

His brow creased. "Then where are you sleeping?"

"I'm not." She laid his hand on the bed. "I'm pulling guard duty until morning."

"That's ridiculous. You can't stay awake all night."

"I can if I'm on my feet, checking all the rooms."

Andrew pushed the blanket back and started to get out of the bed.

"Where do you think you're going?" she asked.

"To a hotel. This place is too big for one person to guard all night. I won't have the same guy who attacked me attacking you."

"Andrew Stratford, get back in that bed before I put you there." She spoke in a soft yet urgent tone, afraid she'd wake Leigha if she raised her voice.

He sat on the side of the bed, staring at her. "You can't do it alone."

"I'm a trained soldier and an MMA fighter. I can protect myself and you two. That's why I'm here. Relax before you make your injury worse. I can't make my rounds if I'm worrying about you."

His frown deepened. "I'm getting rid of this place."

"The hell you are. It's part of your family heritage. You just need to find all the secret passages and seal them. We can work on that tomorrow."

Leigha turned over and sighed.

"I need to leave you two so you can sleep."

"Can't you stay here with us? You can keep your gun on the nightstand."

"What if someone goes after the Kessler twins?" she asked.

"Maybe one of them was the one who hit me."

"No. They were in their rooms when I heard you yell. They couldn't have hit you and run up the stairs without me seeing them."

"So it's not them. Then who was it?"

"That's what we need to find out. We need to discover who would want to hurt you and why."

"Do you think they're after the same thing the Kessler boys are?"

"You'd think your grandfather would have found that treasure before he died. *If* it really exists and isn't some big, whopping lie told to make Peg and Percy Malone more glamorous. I'm going to check the library tomorrow. And maybe Jared and Joe will show me what they're basing their exploration on."

"We'll figure this out."

"Yes. We will. In the meantime, you need to rest and let your head recover from that blow."

He shoved his hand through his hair and felt the back of his neck. Andrew winced. "That's some bump. But I'll live."

"Go to sleep. I'll check on you in a couple of hours."

"Wake me up. I want to know you're okay, too."

"I will." Once more, she tried to leave but he caught her hand and dragged her back to his side.

"Be careful out there." He pulled her to stand between his legs. "Leigha is getting used to having you around." Andrew wrapped his hands around her waist.

"She's a sweet kid." Dix leaned forward and kissed him on the lips. "Sleep. We can talk more in the morning." Once more she bent to kiss him.

He circled the back of her neck with his hand and drew her closer, deepening the kiss, his tongue teasing hers.

Using all of her resolve, she pulled free of his grip and backed out of his reach. If she continued kissing him like that, she would never leave the room. "Rest. I'll be back later." Dix spun and walked out without looking back. She couldn't do her job if she couldn't focus. She couldn't focus when she was around Andrew Stratford. Clearly, making love to her client was a conflict of interest and left her and him vulnerable to attack.

She'd call Fontaine in the morning and ask him to relieve her. Falling in love with a client was not conducive to keeping him and his daughter safe.

Chapter 16

Andrew lay beside Leigha on the little girl's bed, counting the minutes until Dix returned. He didn't like being confined to a bed, but when he sat up, his head hurt and his vision blurred. Granted, it wasn't quite as bad as when he'd first woken in the sitting room. But he wouldn't be of any use to Dix if he fell down the stairs running after her.

Leigha needed someone to fight her dream dragons. Or, to be more precise, rescue her from the fire that had nearly ended her life.

Even as worried as he was about Dix wandering the house searching for bad guys, Andrew couldn't stop his heart from swelling at what Leigha had called him when she'd been so frightened from her nightmare.

Daddy.

He'd told himself it didn't matter that she referred to him as Mr. Stratford. But hearing her call him Daddy had melted every bone in his body and swelled his heart to twice its size. He'd move heaven and earth for that little girl. She was *his* little girl. She had his eyes and his name was on her birth certificate.

He turned onto his side to relieve the pressure on the lump at the back of his neck. It gave him a chance to study his daughter in the soft glow of the night-light plugged into a wall socket.

Part of him wanted to know for certain whether or not she was his child biologically. But another part of him knew she was his whether they shared the same DNA or not. Leigha needed him as much as he needed her.

Brewer stood, turned around three times and lay across Andrew's ankles.

The dog had proved to be a great companion to Leigha, but she really needed some human friends, too. Andrew would consult with Mrs. Purdy about the best way for Leigha to get the interaction she needed. His housekeeper knew everyone in town. Surely she had a contact who could steer him in the right direction.

Tomorrow he'd also go to the local school and enroll his daughter for the coming fall. She'd be old enough to attend first grade. She would make friends with other little girls and, eventually, she might give up her imaginary friend.

The biggest task for the following day would be to find the bastard who was threatening them. Once he was arrested and sent to jail, Andrew, Leigha and Dix could stop jumping at shadows. They wouldn't need bodyguards to protect them. Dix wouldn't have to work for him and he could kiss her all he wanted.

Andrew must have fallen asleep.

A hand on his arm gently shook him awake.

"Hey," a gravelly voice whispered in his ear.

He opened his eyes to stare into Dix's green gaze. "Hey, yourself."

"How do you feel?"

He blinked and thought about it. "My head doesn't hurt as badly and my vision isn't blurry."

"That's a good sign." She took his hand and held it in hers. "You can go back to sleep."

"What time is it?"

"Four o'clock. The sun won't be up for another two or three hours, assuming the fog clears soon."

"Any problems?"

"Not so far."

"Good." He yawned and patted the bed beside him. "I don't suppose I could talk you into staying?"

"Not tonight." She pulled out of his reach, rounded the bed to Leigha's side and pressed her hand to her forehead. "Has she had any more nightmares?"

"She hasn't called out in her sleep, so I assume no."

"I'll check with you again in a couple hours."

"I don't like you wandering around this big old house by yourself."

"It's my job. Let me do it."

His gaze followed her every move. She tiptoed around the room on silent feet, the sway of her hips making him crazy with need. "And if I fire you?"

"I'd still do it. I don't want anything else to happen to you or Leigha."

Andrew sighed. "I'll be up tomorrow and we're going to find out how that guy got in and back out without being seen."

"I think Leigha might be able to help us with that effort. Somehow she knows about this house's secrets."

"She's amazing," Andrew said, staring at his daughter as she slept. "And I haven't paid nearly enough attention to her."

Dix left Leigha's side and walked toward the door. When she reached it, she looked back at them. "Sleep."

Andrew wasn't going to fight her on this. She was the trained professional. He wasn't. In the morning, he would turn the house inside out if he had to.

He closed his eyes, knowing she would take care of them. What bothered him was who would take care of Dix?

He closed his eyes and slept, hoping that by morning, the power of rest would have restored him to full functionality. He'd need it to tear the big old mansion apart to find what he was looking for.

"Daddy?"

A hand on his shoulder woke him from a dream about running through dark, narrow corridors, searching for Dix and Leigha.

When he opened his eyes to see Leigha smiling down at him, he drew in a deep breath, his pulse returning to normal.

Brewer crawled up the comforter, his tail wagging, eager to be a part of a morning wake-up.

Andrew smiled at his daughter. "Hey, sweetheart."

She grinned. "You stayed the whole night of my slumber party."

He nodded, the pull of swelling at the back of his head reminding him of the attack. "I did."

Leigha glanced around the room. "Where's Dix?"

Andrew had been wondering the same. "She probably got up early to help Mrs. Purdy in the kitchen. I can smell bacon."

Brewer woofed at the mention of bacon.

Despite his determination not to feed the dog anything

but the special-blend dog food he'd purchased from the vet, Andrew knew he was given treats by the women in the house. He'd caught Leigha sneaking bits of bacon to him beneath the table. She thought he didn't know. He did, but he hadn't said anything. Mrs. Purdy was just as bad. When she filled the dog's bowl with his dry dog food, she poured bacon grease on the top.

The dog barked again.

"I think Brewer wants to go down for breakfast," Leigha said. She flung her arms around Andrew, kissed his cheek and rolled out of the bed onto her bare feet.

Andrew pressed a hand to his cheek. He couldn't recall a time when his heart was as full as it was at that moment.

He pushed to his feet, happy that he wasn't dizzy. Other than a dull ache at the base of his skull and a knot the size of a guinea egg, he felt as close to normal as a man could after being attacked in his own house.

Andrew opened the curtains to a cloudy day. But the fog had cleared and he could see the bay. "How would you like to spend the day exploring?"

Leigha looked up from rummaging in her dresser. "With you?"

"Yes, with me." He had yet another reminder that he hadn't spent nearly enough time being a father to this child.

"And Dix?" she persisted.

"And Dix." After she had the opportunity to rest. Andrew left Leigha to dress by herself and hurried into his room to shave and put on some clothes. By the time he was ready, Leigha had already left her room with Brewer.

Andrew stepped out into the hallway. He could hear voices below. As he descended the stairs, he looked at his home with a keener eye. Hidden passages had never occurred to him. Now that he knew one existed, he had to know if there were more.

He followed the voices to the kitchen, where it looked like a party going on. The Kessler twins were playing with Brewer, scratching his belly and throwing one of his favorite plush toys for him to retrieve.

Dix stood to one side, talking to the woman Andrew had met the night he'd brought Dix to his home.

The tall, svelte blonde stepped away from Dix and held out her hand. "I don't know if you remember me from the other night. I'm—"

"Nicole Steele." He touched her hand with his injured and scarred one. When she didn't flinch, he added, "Tazer."

She smiled. "I must have made an impression. I hope it was a good one."

He nodded, his gaze going to Dix. "Everything all right?"

She had shadows beneath her eyes, but other than that, she appeared alert and ready to go. "The night was quiet after everyone went to bed."

"I told Dix I'd hang out until she caught a couple hours' sleep." Tazer turned to Dix, her lips twisting. "She says she doesn't need it."

"How are you this morning?" Jared stepped up to Andrew. "That was some nasty bump on the head."

Andrew rubbed the back of his neck. "It's already going down. I'll be fine." His attention remained on Dix. Her gaze hadn't left him since he'd entered the room. "I agree with Tazer. You need rest. Leigha and I can hang out in the study until you've had a chance to sleep."

Dix was shaking her head before he could finish his sentence. "I'm fine. I want to spend some time exploring the house and, if we have time, I'd like to visit the library in town. There has to be more information about your family inheritance."

"Anyone hungry?" Mrs. Purdy plowed through the middle of the adults, carrying a platter full of fluffy scrambled eggs and setting it in the middle of the table. "You might save this conversation until later. Little bits have big ears."

Andrew glanced down at his daughter, who'd been quietly following the conversation like a spectator at a tennis match. Mrs. Purdy was right. They didn't need to give the curious little girl any more fodder to fuel her imagination.

The others shot glances at Leigha and nodded.

"You've gone to all the trouble of cooking for all of us. Let us help by setting the table." Jared grabbed a plate of bacon and one of toast and added them to the offering on the big kitchen table.

Everyone joined in, helping to set the table with orange juice, glasses, butter, jelly, plates, knives and forks. For the next twenty minutes the conversation centered on food and local festivities.

When the plates and platters had been emptied, they all helped carry the dishes to the sink.

"Let us do the dishes," Joe said.

"No, you all need to talk. Leigha can help me." Mrs. Purdy handed Leigha a towel. "I'll wash. You can dry. If we do a really good job, we can have one of those cookies we baked yesterday when we're done."

"Cookies for breakfast?"

"Shh." Mrs. Purdy pressed a finger to her lips and winked. "Don't say it too loud or everyone else will want one and there won't be any left for us."

Leigha grinned and set to work drying.

"We'll be out on the porch," Andrew said.

Once they were all outside, Andrew turned to the twins. "I get the feeling whoever has been attacking me knows something about this house and what might be hidden inside. Do you think the Malones stashed their treasure somewhere around here?"

"That would be my bet." Dix had had all night to think of a motive for someone to attack Andrew Stratford. "You say you moved here with Leigha less than a year ago. Was there a gap between when your grandfather died and when you arrived?"

"My grandfather died two years ago. I came out for the funeral and to secure the house. I had no intention of moving here at that time."

"Then you found out about Leigha and moved here," Dix stated. "There were several months that the house sat empty. Someone could have been in here, looking for the treasure. They could have found some of the secret passageways."

Andrew nodded. "That's possible. When I got here, one of the door locks wasn't working. I had to replace it."

"Who, besides you, knows about the Malone legacy?" Dix asked.

Jared chuckled.

"Practically everyone in town. We went through every newspaper article in Cape Churn related to Peg and Percy Malone. We also looked at everything we could find on Margaret and Percival Mason," Joe offered. "We know for certain that the theft took place. Where they stashed the ill-gotten gains is a mystery."

"We spent time in the Oregon State Library in Portland before coming here and dug up everything we could find," Jared added. "You're welcome to our file of data."

Jared's eyes narrowed. "I don't suppose your family has a blueprint of the Stratford House?"

Andrew shook his head. "If they did, I have yet to find it."

"We'd like to look through the caves a little more thoroughly. There were other tunnels besides the one leading to the beach."

"I have no problem with you looking through the caves. Just be careful."

"You'll be the first to know if we find anything."

Mrs. Purdy stuck her head out the door. "Dave Logsdon is here to pick up the Kessler boys."

Jared grinned. "That's our cue to leave. We'll head back to our hotel and grab what we need for spelunking and come back in our own car."

"I don't know if there are other ways into and out of the caves," Andrew said. "You might have to come through the house. In which case, I'd rather be here when you are."

The Kesslers nodded.

"We understand," Jared said.

Dix probably wouldn't have been as generous as Andrew, but then, the young men hadn't been the ones to hit him and they had helped get him up the stairs after the attack. Her gut told her to trust them.

The twins left a few minutes later.

Leigha slipped between Dix and Andrew and grabbed a hand from each. "Are we going exploring today?"

Andrew smiled down at his daughter. The love shining from his eyes was apparent.

It made Dix's heart squeeze hard in her chest.

"Where are we going?" Leigha asked, looking up at Andrew and then Dix.

Dix knelt beside Leigha. "Remember how you showed me the secret hallway in the sitting room?"

Leigha nodded.

"You said there were others like it." Dix stared into her eyes, forcing a smile when she felt tension building inside. "Could you show us another?"

Leigha's brows knit. "I don't know."

"Why?" Andrew asked. "Have you forgotten where they are?"

She shook her head. "No. But I promised Bennet I wouldn't tell anyone where they are."

Andrew frowned. "Who's Bennet?"

Dix shot Andrew a stern glance and gave a slight shake of her head before she faced Leigha with a smile. "But you showed me the one yesterday."

Leigha twisted the hem of her T-shirt in her fingers. "Bennet said it would be okay."

"Could you ask Bennet about the others?" Dix persisted.

"Yes." Leigha let go of their hands and ran from the room, calling out over her shoulder, "I'll be right back. Stay there."

Andrew and Dix started to follow Leigha. When they reached the door, Dix noticed Leigha was going up the stairs. Brewer followed. "Let her go. She's heading for her bedroom."

Andrew's frown deepened. "Who's Bennet?"

Dix grinned. "Bennet is her imaginary friend."

"Are you sure he's imaginary?"

Remembering that creepy feeling she'd had in the cave, Dix chewed on her bottom lip. "I'm not ready to believe in ghosts, so I'm calling him an imaginary friend."

"Explain," Andrew demanded.

She told him about the trip through the cave and how Leigha had insisted Bennet was in the cave with them, standing beside her.

Andrew shook his head. "I'm enrolling her in school today. And I'm going to find some activity center she can go to during the day so that she can make friends with kids her own age."

Dix nodded.

A door slammed and tiny footsteps sounded on the floor above.

Leigha came running down the stairs, Brewer keeping pace. She skidded to a halt in front of Dix and Andrew.

Andrew dropped to his haunches and caught Leigha in his arms. He hugged her and chuckled, the sound warming Dix's heart. "Well? What did Bennet say?"

Dix was glad Andrew hadn't tried to tell Leigha that Bennet didn't exist. He seemed to know she needed Bennet, even if he wasn't real.

Leigha's face split in a big grin. "He said it was okay. I could show you and Dix, but no one else."

"Great." Andrew lifted her in his arms and turned around in the foyer. "Which way should we go? And do we need anything like a flashlight or a loaf of bread?"

Her little brows wrinkled. "Bread?"

"You know. To leave a trail of bread crumbs so that we can find our way back."

Leigha giggled. "I have a flashlight where we're going. But we don't need bread. I know the way back. And if we lose our way, Bennet will help us get home."

Andrew shot a glance toward Dix over Leigha's head. "Oh, good. I feel so much better, knowing Bennet will be there."

"He's very nice and he takes care of me and Brewer."

Andrew's lips thinned.

Dix could tell he was kicking himself for leaving Leigha to fend for herself while he worked.

Leigha wiggled in Andrew's arms. "Put me down. I'll show you where we start."

Andrew set the child on her feet.

She darted toward the back of the house and turned toward the west wing. "Follow me!" she called, her hair flying out behind her.

"You heard her—follow Leigha." Dix took off at a slow jog, afraid that if she let the child get too far ahead, she might disappear.

Since she'd spent a good portion of the early-morning hours searching rooms, touching walls and feeling for hidden doorways or panels, she still hadn't a clue as to where the other secret passageways were located. They were at the mercy of a six-year-old and a ghost to find them.

Leigha ran halfway down the first-floor hallway of the west wing and stopped in front of a small alcove with an arched entrance. A life-size statue of a Roman woman holding a baby took up the majority of the space.

Dix remembered running across her as she'd patrolled the halls in the middle of the night. She'd walked all the way around her, searching for a doorway, a lever or a switch. The only switch she'd found was a button. When pressed, the light over the statue came on.

Leigha pushed the button and waited.

The light came on. Leigha turned to the statue and grabbed the baby's toe.

Dix leaned closer and noticed the toe moved into the statue.

Still nothing major happened.

Then Leigha pushed the button on the wall again and the alcove, statue and all, rotated into the wall, exposing a doorway.

Leigha started to enter when Andrew grabbed her arm and held her back.

"Wait." Andrew tipped his head toward the wood floor of the hallway.

Dix stared hard at the dark wood. Then she saw them. Footprints. "Sweetheart, let me go first." Her hand went to the gun beneath the blazer she wore.

Leigha looked up at her. "But you don't know the way."

"Brewer does, doesn't he?"

"Yes."

"Then I'll follow Brewer. You can hold your father's hand and help him find the way."

She considered Dix's words and nodded. "Okay. But you'll need this." She reached around Dix and plucked a flashlight from a cubbyhole in the secret passage, switched it on and handed it to Dix. "This hall doesn't have a light switch."

"Nice to know." Dix balanced the light in her left hand, keeping her right hand free to pull her gun, if needed. She focused the beam down the narrow corridor and stepped into the passageway. "Did you put the flashlights in the corridors?"

"No," Leigha said from behind. "They were here. Bennet showed me how to find them."

"Bennet seems to be a handy friend to have," Andrew muttered.

"He's very smart and knows his way around the house and caves."

"I'd like to meet him someday." Andrew's voice carried to Dix.

She almost laughed, wondering how he'd react if Leigha introduced him to Bennet the same way she'd introduced him to Dix.

The corridor made a ninety-degree turn to the left and another to the right. At one point it ended in a T-junction.

"Which way?" Dix asked.

"If you go to the right, it leads to the garden," Leigha said. "Left leads you to a staircase that takes you up to the tower. You can see all the way to Cape Churn up there."

"I'll take your word for it. Are there any other corridors off either of these choices?" Dix asked.

"No."

"Then let's go to the garden." Dix turned right and walked approximately fifty feet to a door. She held her hand up, hoping Andrew would hold back Leigha while she checked to see what was on the other side of the door.

A glance over her shoulder proved he'd understood. He held on to Leigha's hand, pulling her back behind him.

Dix turned the doorknob and swung the door open. Brewer ran out.

Light filtered through a veil of vines.

Dix passed through the door and parted the vines. She stood still, scanning the garden, the bushes and shadows for movement.

Brewer trotted along a stone path, his nose to the ground, sniffing. When he came to a low stone wall, he reared on his back legs, planted his front paws on the wall. The dog looked over the top, his tail still for several seconds, and then he wagged it. Apparently satisfied no one was lurking on the other side, he dropped to the ground and turned back toward Dix as if to say *The coast is clear.*

Dix felt a little bit of relief, but she wouldn't be much of a bodyguard if she based her actions on what she thought the dog was thinking. Dix moved into the open, crossed to the wall and glanced over the top.

She noted the small patch of dirt on the other side. Everywhere else was covered in grass or moss. Peering closer, she could swear the patch of dirt had a shoe print in the middle.

Dix vaulted over the wall, deliberately landing on the grass. Hugging the bushes, she made a one-hundred-eighty-degree sweep of the area around the wall, moving farther into the woods just to be certain no one was out there who could harm her or her clients.

When she was as sure as she could be, she returned to the wall and squatted beside the dirt patch. Definitely a footprint. The pattern indicated some kind of work boot. She straightened and swung her legs over the stone wall.

Andrew stood with Leigha near the vines. "Anything?" he asked.

"It's a lovely garden." Dix bent to pick up a stick. "Leigha, does Brewer know how to play fetch?"

Leigha nodded and held out her hand. "Want me to show you?"

"Please."

She took the stick, walked a few feet away and threw the stick.

Brewer raced after it, snatched it up with his teeth and dropped it at Leigha's feet. She giggled and did it again, moving a little farther away from where Andrew and Dix stood.

"What did you find?" Andrew asked.

"I didn't find the perpetrator, but I did find a boot print in the dirt on the other side of the wall. Whoever hit you last night probably left through the secret passage."

"I suppose I need to stock up on locks."

"You might consider installing a security monitoring system."

"It's on my list of upgrades, as soon as the contractor can get to me."

"You might want to move it to the top of your priority list."

He nodded. "Leigha, are there any more secret hallways in the house that lead to the outside?"

She threw the stick for Brewer once more and came to

stand beside Andrew. "None that lead outside. Only this one and the one that goes through the cave."

"Let's go back inside. I want you to show me the one you showed Dix yesterday."

"Okay." She ducked through the vines, disappearing into the house.

If Dix hadn't known where the door was, she wouldn't have known it was there. The vines and shadows completely hid the door. She was surprised Andrew hadn't discovered it as a boy exploring his grandfather's house.

Brewer followed Leigha, Andrew went next and Dix brought up the rear, closing the door behind her. When she turned, she nearly ran into Andrew.

He hadn't moved far into the narrow corridor. "I'll come back with a lock after she shows me the cave."

Her heart hammered against her ribs. Standing as close as she was to Andrew, she could smell the sexy scent of his aftershave.

He reached out to brush a strand of her hair away from her forehead. "I'm sorry things didn't work out the way we'd planned last night."

She fought the urge to lean her cheek into his palm. Instead she stared up at him, forcing herself to be professional. "It's probably just as well our plans didn't happen. Not that I wanted you to be hurt. It's just that I'm here for the short term. What good is it to start something we both know we can't finish?"

"How do you know?"

"I'm not the right person for you and Leigha. I have too many issues."

"And we don't?"

"Three wrongs don't make a family."

"So that's it?" He tipped her chin up and stared into her eyes in the dim glow of the flashlight he carried in his other hand. "You're not even willing to see what might come of us?"

"I told you—"

"I know. You're damaged goods. I hope someday you'll explain to me how different you are from me and Leigha." He bent his head until his lips hovered over hers. "The way I see it, we have a lot more in common than you're willing to admit." He brushed his lips lightly over hers. "Resist all you want. I like what I know so far, and I'm not ready to give up on you."

Then he deepened the kiss, pushing his tongue past her teeth to tangle with hers. He lifted his head and smiled. "You might think you're all tough and hard as stone." He touched a finger to her chest. "But I'd bet my last dollar you're all soft and squishy on the inside."

"Are you coming?" Leigha asked. "We still have to go through the cave. And Brewer's hungry for one of Mrs. Purdy's cookies."

"Coming," Andrew answered. Then, to Dix, he said, "You heard that. Brewer needs a cookie. But don't forget—I'm not ready to give up on you." He turned and shone the flashlight ahead of him.

Dix stayed rooted to the floor, her lips tingling from his kiss, her heart squeezing so tightly in her chest she was afraid it would implode.

You might not be ready to give up on me, Andrew Stratford. But it's not you I'm worried about. I don't know if I have what it takes to stay.

Chapter 17

Leigha wasted no time leading them to the sitting room and through the hidden doorway in the fireplace. When they reached the door that would lead into the cave, they paused while Andrew worked the combination lock.

Dix led the way through the tunnel, carrying the flashlight.

Andrew was shocked when the tunnel emptied out into the cavern and even more disturbed by the next tunnel's exit over a cliff and down the trail to the beach. The tide was out, so he could see the little strip of sand, just enough for someone to beach a skiff.

"How did I not know about this?" Andrew said as he watched his daughter and Brewer play on the sand.

"The bigger question is how Leigha found it." Dix shook her head. "I can't imagine she found those two passages on her own. Someone had to have shown her the triggers to open the hidden doors."

"But who?" Andrew didn't like it. "All the while I was

working in my office, she was wandering through secret tunnels and caves. She could just as easily have slipped off a cliff or gotten lost in the woods."

"At least you know now and can keep her safe."

He rubbed his scarred hand through his hair and winced when his stitches snagged. "I wish parenting came with a how-to book."

Dix chuckled. "She's amazing. I can't imagine a book would be adequate."

Leigha ran back to the two of them, her hair in disarray, her jeans wet from kneeling in the sand. "Brewer is ready for his cookie."

"What about Bennet?" Dix asked.

"That's silly. Bennet doesn't eat cookies."

"Why not?" Andrew asked.

"He can't." Leigha started up the stone steps. "He's a ghost," she called out over her shoulder. "Everyone knows ghosts don't need to eat."

And so Andrew was schooled on what ghosts could and couldn't do. Never in a million years would he have guessed he'd be living at his grandfather's estate in Oregon, talking to a six-year-old who believed in ghosts. *His* six-year-old daughter.

Leigha hurried them back through the tunnels and cave to the house. Once she emerged from the fireplace, she made a beeline for the kitchen, skipping across the marble-tiled floor, Brewer racing ahead.

By the time Andrew and Dix entered, Leigha was at the table with a cookie and a glass of milk.

"You two look like you need a cookie. Would you prefer coffee or milk?"

Dix and Andrew replied as one. "Milk."

Dix turned to Andrew. "Really? I would have pegged you for a coffee drinker."

"And I am. But nothing goes better with one of Mrs. Purdy's cookies than milk." He leaned close to her as he stepped around her. "Yet another thing we have in common." Before she could protest, he reached for the cup and cookie and took the seat beside Leigha. "Mrs. Purdy, are any of my grandfather's cronies still alive?"

She brought a cookie and a glass of milk and set it on the table across from Andrew and motioned for Dix to take the seat. "Why do you ask?"

"I'd like to talk to them about my grandfather and this house."

She tilted her head and stared at the far corner for a moment, and then her face brightened. "As a matter of fact, Mr. Giddings, the owner of the hardware store in Cape Churn, is still alive and kicking. I think the man is going to outlive us all." She shook her head. "He and your grandfather met for coffee once a week at the café. I believe they used to play cards here at the house when they were younger."

"And he still works at the hardware store?"

"He does. He's got to be pushing ninety. But he likes feeling useful and he knows everything there is to know about lumber, hardware and fixing things. He works a shorter day than his son. If you want to see him, you should go in the next hour or two."

"Leigha, how would you like to go to town with me and Dix?" Andrew asked. "We could run by the school and get you registered for first grade."

"I can go to school?" Her face lit and she practically bounced in her chair. "With kids like me and a teacher?"

Andrew laughed. "Yes. With kids like you and a teacher."

"Yes, please." She leaped out of her chair and ran for the door.

"Leigha," Andrew said, his voice firm.

Leigha slid to a halt on the tiled floor. "Yes, sir?"

"We'll go after we finish our cookies and milk that Mrs. Purdy so nicely provided."

She walked back to the table, slid into her seat and proceeded to gobble up the rest of the cookie and drink her milk. When she set her glass down, she had a milk mustache and a smile. "Can we go now?"

Andrew finished the last bite of his cookie, upended his glass of milk and sighed. "Yes, we can go."

Leigha pointed at him and laughed.

Andrew looked around, pretending he didn't know he had a matching milk mustache. "What?"

"You have milk on your lip." Leigha giggled again.

"Oh, you mean like the milk on your lip?" He grabbed a napkin and wiped the milk from her mouth. "There."

Dix handed Leigha a napkin and she repeated the gesture, wiping the milk from Andrew's lip. "There," she echoed.

Andrew and Leigha turned to Dix.

"What?"

"Are you ready?" Andrew asked.

Dix shoved the last bit of her cookie into her mouth and drank her milk so fast she got milk on her upper lip.

Leigha dissolved into giggles, rolled out of her chair onto the floor.

Brewer saw his chance to lick her face, which made her giggle more.

Andrew loved the sound of his daughter's laughter. And he loved that Dix, the former Army Ranger and MMA fighter, had enough of a sense of humor that she could be silly along with a six-year-old and her father.

He applied a fresh napkin to her lip and wiped the milk away. Then he brushed a quick kiss where the white mustache had been. "Ready?"

She shook her head, but got up from her chair anyway.

Andrew knew it wasn't going to be easy to convince

Dix to stay long enough to get to know each other. But he was up for the challenge. He'd been to hell and back. He could handle it.

Based on Mrs. Purdy's recommendation, Andrew gathered Leigha's birth certificate and immunization record. He, Leigha and Dix loaded into his SUV and drove into Cape Churn. They made their first stop at the school administration building, where Andrew registered Leigha for school. Leigha met the school superintendent and learned the name of the elementary school. She was so excited when they left, Andrew felt bad that he'd isolated her for so long.

After dealing with the school registration, they stopped at the hardware store.

In the front window of the store, someone had set up a display of a small chicken coop and populated it with live yellow chicks. When they went inside, Leigha planted herself in front of the chicken display while Andrew and Dix located Mr. Giddings, the elderly owner of the hardware store.

He was counting wood screws for a customer and dropping them into a thick paper bag. "That's fifty. Is there anything else I can get for you, Mrs. Laney?"

Andrew waited for the woman to pay for her purchase and leave before he spoke. "Mr. Giddings, do you remember my grandfather—"

The old man held up a hand and stared at Andrew through narrowed eyes. "You're the Stratford boy who inherited Thomas Stratford's place. Am I right?"

Andrew smiled. "Yes, sir." He held out his hand. "Andrew Stratford."

"Richard Giddings. But you can call me Mr. Giddings. You're too young to call me Richard."

"Yes, Mr. Giddings." He turned to Dix. "This is my…

friend, Dixie Reeves. We'd like to talk to you, if you have time."

Giddings took Dix's hand in both of his and smiled. "Now, you can call me Richard if you like. Never could resist a pretty girl."

"Thank you, Richard." Dix shot a triumphant glance toward Andrew.

Andrew chuckled. "Mr. Giddings, I understand you and my grandfather were good friends and spent some time together before he passed."

Mr. Giddings released Dix's hand and turned his attention to Andrew. "Thomas was a good man. Played a mean hand of poker, but he was a good man. What's been troubling you?"

"Sir, I've been attacked two times in the past week and I haven't a clue as to why. Once on the cliff behind Stratford House and once inside the house itself."

"Told Thomas his house was far too big when he first brought his plans to me."

"Plans?"

Giddings nodded. "He wanted a house big enough for a whole litter of children."

"My grandfather had only one child that I know of," Andrew said. "My father."

Giddings nodded. "Rowena had several miscarriages before she gave birth to Benjamin. I don't think I'd ever seen her as happy as when she brought your father home." He stared into the distance, a sad smile curling his lips. "She was so proud of him.

"Friends from the church temporarily moved in with Thomas and Rowena to help with the baby, but Rowena never really got over Benjamin's birth. Oh, she lived to raise him, but her health was never the same."

"She died shortly after I was born," Andrew said.

"That's right. Young Ben came back to Cape Churn after he graduated from college. He met Laura, your mother, who was a few years younger, and they fell in love. Ben proposed and she said yes. It made your grandmother happy to know her son was happy and they'd be living close by so that she could watch her grandchildren grow up."

"Only my parents didn't stay in Cape Churn," Andrew said.

"No, they didn't. They would have, but your mother's old boyfriend made their lives hell. He stalked Laura, showing up everywhere she went. Your father came to blows with him after he'd cornered your mother in the grocery store."

"What was his name?"

"Nelson Clayton."

Clayton. The older gentleman who'd talked to him at the Seaside Café. "Isn't he my nearest neighbor?"

"Yes. He bought the property next to Stratford House. I remember he'd said he should have owned Stratford House. He claimed he was Thomas's bastard son, born before Benjamin. Therefore, he should have inherited Stratford House."

"What?" Andrew hadn't heard any of this. "From all the stories my grandfather told me about his wife, they were deeply in love. He didn't have eyes for any other woman."

"Which is true. But before your grandmother came along your grandfather was quite the ladies' man." Giddings leaned against the counter, warming to his story. "He was known to have a fling or two among the more promiscuous women. One in particular. Darla Landis. She set her sights on your grandfather and seduced him."

Andrew chuckled. "I'm having a hard time picturing my grandfather being seduced."

Mr. Giddings smiled and puffed out his chest. "You

only saw him as an old man. When we were young, we were like you—good-looking, viral men about town."

"Oh, I believe you," Andrew said. "Please continue."

"Not long afterward—a couple days, maybe a week—Thomas met Rowena Mason and fell hopelessly in love. They hadn't dated more than two weeks before he asked her to marry him."

Dix snorted. "I take it Miss Landis wasn't too happy."

"Not at all. She tried to break up the wedding. Caused a big ruckus. But when the dust settled, Thomas and Rowena were happily married."

"What happened to Darla?" Dix asked.

"She married Oliver Clayton, an older man who owned a fishing boat. She never was very happy. She had a child right away. Old Man Clayton didn't live long after. He got caught out on the water in the Devil's Shroud and sank with his boat. Darla's baby was only a year old. She started spreading the rumor that her boy Nelson wasn't Clayton's baby after all."

Andrew shook his head and asked, "Could it have been Thomas's?"

Giddings shrugged. "She had the baby ten months after she and Thomas were together."

Dix's eyes narrowed. "I've heard of women carrying their babies for ten months instead of the usual nine."

"It's possible," Giddings said. "Meanwhile, Thomas's investments took off and he became a millionaire practically overnight. He built that massive house to show Rowena how much he loved her. Rowena didn't care about having a big house or fancy cars. She would have loved him if he'd been dirt-poor." Mr. Giddings straightened. "Look at me getting all nostalgic."

"Sounds like Thomas and Rowena had the perfect marriage," Dix said.

Giddings nodded.

"Why did Ben and Laura leave?" Dix asked.

"They didn't want to, but Nelson wouldn't leave them alone. The final straw was finding Nelson in the nursery with baby Andrew. It upset Laura so much, she insisted they move as far away from Nelson as possible." The old man sighed. "Losing her son and grandson threw Rowena into a tailspin. She was so sad. Nothing Thomas did could cheer her up. Then she was diagnosed with cancer and it was all downhill after that. Ben barely made it back before Rowena passed."

"No wonder my parents didn't want to come back to Cape Churn." Andrew had thought they were selfish and hated his grandfather. He glanced up. "Did you know about the tunnels and secret passageways inside the house?"

Giddings frowned. "Tunnels, you say?" He shook his head. "I didn't see anything of the sort in the drawings. Wouldn't surprise me, though. Thomas brought in workers from Southern California to do the excavation and framing. They spent a couple years building that mausoleum. Most of the workers only spoke Spanish, so they kept to themselves. When they were done, Thomas sent them back to California." The old man chuckled. "That would be just like Thomas to do something like that."

Dix tilted her head. "Why?"

"Who knows? Some say he was just a little crazy. Others said he was into smuggling, though the Prohibition was long over. There were the lunatics who tried to convince everyone that Rowena's parents were the famous Peg and Percy Malone." Mr. Giddings's brow knit.

"Is there any reason someone would want me off my own property…permanently?" Andrew asked.

"No one thought you'd come back to live in Cape Churn." The hardware store owner scratched his head.

"Other than Nelson Clayton, I can't think of anyone who'd want the Stratford House. It's got to cost a fortune to maintain. Your heating and electric bills alone would bankrupt most of us."

Andrew's lips twisted. "They aren't minimal." But he could afford it. So what would anyone have to gain by knocking him off? Unless... "Speaking of the Malones, what do you know about them?"

"They were a legend along the West Coast. Supposedly disappeared in broad daylight. They kind of became heroes among the working class. Not many around here were happy about Prohibition. When that big shot from San Francisco turned them in and then sold their whiskey, he got what he deserved."

"The theft of his jewelry store?" Dix added.

The old man nodded. "Since then, there have been treasure hunters who've scoured the coastline searching for the boat they stole." Giddings jabbed a finger in the air. "Just the other day, we had a couple of college students in buying supplies for their own treasure hunt. I heard they hired Logsdon to take them out in his dive boat." Giddings frowned. "I also heard they ended up staying last night at your place. You sure they weren't the ones who attacked you?"

Dix shook her head and answered for Andrew. "Mr. Stratford was attacked on the first floor. I was upstairs, as were the Kessler boys. It couldn't have been them."

Andrew understood how small towns worked. News traveled fast. Still, he amazed at how fast it did travel. "Mr. Giddings, thank you for all the information."

The hardware store owner straightened slowly. "Wish I could help more. Thomas was a good friend. We played cards on occasion and had coffee once a week." He touched a finger to his chin. "Come to think of it, in the last few weeks of his life, Thomas talked about a journal he was keeping. Did you find it?"

Andrew frowned and shook his head. "I've been there for almost a year and haven't found anything like that. I've been through his file cabinets and desk drawers."

"If he was smart enough to build hidden passages and tunnels, he's probably got it hidden somewhere. But that's strange he didn't leave it where you could find it. I got the impression he was documenting things he wanted you to know should he die."

Andrew sucked in a deep breath to ease the tightness in his chest. His biggest regret was not coming back to Cape Churn before his grandfather died. "Again, Mr. Giddings, thank you for your help."

"I hope you find out who's been attacking you." Mr. Giddings straightened a stack of miniature flashlights on the counter. "Hate to think one of our own is causing you trouble."

Andrew and Dix collected Leigha on the way out.

"Could I have a baby chick someday?" she begged. "Please?"

Until he discovered who was trespassing and why, Andrew didn't feel good about bringing anyone, or anything, out to Stratford House.

On the drive home, Leigha fell asleep in the backseat.

Andrew glanced in the rearview mirror at his daughter and then shot a sideways glance toward Dix. "Should I move Leigha and you into a hotel in town?"

Dix shook her head. "Between me and Brewer, we'll take care of Leigha. *You're* the one I'm worried about. You're the one who's nearly been killed. Twice." She held up two fingers to emphasize her point. "Maybe we need to ask Fontaine for a bodyguard assigned to you. Three attacks might be a charm. And I don't mean that in a good way."

Andrew rubbed the knot on the back of his head and grinned. "If I'm not mistaken, you're worried about me. Does that mean you're coming around? Maybe you like me a little?"

Dix rolled her eyes. "That's never been what was holding me back."

"Ah! So you *do* like me." He smirked, his blue eyes bright in the interior of the SUV. "Good to know. Now, let's find my grandfather's journal. I get the feeling it holds the key to why someone would want me dead."

Dix pressed a finger to her lips. "Shh. You don't want to scare Leigha," she whispered.

Andrew wrinkled his brow. "Are you sure you weren't a mother in another incarnation?"

She held up her hand. "Not that I know of. Before I came to Stratford House, I didn't believe in the paranormal, but now..." She shook her head. "I don't know what to believe."

Andrew reached out a hand to her.

Instead of drawing away, she took his hand and held it all the way back to the house.

He called it progress. Now, if he could convince her his bed was the right place to be, he'd cinch the deal.

A glance at Dix's tight jaw and worried frown wasn't reassuring Andrew. But he didn't give up easily, not on something or someone worth fighting for.

Chapter 18

Leigha woke when they pulled into the yard. Though it was cloudy, night had yet to fall.

Dix helped Leigha out of the SUV and set her on the ground. She yawned and stretched. "We didn't get any ice cream."

"I bet Mrs. Purdy has some in the freezer," Andrew said. "Why don't we go inside and ask?"

Mrs. Purdy exited the front door, her purse and sweater draped over her arm. "I left a lasagna in the oven. There's a salad in the refrigerator and green beans in a pot on the stove. I'd stay, but Mr. Purdy is threatening to climb a ladder to clean a gutter on our house. If I'm not there to hold the ladder, he's likely to fall and hurt himself."

"By all means, Mrs. Purdy, you should hurry home," Andrew said.

Brewer squeezed past Mrs. Purdy's legs and ran straight for Leigha.

She flung out her arms and wrapped them around Brewer's neck.

Dix could remember the love she'd had for her dog when she was growing up. Seeing Leigha with Brewer surfaced some very good memories of her childhood. Her heart swelled and she wondered if she really could stay in one place and not feel as if she were going to come apart at the seams.

Mrs. Purdy paused before climbing into her sedan. "Oh, the internet has been out all day. I tried to bring up a recipe on my tablet and couldn't connect. I called the provider. They walked me through several quick fixes and determined the line has an interruption. They're sending someone out. He should be out anytime soon."

"We'll take care of it," Andrew said. "Thank you."

Mrs. Purdy drove away, leaving the three of them alone in front of the big old house.

Dix glanced at the sky. She could just see a bit of the bay beyond the house. Already the water was a steely gray and a wall of fog crept toward land.

"Will you and Leigha be okay if I go inside?" Andrew asked. "I want to check my grandfather's study for that journal."

Dix snorted. "Good luck. The man had a knack for hiding things." She glanced at Leigha. "Do you think Leigha could ask Bennet to find it for you?"

Andrew stared at his daughter for a minute before shrugging. "If you'd asked me that three days ago, I would have laughed you all the way back to Vegas."

Dix's lips pressed together. "Go on. I'll let Leigha and Brewer stretch their legs before we come inside."

Andrew glanced at the bay, his brows dipping. "Don't be too long. Looks like we're in for another foggy night."

"Trust me, I don't want to get caught in that any more than you do."

Andrew touched the side of her cheek and bent to kiss her lips. "Still working on you," he whispered and left her standing in the grass.

Dix touched her mouth where his lips had been. No matter how many times he kissed her, she felt that tingling sensation. Kissing Andrew never got old.

She closed her eyes for a second, wondering what it would be like to stay there. To become another member of the Stratford household. To be a mother to Leigha and a wife to Andrew.

Could they pull together and become a cohesive, balanced family unit?

Dix opened her eyes and glanced around just in time to see Brewer run around the side of the house, Leigha chasing him.

"Leigha!" she called out, already running after her. She didn't like letting the little girl out of her sights for a moment.

Dix raced around the corner. Her heart stopped for a second when she couldn't see Leigha or Brewer.

"Leigha?"

Brewer burst out of a grouping of rosebushes and raced toward Dix, carrying a long string of beads in his mouth. He ran past Dix and stopped, threw the string in the air, let it fall and pounced on it. He grabbed it in his teeth and shook it. The string broke and little white beads spewed across the grass.

"Brewer!" Leigha ran out of the same rose garden. "Give me that! That's mine!" She stopped short when she saw the mess Brewer had made of the beads. Her shoulders slumped. "Now you've broken it."

"We can string them back together. Help me find all

of them." Dix dropped to her hands and knees to help Leigha gather the little white beads. As she collected them, she looked down. They looked like pearl beads, like those that made up the necklace her mother had worn with her best dresses. "Leigha, where did you find these?" She glanced up at the little girl and noticed the bright necklace around her neck. The stones were clear and multifaceted.

Dix's heart skipped several beats as she straightened, still on her knees, eye level with Leigha. "Where did you get that necklace?"

The child touched the jewels around her neck. "I found them."

"Yes, sweetie, but where?" Dix stared down at the pearls in her hand. "This isn't the kind of jewelry you play with. It's the kind grown-ups spend a lot of money on."

"They're mine. Bennet showed me where to find them."

"Oh, baby—"

Dix was cut off by the sound of Brewer barking. He was out of sight on the other side of the rosebushes. Suddenly he squealed and the garden grew silent.

"Brewer?" Leigha turned and ran toward the rose garden. "Brewer!"

Dread filled Dix's chest just as she heard the crunch of footsteps on the gravel path. "Leigha, wait!"

The little girl ran into the rose garden.

Dix leaped to her feet and ran after her. She got there too late.

A big man, wearing jeans and a uniform shirt for the internet provider, stood with his feet braced, holding Leigha around the middle with one arm, his other hand clamped over her mouth.

Brewer lay on the ground beside a marble bench.

Red flushed over Dix's eyes and she barreled toward the big man.

Before she reached him something caught her ankle and sent her flying forward. She hit the ground hard enough to knock the breath out of her. Then someone landed on her back, pinning her to the ground. A cloth covered her mouth and nose. When she tried to breathe in, she smelled something sweet with a hint of a chemical scent. Then the fog from the bay crept over her vision and the daylight blinked out.

Andrew hurried into the house and went straight to the study his grandfather had always used. The study he used now as his office since taking up residence at Cape Churn. He'd been through every drawer and cabinet, familiarizing himself with the paperwork his grandfather had felt important enough to keep.

He went through all of them again, moving swiftly, not really expecting to find the journal Mr. Giddings had mentioned.

When he came up empty-handed, he sat in the big leather chair and stared at the room, wondering if there were any hidden doors, shelves or boxes in the room. He knew about the wall safe behind the portrait of Leigha, but there had to be more. And it had to be here. His grandfather had loved this room and spent hours working or reading there.

Andrew heard the sound of Brewer barking. He started to get up, but the dog stopped. He was probably playing catch with Leigha.

He tapped his fingers on the desktop.

Think.

Where would his grandfather have hidden a journal? The more he tapped, the more he realized the sound was hollow in a place that shouldn't sound hollow. He'd always assumed his grandfather's desk was solid mahogany. But right in the middle where he was tapping his fingers, he heard a hollow sound.

He curled his fingers into a fist and knocked on the desktop in several places, always coming back to the center where it sounded different.

Andrew got down on his knees and looked beneath the desktop. It was a good three inches thick in the middle, much too thick. If it were solid, it would make a dull thump when he knocked. He felt around the underside of the desk but couldn't find a lever or switch. He opened the drawer on the right and emptied it of the papers and documents. Then he stuck his hand inside the drawer and felt the underside of the desk. Nothing. He repeated the same technique on the left-hand drawer. Just when he was about to give up, his finger touched what felt like a rounded wooden dowel. He pushed it. Something clicked and a shallow drawer slid out of the middle of the desk. In it was a small leather-bound journal.

Andrew's pulse picked up as his fingers curled around the leather and he lifted the book out of the velvet-lined drawer. He opened it to the first page and read.

To my dear Rowena,
You will always hold my heart in your hands. Just because you are gone doesn't mean we'll never see each other again. Our souls are destined to spend eternity together. Until then, you have all of my love. Thomas

Flipping through the pages, Andrew shook his head. This was it, the truth about his heritage, all neatly handwritten and documented for future generations of Stratfords to read and know.

"Dix?" Andrew clutched the book in his hand and leaped to his feet. "Dix!" he shouted, running for the door. He couldn't wait to show her what he'd found. This could be what his attackers were after. It spelled out everything.

Andrew raced out the front door.

Dix, Leigha and Brewer weren't there. Then he remembered hearing the sound of Brewer's barking at the back of the house. Holding tightly to the book, Andrew ran around the side of the house and worked his way through the garden maze.

"Dix! Leigha! Brewer!" he yelled.

No response.

Had he missed them? When he went out the front door, had they come in through the back door?

He shook his head. Assuming Mrs. Purdy had locked up before she left, the only door unlocked was the front door, and they hadn't come through from that direction.

"Dix! Leigha!"

A soft woof sounded from the other side of a bank of rosebushes.

Andrew tiptoed into his grandmother's rose garden, crouching low, prepared to react should someone try to hit him again in the back of the head.

Nobody jumped out. Nothing moved but a black thumping tail sticking out from under a rosebush.

Checking the area carefully, Andrew didn't kneel down until he was certain nobody else was there. Then he reached beneath the rosebush, the backs of his hands scraped by thorns, and eased Brewer into the open.

The dog lay on his side, his tail twitching, but he didn't get up.

"Where's Leigha, Brewer?" he asked softly.

Brewer lifted his head and tried to get up, but he fell back. He tried again and this time rolled onto his side. He whined softly and shook his head. Then he lurched to his feet and staggered a few steps.

"That's right, boy. Find Leigha."

Brewer limped a little, fell, got up and limped some more, heading through the garden to the west end of the house.

Andrew knew he couldn't risk going after Dix and Leigha without help. If someone had snatched them, he'd need backup.

He unlocked the door leading into the kitchen, grabbed the phone and entered Tazer's number.

"Yeah?"

"Tazer, this is Andrew Stratford. Dix and Leigha are missing. I think they're in trouble."

"Where are you?"

"At Stratford House. They were playing outside. Then they were gone."

"On our way. Wait for us to get there. We don't know what you might be up against."

"Can't wait. Just get here." He dropped the phone and raced after Brewer, who'd continued through the garden.

If Andrew had waited for the firemen to save Leigha, she would be dead. His instinct had been right to rush into the blaze. He might not be facing an inferno this time, but there were a number of other hazards inherent in living where he was with the cliffs, caves and sea nearby.

He prayed Brewer could track Leigha and find the two women before whoever took them harmed them. He shoved the journal into his back pocket. If he had to, he'd use it in trade for the lives of the two people he cared for.

Inside the journal, his grandfather had confirmed the

identity of Rowena Mason's parents. Margaret and Percival Bennet Mason were, in fact, Peg and Percy Malone, the infamous rumrunners who'd turned the tables on San Francisco big shot Willard Jameson, who'd been in cahoots with the law, stolen their contraband and sold it for pure profit.

The Malones had taken a significant haul when they'd robbed the jewelry store. Not only had they gotten away with thousands of dollars' worth of diamonds and precious gems, they'd taken Jameson's yacht since their boat had been confiscated.

The journal also contained detailed drawings of the locations of several stashes of the jewels from the heist.

Andrew didn't care what happened to the jewels. He'd trade all of them and everything he owned to get Leigha and Dix back alive.

He hurried after the dog, his only hope to find them, praying Leigha's imaginary friend would look out for them until Andrew could get there.

Chapter 19

A high-pitched shriek pulled Dix out of the gray fog swirling around her head. She lay against something hard and cool and, despite the clearing of the fog, she couldn't see much. Darkness surrounded her.

When Dix tried to sit up, she couldn't balance. Her hands were securely tied behind her back and rope bound her ankles.

"I told you—I'm not supposed to show anyone where I found those necklaces. Bennet made me promise. And give them back! They're mine."

Dix lay ten feet away from where the big man she recognized as Dwayne Clayton held Leigha trapped between his hands.

"If you don't want anything to happen to your friend over there, you'll tell us where you found this." The man standing in front of Leigha held out what Dix suspected was a diamond necklace.

As all gazes turned toward her, Dix closed her eyes and pretended to still be unconscious. She peered at the trio through her lashes, tamping down the rising panic of being held captive.

When the man across from Dwayne looked her way, she recognized him as the man who'd introduced himself to them at the Seaside Café. Nelson Clayton, Andrew's nearest neighbor.

Based on the darkness and cool, solid ground beneath her, Dix guessed they were in a cave. Around her were old wooden barrels with metal stays and what looked like the makings of an old still.

If she could get close enough to one of the metal stays, she might be able to rub against the jagged metal and cut the rope tied around her wrists.

When the men redirected their gazes to Leigha, Dix inched her body toward the piles of metal and wood. Just a few inches was all she needed.

"You got these jewels from somewhere in this cave, didn't you? Who showed you where it was?"

Leigha tilted her chin and glared at Nelson. "Bennet told me. He's my friend."

"Where is this Bennet? Maybe we should ask him where you found the jewels."

She smiled. "Bennet's here in this cave. But he's not telling you anything."

Both men glanced around as if expecting someone to appear out of the darkness. When no one did, Dwayne frowned, twisted his fist in Leigha's hair and pulled.

Leigha stood on her toes, her face tensing. But she didn't cry.

Dix was so proud of her. She was probably scared and in pain, but she refused to cry. Dix's fists clenched.

When she got loose, she'd take those two down for picking on a little girl.

She felt around behind her for the edge of a rusty stay. Once she found one, she sawed her arms back and forth, pressing down as hard as she could to cut through the rope chafing her wrists.

Every time Leigha or the men said something, Dix sawed hard at her bindings. When they were quiet, she grew still. But progress was slow and the men were getting impatient with the child.

Finally some of the strands snapped and the rope loosened around her. More sawing took her the rest of the way through the rope and it broke free. Easing her legs up close to her hands, she untied the bindings around her ankles.

The men were so convinced Dix was out cold, they were fully focused on Leigha and the possibility of finding the jewels.

Dix waited to choose the best moment to surprise her captors.

Dwayne raised his hand, as if to strike Leigha.

That was when Dix came unglued. The mama bear came out in her. She rolled to her feet and charged Dwayne like she was on the defensive line of a football team zeroed in on the guy carrying the ball.

Dix hit Dwayne in the side, sending him staggering across the uneven cave floor. He dragged Leigha with him for a few steps before he let go, his arms flying out for balance. He teetered a moment and then crashed like a felled tree.

Leigha fell to the ground and lay for a moment, barely moving. Then she rolled to her hands and knees.

"Run, Leigha!" Dix shouted.

The little girl darted into the darkness, disappearing into a tunnel.

Dwayne roared and scrambled to his feet.

Dix was ready. The man had at least one hundred pounds on her. That didn't faze Dix. She went after him, landing a side kick in his gut.

The man barely doubled over before he came at her again.

Dix threw another side kick, hitting him in the gut again.

He snagged her angle and twisted, sending her flying to the floor. She jerked her foot free of his grasp and swept his legs out from under him.

Once again, Dwayne went down hard. He rolled to his side and started to get up.

Dix was on him before he could straighten, knocking him off his hands and knees. He splayed across the ground, his forehead bouncing off the stone cave floor. He lay dazed for a moment.

Seizing her opportunity, Dix grabbed his arm, shoved it up between his shoulder blades and straddled his back, pinning him to the ground.

"I think we've had just about enough of this," a voice said.

The cool, hard shaft of a gun barrel pressed to Dix's temple. She froze but didn't ease the pressure on the man's arm.

"Get off him," the older Clayton demanded. "Now! Or I'll shoot."

Dix shook her head. "I guess you're gonna have to shoot me. You two have caused enough trouble. I'm not letting you hurt anyone anymore."

"You're not in a position to make that happen. The only position you're in at this time is your last position."

The explosion of gunfire echoed through the cavern.

Dix flinched and held her breath, waiting for the stabbing pain of the bullet to tear through her flesh.

Nelson Clayton staggered backward. The gun slipped from his fingers and dropped to the hard surface. Nelson crumpled beside it.

Distracted by Nelson, Dix loosened her hold.

The man beneath her bucked and rolled, throwing her off.

Dwayne grabbed for the gun Nelson had dropped, rolled to his back and aimed at the man diving toward him.

"Look out!" Dix yelled. She kicked out, catching Dwayne's hand a second after he pulled the trigger. The gun went off and then jerked from his hand, flying across the cave floor.

Still lying on the ground, Dix kicked again, catching Dwayne in the face. The crunch of bone and cartilage meant she'd hit her mark.

The big man slapped a hand to his eye as his nose spurted blood. He rolled to the side, screaming like a girl, and then passed out.

Dix leaped to her feet, secured the gun and ran to where Andrew lay on the ground, his hand pressed to his side. "You're hit!" she exclaimed.

"Either that or it's raining blood in here." He sat up and winced, pressing a hand on his wound. "Where's Leigha?"

"I don't know. When she got loose, she ran."

Andrew pushed to his feet. "We have to find her."

"You shouldn't be on your feet. Let me at least stop the flow of blood before you run any sprints."

"Leigha!" he shouted.

"How did you know we'd be here?" Dix pulled off

her T-shirt, thankful she'd worn a sports bra that morning. With quick, efficient moves, she tore the shirt in two pieces and folded one.

"Brewer led me here." He glanced around. "Where'd he go?"

"Move your hand," Dix commanded.

"Bossy thing, aren't you?"

"When I have to be." She pressed the wad of cloth to the wound and placed his hand on top to hold it while she tore the rest of the shirt into a long strip. Wrapping her arms around his waist, she pulled the strip of cloth around him and tied it in a tight knot over the cloth pad. "That will have to do until we get you to the hospital."

"Leigha!" Andrew shouted again.

Dix turned in the direction the little girl had disappeared. "Leigha, where are you?"

"I'm here," she responded, edging out of a dark tunnel, struggling to carry a wooden box too big for one little girl to handle.

Brewer limped alongside her.

"Sweetheart, what have you got?" Dix started toward her.

Tears hovered on the child's eyelashes. "The treasure. I was going to give it to the men so that you and Daddy wouldn't get hurt." She stared at the blood on her father's shirt. "I didn't want my daddy to die." She sniffed. A tear slipped from the corner of her eye and slid down her cheek.

A flash of movement alerted Dix.

Dwayne rolled across the floor, grabbed Leigha's leg and jerked her hard.

Before she fell, Leigha threw the wooden box at the man's head. Once on the ground, she kicked him in his swollen eye and again in the face, hitting his broken nose.

Dwayne bunched his fist and pulled his hand back, ready to throw a punch.

Dix ran at him and kicked his arm so hard, the bone snapped. With so much forward momentum driving her forward, she tripped over the man and landed on her knees on the other side.

Dwayne roared and swung his good arm at Dix.

Andrew grabbed his wrist and twisted his thumb until he cried out. Then he pulled the handgun from his waistband and pointed it at the man. "Move a muscle and I won't hesitate to end it now."

Dwayne lay still.

Dix scrambled to her feet and away from Dwayne. She scooped Leigha up into her arms and hugged the child close. "You'll be okay."

"And Daddy?" she asked, her gaze going to her father. "He isn't going to die?"

Andrew shook his head, his focus on the man lying at his feet. "I'm going to be around long enough to embarrass you as a teenager. I love you, baby."

Leigha cupped Dix's face in both of her little palms, forcing her to look the child square in the eye. "Are you going to stay with us?"

Those blue eyes so much like her father's stared straight through her, pulling at her heartstrings so hard, Dix could barely breathe. "We'll see, sweetie. We'll see." She couldn't promise that she would stay. Too many variables were still up in the air. And now that they'd found the people responsible for the attacks, her services were no longer needed.

Dix's eyes stung and she fought to keep the tears from falling. Rangers and MMA fighters didn't cry.

But mommies of darling little girls did. At that moment she wanted to be Leigha's mother more than she had ever imagined possible. She didn't even want to think about how much she wanted to be with Leigha's father. A man who'd been through so much, saved his daughter not once but twice and now had saved her... Her heart swelled inside her chest, hurting so much she thought she might be dying.

"Dix! Andrew!" a female voice called out.

"Over here," Dix responded.

Tazer stepped out of the tunnel leading from the house and into the cave, a handgun in one hand and a flashlight in the other. "Did you save anything for us?"

Dix chuckled. "Just the cleanup." She nodded toward Andrew. "My client ended up saving me."

"After she saved Leigha and me." Andrew shrugged and grimaced, pressing his hand over his wound. "It only seemed fair."

Tazer crossed to where Andrew stood holding the gun on Dwayne. "I'll take it from here. You look a little worse for the wear."

"Thanks. I feel like I was hit by a train."

Tazer nodded. "A bullet in the gut has a way of making it real."

Gabe McGregor, Casanova Valdez and Creed Thomas emerged from the tunnel, all carrying weapons.

Dix grinned. "You brought the cavalry?"

Tazer nodded. "Damn right. I didn't know what we were up against when Andrew placed the call that you and Leigha were missing."

Nova shook his head, his gaze scanning the cavern as he crossed to where Nelson lay on the ground. He dropped to his haunches and checked the base of the man's throat for a pulse. "He's still alive." Jerking the man's jacket open, he tore Nelson's shirt and ripped off pieces of fabric to fashion a bandage to help stop the bleeding. "Great place to throw a party."

"If you like dark, cool places you can't find easily," Creed said.

"How did you find us?" Dix asked.

Gabe stepped aside. "I was questioning Jared and Joe Kessler when Tazer called. They thought they might be of some help if you were climbing around inside a cave." Gabe waved his hand. "I didn't know what they were talking about, but I'm glad they came along." His glance came to a halt on Andrew's shirt. "Are you okay?"

"I will be," Andrew said. "I don't suppose you brought a doctor with you."

"Will a nurse do until we can get you to the hospital?" Emma Jenkins stepped from the tunnel, carrying a red plastic box. "I grabbed the first-aid kit from Gabe's cruiser. Who needs it?"

"Andrew," Dix said. "He's been shot."

Emma pushed through the crowd and examined the pressure bandage Dix had applied. "This will hold until we get him out of here." She made her way to Nelson and applied a pressure bandage.

Gabe secured Dwayne by handcuffing his good arm behind his back, clipping the other cuff to the man's belt. His other arm hung at an awkward angle by his side, completely useless.

The odd group of SOS agents and young archaeologists trudged out of the cave and back through the narrow passage.

Gabe and Creed stayed behind to wait for the first responders to arrive with the stretcher they'd need to carry Nelson out.

Tazer and Nova escorted Dwayne all the way out

through the front of Stratford House, just as the ambulances pulled into the yard.

Andrew didn't want to ride in the back of the ambulance, but when the EMTs agreed to let Dix and Leigha ride with him, he acquiesced.

"But who's going to take care of Brewer?" Leigha asked.

Nova waved. "I've got Brewer. I'll take good care of him."

Dix buckled Leigha into the front seat with the driver while she sat in the back next to the EMT who worked over Andrew, checking his vital signs and establishing an IV with fluids.

The ride into town didn't take long, and before she had a chance to say anything to Andrew, she was asked to wait by the ER door until they unloaded him from the back. The driver brought Leigha to her. Together, they watched the EMTs take Andrew into the ER.

Leigha wrapped her arms around Dix's neck and hugged tightly. "I'm scared."

Dix was, too. Gunshot wounds were tricky. Everything depended on what damage the bullet had done inside Andrew. But she couldn't show Leigha how frightened she was.

"You are the bravest little girl I've ever known."

She sniffed and leaned back to stare into Dix's face. "Me?"

"Yes, you." Dix smiled and brushed a strand of spun-gold hair out of Leigha's face. "You went to get the treasure to save us. That was very brave of you, when you could have run all the way back to the house and stayed safe."

"But you and Daddy were still in the cave with those bad men."

"Yes, we were. And you saved us." Dix hugged her, her eyes stinging again. Whoever married Andrew Stratford would be one lucky woman. Not only would she be getting a wonderful, sexy, handsome man to spend her life with, she'd also get the huge bonus of being a mother to Leigha.

In that moment Dix envied a woman she didn't know and who might not even exist.

Shortly after Andrew was wheeled into surgery, Tazer arrived in the surgical waiting room. "I hear Stratford's in surgery."

Dix nodded, unable to say anything for the lump lodged in her throat.

She didn't have to. Tazer continued. "I checked on Nelson and Dwayne Clayton. Dwayne had his arm set, his nose splinted and he was escorted to the county jail. Nelson is next in line for surgery."

Dix didn't care about either of the men. As far as she was concerned, they could die and the world would be a better place.

Tazer arched her brows and stared at Dix. "Hmm. Real talkative, I see." She fished in her purse and pulled out a deck of cards. "You might want these to keep your mind off things."

Dix pulled the cards from the box and shuffled several times before dealing three hands of Go Fish.

"I reported what happened to Royce."

Dix glanced up. "He should fire me."

"How do you figure?"

Tipping her head toward the hallway, she said, "I'm not much good as a bodyguard. I mean, look where my client is."

"The way Royce sees it, you've proved yourself as

an SOS agent. He's already looking for your next assignment."

Dix frowned. Anywhere else she'd been, she'd been ready to leave within weeks of getting there. The only reason she'd lived in Vegas so long was that her fighting had taken her all over the country and sometimes all over the world.

Staring down at Leigha's golden hair, her small hands holding on to the cards, Dix didn't want to leave.

"You do know that quite a few of us work out of Cape Churn. We leave to perform our assignments, but we always come back. It's home."

"Are you all from Cape Churn?"

Tazer snorted. "Hardly. But we've found our homes here." She smiled. "Strange how that old saying 'Home is where your heart is' holds true." She touched Dix's arm. "So, have you found your home?" She tilted her head toward the hallway.

The word *home* made Dix long for so much more than what she'd had since returning from the war. "I don't know. I've only been here a few days."

"Your heart knows. Trust it."

A man in green scrubs stepped into the waiting room, untying the mask from around his face. "Are you the family of Andrew Stratford?"

Leigha, Dix and Tazer stood.

"Yes," Leigha said.

"Mr. Stratford came through surgery just fine. The bullet managed to miss all of his organs. Other than losing a lot of blood, he should recover nicely."

"My daddy's going to be okay?" Leigha asked, tears filling her eyes and spilling onto her cheeks.

The doctor knelt in front of her. "He sure is." He lifted her little hand that still held cards. "Are you winning?"

She nodded and turned to Dix.

The doctor straightened. "The nurse will let you know when he's awake. You can visit, but not for long. He'll need rest." The doctor left them in the waiting room.

Dix lifted Leigha into her arms and hugged her. "You hear that? Your daddy is going to be okay."

Even if she didn't stay in Cape Churn, she'd leave knowing Andrew would be okay. The bad guys were neutralized and Leigha would have her father for a very long time.

When she thought of leaving, her chest felt hollow and her belly tightened.

Was Tazer right? Did her heart know what her head couldn't comprehend? Was she falling in love with her client?

Or had she already fallen?

Chapter 20

One night in the hospital was all Andrew could take. He barked at the nurses, growled at the doctor and nearly tore his stitches getting out of bed too soon after surgery. He was up and dressed by the time the doctor made his rounds the next morning to sign his discharge papers.

The doctor chuckled. "Anxious to get home?"

"I never liked hospitals," he grumbled. "No offense. You and the staff are doing a great job."

"You don't have to explain. I get it. I'm one of the worst patients when I'm sick." He scrawled his signature on the bottom of Andrew's chart. "You're free to go as soon as the nurse gives you discharge instructions. Remember when I told you not to fall off any more cliffs? Well, try not to catch any more bullets, as well." The doctor left and the nurse came in to go over the discharge instructions, and still Dix hadn't shown up.

She'd been there the previous night up until the pain

meds had kicked in and knocked him out. He'd woken once, and Dix had been by his side. She'd told him Molly had taken Leigha to the bed-and-breakfast. Brewer was at the vet's office overnight for observation. They said he had some broken ribs and a mild concussion, but he would be all right with rest.

A knock sounded on the door.

Andrew's heart sped up as he glanced up from the documents the nurse handed him. When he saw a fit man with white hair standing there, he couldn't help the disappointment welling in his chest.

"Mr. Stratford?" the man said.

"Yes," he said, carefully shrugging into his jacket.

The man entered with his hand held out. "I'm Royce Fontaine."

The feeling of disappointment turned to a solid ache. "Dix isn't here."

He smiled and nodded. "I know. I asked to be the one to take you home."

Andrew's eyes narrowed. "Why?"

"I wanted to get feedback on one of my newest agents, and to make sure you were okay." He held the door for Andrew and waited until he passed through.

The nurse stopped him before he could go three steps. "Sorry—hospital policy. You have to go down in a wheelchair."

Andrew growled. "I don't need one."

She smiled cheerfully and pushed a wheelchair in front of him. "Sorry—it's policy." She pointed. "Sit."

"I'll push it," Fontaine offered.

The nurse gave him a narrow-eyed glance. "All the way to the exit?"

Fontaine held up a hand. "I swear I'll keep him in the chair until we reach the vehicle."

She stared a moment longer and finally nodded. "Okay. Mr. Stratford, please follow the post-op instructions. I don't want to see you back here anytime soon."

Andrew eased into the wheelchair, muttering curses beneath his breath.

Fontaine stepped behind the chair and pushed it toward the elevator.

"So, what do you want to know?" Andrew started the conversation. "Did Dix do a good job? Was she professional? Would I do it all over again?"

Fontaine stopped the chair in front of the elevator. "For a start, yes."

Andrew punched the down button. "My answers are yes, yes, and I don't know." The door slid open.

Fontaine backed Andrew into the car and stood beside him, his brows knitting. "What do you mean *I don't know*?"

"Look, I have a little girl. I come as a package deal. What hurts my little girl hurts me. And I think it goes both ways."

Fontaine shook his head. "I still don't get it."

Andrew sighed. "I don't regret hiring Dix. She saved my girl and me. But I will regret losing her."

Fontaine chuckled and shook his head. "I don't think you have to worry about that."

It was Andrew's turn to frown. "No?"

"No." The elevator stopped and Fontaine pushed Andrew through the lobby to the exit where a rental car waited in the pickup area.

"We're out of the hospital. I can take it from here." Andrew stood and walked toward the car.

Fontaine pushed the wheelchair away from the curb and set the brake. Then he hurried to open the door for Andrew.

Andrew didn't like to have people fuss over him and he didn't even know Fontaine. But he needed his ride home and he didn't have another one waiting. He swallowed his pride and the curse words he wanted to let loose, and he got into the car, jolting his wound as he settled back against the seat. He winced and bit down hard on his tongue.

Fontaine slipped into the driver's seat and started the engine. "Ready?"

"I was ready an hour ago."

The older man smiled and drove out of the parking lot. "Though Leigha was worried about her father, she had a good time staying at Molly and Nova's place."

"If she's still there, could we stop by and pick her up?"

Fontaine shook his head. "Molly and Nova brought her home. Your housekeeper is watching her."

"What about Brewer?"

"Already home from the vet clinic. The vet observed him overnight, but by morning he was ready for release." Fontaine raised his hand. "Not to worry. Creed and Emma took him home. He'll be there with Leigha when you arrive."

Fontaine had mentioned Leigha and Brewer would be at home, but he still hadn't said anything about Dix. Had she been reassigned? Was she already gone from Oregon on her way to her next dangerous mission?

Andrew's chest hurt even worse. Not in the area of his wound, but in his heart. He hadn't known Dix long, but she was an amazing woman. With her gone, Stratford House would feel even bigger and emptier.

Dix had been right. He needed to turn the place into a hotel or bed-and-breakfast. It was too big for him and Leigha by themselves. It needed to be full of happy people.

He'd be happy to see Leigha and Brewer, but part of

him didn't look forward to going home to the house with Dix gone. He sat in silence, dreading walking through the door and not seeing her smiling green eyes. Hell, he'd let her throw him again, if it meant she was staying a little longer.

Fontaine fell silent until they were well out of Cape Churn and almost to the gate to his estate. The quiet suited Andrew. He didn't feel much like talking.

And then Fontaine broke his silence. "You know, I was thinking, with as many of my agents out here on the West Coast, I could use an office with support staff here. I don't suppose you know of a suitable building that has sufficient room in a secure location?"

Andrew had to let Fontaine's question sink in before he could respond. "I'm not that familiar with what Cape Churn has to offer."

"I've been thinking it would be even better to have an office away from town, in a secluded area. Maybe a gated location."

"Sorry." Andrew started to shake his head but then he frowned. "What are you asking for? Just spit it out."

"Mr. Stratford, would you consider leasing space in Stratford House for our West Coast operations?" Fontaine pulled up to the gate and turned to Andrew. "It would be a perfect location to set up computers and satellite communications."

Andrew's frown deepened. "My home is not for rent or lease."

Fontaine nodded. "Just think about it. No pressure. It just seems a shame to let all those rooms sit empty when you could put them to good use." The SOS leader leaned out the window and pushed the code for the gate entrance.

"How did you know my code?"

"I have people who specialize in code cracking." Fontaine's mouth turned up on the corners. "And if all else fails, I asked the housekeeper, Mrs. Purdy. She's a wonderful woman and she cooks a mean meat loaf."

Andrew sat back in his seat, not sure he liked that Mrs. Purdy had given his gate code to a stranger.

When they rounded the last bend in the driveway, Andrew leaned forward. "What's going on here?"

Half a dozen vehicles lined the drive. He recognized two sheriff's SUVs and his pulse kicked up its pace. "Is everything okay?"

"As far as I know, everything is fine." Fontaine parked the car and rounded to the passenger side to open the door for Andrew. "A few people wanted to come by and wish you well."

The last thing Andrew needed was a houseful of guests. His chest hurt, his hand hurt, and all he wanted was to hug his daughter and spend time with her.

He sucked in a deep breath and climbed out of the vehicle. As much as he'd like to tell everyone to get lost, he had to remember they were part of the team that had helped him when he'd needed it. They were part of the community and he needed to get more involved with them. He couldn't let his scars hold him back. Nobody had seemed to be turned off by them. They'd helped him unconditionally. The least he could do was thank them.

When he walked through the front door, nobody was there to greet him.

He followed the scent of charbroiled steaks and hamburgers coming from the back of the house. He could hear voices in the kitchen and Brewer barking.

When he arrived in the kitchen, Mrs. Purdy was chopping onions, alone. "There you are. We were waiting to eat until you got home."

"We?" Andrew asked. "Where's Leigha?"

"In the garden with the others." She waved her hands at him. "Go on. I'm just finishing up the potato salad and then I'll be out there, too."

Andrew stepped out into the garden and followed the voices to the patio overlooking the cape.

More than a dozen people were seated in lounge chairs, at the tables or standing near the barbecue grill.

Gabe McGregor spotted him and shouted, "He's here!"

A cheer went up from all of the people there.

Andrew stood stunned for several seconds. Then Leigha grabbed his hand and pulled him into the crowd. "We're having a barbecue. Come sit with me and Dix."

His heartbeat ratcheted up, pounding against his ribs. Then he saw her and it was as if everyone else faded into the background.

Leigha led Andrew to where Dix sat at one of the tables.

As they approached, Dix stood, a smile spreading across her lips, her gaze sweeping over him. "You look great for having been shot," she said, her voice soft, controlled.

"I thought you'd left."

She shook her head. "I couldn't." Her eyes grew glassy and a single tear slipped from the corner. She brushed it away and reached for his hand. "I didn't think I could stay in one place without feeling as though I were a captive again in a Taliban village. But when I thought of leaving Leigha, Brewer, Stratford House…and you, I couldn't."

Andrew drew her into his arms and smoothed his hand over her hair. "I'm glad. You've only been here a few days, but this big place wouldn't be the same without you in it."

Leigha squeezed between the two of them and looked up. "Does that mean Dix is staying?"

Andrew held Dix's gaze.

Dix nodded. "Yes. If you two can stand to have me around."

Leigha hugged her around the middle for a long time and then turned and hugged Andrew.

"What about your job?" Andrew asked softly.

She smiled. "My boss tells me I can base out of the West Coast office of the SOS."

Andrew smiled. "That's perfect, because I'm going to lease the west wing of Stratford House to SOS for their new offices." He kissed Dix and stood back, grinning. "I told you I'd convince you to stay."

"Yes, you did. And just look at all the friends you've made in the past few days."

Andrew dragged his gaze away from Dix long enough to appreciate all the people he'd met.

Gabe McGregor, the sheriff's deputy, and his wife, Kayla Davics, were there with their teenage son and newborn daughter. Sheriff Taggert and his wife, Nora, were talking with Tazer and Dave Logsdon, the dive boat captain. The newlyweds, Molly and Nova, were laughing with Creed Thomas and Emma Jenkins. Even the Kessler twins had come by.

Royce Fontaine stepped up to him and laid his hand on his shoulder. "Glad you're on board with the whole SOS West Coast office being based out of Stratford House. Can't think of a better place."

Andrew nodded and smiled. "Me, either. It means I'll have Dix close by."

She leaned into his uninjured side and wrapped her arm around his waist.

Watching Leigha play with Nova and Brewer, Dix pressed against his side, and new friends gathered around, Andrew finally felt like he'd come home to stay.

* * *

As the sun dropped below the horizon, the guests, full of steaks and hamburgers, left for their own homes, stopping to congratulate Andrew and Dix on a case closed.

When the last person left, Andrew walked Leigha up the stairs to her bedroom.

Dix followed, feeling more settled and happy than she had in a very long time.

"Daddy?" Leigha leaned up to kiss him good-night. "Do you think Bennet will ever disappear?"

"Since I haven't seen him, I couldn't say," Andrew said.

Dix smiled. "Even if he does disappear for you, Leigha, you will always have him in your heart." Dix dropped a kiss on her forehead. "Sleep tight, sweetheart."

"I will." Leigha yawned and rolled onto her side, her arm draping over Brewer's neck.

Dix walked with Andrew into the adjoining room. "After all that's happened here, have you changed your mind about ghosts?"

Andrew turned Dix to face him and touched his lips to the tip of her nose. "You mean, do I believe in them?"

Dix nodded, loving how tender he was.

"Jury's still out, but I'm leaning toward yes." Andrew brushed his lips across hers. "What about you?"

She captured his face between her hands and stared up into his eyes, loving the blue depths more and more. "Yes. There's no other way to explain everything that has happened. And I kind of like the idea of having a benevolent ghost looking out for Leigha."

"And I like the idea of you being here with us. Anytime you feel the need for space, just let me know. I've got a yacht at the marina. We could sail away from everything."

"If it's all right with you, I'd just as soon stay here with you, Leigha and Brewer. I think I'm falling in love with all of you, and I'd like to see where it goes."

"I knew it the moment you threw me on my back— you were the woman for me." Andrew drew her into his arms and kissed her.

* * * * *

SPECIAL EXCERPT FROM

⊕ HARLEQUIN®

I N T R I G U E

*Jen Delaney and Ty Carson were once sweethearts, but
that's in the past. When Ty starts receiving threatening
letters that focus more and more on Jen, he'll do
whatever it takes to keep her safe—even kidnap her.*

Read on for a sneak preview of
Wyoming Cowboy Ranger *by Nicole Helm.*

Jen Delaney loved Bent, Wyoming, the town she'd been born in,
grown up in. She was a respected member of the community, in
part because she ran the only store that sold groceries and other
essentials within a twenty-mile radius of town.

From her position crouched on the linoleum while she stocked
shelves, she looked around the small store she'd taken over at the
ripe age of eighteen. For the past ten years it had been her baby,
with its narrow aisles and hodgepodge of necessities.

She'd always known she'd spend the entirety of her life happily
ensconced in Bent and her store, no matter what happened around
her.

The reappearance of Ty Carson didn't change that knowledge
so much as make it…annoying. No, annoying would have been
just his being in town again. The fact their families had somehow
intermingled in the last year was…a catastrophe.

Her sister, Laurel, marrying Ty's cousin Grady had been a shock,
very close to a betrayal, though it was hard to hold it against Laurel
when Grady was so head over heels for her it was comical. They
both glowed with love and happiness and impending parenthood.

Jen tried not to hate them for it.

She could forgive Cam, her eldest brother, for his serious
relationship with Hilly. Hilly was biologically a Carson, but she'd
only just found that out. Besides, Hilly wasn't like other Carsons.
She was so sweet and earnest.

But Dylan and Vanessa… Her business-minded, sophisticated older brother *impregnating* and marrying snarky bad girl Vanessa Carson… *That* was a nightmare.

And none of it was fair. Jen was now, out of nowhere, surrounded by Carsons and Delaneys intermingling—which went against everything Bent had ever stood for. Carsons and Delaneys hated each other. They didn't fall in love and get married and have *babies*.

And still, she could have handled all that in a certain amount of stride if it weren't for *Ty* Carson. Everywhere she turned he seemed to be right there, his stoic gaze always locked on *her*, reminding her of a past she'd spent a lot of time trying to bury and forget.

When she'd been seventeen and the stupidest girl alive, she would have done anything for Ty Carson. Risked the Delaney-Carson curse that, even with all these Carson-Delaney marriages, Bent still had their heart set on. She would have risked her father's wrath over daring to connect herself with a *Carson*. She would have given up anything and everything for Ty.

Instead he'd made promises to love her forever, then disappeared to join the army—which she'd found out only a good month after the fact. He hadn't just broken her heart—he'd crushed it to bits.

But Ty was a blip of her past she'd been able to forget about, mostly, for the past ten years. She'd accepted his choices and moved on with her life. For a decade she had grown into the adult who didn't care at all about Ty Carson.

Then Ty had come home for good, and all she'd convinced herself of faded away.

She was half convinced he'd returned simply to make her miserable.

"You look angry. Must be thinking about me."

Don't miss
Wyoming Cowboy Ranger *by Nicole Helm,*
available June 2019 wherever
Harlequin® Intrigue books and ebooks are sold.

www.Harlequin.com

HIEXP0519

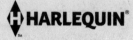

Reward the book lover in you!

Earn points on your purchase of new Harlequin books from participating retailers.

Turn your points into **FREE BOOKS** of your choice!

Join for FREE today at
www.HarlequinMyRewards.com.

Harlequin My Rewards is a free program (no fees) without any commitments or obligations.

MYR18